Wood Point
A Novel By

Paul Kestell

To
Rod & Geraldine
best wishes

Paul

Thorn Island Books
House 3 NO-2 Hamilton Row
Main Street
Courtmacsherry
Bandon Co.
Cork

First published by Thorn Island Books, 10 /12/2011
©2011 Paul Kestell. All rights reserved.
Isbn-13 978-1467981996
Isbn-10 1467981990

Cover Photograph by Thorn Island Films.

Father went to heaven the following April, and life was never the same again for me or my little brother. Years later when I returned I sat on the boot of my car, my feet resting on the sea wall, and I saw Galley Head and then the little house where the lady gave us eggs and milk and I remembered Mrs. Peeping Tom.

I thought so much about time and our place in it—how it passes so slowly as we live it, but when we reflect it has gone by so fast. I dreamed there so often as it is only a place to dream, but my dreams now are mixed with the dreams of long ago. Yet I am frightened by life and how cruel it is, and as the sea washes to the small beach with the sad stones I see him there watching me as I stand in three feet of the Atlantic Ocean.

Beyond the horizon is the highway to America and the world is fast and cold, but I see it still as a child—the fast cars on the highway break my spirit, sending waves of such power and force to damage my cliffs. They cry with me as yellow oil spills tears. Then peace descends from the Marian statue and the small boat appears, riding white horses to crash land with loaves and fishes, the silver sparkle, and I remember him, how he looked so tired, so sad, as he was watching me.

From Memories of Ballinglanna

For Mammy and Daddy

And

For John

Music by Ennio Morricone

"A Fistful of Dynamite"
"Once Upon a Time in the West"

Available on Virgin Records
ISBN 724373901326
Film music by Ennio Morricone

The author advises readers to listen to this music whilst enjoying the book.

Acknowledgements

Thanks to Carolann for help with the library and bookshop readings –and to Stephen for everything.
Thanks to Damien Enright for his insight into the local wildlife and fauna. Thanks to my family for their support throughout this process.

Foreword:

Some time ago I met Jack Browne. He was doing what he usually does: sitting and watching container ships go in and out of Cork Harbour. He joked that he had just invented a new hobby called ship spotting. He told me he had written a novel, but nobody was interested in it because he was an unknown. So then he wrote a screenplay based on the novel-but still nobody was interested. He said he had heard I was a famous novelist, having written the best-selling Viaréggio, so he handed over his screenplay and asked me if I could make a novel out of it.

I have done my best with it, cutting out all the crappy bits—well, most of them anyway. When I showed Jack the final product without some of his favourite bits, he said he didn't mind as he was well used to humiliation and another lot of humiliation wouldn't do him any harm. He asked me to point out that Wood Point of course is really Courtmacsherry where he lived for a few years, but he changed the name as you do.

My final word is simple: we all know that Jack is as daft as a brush, thinking he can write and all of that, and of course most of what happens in this novel belongs in Jack's imagination and therefore is strictly within the realms of fantasy. The action begins as the rostrum camera falls from the clouds to zoom in on Kate Donovan on the walkway between Wood Point and Timoleague.

Wood Point A Few Years Ago
1.

Kate fixed the buggy harness; she slotted the straps into the receivers. Sarah stared into her mother's eyes, her cheeks red. The wind hushed the tiny hairs stranded on her head. Kate pulled up her hood and fastened the top button. The wind, westerly from Timoleague, wasn't cold yet; it gusted and almost blew her backwards. She lifted the buggy over the stretch of matted grass, round the exotic tree that didn't quite know of the prevailing wind.

Across the estuary the tide was on the turn. A small boat moored at Burren Pier bobbled as if excited it was allowed more water. The cattle still on the side of the hills looked odd; she felt they might fall over as they stood statuesque just below the ridge. Aunt Myrna was minding Fiona. A blessing to get out in the air. She was grateful for the pathway, again the first of the new tide against the sea wall.

She rounded the bend below Lyall's farm passing the spouting foam, the silver shadows of elusive mullet. The wind caught her auburn hair, allowing it to fall beyond her ears onto her shoulders. Small finches from Disney danced before her, taking refuge in the scrub at Abbeymahon. Pushing onwards round the slow bend at the white gates, the wind found gusto.

She checked Sarah again; Sarah slept peacefully. Gulls glided in the air above her before landing in the sliding field to her left picking worms. Through a small gate an ugly horse too fat stood abreast of a pony they looked downtrodden and sad. Was it these horses he spoke to? How did he learn to speak fluent horse?

Timoleague was lost among the gales of cloud, the church towering over the village, the old abbey chilling the river and reminding of hope and need. The men who sailed up this estuary so long ago in search of God, the shrines they built crumbled now.

The tide had still to reach the bridge, and the river was faint like it was hiding dark salmon immersed in the mud. Loose branches and dead stone formed a causeway to the duck pond sponsored by the local gun club. A boy kicked a ball against the gable end of a farmhouse—a lonely place for a boy to kick a ball.

She heard the ball thud; it was greeted by the shuddering of the road on the far side. A large truck packing gravel grated along, making cattle grill sounds, shaking the earth till at once she found the sky was too big. The blue canvas above narrated into a smelling grey that ran a thin line over Kilbrittain, this world suddenly huge and forceful devouring them.

Turning back, the wind chimed against her back; the sand was becoming the sea. Small pools engulfed the plover and terns, but they escaped without fuss. The new sea reflected the grey of the cloud brushing from the coast, and the buggy moved faster. Though asleep, Sarah dropped her hands to filter the air. Lyall's farm was darkening; the sheep had moved nearer the house, huddling under the candlelit windows drawn secretly in crayon.

By the time she reached the matted grass, traffic coming home flew by urgently on their way to Clearwater up Ramsey Hill. Was Jack Browne on his way home from Timoleague? Sometimes he went to get the newspaper. Wouldn't miss his old car! A truck passing splashed through a small puddle; it drenched the grass in front of her but missed her.

Back on the pathway she gained speed. Sarah was waking like she sensed the arrival of the smoke hanging in the air, the sweet tobacco scent of burnt wood. In the fields up the back road three ponies played in the corralled garden of a bungalow. She heard screams in the distance—as though a man screamed for help—then she heard the hounds baying and the crows take flight.

Gulls hovered but didn't land, the hounds' throats hoarse from breathing fast, the excitement owned by their breed,

centuries of torment reincarnated by the sound of a
screeching human voice. Breeding terror manifested in the
dark throats of the hounds, the wily fox listening from a
distant covert. His instinct readied him for the chase—he
would have his revenge.

In Wood Point she felt the wind no more. She turned the
final bend, allowing it to blow seaward and shake the small
craft moored at the harbour. A swim from the pier, the
floating orange lifeboat rocked in the water. Small boats like
discarded bathtubs surrounded it. The stench of rotting from
fish caught days ago stuck to the air, the fragrance barely
diluted by the wash.

The wind returned to her over the cold concrete to be
swallowed by the trees at the point. Lights were on in the
houses down the street, the lamplighter taking his time. She
saw Thomas Crowe set from a battered van and make his
way down the side alley of his house. Even from across the
street she could see his boots and pants spattered with paint,
the stains derived from old colours of white and red and blue.

He hunched like he knew she was looking at him, his soft
woollen cap sitting oddly on his head more like a tea cosy
than a hat. He vanished through the back gate, closing it
slowly. Kate pushed on feeling the fresher air. The trawler
was coming down the channel, the gulls screeching, the flock
dancing up and down like on occasions they were afraid.

Bill Thornton was at his window pulling the drapes. He
looked over her, pretending to look at the last of the evening
sky. Kate didn't mind; she knew he didn't like her. The lights
were blinding in Detta's grocery as she prepared for the busy
time of day. Further on the pubs, Harrington's looked closed
with the blinds pulled full; the place always looked like
death, she mused. The Fisherman's wasn't open yet, its
bright red door impersonating a private house.

Not long to go to Myrna's. She hoped Fiona wasn't cross.
Sarah was so placid by comparison. Fiona took after her
father, taking the hump so easily and then retreating to

silence. Sometimes she screamed, her face going bright red, and she could hold her breath till on the verge of passing out.

The first of the rain fell on the line of cars passing on dipped headlights. She saw it splash off the flashy bonnets, yet some of the occupants chose to wear sunglasses. The rain brought with it a new cold that made her hurry. Running out of footpath she crossed, lifting the buggy on the far side. It was easier to push, the surface better.

Later that evening, the kids sound asleep; she poured herself a deserved glass of wine. Only a month to go in the rented house, then a move to the Anchorage. Ted O' Reilly didn't know what he had done. For the first time in his life he had worked and saved for something, spending three months at a time at sea. The money was good, but the life was hard. When he rang home she could tell he missed his children. Did he miss her? That was another thing.

Hardly the kind of thing she could ask without appearing damn foolish. Ted was always matter of fact. "Miss the kids, Kate."

Then he would hesitate. Kate helped, saying, "I know you do. It must be awful for you."

"It is," the muffled voice would say from the other side of the world.

Sometimes his voice would drown, and all she heard was static. Slowly his sound returned. Kate felt guilty she didn't mind him gone. Trying so hard to be upbeat, she would say, "You went away for a minute, but you're back. What were you saying, Ted?"

Ted said, "Ah, nothing really, just saying the weather's been mighty this past week. Pity I can't bottle it and send you some."

Kate laughed. "It's been terrible here for a month—wind and rain every day."

Ted was gone again, the static deciding to whistle till eventually silence descended. He was gone; he never tried to call her back.

Kate drank a swallow of wine; it tasted sour, but when she held it on her tongue it seem to blend to her taste buds. Swallowing it eased her tummy, which was hopping up and down. Jack Browne—why did he pop into her head? He was from Dublin and was much older, at least ten years if not more. He had been married and had a grown-up daughter. Why would a man like him end up in Wood Point alone? He rented a house a few doors up; she saw him daily as she walked by.

Jack sat at his window typing his novel on the laptop. He said he was a writer, but she had never heard of him. If he was a writer, then he wasn't famous. He did type away, though, but maybe he was only fooling everyone. He didn't talk like a writer, all intellectual. He was quirky, though, talking to horses. She smiled thinking of the idea and the way he said it—quirky!

Her ramblings emptied the bottle of wine; she was sorry, looking at the empty bottle.

Why does everything happen at the wrong time? She mused. Life is so full of tricks.

There was a time when she was sure she missed the boat. Aunt Myrna said nobody would ask her. She let it go too long, hanging out; not taking anything seriously enough till along came Ted O' Reilly. His people were from near Timoleague. They were rough, but Ted was noted as a big softie who had gone to school and had tried to better himself. Ted, who made her laugh. He was quick with the smart remark. The days of drinking, wild nights, singing, and messing about—those were the days. No responsibility—just go to the Fisherman's; go dancing in the Emmet Hotel. Ted was a good dancer.

Jack Browne doesn't dance; he said he hates dancing. What type of man hates dancing?

*

Bill Thornton watched her, pretending to concentrate on the drapes. She looked cold and worn out as she pushed her buggy, crossing the road just below the pier.

He turned to Danny Murphy and said, "More rain forecast. Nothing but rain." He rearranged beer mats as he went on. "Rain isn't news. When its stops raining we will have news. Maybe I will move to the Salou permanently—what do you think? Herself will be made up. When she is made up aren't we all ahead?"

"It is grand for you, Dan, to have the money for a place out there. She will get herself a nice tan and you will have the pick of the golf courses. Great to have the readies, huh?"

Danny Murphy lowered the drains of his pint watching Bill go through the side door, only to re-emerge from the kitchen going to the Murphy's tap. Danny watched the stout swirl in the glass; it was light brown and soon it would turn black. Bill, who was small in stature, lifted himself to his full height.

"You missed the krauts, Danny. They took over the place. Yer woman, the producer, a right bitch. She said they had their own chuck wagon. They didn't even buy a mineral! Now can you credit that? With all their hi-tech cameras and fancy trucks, they gave me nothing, not a farthing. I asked Madge Butler to make sandwiches, but, sure, it wasn't sandwiches they wanted. She said they were rushing to get it done before it rained, and of course there wasn't a drop. Laying down rail tracks. They turned the whole pier into a fish market like something from the nineteen thirties. They were all wearing soft caps and the woman with dresses on like they were off to a wedding. My God! When a fella can't make a bob out of that, it says something."

Taking his pint, Danny said, "So that was all the fuss Herself was on about. She saw them over at Lyall's farm earlier. She wouldn't shut up about it. Are they making a film, or what is it?" He sipped at his pint.

"Some German soap opera," Bill said. "A flashback scene. It must have cost them a fortune. There must have been twenty of them and the gear they had."

He pretended to clean the spillage tray by taking the lid off and draining it in the sink, scratching his bald head in the process. His habit was to run his fingers down to his right ear where he still had the remnants of sideburns.

"Those things cost a fortune," Danny said, drinking more of his pint and adjusting the beer mat to receive his glass.

Rita walked in. She was caked in fake tan, making her young looking from afar. Her breasts were ornamental over her tummy. She wore a tight tee shirt and was good for her age. Bill eyed her appreciatively; she was still good looking, her dark eyes announcing her.

"Congratulations," Bill said taking a new glass from the shelf.

Rita looked at her husband blankly.

Danny, smiling at her, said, "Salou!"

"Oh," she said off handily. "It was either we bought or stopped going altogether." She gave Danny an undignified look as Bill handed over her gin. "It is the time to buy, Bill Thornton, when the money is so cheap. Why wait till we are old and weary and we can't stand up to enjoy ourselves? It's only money. We are right on the beach—well, almost. What is it, Danny?"

Drinking his pint, Danny made her wait until he said, "A hundred yards exactly. I measured it myself."

Bill, seeing he was low, started another pint.

Rita said, "He can play all the golf he likes as long as I get a tan and a toy boy with it. I tell you, Bill, you want to see the boys on the beach playing soccer and volleyball? He can sweat it out on the golf course if he wants. I know where I will be!"

"I hear you saw the Germans," Bill said finishing off Danny's pint. "Was that them over at Lyall's? They had all these screens and a beautiful white pony."

Rita sipped her gin.

"They are making a German soap," Danny said knowledgably. "Evidently they turned the pier into a fish market from the nineteen thirties and were gone away in an hour."

"They didn't spend a red cent either!" Bill said. "Probably got a heap of grants and incentives from the government and the film board. For what? Not to spend a dime in the village.

What good is it to us? We may not even get a credit. The Germans won't know any better. It could be anywhere."

Bill allowed a hang-dog look.

Wood Point, Many years ago
2.

When Mammy Rosie said it to me, she stuck her big fat pig face into mine. I could smell the stench from her breath like she had eaten a sack of onions. In fact she just had rotten teeth, which was a shame. In some ways it was more a shame on my father, Michael Harrington, for allowing her get to the way she was.

It wasn't like she came from the poorer classes. My grandparents (both dead now) had a hundred acres near the Pike. I know because I heard Michael Harrington argue with her one day as to why it all went to her older brother. Evidently Mammy Rosie didn't get a dime and she said she didn't care about it either, which vexed Michael Harrington more than anything else.

"It's hard enough, Sean, when you can talk and argue like the rest of them. Fight your corner. But you poor gobshite can't make any more sound than a cat, and who ever listens to a cat? So you better be something special, my boy. No use in you going around sticking out your tongue at strangers or squashing your face against the front window. They will lock you away if you keep doing that. You know what your father is like; he doesn't have the time or the inclination!"

Her face became huge, and her eyes, red in their sockets, looked ready to burst. But I didn't mind Mammy Rosie or what she was saying. Even at seven years old I figured she was in far worse straits than me.

For a start she was a sight, her obese body hardly able to move about and blood flooding her face. Michael Harrington said she had diabetes, chronic lung failure, kidney failure, and complete heart failure. The doctors in the Mercy Hospital had all but given up on her. Worse than that, she couldn't drive properly and was a danger to every other road user and herself and, by extension, me in particular. Yet when she wiped my face with the rag of the tea towel, I saw her eyes moisten for the first and only time.

"You would best stay cute, Sean Harrington, 'cause I won't be here to save you. I will be gone back to where I came from to be rid of this dreadful man. Surely you most know he doesn't love either of us. How he can stand himself is beyond me."

She wiped more spitting on the cloth to remove a hard dry stain. Her rubbing hurt.

"We will take your net and go over to Burren," she said. "That's what we will do, put in the morning. We will call and see Mr. Sexton. He might give you a lollypop. I need to get my tablets."

She rose suddenly from her chair, dragging her right foot as she made to the filthy sink. Mammy Rosie started to sing as she always did when starting to wash up. Her voice was sweet for such an ungainly woman. She was like something from a fairytale—a beautiful girl trapped in the body of an old hag.

"The face that holds such sweet a smile for me...," she sang, clattering the dishes dangerously. The plates and cups ended clean on the draining board. Most had tiny chips, the cracks appearing like the faults of the earth.

She was right on old Sexton: he gave me a yellow lollypop. He watched as I experimented with it, putting it up to my forehead, trying to make it stick, till the exasperated Mammy Rosie stuck it in my mouth. Mr. Sexton made his way to the dispensary counter slowly. Two elderly people sat on the battered chairs provided whilst Mr. Sexton's eldest daughter, Brida, served plasters and ointments and the like.

"He is fine and handsome, Mrs. Harrington," Brida said kindly, placing plastic packs of teats on plastic hooks.

Mammy Rosie replied, "The world of good it will do him, unless God regains the world and all our souls with it. The poor child has the blight."

Brida went red, surprised by Mammy Rosie's outburst. Mr. Sexton lifted his head from the list of prescriptions he surveyed.

"I hear they can do great things now," he said in his low gruff voice.

Mammy Rosie looked at me, patting my head, and addressed the embarrassed Brida.

"I need a cough bottle for him. He wakes every night with a tickle in his throat. Takes me an age to get him settled. Give us your own mixture, and we will see how it goes."

Brida was relieved the request was an ordinary one.

I could see the sweat pump, the back of her neck sapping wet; she avoided the ruins of the abbey by sweeping past the church, taking the sharp bend right, then left across the Argideen. Wood Point looked different from Burren. The small birds crept closer from the vagrant pools left by the tide, and weed clung to the walls. It was a dour mix of sea and land with the grey shale mocking the dark fruits of the sea.

Mammy Rosie lost control of the car twice as she looked back over her shoulder, regaining control as the car veered from right to left. The wheels scraping the sharp stones embedded in the verge, narrowly avoiding the tiny drains filled with mud and bog water.

Of course that was some time ago, and Mammy Rosie is dead nearly seven years now. My father used to draw me pictures of her, little sketches, and I would draw her alongside. Michael Harrington would study mine for ages every now and then, referring to his own work.

"That isn't the woman I married, Sean," he said, going to the sideboard and pulling open the top drawer. There were hundreds of photos of him and Mammy Rosie smiling and laughing, out on Galley Head, the two of them staring down the blowhole.

"You see, Sean," he said. "See how pretty she was. Not like you are drawing. Why, you don't draw her nice like in this photograph."

Eventually he gave up, going back to the bar, cleaning glasses by hand, whilst Madge Butler served the customers. My father mingled, making small talk. Every now and then he eyed the kitchen to check if I was still seated, scribbling in my copy book.

Wood Point, A few years ago
3.

When Kate tried to sleep, the pain in rear of her head got worse till she shot up in the bed, turning on the bedside light. The light blinded her, causing black dots to change shape along the walls and up to the ceiling. She heard Sarah mutter, but the child was dreaming and the soft sound soon disappeared. Kate listened intently till at last she could hear the soft breathing of before. Fiona was quiet next door; she slept soundly without noise.

Kate took a swallow of water; her head still ached.

It must be a muscle, she reassured herself. It is only there when I move.

The water all gone, she slipped down the tiny stairs to the kitchen. The tap water was warm, but she rescued a drain of spring from the fridge. The door made a clicking sound, something she never noticed in the daytime. The light from outside was climbing through the blinds and through the open door the bay window, allowing a piece of the estuary. The tide was out and not even the birds were bothered with the hills and hollows of the hard sand. An old tyre stuck to a block of dark concrete, part hidden as if someone had just planted it.

She wondered about Jack Browne, and she wondered whether a cup of tea would make her head better. Wearily she put on the kettle, trying twice to find the correct wall switch. That house had been empty for over a year before he came. He brought it back to life, sitting there day after day; playing his laptop like one would a piano. Head down, portable bald spot depending on how he moved his head.

What life did he bring to Seaview? He walked every day and he drank down the village at weekends, but the people didn't really know him. He kept to himself. Aunt Myrna said he didn't go to mass, not that she cared personally, nor did anyone really give a damn anymore. No, it more summed him up as a heathen.

"All those Dublin fellas are heathens," she said laughing. "Nothing's sacred with them. He would have the pants off you while you are trying to remember his name. They ride bare back too," she said laughing again. "Anyhow, he is closer to me in age than you, Kate. Now drink up your tea, and get back to your bed."

Kate imagined her present, mimicking her word perfect. She wondered about him—was he awake? Do all those arty types wake early? Maybe he never slept, like a vampire. He closed the curtains during the day, leaving those awful walking boots on the sill to dry, to kill his foot odour.

The other night he passed by the kitchen window while she washed up, a smile and a nod. She nodded back, wondering should she recoil into the bad light. No, she stayed put till he vanished round the corner, and then she got this dreadful urge to run to the bay window to see him again. He didn't look in, and she stayed well back. She knew with the sun gone to Timoleague he was blinded, but he didn't look in anyhow. She saw the top of his head—the old bald head and young man's eyes. He bobbled along hen-like, inspecting his own garden like he was looking for something.

She guessed he was asleep. He often worked late in the evenings. Sometimes when she and Ted O' Reilly drove past he was there, his shadow hunched through the drapes. Ted didn't comment but she saw him, noticing it was 2 a.m. Another late night in the Fisherman's. Why did he sit there all night? What on earth was he writing about?

Did he notice her makeup, Kate wondered. When he arrived she was plain Jane.

I mean, who needs makeup? Two small kids, hubby away for most of the year. The deli counter in Clon part time three days a week if she was needed.

What was the point? Her social life revolved around the weekly visit to her parents. Both her brothers and her older sister, Francis, had flown the nest with one brother away in England and the other two in Cork City. There was little to be doing.

Kate was thinking how much things had changed even in just a few years. She thought of Tim, her older brother. She remembered watching his smiling face as they pulled alongside in old Hannon's trawler. Sometimes he would bring some fresh fish and even crabs home. He showed his delight by giving her a hug as he secured the lines of the old boat. Now, no sooner did the fish land but they went to the fish market in Cork or Skibbereen. If you ordered fish in the hotel or the Fisherman's you would get fish from the freezer.

Kate took to surprising him in the early afternoon when she collected Fiona. She could see he had a grown-up kid himself, the way he eyed them. He was patient with Sarah who was into everything. Fiona did a pooh but he laughed, citing the amount of nappies he had changed.

The fire grate was ready to go; he anticipated the fury of the evening. He sat by the table with his computer papers tossed idly. Some had slipped on to the floor. Kate laughed nervously at everything he said. He offered her tea or a beer, which she refused but only half-heartedly. How she might have gone for a beer!

Fiona was pulling at the kitchen drawers. Kate lifted her away as she sensed his patience exhausting, like somehow it reminded him of mayhem. Kate was all apologies. Sometimes she felt his stare too, like he suffered some kind of longing. She turned quickly towards him, but he had gone to offer Sarah some small ornament to play with.

Then she might not see him for weeks—maybe catch the odd glimpse of him on the walkway. His boots were for trekking, not for power walking, but he didn't seem to notice, leaving them to air on the upstairs window sill. Kate passed by smelly boots airing, the curtains closed at all times of the day. This man slept more than anyone.

One day he was going to his car wearing only his dressing gown. Embarrassed as she approached, he held the gown tight round his chest. Kate really just wanted to pass the time of day.

"I have an ugly scar," he said trying to smile, but she knew he wasn't comfortable.

"What's the worry?" Kate said kindly. "Don't we all have them?"

He pulled the dressing gown tighter like his embarrassment got worse. Kate was sorry she said anything as he withdrew through the hall door.

"I left my hair brush on the back seat," he explained. "Always the same. When you step out of the shower you can't find it. Not that I have much hair to worry about."

"You have enough," Kate said. "Ted is home at the weekend. She is all excited."

She pointed at Sarah who was trying to sit against the bonnet of the car, but she kept sliding down.

"Mind Jack's car, you. I will have to pay him for the damage," Kate said, laughing at the idea. "It is all you need now, a broken headlight."

He didn't flinch when she mentioned Ted; it was like he wasn't really listening.

"Better let you go get dressed before you get pneumonia on top of everything else. Your car will be wrecked. She's falling asleep. All this child does is sleep. Misses her daddy, don't you?"

Kate spoke softly to Fiona, gently rocking the buggy as the child rubbed her eyes.

Wood Point, A few years ago
4.

Caw heard him come in, flapping his wings twice to clear
the air, and somehow it made it easier to listen. He was in the
kitchen making crackers and cheese. Caw heard the whistle
of the kettle. Jack dragged a tea cloth with the shoe on his
right foot to clean the dark stains ingrained on the tiles. He
was leaning back against the work top, bits of cracker
breaking off his shoe to scatter beside him to crumble, some
pieces under the kitchen table.

Caw heard his footsteps as he went back to the kitchen
twice to check the electrics. Plodding his feet on the short
stairs, pausing momentarily on the landing, he opened the hot
press door to check on the hot water. His pee started and
stopped, but at great velocity, making a strong pouring
sound, stopping then starting again till it was no more than a
drain. The tap water was quieter. He scrubbed his face with a
special rub for oily skin; it was akin to washing your skin
with sand. Lying in bed he sighed heavily, turning over on
his side, eventually turning on the radio.

The music was soft a ballad from far away. Caw liked the
sound. It reminded him of wide open spaces. Caw strained to
hear as Jack was so quiet. He was tapping the letters on his
phone, texting a late-night radio show. What a life. The thrill
when the DJ read his name.

"Jack from the Point." The presenter made it funny. After a
gap Jack was snoring. This worried Caw as he couldn't sleep
himself, especially if it was cold. But this night was warm.
The cloud had covered the whole of Wood Point with a
blanket. The boys slept soundly, not a sound from anywhere.

Perhaps it was only now he really missed his wife, all
those years they lived on Ramsey Hill. How she insisted they
move out, with the crumbling walls and the rats crawling
through the gutters. Some of them were all right, sleeking by,
saying goodnight, but she didn't trust them. She said how

she remembered when she was a kid, rats feasted on the body of her only brother. Caw moved uneasily in the nest, a loose slate striking off another, the same shrill sound the rat made.

She liked Seaview. The houses were new, the dustbins full, no more begging from the wood pigeon who kept the sycamore. More undesirables in there, picking at the hotel bins after a function, all sorts of funny-looking crows with their grey uniforms. Why did she come here? A better address but too near the walkway, the truck delivering beds to the Anchorage, a new estate next door.

Caw found nothing of her spots of blood—a severed head welded to the concrete, her lower body removed by the rats or starving gulls. Now he was left to mind the boys, keep them safe till they could fly away on their own. They were trying, sometimes making it to the edge of the roof, but their flapping was either too fast or too slow. Caw encouraged them, giving them some extra maggots for trying. He found a half-full bag of crisps on the pier. He broke off the sharp ends, feeding them the treat.

In the morning they would wake first, bellies sore from hunger. They would cry, "Caw, caw" with great consternation. He would fly low near the upper houses where they deposited their black bags first, pecking, ripping, minding out for glass and sharp cans. Breakfast would be had, and the writer would wake to hear "Grand Central Station."

Roof games, slates moving on their own, the squawking Caw, the boys' mouths open feed, and sore bellies breathe. He would see shadows flap by the curtains, older crows stopping to beg for scraps but Caw would only barely have enough for his own. The shadows would migrate, the writer would be half awake wondering about the crows and why they are so chirpy at this hour of the morning.

*

I never understood what Michael Harrington saw in Madge Butler. She would hardly win any prizes, yet there is no accounting for taste. Whatever he saw in her was in general good for him, as it perked him up after what they still refer to round here as the tragedy. One day Mammy Rosie was feeding me at the kitchen table and in she walked.

Even I noticed that her hair was dyed off her head and she had enormous breasts, which sagged to her waist. Maybe it was because she was a great cook and made a super sandwich. She made all the food for the parish committee who met the first Tuesday of every month.

Madge could pull a pint as well, and Michael Harrington swore some of the dirt birds only came out to catch a glimpse of her giant melons. She wore low cut blouses and her dresses were a size to small, but she was hardly God's gift either with her white cake of makeup and lipstick that was pink or orange, making her look ridiculous. Mammy Rosie never missed her chance to get stuck into Michael Harrington about her, mimicking Madge redoing her lipstick in the bar mirror.

Michael ignored her for the most part until Mammy Rosie said she would have to go. She accused her of being indecent and she most likely had her fingers in the cash drawer.

Michael banged the kitchen table with his fist saying, "Enough, woman, and in front of the child."

Mammy Rosie gave me a pitiful look like she was thinking I hadn't got the brains to be listening, and what of it? I wouldn't understand anyhow.

Michael Harrington stood and said, "I need the help behind the bar. She makes sandwiches for the footballers and the hurlers. She is a good cleaner and the customers like her, young and old. How am I to diversify if I haven't got the help? You spend all your time with young Sean. The business is too much for me."

Mammy Rosie came to me, placing her fat hand on my head.

"No need to bring him into it. He has the blight; can't you see it? Your profits won't save him one way or another."

Michael gave her a desperate look.

"I hear they have a good place in Celbridge," he said, brushing by us to get to the bar. "So you want rid, is that it? Send him away out of sight."

Mammy Rosie patted my head harder than before.

"I want what's best for him, Rosie. Whatever is best. Or is this the way you want him, sticking his tongue out at passers-by, licking the dust and soot off the windows, watching endless television? Even the snow excites him when the channel is down!"

Mammy Rosie eyed him coldly. "Remember, he is as much yours as mine. I brought him into the world for sure, but you played a hand, hah?"

It was the only time I ever heard them row, but I am sure they rowed constantly. I was just not tuned in to hear it. After all what do you do when you have the blight? Sit and watch television, draw pictures, eat, and shit. That's what I did. I suppose it was the one thing I had in common with Caw. We both sat around all day shitting.

Caw didn't take to me at first. I can hardly blame him with my face all squashed against the window. Sticking my tongue out at him as he sat tired on the wall opposite. I knew he was trying to ignore me. His head bobbed up and down every now and then as he would stoop to clean his rear. His feathers would be wild from the wind and the stray branches of trees. Eventually he gave up and stared me out of it. He looked nervously skywards from time to time like he was reluctant to fly because he might not make it and suddenly fall back to earth.

One day I was sitting on the fish boxes watching for the trawler when Caw landed beside me. He didn't say anything at first. He just did what he usually did—cleaned his back feathers, bobbed his head a bit, did his, "Caw, caw" thing. He eyed other crows contemptuously and glared at any gulls that came near. After a while he started to tell me stuff about Jack Browne and Kate Donovan. I had no particular interest in either of them. I am not romantic or anything. Anyhow Caw seemed to think it was of great interest, and I didn't want to disappoint him. Then he said he had overheard Jack Browne read aloud from some stuff he was writing, and you would never guess but Caw said I was in it.

Wood Point, Many years ago
5.

When the sun beat off her shoulders she ducked under, tasting the salt in the sea.

Georgina watched nervously as Kate dived, submerging her whole body before standing upright to drain the water swishing from her bathing cap sapping her shoulders. Her one-piece swimsuit looked weighty.

"Do it again, Kate, go on, will you? I promise I will pay attention this time. Go on, just do it once more for me, will you?"

"No," Kate said, looking away out to Kilbrittain.

The wind was making shadows dark on tiny pools beyond; along the lower hills small settlements of evergreens were bitterly divided. Over the hills she imagined valleys of lush farms and whitewashed houses.

"Please, Kate, come on. I'll teach you to play tennis. I swear I will pay attention this time."

Kate did the breast stroke, clearing the cloudy water for a split second so she could see the sandy bottom.

"Bring your hands right in to your chest and then push," Kate said, looking strangely boyish. Georgina tried, failing miserably.

Standing upright frustrated, she said, "I will teach you to play tennis better than this. I can't see the stroke; you will need to show me above the water, like this."

Georgina pulled her arms into her chest then pushed away like she was removing a dead weight.

Kate laughed. "You have to kick your legs, Georgie, and point your fingers."

Kate bent her fingers till they looked thin and sharp like a fish fin, then launched into a swim shouting, "Look, into the chest, then wide out like that!"

She stood abruptly, much to Georgina's disgust.

"Try it again," Kate said, noticing a crowd of youngsters gathering on the low wall by the road.

"Wait till you have a tennis racket. I will make a fool of you." Georgina looked at her pathetically and then said, "Is that Barry Cousins and the crowd over by the road?"

Kate, floating on her back said, "It is, I think, with his followers from Wood Point."

"I heard he is going out with Ann Marie McCarthy from Barryroe," Georgina said sadly, trying to identify the crowd.

"Barry Cousins has loads of girls," Kate said, standing by her friend.

Georgina moved away from her as the water dripping was cold. The wind was picking up around the point, disturbing the tops of the trees with a hair brush. Without discussing it the two girls made for the shore, the water heavy against them. Swishing, their movements laboured, the sand softer at the waters edge. The beach was stony and hot where there were small patches of sand. They walked slowly up to the wall to collect their towels.

Drying off, Kate heard one of Barry Cousins' entourage cry out, "Hey, young one, have you ever seen a prick?"

The rest of them laughed, and Georgina smiled, unperturbed.

"Do you want to see one?" the same voice shouted. Again, a huge guffaw of laughter.

Georgina turned her back on them wrapping her towel round her waist.

"Hey, young wan, you have a fine arse on you." A different voice this time.

Going red, Georgina said, "Is that him, Kate?"

Kate peered round her and whispered, "I don't think so. He is sitting on the wall quietly." Kate stopped peering.

"Is he looking at me?" Georgina pretended to dry herself with a second towel.

"He is not," Kate said caustically, "He is looking at the yacht going down the channel. Now will you stop asking me questions, girl, and look for yourself?"

Georgina retreated to the wall, sulking. Occasionally she sneaked a look, but Barry Cousins was lost among his admirers. Kate sat below her, using the wall as a rest. The sun returned and it sparkled against the damp of skin, sparkling with tiny hints of sand like precious stone.

A brother and sister from Timoleague who were both obese waddled their way onto the beach further down. The roaring crowd didn't notice them at first. They shouted abuse at a few young girls from the riding school who trotted past on horses that seemed much too big for them.

"Glad to see you can ride!" shouted one of the lads.

Then Barry Cousins came to the fore with, "Hey, have you got a posh pussy?"

All his fans went into kinks, some of them doubling up with laughter, their faces red and ridiculous.

Georgina smiled up at them whilst Kate stared straight ahead, loving the light warming her face. The leader of the riders kicked heels, and all four horses trotted on till only their big wide behinds were visible. One of the group fired pebbles after them, but they moved fast and the pebbles sprayed harmlessly on the road, the horses and riders oblivious to any wrongdoing.

"Posh bitches," Barry Cousins said to the grunting of his mates. They were quiet for a while, talking amongst themselves, the occasional loud guffaw. Barry Cousins, the best young hurler in Barryroe, was the centre of attention.

"Do you think he notices me?" Georgina said out of the blue.

Kate's eyes were closed. When she opened them the sea glistened like milk bottle glass.

She closed them again. "Go way with you, Georgie. I told you he is with Ann Marie McCarthy. She'd take the eye out

of you, as quick as she would look at you. All the girls round
the parish are afraid of her."

"I was only asking. That's not a crime is it?"

Kate, hesitating eventually, said, "I'm not looking at him
anyway; there is nothing to look at. I love the sun on my
face. I have to keep my eyes closed. Anyway he is nothing to
look at. The tiny nose on him…it will be years till he sees a
razor. He might be the best hurler in Barryroe, but that says
nothing for the rest of them. Doesn't his father select the
team, or is it his uncle? I dunno."

With her eyes closed fast Kate felt Georgina adjust her
sitting position on the wall; the damp round the seams of her
bathing suit was starting to itch. The obese brother and sister
had made it to the water's edge where the girl flirted with the
surf, her brother clearly coaxing her to step in and get wet.
The girl, her hair tied up in a bun, was falling out of her one-
piece swimsuit. The boy looked around him, cautiously
happy the crowd of boys on the wall were distracted, and he
took the plunge himself.

Stepping in, bending forwards, he scooped handfuls of
water on to his midriff and over his shoulders. His sister tried
to follow but again stepped back. She stood rigid as though
the ice cold water had numbed her entire body.

One of Barry Cousins' crowd shouted, "Are you afraid of
it? Go get in, will you? Blocking the sun off us all over
here!"

The crowd laughed but the girl pretended not to hear.

Barry Cousins, who had slipped onto the sand in line with
Kate, shouted, "What the fuck are you at? It's only a fuckin'
inch? The size of you blocking the sun off of me, can't you
get down?"

Georgina giggled but Kate barely opened her eyes
squinting at the fat girl at the water's edge. She had her head
bowed forward like she was ashamed.

"Are you afraid you will cause a tidal wave?" Barry shouted. This time the girl placed both hands on her face and walked slowly back to where they had left their clothes. The crowd clapped as she picked up her towel. Turning away she pretended to dry herself. Her brother, struggling with his weight, made his way up the small beach to confront the crowd.

Kate opened her eyes fully. Georgina made a small screeching sound. The boy was younger than Barry Cousins but around the same age as most of his companions.

"Why da fuck did you do that?" he addressed Barry who regarded him calmly. "Why say all that to her? She can't swim yet, she is learning!"

"The rest of us are here for the sun. She was blocking the sun, so I told her to get in or out," Barry said to the loud amusement of his cronies.

"How would you like it? You wouldn't like it at all!" the boy said, half turning away. "Anyhow," he said turning back, "a person won't block the sun from over there. You are very smart."

"Depends on how fat you are!" Barry said laughing.

The fat boy didn't find it funny; he kicked a mix of sand and small stone in the direction of the crowd. It dusted off the base of the wall.

Barry Cousins was on his feet, his cronies bouncing on the wall in various stages of excitement.

"What a ballocks!" Barry said. "See that?" he looked back at his friends with practised hurt. "The fucker wants to blind me and put me out of the county trials! The only player from Barryroe in with a chance, and he tries to blind me!"

The fat boy got scared and marched off towards his sister, his feet making deep holes in the clay. Barry Cousins rushed after him, letting out a huge roar. His anger exaggerated like he was dragged into temporary insanity, and with a mighty scream he brought his right fist down on the boy's shoulder.

The boy winced and turned only to meet the same fist hard against his nose.

Georgina laughed and the entourage clapped as the boy fell to his knees, blood spurting from both nostrils. Barry Cousins examined his victim to see if he needed more, but the cheering crowd and the boy's whimpering forced him to withdraw to his seat. The boy, watched by his bemused sister, took an age to get up, plodding his way back to his towel and his clothes. His sister whispered something to him, and he nodded his head, holding the towel to his face for what seemed like an age.

Wood Point, Many years ago
6.

Later Bob ran to meet them on the gravel path; the dense hedge hid them from the cars on Ramsey Hill. The Labrador skidded to a halt, licking Georgina's bare knees before jumping on Kate. He licked her arms and turned, picking up a stray piece of wood before racing across the lawn and eventually sitting and spying from under the sycamore. The sun found them through gaps in the branches; the tree looked pinkish in the glow.

They rounded the house. Madge Butler was washing cups at the sink; she smiled through the fly window as they approached the open door.

"Don't let the dog in, Georgie," Madge said, meaning business. "I have just cleaned out his bed. I have no need for his slobbering all over it till I at least get his blanket dry."

"Go away, Bob!" she shouted at the dog. Bob had followed around the side of the house; the confused Bob went to roll on the back lawn.

Georgina said, "We need water, Madge, badly. I am dead after the walk."

Madge filled two cups of water. "Many down at the beach?"

"A good few…not that many, though," Kate said sipping the cold water and watching the dog turning over franticly, then trying to catch his own tiny tail.

"People don't trust the weather, so they go elsewhere. Who wants to sit on their backsides freezing cold with the kids full of muck?" Madge said with authority.

"Is Mum home?" Georgina asked casually.

"Not yet. It's not half-four yet. Your father was home, but he went out again."

"We are going to the court, but I think I will lock Bob in the tool shed."

Madge looked at her then quickly at the dog's bed.

"Why would you do that? It is such a wonderful day."

"He chases the ball, Madge. We won't have a second's peace. I am going to give Kate a few lessons. She is teaching me the breast stroke, so I am teaching her tennis."

Madge, laughing said, "Good for you, Kate. We could do with more tennis players round here. Years since I hit a ball, never mind had a racket. Okay, give him his water if you are going to lock him away. I hope he is not going to bark the place down now. I still have upstairs to clean, and my head is bursting already."

*

"I don't know why she asks you to clean the study. She knows I do my accounts on Fridays. Might as well take all of this with me down to the hotel. At least Mrs. Edwards affords me peace."

Donal Travers looked her up and down, making her feel smaller than she actually was.

"I will leave this room till last so," Madge said fixing the curtains. "I don't see what all the panic is about, Donal. I will give a lick, five minutes max. She is sure to check it over. You know she checks everything I do."

"She is paying you!" Donal snapped, reading a bank statement every now and then he peered over his glasses at her. He lifted his head as Madge came close, covering the statement with his right hand save she could read it over his shoulder. Madge arranged the bellows behind him, then she started clearing the grate with the poker. She forced loose bits of burnt coal through the gaps.

"How are things anyway?" Madge asked.

"Things are hectic. I have the phone off the hook in case they ring me with some other stupid query, or herself is pissed in Clon and needs a lift. Things couldn't be better, except getting the money in is still the problem. Why is it,

Madge, people want everything for nothing?" Donal said
turning around to see her behind. "You're everyone's friend
until the fateful day they have to part with the cash."

"True for you," Madge said, walking in front of him to
retrieve her furniture polish and duster off the hard chair by
the sideboard. "You should call the heavies…might wake
them up. Has Bill Thornton paid up?"

"Bits," Donal said folding the bank statement and covering
it with a file he was studying earlier.

Madge started to polish his desk. The spray, white, turned
clear as she rubbed vigorously.

"Call in the heavies, I say, then you won't have trouble,"
Madge sighed heavily as Donal watched her fluff the cloth
along the desk surface. Her huge breast followed, rubbing the
hardwood.

"Are you going down to Mrs. Edwards, or where are you
going? It's nice out. You should walk to relieve the stress.
They say it is the 'in' thing these days. Walking takes away
stress and repairs the ticker. Even for five minutes," Madge
said lifting herself upright.

Donal walked to the window taking his glasses off and
placing them neatly in their case. The garden was losing the
run of itself. The weeds were taking over, the tree needed
surgery, and moss was thriving in the shade. The loose stones
marking the gravel path were uneven with some on their side.

"He doesn't owe you, Donal, does he?"

Donal turned back to her, surprised. "No, he never would.
You know that. He wouldn't allow it, never. I asked him, did
he want in, but he said no, and he wasn't very gracious about
it either. You would swear I asked him to cut his own throat.
There was way more than him who wanted a part in the
development. What is he making from the pub? Only he
owns the freehold."

"The summer is good, and he has his locals, but you're
right: Michael Harrington is not one to gamble. He is suitably
scared of you, Donal. He doesn't approve to be honest with

you. Michael's people are a wary sort. They wouldn't even
go to the bank for money, everything is hidden under the
mattress. Do you want me to Hoover, or will I leave you in
peace? She isn't back yet, so she might go straight upstairs.
Sometimes she does when she's in a state."

"Go ahead, woman, I am going down to the hotel. I might
get some civilised conversation there and a bite to eat. I left it
for you in the drawer, just in case you are wondering."

Donal left, leaving the door swinging. Madge heard him
almost take the front door off its hinges. His jeep started and
she could hear the deep throaty sound of the diesel engine.

He should walk, she thought. He will be footless later. He
wasn't looking well—more stressed than before, in fact.

She walked to his desk, sliding open the drawer. Out of
habit she listened, just in case Madeline was back. No sound.
The envelope lay there, untitled. She opened it, checking the
contents. All there, as usual. Last Friday of the month, like
clockwork. Michael was so impressed with her. A woman
able to fend for herself, look after her sick mother, run her
own car—he thought her a great catch.

*

Madge heard her car and then herself opening the front
door, picking up a plate as the kitchen door opened. In
walked Madeline, her face pale, the lipstick too thick for her
lips. She had painted oddly, too, missing the corners of her
mouth.

"Where is Bob?" Madeline asked, looking past her and out
the kitchen window.

"Georgina put him in the tool shed. She is up on the court
with Katie Donovan."

Madeline made a long face, exaggerating her emotion.

"The child plays tennis, the dog is locked away, and I must
pay you before you go away."

Madge kept working, stacking the plates on top of each
other in the cupboard.

"Would you care for some tea or coffee, Mrs. Travers? The
water is not long boiled. It will only take a second to boil up
again."

Madeline, feeling the worsening effects of drink, sat down
on the nearest chair. It was still half under the table and she
nearly slipped off its edge.

"I rambled here and I rambled there, and then I got no
bloody where, and the road from Clon is gone, is gone. Do
you know, I think I killed a fox. I was just passing the road to
the agricultural college when it ran across in front of me. At
first I thought it was a cat, big bushy tail, then I heard
BANG!" she said loudly, startling Madge.

Madge placed a mug of coffee beside her; Madeline stared
at it like she didn't know what it was or where it came from.

"I don't like coffee or men. I prefer men to coffee. No,
really, I prefer coffee to men, and I must pay you, Madge,
before I forget. We had a meeting in the Emmet, and I'm
afraid it ended up a liquid lunch. Lots of vodka. It is twenty,
isn't it?"

Madeline fiddled for her purse. "I keep meaning to leave it
for you before I go, but you know what it's like, last-minute
stuff, keep forgetting."

"Shall I make you tea instead? I thought you liked coffee."

"No, I like coffee, but I don't like men. He was the size of
Bob, but he had a big bush of a tail. I think I might have
killed him, Madge. Imagine that—killing a fox. Does it bring
you luck to kill a fox? Is that lucky?"

"I will make you tea," Madge said, taking the coffee away
and emptying it in the sink.

The tea sobered her a little. She steadied herself holding
her head more aloft. Madge envied her looks and her figure,
the money to take care of herself all these years, yet she was
no spring chicken—at least late fifties. Georgina was a late

baby. Mrs. Edwards swore she lost a few before that, but Madge never got the truth of it.

"I don't think killing a fox is anything, you know, like killing a spider. Never heard anyone say it was good or bad luck. It's lucky it wasn't a child that ran across the road."

Madge hesitated, unsure as to how Mrs. Travers would take her comments.

Madeline, considering what she said, shrugged.

"It wasn't a child, Madge, it was a fox," she said seriously, as Georgina and Kate arrived at the back door.

Georgina burst in. "Water, water, please, it's scorching out."

Madge went to fill two tumblers including one for Kate who had followed in.

"Hello, Mother," Georgina panted. "Good lunch?"

"Hello, Kate, you got the sun!"

"Hello, Mrs. Travers," Kate said shyly.

"How is your father? I heard he wasn't well. Is he any better?"

Kate, sipping her water, said, "He is much better, thanks. My mammy said he'll be home next week."

"Very good," Madeline said and was about to ask another question when Madge intervened.

"Let Bob out now, Georgina, the poor thing will die of heat in there. Here, I will get his other water bowl for you."

The two girls set off down the garden to the tool shed, Georgina carrying the water bowl. It was heavy with water, so she set it down on the small path. Bob exited lazily as if he had just woken up, shaking himself till he got his bearings. Georgina tapped the bowl of water. At first he appeared disinterested, a few licks before turning away, but he took control again after smelling Kate's feet. He allowed his thirst to come to the fore, scooping the cold water with his tongue, splashing and swishing until the surrounds of the bowl were wet.

Madeline turned to Madge as she was leaving to go upstairs to the drawing room.

"Tell Georgina I am off for my nap. She won't mind a bit, she knows when Mummy's tired."

"Will I leave you some dinner, or do you want to do something later?" Madge asked, peeling the spuds and cutting away the rotten bits. The potatoes were poor.

"I intend to go join my husband later in the hotel. I may eat down there. Don't you worry about it. If Georgina is fed, the job is done, as they say. I am off to dream of foxes!"

Madeline closed the heavy kitchen door behind her. Madge heard her sharp footsteps on the stairs. She would never make the hotel later with a bottle of vodka unopened in the drinks cabinet. No, Donal would have another night to himself.

She is in a funny mood, Madge concluded. She is often drunk and full of nonsense, but she is normally more curt and formal. Maybe she did think killing a fox was unlucky only because she was so drunk. Of course, when she is sober she is a right scourge, following you round the house, offering to help, checking your work, commenting on tiny specks of dust missed on the sideboard or the piano in the study.

The girls walked back through the garden slowly, the tennis rackets abandoned by the flower pots below the window.

She doesn't do the garden much now, only the odd time if she is sober. For a while the bedding plants have looked dry and tired in need of water. Maybe she would water them before she left.

The whole place has an overgrown feel to it. The old hedges needed clipping. Only the Montbretia thrived, gathering in clusters around the dark borders, the flower of yellow and purple with a shadow taste of orange.

"Mum is drunk," Georgina said, sitting on the grass. Kate followed suit but didn't comment on what her friend just said.

"Mum is drunk every day. At least Dad only gets drunk at the weekend. Do your parents get drunk, Kate?"

Georgina started to pick strands of grass and just fire them aimlessly, small bits landed on Kate's ankle.

"Daddy does sometimes, but I never seen Mammy drunk."

Kate was watching the dog who was investigating something moving under the tool shed. The sun was giving up. At last the warm air was replaced by a cool breeze imported by the Atlantic cloud.

"Mum drinks upstairs. She sits by the window for hours looking out over the bay drinking, the dog lying at her feet. Sometimes she drinks herself to sleep. I have to get a blanket to cover her, and she stays there all night."

Georgina moved on to her side.

"My bum is sore from the tennis," she said.

"So is mine. My knickers are too tight."

They both laughed. After a pause Georgina said, "Do you think Barry Cousins fancies me at all? Now tell the truth, don't be jealous or bitchy. Does he?"

Kate started to mess with the strands of grass herself. It seemed like the thing to do.

She smiled at Georgina. "I don't know, honest. I suppose he would, you know, with your good looks and this big house and all the money your daddy has."

Kate took a clump of grass, unable to continue as she knew she had already repeated stuff she had overheard her mother saying.

"What's that to him? We're not marrying yet. Maybe he thinks I am posh, you're right, and a catch. Do you think I will get him? Hey, do you know something?" Georgina brought her face right close to Kate till their noses were almost touching.

"What?" Kate said eagerly.

"Daddy has these builders over in Butlerstown. They're building these houses for him. They're nearly done, and as soon as they're finished he is going to get them over here, and guess what?"

Kate said nothing; she just shook her head.

"I am getting a tree house in the sycamore out the front. We will invite them all, see. Maybe Barry Cousins will come over, Kate! Dad says it will be huge, the biggest ever in Wood Point."

Kate was quiet; she turned away from her friend. Bob ran towards them, having given up on chasing whatever it was under the shed.

"We were going to build one once, but Daddy said no, it was too dangerous, we might fall out of it and kill ourselves. So we never did it."

It was Georgina's turn to go quiet. "Kate, you don't have a tree in your garden. You have a few bushes and the old apple tree at the top of the bank. If you stepped on a branch of that thing it would snap in two. To have a tree house you need a proper tree."

Bob started to lick Kate's cheek, but she brushed him away. Bob, unperturbed, went to Georgina who hugged him tightly.

Wood Point, A few years ago
7.

The day Jack Browne sat at the bar with my father and Pee
Wee Flynn, he was holding forth about lots of things do with
the arts, mainly, but also stupid things like the list of side
effects listed on the pamphlets that came with his
medications. Don't get me wrong, Jack didn't say much
about what was ailing him. More, he had them all laughing
when listing some of the worst of the side effects of
consuming his tablets. The pamphlets warned of things like
dizziness, red eyes, swollen tongue, vomiting and diarrhoea,
sweating, palpitations, rashes of every kind, mild epilepsy,
heart failure, kidney failure, but the biggest and most
wondrous side effect was the anxiety that his anti-anxiety
medication could cause.

I was watching "A Fistful of Dynamite" with James
Coburn and Rod Steiger. Father made me turn the sound
down, but I was determined to turn it up when the bar scene
in Dublin came on. I awaited the soundtrack playing, "Sean
song, Sean song."

Jack looked over at me from time to time. I stuck my
tongue out at him but he didn't seem to mind, ordering
another pint, sitting and listening to my father argue with Pee
Wee about hurling. Pee Wee was nervous around my father,
so he tried to keep his English accent light.

When father said that Danny Fitzgerald was the best
goalkeeper in the parish, Pee Wee countered with, "I know,
Michael, but you have never seen John Hurley. I'm telling
you, mate, he carried us against Charleville."

My father's eyes strained under the thick grey brush of his
eyebrows. I could see he was trying to put his emotions into
context, but such was his frustration his cheeks burst rose
red.

"I have so! Didn't I hurl with his father and his uncles for years? And I watched him grow from a nipper to what he is now. I will tell you, Pee Wee, he is not half the player his father was, and if Seanie Hurley wasn't a selector he wouldn't see the light of day. Come on now, man, one good game against Charleville, who are poor. Tell me, why, then, is Danny Fitz on the Cork panel if Hurley's so good?"

Pee Wee was slightly taken aback by my father's conviction and tried to back pedal.

"I know, Michael, I know Danny Fitz is a class act. We all know he is the business. I'm only saying that Hurley is pushing him. It can only be good for Barryroe."

Not convinced, my father rounded the bar to pull more stout.

Pee Wee who was still trying to conciliate said, "I think it is going to be a great year this year. We finally have a team that can do it!"

My father, resting the stout on the draining mat said, "We won't beat Kilmichael. I would stake my life on it, no matter what team we have. We don't have the beating of them, not yet, so unless someone else does us a favour and then has an off day we can say good night to it."

Pee Wee dropped his head in reflection. Jack Browne thanked my father for his pint then looked over at me. I stuck out my tongue. He smiled. Walking over, he stood watching the screen.

Rod Steiger walks to James Coburn, who is lying back, resting under a tarpaulin in the rebel camp.

Jack listened to the dialogue intently.

RS—"What is that?"
JC—"It's a map."
Steiger lies down, using it to rest his back.
JC—"It's your country you're lying all over."

RS—"Not my country. My country is me and my family."

JC—"Well, your country is also Huerta [Rebel Leader] and the governor and landlords. And Gunther Ruiz and his locusts. This little revolution we're having here."

RS—"Revolution? Please don't try to tell me about revolution! I know how revolutions start. People that read books go to the people that don't read books and say –'The time has come for change.'"

JC—"Shh!"

RS—"Shh! Shh! Shh! Shh! Shh! Shit, shush!"

RS—"I know what I'm talking about when I'm talking about revolutions! The people who read books go to the people who can't read and say, 'We need change,' so the poor people make the change! The people who read the books sit around big polished tables and talk and talk and eat. But what has happened to the poor people? They are dead! That's your revolution. Shh! So please, don't tell me about revolutions! Then what happens? The same fucking thing starts all over again!"

James Coburn, taking a puff from his cigar, closes the book he was reading—The Patriotism—and he drops it in the mud.

Jack was really impressed. He stuck out his tongue at me before returning to the bar and his pint. I couldn't see what Caw was going on about; he was the best of chaps to me. I liked the way he communicated through his eyes. I dunno, I suppose Caw, living in his roof, saw another side of him. Then there was the tragedy with the boys, and Caw held him responsible for it. I couldn't talk to Jack about it, so it was best left for Caw to deal with.

Margaret from the Fisherman's came in. She was on her lunch break, and when the mood took her she came by to see me, sitting herself down beside me like I was her boyfriend. Caw told me Jack Browne was besotted with her. Evidently one night when he had drank a load of stout he just stared at her endlessly. Earlier she sang in the Fisherman's talent contest, and Caw said that Jack just fell in love with her voice.

I was waiting for Caw to say something about him—you know, like he was a real pervert or something—but he didn't. He said when Jack was reading his stuff aloud he referred to Margaret as the beautiful girl with the golden voice. Caw said Jack wanted her to be the voice when he played the themes from "A Fistful of Dynamite" and "Once Upon a Time in the West" in his head. He must really have been pissed that night as he paid no attention to her now.

Margaret said to me, "What's this, Sean? I think I saw this, didn't I? I did. Love the music."

She skipped to the bar and Michael gave her a Coke and a packet of Tayto crisps. Then she came back to me, squeezing up against me till I felt the full weight of her. Jack gave her a quick glance as she crossed the floor, but he returned to his company like he just gave up. Pee Wee kept looking at her before looking away, hoping nobody would notice, but I did. Dirty pervert Pee Wee. The music came on so I turned it up a little.

"Sean, Sean, Sean, da dada dada da dada." And Margaret got the microphone, her voice piercing the air with Jack and Pee Wee playing the violin. Suddenly I was outside, leading the parade, the whole village behind me. People passed by on different coloured floats, more violins, more dancers, young boys lash the air. They phantom hurl with invisible ash. Caw on my left shoulder, the women dancing in old-fashioned ballroom dresses, the men neat in black tie. The elders on floats, sitting, smiling.

"Da da dad a da dad, dad a dada da dad dad a, Sean, Sean, Sean."

Little children ran alongside, Caw cawing, Michael Harrington laughing, the violin players were outdoors, and Kate led the way. Margaret, still her face pale 'neath her blonde hair. She was serious, squeezing ever closer till her heat grabbed my heart. Her hands in my brain massaged the tiredness, the numbers. She saw Caw.

"Sean, Sean, Sean."

I am under water blowing dark bubbles, my face compressed. My hair stands like rushes pulled from above. I am looking for Mammy Rosie, and I can't find her. It is all too dark.

Mags sings, "Dah da dad a dad dad dad a da." The bubbles lessen; they are filled with dry air.

The darkness recedes; the parade is over. Dancers stop; the floats are gone. There is just me and Caw.

Margaret kisses me gently on the cheek. She goes back to work.

Wood Point, Many years ago
8.

Mrs. Edwards watched Donal.

There were so many things she didn't like about him. The way his hair had only partly receded, leaving a tuft glued to his forehead. She didn't like the fact he hid his glasses in their case in his inside pocket, his vanity refusing the permanent display of the same. Yet she knew he needed them to read and to watch television. Also his suit was good, but he was sloppy, not pulling the jacket up correctly, the collar splashed with dandruff, his hair damp with oil spoiling the line of his shirt.

She didn't like the way he drank a pint of stout with a brandy chaser. Why both when one would do? Go either a pint or a brandy, but both together? Fred liked him and relied more on him now since he bought the land out in Butlerstown. Donal Travers was doing well when all round him were afraid. If only he could put the face of enjoyment on it all. He was always tired and miserable looking, just waiting to make a complaint.

She noticed he did strange things with his hands when ordering a drink, waving them about like he was making a sign of the cross. Young Brennan behind the bar was used to him and hopped to exaggerated attention, knowing it pleased Donal no end. He was good for a drink, though, buying for the company and sometimes even for a straggler from the village who was counting out their change.

"Are you eating, Donal?" Mrs. Edwards asked, gathering up unused menus from the tables.

Donal gave her an intense look like he wasn't expecting the question, like nobody had ever asked him such a question before.

"I will," Donal said, resting his right elbow on the bar. "What's the special?" he asked gruffly, imitating some of his workmen.

"Fish pie. Will that do you?" Mrs. Edwards looked at her husband who was looking sleepy. He wouldn't last the evening; he needed his nap.

"The fish pie is delicious," Fred said to Donal, like he was telling him a prized secret.

"I don't want fish. It sits in my gut for days. I will go a rare sirloin and chips, onions and mushrooms—the business," Donal said, pointing at Mrs. Edwards.

It made her uncomfortable, and she gave him a false smile before leaving for the kitchen.

Later Donal, slouching over his, plate muttered to himself. He called the young waitress every minute or so, each time asking some more ridiculous question or commenting caustically on the fare before him. He drank red wine with his meal—it had to be French, strong and fruity. Every now and again he would belch.

The restaurant wasn't busy. A young couple sat lazily at the far end near the door, whilst two elderly guests picked at their food, oblivious to him. They were more interested in the photographs of the West Cork coastline adorning the walls.

Edwina Edwards brought him his coffee. He looked up, surprised to see her.

"Is he still inside, Edwina?" Donal asked, wiping his fingers with his serviette.

"No, Donal, I sent him to bed for a rest. You know he is hardly able for it anymore, if he ever was."

Donal waved his arms like he had just accepted the loss of something.

"He should have gone in with me on the financials, you know what I mean? They are all pissed with me, you know? But you see, Edwina, they didn't listen when I told them. Land will be the thing in years to come. Property will be the key. The people who own it will do nicely. Those who don't will struggle, believe me. It will happen."

He finished his wine, swallowing the glass whole, then stared at his coffee like it could make him ill.

"It will do you good, Donal. A long night of it yet. Are you going to the village? I can get young Brennan to run you over. Come back for the jeep in the morning."

Donal wiped his chin with the same serviette he used for his fingers.

"I might walk over. It will clear my head, but, sure, I may have a few brandies beforehand. Helps digest the food. I have to tell you, Edwina, compliments to your chef. Very nice indeed."

Mrs. Edwards blushed. He was never amorous or particularly mannerly despite the trappings of wealth.

"How is Madeline?" she asked, taking the wine glass.

Donal moved his right hand nervously to his chin, pondering her question.

His voice softening, he said, "Madeline is fine. She has the Lions Club. Gives her plenty to do. You know what she is like, always wants to be involved, never the one to lie down. She runs it, you know?"

"They do great work locally, don't they?" Mrs. Edwards had removed the soiled serviette as well. "Aren't they raising money for the hospice right now? Someone said they are having show jumping over in Ring in May."

Later she watched as Donal staggered his way across the drive. She watched with young Brennan on standby in case he should try and take the jeep. But he didn't, he was walking erratically with exaggerated purpose.

*

Bill Thornton smiled. Donal hadn't graced his door for a while, and they had things to discuss. Also, he was very likely to drain most of the bottle of brandy he had opened the previous day. Donal sat at the end of the bar near the fire; the television was turned off.

The small group of local arty types, men and women, sat at the opposite end near the door. Donal, his head bowed, ordered a brandy, his hand hitting his eyebrow. He then slapped his right cheek with the palm of his left hand. Nobody took any notice of him. They had all seen it before many times. He muttered under his breath.

Bill didn't ask him to repeat what it was he had said. Ignoring it completely he said, "Many down below?"

"Quiet," Donal said, like he was suddenly sober. "They have nothing on for anyone; the punters can't afford to eat out, not at their prices. She won't let him do a thing with it. You would be better on your own, like you, Bill, calling the shots yourself. Who wants a cackling woman calling things? She has a restaurant fit for kings and queens, but you don't have many queens and kings in Wood Point. She spends her life picking up the bar menus off the fucking tables. All the classy French names and the fine wines. When the local has never seen France, he doesn't even know what wine tastes like, huh?"

Bill, used to him, agreed for the sake of it. There was little point in causing a disagreement, even if he totally disagreed with him. In his mind Wood Point needed to improve its standards big time, attract the more discerning customer holidaymakers with money to spend. Edwina Edwards was right to give it a go. What harm? The locals wouldn't even take charity if it were offered.

Donal allowed his head drop over the counter as Bill made small talk with the arty crowd at the end of the bar. Then Danny Murphy came in, sitting on a stool two away from Donal who didn't lift his head to salute him. Nor did Danny make any special effort say hello.

"Sick of the weather," Bill said, handing over a stout. Danny who was discommoded by Donal looked exasperated, lost for an answer.

"No sign of a change," Bill added. "It is early yet, but it could be another bad year. They are not confident it will change." He was pressing buttons on the cash register, the drawer opening and closing quickly. "The weather. All people talk about around here is the weather. The fucking rain and the farmers and their fuckin' tractors getting stuck in the mud. What can we do about it?"

Donal waved his arms addressing his statement at Danny who, smiling at him, said, "Nothing. Not a thing can be done."

Donal grimaced liked he had contradicted him. "Why they fuckin' talk about it endlessly beats me, you know? It rains, it pours, it fuckin' snows, the sun shines—so what?" He moved the palm of his hand down hard, hitting the bar. "So what?" he repeated.

Danny smiled at him, sipping his pint.

"Makes conversation," he offered.

Donal, highly offended said, "Conversation must be very poor if a fella can only discuss the weather. Like a fella thinks he is imparting news to the world around him. Can't people see for themselves through their own eyes? It's wet, it is dry. Fucking farcical. Here, Bill."

He slapped the bar hard. Bill shuffled along to refill his brandy. Soon Donal succumbed to a kind of mummified stupor. Danny Murphy noticed how red his whole complexion was, like a button was pressed and red dye injected. Every now and then he would mutter. It was indecipherable to anyone else. Danny was satisfied with just a couple of pints. He left to avoid the company and make his bed early.

Bill gave him one more for the road. Donal struggled to hold the glass steady.

"I can't do that this month, Donal. It is poor enough, you see for yourself tonight. Less than ten people. We will have to talk about it when you are sober."

Bill poured himself a glass of orange. Sipping it slowly, he placed it 'neath the spirit dispensers away from Donal, save he should get one of his sneezing fits.

"You missed last time, Bill. You shouldn't have come in if you can ill afford it. If everyone misses, then I have to pay it all myself. Makes fuck all sense to me, and none at all to the bank manager."

Donal was surprisingly lucid, the mention of money dusting him down.

"We can make it up, Donal. Keep me in; we will catch it up. I need more time. We are heading into the summer, the good months. I will catch up then. Just keep me in till I am able to keep up."

Bill tried to sound hard, but Donal, drinking his brandy down, said, "I have nobody left, not one I can trust. I started with four, and you people out there think I can manage while you live on my hard earned. That is people for you, Bill—greedy, only out for themselves. If you don't pay up then I am screwed, and the next person who comes to me has to wait till I am paid before we can re-invest. What good is that? Action will have to be taken before it is too late. And you, Bill. I need double next time, or you are out and you will still owe me for when you were in. I will have to sell it on if you fuckers don't pay! As much as it kills me, but you will leave me with no choice!"

Donal slid off his stool. He moved carefully in the bad light so as not to trip over anything.

"Good luck to you!" He waved his right arm aggressively.

Wood Point, Many years ago
9.

When Kate and Georgina walked through the woods, they got a sudden fright. Thomas Crowe appeared. He carried a dull white sack, black on the inside, full with periwinkles. Kate greeted him with a smile whilst Georgina cowered behind her.

Thomas said, "Where are you girls off to? It's a great day for hanging around."

"Nowhere," Kate said cheerfully. "We might go out as far as Broadstrand, but our legs might give up before that."

Thomas was only twelve years older than Kate, but he assumed a fatherly role.

"There's a crowd of lads out by the pan. Up to no good. Some of them are fishing; the others are swimming. They don't know what they're at. All I say is they're making plenty of noise. And watch out for O' Regan's bull. I heard he is tearing around the place chasing walkers and bullying the young horses."

Thomas laughed. Moving on a little, he addressed Georgina.

"Does Madge Butler want any periwinkles? I could call by. What do you think?"

Georgina, still cowering behind her friend, said, "No, we don't eat periwinkles in our house. They make me sick, and my mother can't stand the sight of them."

"Fine so," Thomas said walking a pace. "Katie, I will call see your mother. She loves her wrinkles."

Kate, who was starting to walk, looked over her shoulder at him shouting.

"She will for sure, Thomas."

He was gone round the bend of the track, his soft cap stuck to his head with the heat of the sun.

"I hate him. He gives me the creeps," Georgina said sulkily. "He wears the same clothes summer or winter. You think he might change his clothes every now and again. And he smells, Kate. I wouldn't trust him, walking along here on my own. I am so glad you are with me."

"Not an ounce of harm in him. Sure, he is knocking around for years. No stories about Thomas save for his drinking and a bit of fishing."

"Don't talk about him. I feel like there is something crawling inside my flesh," Georgina said, looking genuinely worried.

They stepped from the wood over some hard ground before stepping over the stile into O' Regan's field. They both stopped, inspecting the young horses grazing in the lush grass, the breeze gentle over the thick gorse that spread along the cliff edge. Beyond, through gaps, the sea appeared in a deep blue with the land on the other side brown and dark, the surf dancing at its edges all the way to Barry's Point.

"No sign of O' Regan's bull?"

Kate sounded excited, but Georgina said nervously, "Is he out, what do you think? I am not taking another step if he is on the loose. I mean, how will we escape if he comes rushing over the hill? We can't run into the gorse. We will never make it to the next field!" Georgina stood firm, her body rigid in refusal.

Kate, laughing said, "I am going on, bull or no bull. If you want you can stay where you are, Georgie. Two of us, we might confuse him. The quicker we pass through the better."

Kate started to run, but her stride was leisurely and displaying no fear. Georgina paused for a moment before running after her madly. She had a suspicion that Barry Cousins would be with the crowd at the pan. She was dying to see him. This time she would make him take notice of her.

Four of them straddled the water's edge, the frying pan dark from the continued attentions of the sea. One boy was fishing aimlessly with a spinner, cast after cast, reel after reel, then nothing. Off he would try again.

Barry Cousins sat on the far side with another lad round his own age. They wore swimming trunks and sat on good beach towels to stop the jagged rocks from spearing their behinds. The youngest, a small fair-haired fella from near Broadstrand, was sitting alone at the edge paddling his feet. He wore a tee shirt to keep warm. As the wind picked up, the water swished over the frying pan every so often.

Looking out to sea, Kate noticed the gannets diving. They were expert fishers. The boys were excited by the arrival of the two girls, shouting comments as Kate and Georgina climbed down the rocks from the cliff face. It wasn't dangerous just arduous. Kate was down way before her friend.

"We are all right now, Barry," Kevin shouted, though he was right beside him. The boy fishing glanced up but paid no attention, pulling on the fishing rod then allowing more line. The sun came out under a small white cloud, and suddenly it was warm and the breeze retreated back out to sea racing to the seven heads.

"It's your wan with the nice arse again, Barry, and Donovan from the village." Kevin said but not as loudly.

Kate paid no notice. She wasn't ready to look her best—not yet. She often spent time staring in the mirror, and she liked what she saw.

Georgina stepped forward. Her body was compact, and she wore tight jeans that were complimented by a white top. It was also tight, making her breasts look stronger than they were.

"What are you up to? Are you fishing or swimming?" she asked, looking at Kate for support that never came.

"Michael's fishing. We were swimming earlier, but it got a bit choppy so we're chilling out now. Hey, come on over. You can sit on our towels."

Barry Cousins was on his feet.

"Come on," a delighted Georgina said, but Kate was hesitant. She walked to where the fair-haired boy swished the water with his feet.

"Cold, is it?" Kate asked, like she already knew the answer.

The boy was shy. He muttered, "It's not so bad. After a while you get warm, but at first it freezes the balls off of you."

He was then joined by Kevin who had abandoned Barry.

"That's if you have balls," he said, sitting down and making his friend Tim move over.

Georgina sat beside Barry Cousins who folded his towel to take the worst of the rock edge away.

"I know you," Barry Cousins said. "You're from up Ramsey Hill. You live in the big posh house."

Kevin laughed like he overheard something really funny. Georgina, going red said, "We all live somewhere."

Barry, warming to her, was taking an interest in her tanned complexion and the soft brown of her eyes. She had nice hair too, long and dark.

"Do you do a trick?" Kevin shouted, his words sailing over his younger companions' head.

"Shut up," Barry scolded him. Kevin still finding it funny, was on his feet, dragging Tim to the other side to see how the fishing was going. Kate watched them cross over the flat stone, their sneakers attacked by the trapped sea water.

"How come I don't see you around much? You're too young for Clon I suppose?"

"You're not much older," Georgina countered. "My father's very strict. Anyway, it will happen. Next September I am sixteen, so I will go whenever I want."

Barry was taken with her independence and the posh touch to her voice.

"She is your mate, so?" he looked disparagingly at Kate. "She isn't friendly; I hate girls who aren't friendly. I don't bite."

"I hear you are a great hurler, and all the girls are after you." Georgina bit her lip, afraid she had said too much. Barry Cousins dropped his head, but when he lifted it he was smiling.

"Not bad, yeah. I hope to make the junior team next year and then maybe the under–twenty-ones after that. We will see. My father says I have the gift but we will see."

Georgina laughed for no reason. Kate glanced at her but away again just as quick. The fishing line was tangled in the rocks about ten yards out. The boys were lifting and dragging the rod, placing it up and down, sideways and then horizontally.

The small fella tried to pull it by hand; Michael chastised him shouting, "Stop it, Tim! You will break it, for fuck sake! I can't afford a new line. My mother will kill me if I go home without it; she is sick of forking out."

Barry Cousins shouted over, "Cut the fucking thing, will you? It is not worth the fucking trouble."

But the boys continued tirelessly, trying to free the snag.

"Do you want to lose her? And we can go up to the fields," Barry whispered.

Georgina, surprised said, "I am happy here. What's wrong with here?"

"I can't kiss you here, can I?" Barry said taking her right hand and squeezing it. "Don't you want me to kiss you? If you do we better go up the fields, girl. I can't kiss you here like."

Kate went to assist the tangled fisherman. Reluctantly they gave her a go; after all, her brother once helped out on the trawler.

"I dunno," Georgina said. "I don't think it would be nice to leave Kate on her own. Besides they would all know where we were going, wouldn't they?"

Barry Cousins laughed mockingly. "Do you care? We could be just going for a walk. I am not asking you for a ride, like!"

Georgina was confused. She had never been with a boy, not really, save for Spin the Bottle. This Barry Cousins knew too much for her.

"I dunno."

She looked over her shoulder at Kate who was doing her best to release the line, trying as best she could to go easy, in case she was blamed if the bloody thing snapped.

"Nah, it's no good, it's stuck," Michael said sadly. "Nothing for it but to cut the line."

Barry Cousins, by now exasperated, shouted, "Hold on, Michael boy. I will swim over and grab it from the back. I will pull it back around for you. Job done. Your mother will love you."

Barry the hero walked to where the boy had been sitting earlier, testing the water with his feet, stepping on to the ledge below. It was slippery with weed. He allowed himself to go, his body splashing, leaving handfuls of surf in his trail. The rock was no more than ten yards from the pan, but even before his sleek body got near it they could see him struggle. It wasn't as if the sea got rougher in any way; if anything it was flat calm. Yet the current was dragging him away from his intended target. So he put up a fight, and the more he fought the more tired he was.

Kate watched him struggle. He tried to take breaths at one point. She imagined he planned to rest on the protruding rock as soon as he reached it.

Georgina didn't sense any danger as such. She thought him brave for trying it and was sort of disappointed to see him struggle.

His friends started to panic.

Kevin ran as close to the edge as he could, shouting, "Come back, Barry. Leave it, boy. Come on back."

Michael dropped the rod on the slab and screamed, "Leave it, boy! I will cut the line! Sure! What the fuck, it is only a rod!"

But it was Tim who saw the danger first. He rasped, "He's drowning, for fuck sake! Jesus, what will we do? He is drowning!"

Georgina stiffened as Barry's head was now immersed, his arms flailing. The sea had turned from blue to grey, his arms churning dark colours from the deep.

Michael considered diving in and was down to his togs, but he hesitated hoping Barry was somehow out of danger.

Kate dived in from the far side. The boys had never seen the like of it. She had removed her clothes so fast and was down to her underwear and then falling into the sea. She swam fast, assured. Within seconds she approached the almost-lifeless Barry from the rear, pulling him by the hair till his head was above water.

He appeared semi-conscious. Kate glided, her movement so easy, till she got him alongside and the boys dragged him ashore. There was no time for modesty. She climbed out and proceeded to turn Barry on his side where he spat out green water and was sick before the colour returned to his cheeks.

Georgina covered the shivering Kate with the towel she was sitting on. Barry was shivering also, but soon he came round and had the strength to sit up.

Tim said, "Fuck it, boy, she saved you're life."

"She did not!" Barry said. "I just felt sort of funny for a few seconds. Thanks, anyway, but I was all right in myself."

Kevin looked at him in disbelief as he cut the fishing line with a lighter, the tackle lost forever. Michael dressed meekly like he was re-examining his very existence.

Georgina started to shiver. The evening was closing in and she fetched Kate's clothes for her. She watched the boys leaving slowly to give Kate time to dress.

"Thanks anyway," Barry Cousins said to Kate, who sort of smiled back at him.

Georgina looked to the sea. The tide was turning, the nooks and crannies filling, reclaiming much of what it had lost earlier in the day. Beyond, the gannets dived, making white foam as they did.

Wood Point, A few years ago
10.

Kate saw him drive past the hotel and on to the car park at the foot of the woods; maybe he was going to do the Fuchsia Walk, she mused. Her niece and her friend were digging in the sand, mixing cement in the small bucket. Every now and then her niece would toddle off to the water's edge to fill up, and then begin the heavy journey back with the bucket strap straining.

Myrna had Sarah and Fiona for a few hours, just for a break. Then she would get landed with her niece, Bronagh, who she loved, so it wasn't a chore. She adjusted her sunglasses; the wrong size, they kept slipping down her nose. Then his car pulled alongside the wall and he put the driver-side wheels unto the small pathway.

"Hi, Kate," Jack said through the open window. "I wasn't sure it was you, you flew by. But then I thought nobody else around here has a car like that."

Kate beamed.

"I went for a drive, brought the camera." He showed her his video camera. "Such a nice day, I had to get out. I went out to Butlerstown and Dunworly and on to Ballinglanna."

Kate, eyeing Bronagh and her companion, smiled at him.

"Lovely drive. Did you do your thing?" she asked, pointing at the camera.

Jack nodded putting the video camera on the passenger seat out of sight. "Where are your two?"

"Myrna has them for a few hours. Ted is having a nap; he is exhausted since he arrived home. I went down to my mother's, but look what I was landed with! Ah, no, Bronagh is really cute and her little pal."

Jack then said, "Having fun anyway, plenty of sand for the bucket. I'd say the water is cold. It might only change by a degree winter to summer, a little more at the shoreline, I reckon."

Kate turned towards the water. It looked so inviting, a yacht drifting down, the sound creating delayed ripples that were unexpectedly angry. The crew, clearly visible, were all decked out in orange and yellow, and for a split second Kate longed for a swim.

Feeling suddenly warm all over and needing to cool down, she fanned her face with her right hand and said, "You been chatting to horses lately?"

Jack, smiling said, "The horses in Butlerstown are pure culchie. They don't understand a word I am saying!"

Kate laughed, moving one leg over the wall. It was easier to talk to him that way and still keep an eye on Bronagh.

"I hear poor Thomas had an awful time of it in Clon last night," Kate whispered and Jack strained to hear her with the general noise around. "He didn't know who he was. The guards asked him for his name and he didn't know. He was very bad!"

Kate raised her head to the heavens to punctuate her statement before throwing an eye to see the girls sit down at the water's edge together.

"He's getting worse and becoming a real nuisance around the village. I think Michael Harrington has barred him for life, and Bill Thornton doesn't want him around at all. Says he brings the tone of the place down."

She held the tip of her nose mockingly. "He is always annoying young Margaret in the Fisherman's. She is good about it, though. Barry Cousins is going to bar him if he doesn't stop it. Imagine the guards finding him lying face down on the street by the Emmet, his cap glued to his head and the guard not certain if he was alive or dead! I think the strain of minding his mother is getting to him. It's a full-time job, and sure he has to go out do a bit whenever he can, or he will starve."

Jack was blinded by the sun temporarily. He put his right hand between them so as still to see her. She was white under the dark shades, her auburn hair lending pink to her pale skin. He liked the smooth skin of her neck and he longed to touch it.

"Somebody said he studied for the priesthood," Jack said kindly.

"A priest? Thomas? Are you mad, man? He was an altar boy here in Wood Point, that's as far as he got. No, but he's a clever bucko. Don't be fooled. I think years ago he had ideas about teaching, but then his father died and it all changed. He never followed it through."

"Pity," Jack said without conviction. "My mother knows the guard's wife in Timoleague. She says they're watching for him now, save he kills himself or someone else."

Kate, leaning forward, said in just above a whisper, "Don't say this to anyone, but Barry Cousins would want to be careful there, watching the place for you know." Kate imitated someone snorting through their nostril.

"Do you ever see his eyes? Not the same lad since he stopped hurling."

"No," Jack said laughing, feeling like he was trapped in lift with a gossip. "Terrible I am, but, sure, I hardly ever get to give you the news."

Trying to be funny, Jack smiled at her when he said, "What's the story with Madge Butler and Michael Harrington?"

Kate, glancing at Bronagh, seemed surprised by the question. She fiddled with her shades, keeping them straight.

"Rumours, that's all. Going on years ever since his poor wife died. Rumours, but you wouldn't see them carrying on."

Jack was clearly enjoying himself. "What about Bill Thornton, did he ever marry?"

Kate was shouting at Bronagh to tidy up. The cloud was thickening and the sun lost momentarily.

"He's too mean. Nobody would have him. There was talk of some woman years ago from the west of Ireland. They were nearly engaged. She worked a summer in the hotel. He's supposed to have made a move on her—even went across the country to her place. Nobody knows what happened because when they came back she was acting different, you know? She was gone very soon afterwards, leaving him on his own. The miserable bastard is on his own still."

Kate laughed as Bronagh and her friend came up to her. "These are my girls, Jack. Do you think she looks like me? My sister says she is head off of me but I can't see it."

Jack struggled to find a resemblance—the child was dark and sallow. Kate was pale with auburn hair.

"She's the head off you all right," Jack said, wondering whether he should say anything about his dinner date with Judith Tebbut.

"Ted and I are going for a meal tonight in the hotel, I hope you know." Kate was settling herself. She was standing on the path, the two girls climbing over the small wall after her, scraping their buckets on the smooth surface.

Jack didn't comment, but Kate urged, "Have you ever eaten there, Jack? It is lovely."

"No. I like to cook myself or have a bite in the Fisherman's. I am sure it is the business."

Kate laughed, "Come on, girls, I will get you a lemonade in the hotel."

Turning to Jack one last time, she said, "Ted and I don't get out much with him at sea. I am looking forward to it no end. We probably will go down the Fisherman's for a drink after. Will you be in there?"

Jack hesitated, thinking of Judith Tebbut. "Maybe. I will have to see."

Kate sailed across the narrow road with her two followers loyally behind her; Jack sat, watching her till she disappeared into the drive of the hotel.

*

I will tell you the story but not as Caw told me. You see,
Caw has a problem communicating. He is all shaky in the
head and spitting out. It takes him all day to get to the point,
so I will tell you my version of what Caw told me and you
can make up your own minds on it.

As you know, Jack Browne has a problem sleeping and
Caw spent long hours in the gutter listening to this restless
soul knocking about. It all started on one of those restless
mornings when Jack was up and about, staring out the bay
window at the hard sand of the estuary. He had two things
hanging on the wall behind him that he constantly looked at
as if he was seeking some kind of guidance, some steerage to
make some kind of sense of his life.

The first was a wooden cross with the semi-naked figure of
Jesus painted in gold, the arms outstretched beyond where
normal arms could reach. Jesus' head was bowed slightly
with his golden crown of thorns, the torture complete; yet the
figurine held a kind of serenity. Alongside this, hanging
from a thumb tack high, almost at the ceiling, was a gold
chain with a butterfly hanging midst a series of soft bells.
Only when he opened the fly windows and the wind filtered
through did they ever move, the jangle faint, only
whispering.

Jack proceeded to put on a wash. His clothes crumbled in
the small clothes' basket he had bought in the Barryroe Co-
op for four euro and ninety-nine cent, as good a bargain as he
ever got. He emptied the contents into the washing machine.
There was a faint smell of must along with the acidic odour
of sweat. The clothes at the bottom of the basket were damp.

The machine started quietly before rattling along on
extract. It was like a plane taking off. Caw flapped his wings
in a vain attempt to disperse the noise, but soon the machine
went quiet again as it came to a slower cycle, making a calm
humming sound like a car engine when a good driver drops

down the gears rather than slams the brake. Jack was emptying the kitchen bin, a mixture of paper and stale food, dinners that were stored in the fridge overnight with the misleading intention of consuming the next day. Caw knew Jack never intended to eat the leftovers; his paranoia on food poisoning wouldn't allow it. Yet it never crossed his mind to leave it out the back door for the birds to feast because he was too afraid of rats. Why are humans so goddamn afraid?

Jack's black bin bag was so full he could barely tie the top. He heaved it, dragging it out the back door. The smell was revolting but he would have to wait till he dressed before throwing it in the boot of the car and driving up to the waste management area. Caw saw his chance. Jack was back at the bay window. Caw to his surprise was joined by the boys. At last they had made it off the roof.

They were attacking the black bag with him. Caw warned them against tins and glass and anything sharp. Peck, peck—a chicken bone. More pecking, and some peas, and the boys found a carrot. All was going swimmingly when suddenly the back door opened and there was Jack, with his dressing gown falling away. The belt was tied in so many knots he couldn't devise one to keep it closed over.

Caw flapped to the lower end of the garden followed by the boys. Jack, muttering expletives, went red in the face as he picked up the torn bag, more goodies falling unto the gravel. Fetching a fresh bag, he then got a dust pan and brush to tidy the remnants. All the time he kept repeating the word, "Bastards."

This irritated Caw who cawed at Jack from a safe distance.

Jack carried the new bag through the house and out the front door, depositing it safely against the drainpipe. Checking for any would-be scavengers, he saw none. He returned satisfied to his window, watching as the tide stretched from the harbour to fill the tiny crevices in his view.

Terns appeared from the shadows, moving excitedly like commuters. Jack heard the noise. Caw and three other adult crows had made it to the front door. His boys, exhausted from their exertions, rested beneath the bay window. Peck, peck. The crow slit the bag, his beak like a knife. More odds and ends, another chicken bone, the top of a beans tin covered in sauce. Dangerous but nice. The stones of two plums, one with delicious mould, tea bags fermenting on the side of the path.

Jack reappeared, his face redder than before. "Bastards."

He screamed, but the crows kept working, trying to drag the beans lid away.

Out came the dustpan and brush and a new bag. This time Jack left the bag inside his front door till he got dressed and found the time to throw it in the boot of his car. In all it was a thirty-second drive uphill to the waste management area.

Caw went back to the boys, only to find them cowering under the bay window. In their excitement they had followed their father, but neither had the appropriate skills to fly and return to the gutter. Caw gave them some food, which they took delightedly, yet as soon as they had eaten they retired to the shadows beyond two abandoned cement blocks.

This was a fix. Caw wondered what he was to do. Neither boy was proficient in the art of flying. Maybe he could frog march them across the main road to the wild bushes that straddled the sand. That place was full of rats and other vermin.

Jack was back at the window now. Dressed, he sat typing away; every now and then he would stop to consult some notes he had or pick up some pamphlet or book. He then resumed his monotonous typing. Sometimes he stopped, bracing his shoulders, rubbing his neck with his right hand. Yawning, he would get to his feet and walk aimlessly around the room. Stopping the odd time to examine his cross, he would open the fly windows in the vain hope of attracting the wind.

Jack pressed his face up against the window and watched girls set off down the walkway with their regular boyfriends or husbands. He watched their sturdy bottoms or marvelled at the golden legs glued to thighs. People passed him all day, and Jack watched them: young men, training hard, running distance; the old man who waved every day at six p.m. who crawled by with his walking stick; frumpy women in their forties trying so hard to remove the stomach flab that arrived so easily. Jack saw them all. He lusted, pitied, and sat in awe every day.

The only thing he failed to see out that window was Caw sitting on the garden wall, his head shaking from worry. The strong fluff of dark feathers beneath his wings sprouting grey, Caw feared the worst. The evenings brought the cold and the sun sank low in the sky over Timoleague. He sat on the wall wondering what to do. Maybe he could make a nest beyond the two concrete blocks—but what madness ran through his head! The rats could find it or other birds would attack. Yet the real danger was the night creature—the fox.

He told the boys to be still, not to wander. He had to go away, but he wouldn't be very long. He instructed them not to leave the shadow of the cement blocks for any reason. Caw fluttered his way to the wooden steps that let the gravel garden drop to the lower level. He flapped because the two boys had followed him. Jack Browne was watching from the bay window; Caw could see he looked concerned. Caw gave the order, and the boys rushed back to the shadows. Taking off he rested briefly on the westerly breeze.

Wood Point, A few years ago
11.

"I don't mind who you talk to, that's your business. She is friendly with my daughter. News travels fast around here, Jack. You should know that. Anyway, she said you were a nice man, if it makes you feel a little better."

Judith studied the menu, refusing the temptation to fetch her reading glasses from her handbag.

"Her old man does well for himself; I hear he has a new novel out," Jack said, watching her pick up her water and take a sip. "He lives in the cottages down by the river. Evidently he trades in his woman every couple of years for someone new—and younger of course—and the daughter lives on the continent with a woman, I believe."

This time Judith ventured the red wine. She sipped it like the experience was new to her.

"I wouldn't go there, Jack."

"She's pretty," Jack said, before venturing further. "It is a pity, as they say. A waste."

Judith laughed and bravely took a more worthy sip of wine. "A waste. Only a man would say that. I doubt if her partner would agree. What are you ordering? I might go with the lamb. It is the specialty in Kilbrittain house."

"So you have been taken here before—well now!" Jack laid his menu flat on the only space available to him.

Judith looked at him blankly. "We do have birthdays and anniversaries, you know, when Gareth comes home from England. He always brings me here, and when Father comes in the summer we come here at least once, maybe twice if he is feeling up to it and flush. It's not cheap." She whispered the cheap bit.

"I think I will go with the lamb as well," Jack said, picking up the menu and quickly reading it. "Sounds delicious, and served with roast potatoes. I thought custard and roast potatoes were a thing of the past."

"Custard?" Judith said astonished. "When does anyone ever order custard?"

"Me! I love custard, but it has gone out of fashion. You can get cream with everything, but if you ask for apple tart and custard they look at you like you have two heads and Byrd's never existed. I wouldn't mind, but you can buy it ready-made. I guess someone just decided it wasn't cool to serve it anyplace. I don't think you can even get it in McDonald's."

Jack helped himself generously to the wine, checking how much remained in the bottle, but he was all right as Judith was only a sipper.

Judith stopped for a breather. The lamb was succulent and very hot. She drank water, sighing as if the whole experience was too much for her. Jack admired her. She was a couple of years older than him, touching fifty although he hadn't quite the courage to ask her to verify his guess. She was fine and natural with light brown hair she kept over her shoulders. She had an easy way about her, which he liked. She was English, of course, but had lived in Ireland via Zambia for twenty years.

Noticing his stare, Judith interjected with, "I don't know how much longer I will last with Barry. The place is a mess over there. I spent the first week in the kitchen just scrubbing. I found salmon in the deep freezer. It was rancid. I feel a loyalty to him, you know. I just wanted something to get me out of the house. But do I need him and all that goes with him?"

Jack smiled, sensing a lightness of tone that he hadn't figured her for.

"I know he is a bit of an oddball, but I have seen worse. Of course he is not helped by some of the idiots he has working there. I would say it is hard to make it work with all the staff and the place empty from Monday to Friday. He likes the young ones and the bright lights of Clon too much."

Judith laughed, returning to her meal. After swallowing another mouthful of lamb she said, "Indeed, and he is getting on a bit. Wants to find himself a woman in a hurry, or he will get left behind."

"He always has you," Jack said, upset straightaway he had said it. "He wouldn't be for you, Judith. Not your type is he?" he said trying to retrieve the situation.

"If I wanted a man, that is? Since I divorced Ronnie Tate, I haven't even had a date. Not till now, if you can call this a date. But you know what I mean?"

She took the last spoonful of vegetable, shaking her head when Jack tried to fill her wine glass.

"I will be tipsy if I drink another drop. It doesn't do to get tipsy round here 'cause everyone knows you, and I will be the talk of the place. It drives me mad, like isn't there enough to be spoken about with the crowd from Timoleague not liking us from Kilbrittain and the people from Wood Point not liking either of us, and you a runner in, wanting to set me up with Barry Cousins? I am afraid he would be too coarse for me, and I hear he is into drugs." Judith lowered her voice as the proprietor passed their table. The small slim lady smiled at Judith.

"She's Canadian—French Canadian—and he's from West Kerry. They fight like mad you know? He is the chef, but she runs the place. The shouts from the kitchen—sometimes they forget, they really do!"

Judith studied her younger companion as she swirled the last of the wine in her glass. Jack was admiring the flowery dress she was wearing. They were like unhooked curtains pressed and adapted to wear.

"I like you, Jack," Judith said suddenly, shocking herself as much as Jack.

Taking his gaze away from her dress he simply said, "Are you having a dessert? I can't, you know. Health reasons."

"No, no," Judith said raucously feeling her midriff with the palm of her right hand. "I will be as fat as a fool. This dress barely fits me as is. I will have a coffee, that's it."

Jack ordered coffee. It came in tiny cups but was strong, marked with a residue of coffee bean skimming the surface.

"The dogs will be missing you. Are they all right on their own?" Jack asked to break her concentration.

Judith smiled immediately. "I leave the kitchen door open so they can come in and out. Byron stays in—he likes the heat—but Shelley is a devil. He chases rabbits and anything that moves in the garden. He's the guard dog whereas Byron is the old fool. How is your coffee? You do like coffee. From what you are telling me, it seems you are not a great food fan. Were you always like that, Jack, even when you were married?"

Jack watched as she wiped her lips dry with a napkin. He finished the bottle of wine before downing the tiny drain of coffee.

"I ate too much when I was married. I made myself sick eating so much. How hard is it to get a taxi out here?"

Judith looked puzzled, but holding her dignity, she said, "I offered to drive you. I hardly drink much now. I suppose it depends. We might be lucky, but sometimes they have to come from Ballinspittle and that takes an age. Ask her."

She pointed discreetly at the French-Canadian lady. Jack paid the bill as Judith studied his writing of the cheque like it was the first time she had ever witnessed such an undertaking. Judith knew the taxi man. His family once had a grocery store in Timoleague.

He revved his car up the gravel hill of her driveway. It was pitch dark save for a faint sidelight. Shelley barked. Jack could see his shadow beyond the side gate, and when the taxi driver turned off the engine Jack could hear his paws scraping against the wood.

"I will be going on home," Jack said.

Judith looked stunned.

"I have medications to take later. Thanks; it was a lovely meal," he said, smiling.

The taxi driver who was looking over his shoulder corrected his gaze, and Judith gracefully said, "Thank you, Jack. I better go tend to the dogs."

She stepped out into the dark, walking gingerly to the side gate without looking back. The taxi started up and the driver let it roll to the roadside edge.

"Where's home?" he asked.

"I have to meet some friends."

The car turned right onto the road.

"Fine," the driver said. He sounded confused; like he was privy to something he found a little offensive.

*

Adam made such a fuss.

"You bastard, she is here. I show you; come with me."

He pulled at Jack's hand till he gave in, Jack following him smiling. They finally arrived at a pretty girl of around thirty; she sat nursing a vodka.

"This is him, the bastard, hey. He is the writer, very good, hey!"

Adam's girlfriend was from Dublin. She came see him the odd weekend.

"A writer?" She looked at Adam to see if he were serious.

"I buy you a pint, hey. I need a pint and two vodka and Coke, thank you very much."

Margaret behind the counter was on to it.

"So what is this book about?" his girlfriend asked, brushing her hair from her face.

Jack found her attractive in a sisterly type of way. She had brown eyes, which to him always denoted a bad temper. Yet she possessed a coolness he liked.

"It's about a guy recovering from illness. He is writing this book."

When the vodkas and the pint arrived she said, "Adam, I thought you were going on to the JDs."

"Not yet. I will go with the vodka. Hey, when is this book due? I wanna see this book!" Adam said, putting his hand on his girlfriend's shoulder. "I think you sit all day and watch the porno, hey, Jack? Porno, hey?"

Jack, laughing, glanced around. The bar was getting busy. There was no sign of Kate. Maybe she changed her mind.

"You haven't introduced me to this lovely girl yet," Jack said kindly.

Adam, laughing nervously, said, "This is my girl I tell you all about, my Anna, and you don't remember her name. You are drunk as usual."

Jack swallowed a mouthful of Guinness.

Anna said, "So where in the big smoke did you spawn?"

Jack replied, "I am from Sallynoggin."

"Dundrum." She was cool, letting the vodka sit on her tongue before swallowing.

"We could have thrown stones at each other. How come you can leave the delights of Wood Point? Don't you miss him?" Jack asked, making fun.

Anna smiled at him. Self-assured she drank her drink down.

"Come on, Adam, smoke. I think I will go a JD myself. See you in a minute."

They left through the side door; Jack could see them chat through the window, their heads moving. Anna leaned over to get a light; Adam was on his best behaviour, whispering things into her ear.

Kate walked in first with Ted behind her. She stared into space, the crowd blending into her vision. She struggled through the rabble, eventually settling at the far end. Luckily two women got up to leave, and they grabbed two small stools.

A ballad singer started his set, and suddenly Jack felt tired. His pint was warmish, and he longed for the coolness of the table water in Kilbrittain house. He felt bad about Judith. She was so nice. He pictured her sitting by the fire; her two dogs keeping her company, Judith cosy warm but alone.

"Hey, you bastard, did you order me a vodka?"

"No, I was going to order you JDs."

"No, don't do it, don't do it. You see, she doesn't like that. Anna wants to buy you a drink first so you can have two pints from us, and then we can have JDs. But we pay, you bastard, because you are a poor writer. "

Adam leaned over slightly so Anna could hear above the sound of the balladeer.

"Poor bastard follows Shelbourne. He never heard of Banik Ostrava, poor bastard."

Anna ordered a round and the balladeer played "Hallelujah" by Leonard Cohen. The whole pub sang the chorus with him, the barmaids and all. Jack wondered what it was with people. Next he expected a lot of Baaas, but then he found himself singing along when the singer sang the last chorus.

Adam went to the toilet, so Anna, leaning forward, asked, "Did he show you pictures of me on his phone?" She asked the question innocently like she was asking about the weather.

"His phone?" Jack said surprised. "No. He told me he had this beautiful girlfriend in Dublin, but he never let on you were so beautiful. He would have us all jealous," Jack said, remembering the semi-naked photos Adam had shown him of some sex romp, where she was crawling on all fours on the carpet. Adam was dressed up as a Roman centurion. It looked like they were having great fun.

Anna, eyeing him suspiciously, said, "I will kill him if anyone ever sees those photos. He promised me he erased them."

Jack looked at her awkwardly. Adam returned, looking at both of them curiously. He said, "Right, you bastard, I will buy you another pint."

"Anna wanted to know if you showed me photos on your phone," Jack said.

Adam went white. Jack watched as his eyes widened incredulously.

"I show him photos of Sweetie that is all. He loves little dogs, don't you, Jack? His favourite is the Chihuahua. Isn't that right, you bastard?" This time Adam spoke with real feeling.

"Yeah, sure," Anna said picking up her packet of cigarettes from the counter. "The dog. I remember now. Was that you who showed me those photos? Sweetie is a lovely little dog."

Jack reached for his pint awaiting her reaction.

Anna smiled at him. She glanced slyly at Adam who, sensing her soften, said, "I love this guy. I really love this guy, Anna. If you were not my girl, I would want you to meet a man like this guy." Adam lowered his drink, the colour returning to his cheeks slowly.

Soon Jack, feeling the effects of his cocktail of wine and stout, was close to exhaustion and was ready to go home. Anna calmed as the alcohol massaged her curiosity. She no longer spoke of the phone pictures but had turned her attention to Sweetie instead, saying the next time she visited Wood Point she would bring Sweetie with her, so everyone could see for themselves what a beautiful little dog she was.

The ballad singer finished with an inane rendition of the national anthem. People who were sitting stood to attention. One particularly fat woman had just managed to get to her feet when he finished. It took her nearly as long to take her seat again.

Kate was leaving. Ted, walking behind, her was distracted by an older man who spoke secretly into his right ear.

Kate smiled but looked embarrassed as she passed Jack, who said quietly, "The best looking woman in Wood Point."

"Quiet, you," she chided.

"It's the truth," Jack said louder. Adam looked on interested.

Ted had caught up. He nodded at Jack who watched as Kate slipped out the centre door gracefully.

"You, bastard, have a problem. Hey, she is married, man. You can only wish. She is taken, my friend. Come to Dublin with me. I will show you Anna's sister. She is hungry for it, yeah?"

Anna slapped him playfully across the back of his wrist, and Adam feigned pain.

"She is my neighbour; we are friends." Jack made his excuses, finding the last of his Guinness warm. The froth was disgusting as it lodged in his throat.

Wood Point, A few years ago
12.

Caw was rightly vexed when he came to me. He was
trembling, the blue of his feathers fading. He had lost weight
and only yesterday had a real fright when he was caught in a
skip at the Barryroe co-op. Some guy emptied a pallet of old
tea chests into the skip on top of him. He froze, sticking to
the corner in a tiny air pocket. He stayed trapped until they
moved the skip across the yard and a falling tea chest
allowed him room to escape.

Caw was rightly pissed about it. He kept referring to the
injustice of it all. At his time of life the boys would have
come into their own, hunting in pairs round the co-op car
park, their feet strapped to the railings. They would be
feasting on food spilled from the windows of cars as travelers
ate lunch and truck drivers discarded crusts and sometimes
crisps.

Right now weak Caw must fend for himself in many ways,
he confided. Life just wasn't worth living any more. He told
me how close he had come to ending it all.

"Simple," he said. "Just fly into some poor sod's window
as he drives past. Thud! Bang! I fall on the bonnet. Do you
know some of those poor sods would actually bury you?
Some humans are that soft. I know it is hard to figure when
the same fuckers lay poison because we might help ourselves
to a few seeds from their field, but that's humans for you,
Sean."

Caw does like to go on. He didn't seem to mind the cold of
the pier that day, though I myself was frozen waiting for old
Hannon's boat. Maybe he did sense there was something
amiss with me 'cause after a while of him moaning and
giving out he started to tell me about the fox. I suppose it
amounts to the same giving out like poor us and the fox type

of thing, but Caw tells this story lovely, like you really get a sense of being there.

It reminded me of nights Michael Harrington would slip Madge into his room, and there I was at the upstairs window in my pyjamas as cold and as hard as fuck staring at the only street lamp illuminating the pier. I was watching for the sleeking cat or the busy dog smelling around. I might even see a fox come down to steal some of the rotted fish left in the boxes. Later I listened as Michael Harrington slipped her back out. There was the fox splashing through the small rain puddles, a mixture of fresh and seawater and lots of diesel oil.

Caw could hear the snores of Jack Browne, the radio switched off, the late night music long over. Every now and then he would sigh, turning in his sleep. Then all would stay quiet for an age.

The fox travelled a great distance. He wasn't full red or dog-like, his fur greyish, his movement like an overgrown rat. Rabbits hiding in the hedgerows consulted one another as he crawled through the long grass. They smelled him close, his coat damp, and slug spit suffocated his tail like the web of spiders long gone. Small birds tweeted suddenly and out of place. This made the fox pause as he watched for men, listening for the hoarse sound of the hound. A light van came fast down the side road that fed the walkway. The fox let it pass. The driver turned right towards the village. He waited for the darkness to return.

Caw tried to sleep but he couldn't get comfortable. The boys had woken and they chattered endlessly, so Caw shouted at them to be quiet or they would attract the rats. The boys gave in. Closing their wings, they conserved the heat from the concrete slabs beside them.

Caw thought about the advice he had received earlier from the murder of crows. The advice was hardly worth it, and in the end he was sorry he had left the boys at all. The murder advised him to hide the boys as best he could and feed them ferociously until they had the strength to fly. But he knew in his heart of hearts that they were at least two weeks away from full individual flight, and hiding these noisy specimens was virtually impossible.

The fox waited in the verge. A car appeared on the far side of the estuary. It came from Kilbrittain; its headlights made stabbing images across the water. The fox's eyes were transfixed until the car completed the bend. Then he allowed himself to fall into the narrow ditch. It was muddy with a trickle of dead water. He waited for a moment, resting, his tail sapping gently the dark puddle wetting and cleansing.

Caw felt his eyes closing ever so slowly. Not a sound from the estuary—not a bird or a ripple of water. No cars or even noises in the distance to disturb him. The moon appeared, the clouds separating like they were cut by a wounded spirit. Such was the blood he saw as he stirred. Moonlight filled the garden, and searchlights chased with ruthless efficiency.

The boys screamed the fox sleek and wiry as he looked at Caw with eyes dead and cold. They didn't sneer but instead offered an alternative terror. He threw the screaming boys through the hard air to land stunned on the gravel. Then he pounced with his paws, and the sharp teeth sent blood spouting over his face and mouth. Once more he looked at the terrified Caw, this time mockingly.

Caw knew it was too late. It was too late to do anything. The fox decapitated the boys, their torsos shaking, gravel stones stuck to feathers hardened with blood. The fox stood on the garden wall cleaning himself, glancing at Caw one more time before he was swallowed by the night.

I know that fox, and, believe me, he is not very nice. Stories of how his kin were hunted down by hounds and horses have marked him badly. He is no longer balanced in the way the average fox might be. He reckons having to scrimmage in waste bins and boxes of rotted fish just about tells its own tale, so he is set on revenge against the world and, sure, what does the world care? He makes do as best he can. A loner, he likes to prowl the night looking for easy food.

Who can blame him really? Of all the animal kingdom, I reckoned that the fox is just about as blighted as me. At the mercy of the hunt, disease, and starvation, he has lowered his standards in order to get enough food. No longer can his kind dance around the drumlins and the fields flashing their bushy tails. It's down to business with the crows and the rats.

Maybe that is why he killed Caw's two boys, to cull the opposition. It is, in animal parlance, ethnic cleansing. I wouldn't mind, but he didn't eat them as such. He just bit off their heads and swallowed them whole. He left the rest of their bodies for Jack Browne to clean up, and Jack did about two weeks later. He used the coal shovel so his hands wouldn't get infected. He emptied the headless stiff bodies over the garden wall.

Caw watched, disconsolate, from the roof. Jack went immediately indoors to wash his hands. Caw flew onto the garden wall cawing abuse at Jack, who took his seat back at the laptop. He was oblivious to Caw's taunts. Jack typed away, and every now and then he stopped to rest his fingers and stretch his neck. The sun shone on the pathway opposite. Pretty girls from the village were going on their daily run. They were followed by a middle-aged man and his wife walking greyhounds restrained on chains. The dogs, muzzled, looked eager but confused.

Jack started typing again. Caw wanted to fly into his bay window and give him a fright, but his nerves got the better of him. Since the boys died Caw had gone very sketchy. He didn't take risks anymore, whereas in the old days risk was second nature—he had thrived on it.

After an hour Jack had had enough time to light the fire, stretch the legs, and watch some television. Stepping back to the shadows, the room seemed strangely barren from the road, the laptop bored and the printer dead-looking, idle on the table. Jack saw Kate as he turned. She was pushing the

buggy, appearing from a line of dead bushes. She couldn't
see him, but he could see her.

She studied the house, starting at the upstairs window. Her
eyes fell to the bay window where he normally sat, and he
sensed her disappointment. She was searching for him,
allowing a sense of wonder to develop like she was anxious
as to his whereabouts. Kate, dark red, her face paling to
handsome, her features strong and alert. He wanted to show
himself, but he couldn't do it. She passed by reluctantly.

Jack moved to the window, his head pressed against the
cool of the glass. Before she disappeared he noticed the
strength of her shoulders and the proud way she carried
herself. When she was gone he stayed where he was, feeling
the cold of the window pane soothing against the heat of his
forehead.

*

Bill hated the nightly ritual of checking that all the doors
were locked and re-checking the door to the yard. It was dark
and shadowy, just the place for a lout to stake out. He
checked the small yard twice and bolted the door when he
was satisfied. Knowing that a cat setting off the sensor would
most likely wake him later, he imagined the pit of his
stomach swilling like it released the putrid juices of a rotting
lemon. The pleasures of living alone.

He climbed the stairs, sliding his hand off the side wall,
following the permanent stain the years of climbing had
made. The toilet door stood slightly ajar, stale urine tainting
the air. He must do something about that—fill the bowl with
Domestos and place one of those soap things in the cistern.
Woman's work, he concluded that and making sandwiches.
That is why women were put on earth, and they can make
good tea as well.

He ventured in, pulling the chain and watching the water level rise in the bowl. He pissed, cursing as he pissed a tiny dart right and unto the discarded cardboard inside of a toilet roll. Re-directing his aim he enjoyed the pressure he made, watching it die slowly till it was just a mere trickle. He was doubly careful not to splash his pants or wet his fingers round the fly. He brushed his teeth, noticing trickles of blood on his upper gums. He rinsed till it finally went away as fast as it had arrived.

His room was tidy, but the old furniture was shabby. Yet it had been good in its day. The curtains were torn at the side and at the bottoms. The net curtains on the window were yellowed with time, and the carpet smelled of must for the want of a shampoo. A man alone, he lamented, sitting on the side of the bed. His belly ached as he leaned over to untie his shoes.

"A man alone," he said out loud with no scent of a woman to show him comfort at least. In bed he was restless. He tried reading a book about the seven heads, written by a local who lived beside the hotel. But after a few minutes he gave up. The bulb in the lamp wasn't strong enough, and anyway there was nothing about the seven heads he didn't already know about. Wood Point hardly needed some runner in from Donegal becoming an expert on the locality as bad as those Germans and their soap opera.

He turned off the lamp, lying quietly for a few moments, listening for a sound that never came. The odd car travelled the street outside. The harbour, though, was quiet. Only the bobbling lines of the small craft gave tell of the swishing tide. A warm night in bed but damn cold to be sitting on one of those little things. Further out it would be choppy enough. Wood Point was well protected. Wasn't that why it was chosen to station the lifeboat all those years ago?

Bill hopped out of bed to look out the window. After the sensor light came on, he could see nothing as it faded quickly to pitch dark. A cat scurried along the back wall, crawling beneath him before pouncing over the back gate like it had spotted something move. Bill didn't like cats. He cursed under his breath while returning to his warm bed, drifting to sleep. Soon he was snoring, the sound intermittent as he stopped breathing, sighing in slumber. He then started the process over again.

He woke again at half-past-three. The old alarm clock ticked too loudly. He checked his wrist watch on the bedside locker to validate the time. The alarm clock didn't lie. He sat up for a good five minutes trying to figure out what in the name of God had him awake. There was no security light or sneaking cat now. Should he go down, he wondered, and check the bar? Maybe something made a noise to wake him. Yes, and all was quiet now because the thieves heard him stir.

Unsteady on his feet, the blood rushing to his head, carefully he took the stairs step by step till he reached the doors of the bar. It was still and dark. Pressing the light switch, he was blinded by the sudden surge. There were strange black blobs in his line of vision.

Angry with himself he walked to the window, swishing back the heavy curtain. The dark harbour kept the small craft hidden. He knew most of them. He knew who owned them—he knew them all. It was his business to know everyone. He knew why the boats were called "Sea Biscuit" and "First Lady." There were lots of things a man in his position would know, things other men wouldn't.

Idle words slipped out, men the worse for drink confessing their sins. He had that weight on his shoulders. Maybe it was the reason he couldn't sleep. He plodded up the stairs to his room again, but before he could settle he had to return to the toilet, his bladder full. This time his aim was steady. His bed cooled down, he tossed and turned to get warm and fiddled with his pillows, finally settling on two of them to support his head. Julia came rushing back. But why, when a man just wants to sleep?

Julia came from nothing. She arrived in Wood Point one summer a long time ago. She was half his age. Her people were from Belmullet, but it wasn't till after her father died that she showed any interest in going back there. She started with Mrs. Edwards, cleaning rooms and working in the bar. That was where he met her. He was invited to Fred's birthday party.

She was a strapping girl in a country way, built for comfort rather than speed. She wasn't very attractive; her lips twisted slightly to make her sour. Her eyes were small, sunk in her head like she had inherited some masculine traits. Yet she had a good figure and tidy breasts that were of the hills, but Bill thought they churned for an age.

Mrs. Edwards spoke down to her, but Julia didn't mind. She introduced Bill as the proprietor of the Harbour Bar no less. Julia was impressed. She offered him his choice from a plate of finger food. Bill made a point of speaking softly in a polite way. Julia smiled at him. Whatever effect it had on the creases in her skin, it made her look desirable in a flirtatious way.

So Bill flirted with her at every opportunity. She came by with glasses of punch or wafer crackers with cheese and pate, the type of things women invent. Julia made sure he got first choice when new plates of delights were brought. She was adept at keeping in Edwina's good books by wiping tables and filling jugs of water. She tended to the older people like she was a trained nurse.

Bill had eyed her, feeling uncomfortable. It was so long since he had enjoyed the pleasure of a woman. It must have been three years or more since he had sex. He remembered it was a most unfortunate affair with a prostitute down the docks in Cork, staying in town after a hurling clash with Tipperary, which Cork had just about won. At the time he was a serious drinker. Too many pints followed by a posse of chasers led himself and a companion down to the docks where the prostitutes varied from the underage to the senile.

This was the very catalyst that led to him giving up on the drink almost completely, save for a special occasion. More than anything, he might go for a glass of punch. The hag just took his money; she was a worse drunk than himself, apologising every time she got rough with him. There was no pleasure in it, her flat beside a disused scrap yard crawling with rats.

The memories still turned his stomach. Julia offered to refill his glass of punch, but he refused, wondering whether he should mingle. Perhaps she was just paying him attention because he was alone standing in a room crowded with people.

Edwina came over, either spotting his predicament or to genuinely chat. She was full of Freddie—how wonderful he was and how he was the love of her life. Fred, who was suitably pissed, chatted to all and sundry, but he took a great interest in the young girl from Lislee who was carrying trays of sandwiches. She didn't look any older than sixteen.

"So, she is Mayo girl?" Bill said without any lead in.

"She is," Edwina said warmly. "Her mother has relations in Butlerstown. You know Binny Farrell?"

Bill looked puzzled for a second, but then he turned to Edwina saying, "Binny Farrell. Slaughterhouse Binny!"

"The very man," Mrs. Edwards said, grabbing hold of his arm. "Her mother is his first cousin, and that's her youngest daughter. So, small world isn't it? She has the Farrell charm."

Mrs. Edwards was smiling at Fred, who in turn was having a quick stare at the girl from Lislee's backside.

"Is that where she stays?" Bill asked, drinking the last of his punch.

Edwina, ignoring her husband's antics, smiled. "No, Bill, she lives in. We only have her for the season, but she is good.

Worth two of what I normally get. I might get her to stay on a bit."

"Yeah," Bill said, trying to show support as in all business people should stick together, especially concerning staff.

Soon he started to see more of her. She worked the bar on Wednesday evenings, so Bill arranged for Madge Butler to fill in for him. She was reliable, even if she didn't do things his way.

"It's you again, Mr. Thornton." Julia gave a very welcoming smile, which at once put him at ease. He ordered a pint of lager, which he nursed.

When things went quiet, Julia placed her elbows on the bar like she was taking the weight off the world around her. Somehow she made him feel all right in himself, even though he was twice her age. Their chat was natural and easy.

"Have you ever been in Belmullet?"

"Can't say I was. Been everywhere else, mind you, in my younger days. I was a travelling salesman. I sold car parts to motor factors. I travelled the twenty-six counties, Mayo included. Castlebar, Westport, Charlestown—but I can't honestly say I was ever in Belmullet."

"It's a pretty place. A bit like Wood Point, only it's flat and the sky sort of touches the ground."

"I hear if you step too far you will land in New York. Isn't that right, Julia? The next step is America?"

Julia laughed at the ridiculousness of him. "I would say you might want to jump pretty far. But it is wild, and we have beautiful beaches. Some of them stretch for miles."

"Is that right?" Bill watched her behind as she reached into the till for change. She was well-proportioned, with right child-bearing hips on her.

"Were you a salesman for long?" she asked, turning round.

"Over ten years till I ran out of rubber, and my grandfather died and left my mother the pub, Lord rest her. Some would say I was lucky, but when you're quiet like I am...."

"Sssh, now, Mr. Thornton, don't you do well enough?"

When she smiled she bowed her head, slightly embarrassed. "I'd love to own my own pub. It is a dream I have. There is a little place out near Elly bay. It is always for sale. I promised myself if I ever get to go home, I will buy it. I will keep an open fire like you and have musicians play as they will. I've worked it all out with pub-grub like lunches and the like. Maybe when I get it up and running, I might get a really good chef and do evening meals. We don't have any nice restaurants in Belmullet."

Bill interjected. "Julia, if you need any advice or help you know it is my forte, but the pub business isn't what it seems, you know. The public don't see the half of it. People think because there is a half-dozen customers the publican is raking it in. But the government gets most of the takings, and half of our opening hours are spent stocking shelves and tidying up. Sometimes I can go an hour without seeing a soul. You might get busy the last few hours of an evening, and people think you're made and rich."

Bill stopped himself before adding, "Of course, I do all right, but I am a long time in the business. I have learned the tricks of the trade, you know, the hard way at times, but you have to keep a tight ship, know the customers, give them what they want. And people can be very demanding and fussy when it comes to drink, especially women. And they watch the price. If I am a few pence more than Michael Harrington they complain, despite the fact you give them comfortable chairs and stools. And I keep the toilets clean!"

He stopped himself once more, but he was pleased Julia was listening carefully to everything he said, so he continued. "Life is funny. Maybe you won't have to go back to Mayo to realise your dream. There is many a good pub for sale or rent around here, some of the best pubs in the country. For one reason or another they come on the market."

Julia laughed. "I don't have the means, Mr. Thornton. I am thinking twenty years down the road when I can build a little nest egg." Julia placed her hand on the counter to rest.

Bill thought of covering it with his own but the thought
collapsed when Mrs. Edwards appeared greeting him
warmly.

The cat was back. He couldn't shift it as it scraped along
the high wall. Soon it would slide onto the paved stones
below, clatter its way beyond the ashes bin, and then scale
the wooden fence dividing the next level. And that needed to
be dug as soon as he could find the time to do it. Bill yawned
and held his stomach. Immediately the ache attacked the pit
of his stomach, just enough to let you know it was there but
hardly worth mentioning to the quack.

The night had succumbed to the early hours. Dawn was
queuing way out to sea, and the tide parted like friends tired
after a long night out. At the mouth of the estuary, horsemen
waiting to gallop restrained white horses as the dark knights
returned lonely and bitter, their night's work yielding
nothing. He thought of getting up altogether, but what would
he do, sit in the damp kitchen drinking tea and reading old
copies of the Bandon opinion?

He closed his eyes, concentrating on the darkness beyond
the canvas pulled tight and nailed on. Tiny flickers of light
from outside the cat had met a foe, and it screeched like a
child on its last, the sound chilling above all the others. The
house expanded—the ticking clocks, the faint sound of a
tractor starting in Kilbrittain.

Bill opened his eyes, cursing the cat and promising to lay
poison for it. On his feet, he made the toilet. His urine was
dark and unusually yellow. He should never have gone to
Belmullet with her. That's where it all went wrong;
everything had been fine up to that.

Washing his hands, he noticed how tired his face was. The
mirror was old and it was usually kind to him. But his eyes
sank in their sockets with lines beneath them, creases
deepened by swollen circles of skin. He needed a complete
revamp. This was where a loving wife could come handy.

Never let you slip into the mire, keep at you, nag you till you
looked your best. Made you wear the nicest of clothes,
making you the perfectly groomed man, accepting the last of
middle age full of grace.

Wood Point, A few years ago
13.

Thomas Crowe didn't regard Jack as a rival, not in the same way he envied Ted O' Reilly. The truth of it was that Jack Browne was only a little better off than himself, and when all was examined in the cold light of day it was Ted O' Reilly who had married her and he held ownership in that sense. So Jack Browne for all his high and mighty chat could lump it just the same, as he was no better off. Thomas knew that there was something at the core of him that wouldn't allow him to feel hard done by or cheated. Anyway in his life disappointment and tragedy were served on a silver tray. It was the truth: some people got it easy. Others struggled eternally. He often thought he might be serving time for sins committed in a previous existence.

Sometimes he stopped where the woods ended, and he could sit among a series of small rocks embedded in the grassy mound sitting by the beacon with the ladder resting alongside of it. He wouldn't stay long at all, just enough time to stare out at the tide and see the land, dark brown, sink to the blue of the sea. Since his father died he made it a habit, as it was this place they walked every Sunday. If it didn't rain his father would plonk down on the grass bank for a rest and to spout some wisdom, and even at the time Thomas guessed his father was exaggerating. But he still loved the way the old man paused between sentences, like he was arranging his thoughts with order.

In the winter he wouldn't sit. But he would stand tall looking at his son directly, his back to the great view of the seven heads, his voice fighting the wind. And when it was really cold, his words hung in smoke clouds in the harsh air. The old man was getting frail but was still hardy enough to warn him about his mother and how she would need locking up after he was gone. The next time she and Brid Dargan went off to the woods for one of their pixie visits he might lock her up himself. At last, peace before the Lord took him.

Thomas smiled at him as the old man dusted himself down before moving on, brushing dust from his suit trousers before fastening the bottom buttons of his overcoat. Thomas stood in such a way that his father could lean on his shoulder as he stepped over a protruding rock.

Looking at his son's head he said, "I lost the top of my head when I was twenty-eight years old, and I had never set sight of your mother. Declare to God, didn't the shock of meeting her make me lose the rest of it, so I wear a permanent hat and I sport a good tache to make up for it. Whatever about the tache, you will need a hat. Get a good hat, son, and nobody will notice."

Thomas, grinning, was thinking he might inherit his mother's head with her dark looks. She had the hair of a witch, thick as rope, and in sober moments she made him comb it for her. After she had washed it, she said it soothed her mind, slowed it down. As soon as the drink came on her again she might not bathe for six months, and the same hair she tied up till it resembled a brown sack full of maggots.

The old man was right, of course, and Thomas lost most of his hair before he was twenty-six. Taking his father's advice, he bought a nice cap in Bandon. It fitted perfectly and he thought it made him look sophisticated when in company in Sean Harrington's or in the Harbour Bar. He also owned a series of woollen hats suitable for the sea. He liked them because the wool pulled round his ears, protecting him from the wind. Also, strangers would know he was a local and a man of the sea deep, knowledgeable and drunk—the price you pay to be a celebrated character.

His father never really got the plans for his mother straight in his own lifetime. He threatened to have her committed on several occasions, but something or someone always intervened at the last moment. His dreaded sister, Eileen, had sabotaged the plans on one occasion, intruding with her English lawyer boyfriend, a little fat fellow with glasses. Thomas hated him immediately; he was runt-like with rose red cheeks. When he spoke it was like listening to a girl or a deballed man.

They rounded on the old man, claiming the cost of incarceration would be enormous and the whole exercise would lead to his financial ruination. Pleading that by proxy all family assets would be used up and thus eliminate any prospective inheritance for Eileen and Thomas, (citing his welfare as their chief concern,) they used him as the lever of persuasion. Finally the old man, having enough of them interfering, wanted to know: would they take her to Dublin and look after her so as he and Thomas might have a life? Of course, they used work commitments and the unsuitability of the apartment they leased as an excuse.

The cure came from an unexpected source. After one fateful day of drinking with all the additional debaucheries, Annie arrived home cursing the pixies and shouting jealously that they preferred the pissing Bríd Dargan to herself. She said they were laughing at her, and when she overhead them sniggering and sneering about having their way with the young maidens that strolled through the woods she had enough.

When she sobered up, she said, she wanted to change, make herself well and warn the young girls of the parish to stay away from the wood. What a price they would pay, as the pixies were made of bad stock and they tricked the young maidens to sleep whilst they had their wicked way and the girls were no wiser till it was too late. So she cried by the fire for an hour, her husband staring at her like it was the first time he ever laid eyes upon her. On and on she wailed, and then suddenly she stopped and quite rationally said she had heard of a nurse from Barryroe who knew about the pixies and their spells.

Annie stayed sober, and (despite a few blips in the early weeks) she did, much to her husband's surprise and to the celebration of her son. The only one who was pissed with the situation was Brid Dargan who sat up in the woods alone, wailing and shouting. After a time she got bored with herself and gave up. She stayed on the sup but drank at home where she could stay warm.

Annie was a revelation and the nurse beautified her. The hair stayed immaculately clean, and the nurse brought her second-hand dresses, hand-me-downs from a rich aunt. Annie didn't care and she looked well in them. The rich aunt was her perfect double as the dresses looked like they had been made especially for her. Patrick was delighted. His wife now had been to the dentist, and her teeth were cleaned and the rotten one, which fouled her bottom lip, was extracted. After a few months the shine returned to her eyes, and a richness that had vanished for years returned.

Annie pontificated over Sunday lunch. She went on endlessly about the well-off classes and how they inherited the state from the British. She didn't ease off her theories, much to the delight of Thomas who fired a fake rifle each time she said the word 'Brit.' Patrick was bored by it all, yet it tickled him to hear her come back to life. She hadn't ranted on for years, and whilst it was boring always it brought a certain pleasure to hear her at it again.

"James Connolly, a lovely man. No wonder he was one of them they shot. Made sure they got the socialist, hey, Thomas?" she said winking at her son, who did a silly fake rifle shot for no reason. "Patrick, don't you know they handed the state over to the West Brits? The likes of the hospital consultants and the Protestants, those fellas up in Trinity College, and even when De Valera fought them, sure, they bought him out too. A new ascendancy was created, aren't I right, Patrick? The Irish ascendancy. If you belonged to the party you were looked after, but if you didn't…"

Annie looked at Thomas, her eyes on the brink of exclamation. Thomas, sensing the intensity of her stare, bowed his head slightly.

"Even here in little places like Wood Point, the divide is here still. Look at them all over the far side, farming the land stolen by Cromwell. They are all still around here. All the same, Patrick, all of them privileged."

"You will blind the boy, Annie. You have already recruited him for Sinn Féin. Now you want him to join the Communist party. People live, Annie, I keep telling you that. People live and get on with it. Their routines, the ups and downs of life. There is no time for thinking the tripe you spout. What of it if a few of them have more than we have, and, sure, if they served to free the state from the lousy English? Were they not entitled to some class of a reward? So be it. If their descendants benefited without these people, we would still be enslaved to foreign rule. I, being only natural myself, wouldn't I take the gifts if they were handed to me, just the same as the next man?"

Patrick went to get up from his chair but sat down just as quick before adding, "The landowners your mother refers to, Thomas, these people in the main are hard-working and frugal. They don't waste like the poorer classes, spending needlessly on items surplus to requirements. These people know how to invest and through their indigenous networks they make cautious investments designed to produce money, cash money long after they are dead."

Patrick used his fingers to signify money trickling through onto the table cloth.

"They are not only frugal, Annie, they are planting the seeds of ethnic survival, generations of their likeness spawned by foresight and forbearance."

Annie, looking blankly at her son, snarled. "So it is the same for the rest of us, Patrick. Is it that we plant the seeds of gombeenism, the mighty working man or the farmer with a headless shovel? Aren't we all planting seeds for generations? But, sure, if I haven't the means, it will be the poorest crop that will sprout in my field. Where did they get their hands on the good land? The lush hills of Kilbrittain—they go back as far as I can see. Look, Thomas, look out over the water to the other side look at them!"

Patrick started to lift the dinner plates, stacking them, careful to remove the knives and forks, first cleaning them dry with the paper napkin. Thomas looked out; it was overcast and cold but not a bad day. The rain had stayed away and at this time in the afternoon it was unlikely to come at all. The tide was still, the only movement ripples separating fake rivers. The odd car passed by, their sidelights throwing light over the sand just to confuse these idle rivers even more. They strived to gel midst false waves, the wind built with small pieces of surf.

"Look at the wealth, Thomas, and the further up the hill you go, doesn't the land get better? And beyond, where we are blinded, it is the best of all lush pasture, the best in the county."

Patrick rattled the plates nervously as he made for the parlour door, Thomas his eyes searching on his mother's instruction.

The afternoon was closing in. Even the seconds made a difference. The stray trees were suddenly darker, their shapes soon to fall to the enticement of the evening. Two large trees stood like two lovers, big and bold, but nearby their children scattered in an errant line. Yet more lovers hugged the brow of the hill. He tried to look beyond, yet the curve of the hill didn't allow it, stopping him and his imagination.

His mother's words were correct. In the distance the land was calm with cattle and farmhouses like shrunken models. These hills rolled on with the cattle becoming small black dots. Thomas imagined the faint whitewash of stone walls. His imagination rushed on to the next valley and the lush grass and the big heifers and the prize bulls and the dairy cows lost midst stacks of hay.

Annie stayed on the dry for two years solid. She didn't even stray when collecting the pint bottle of Guinness from the Harbour Bar and bringing it to her dying friend who seemed to return from death's door every time she drank stout. Annie would sit with Bríd for hours whilst they relived their long days in the woods and the chats they had.

Bríd repeated, "It was always you, Annie, that went for the pixies, and the people who don't believe us, aren't they made of ignorant stuff? But you, Annie, you saw the good side of them too. Isn't that why they liked you and left you be? They never bothered you like they bothered me. What about the fella who followed me home? Do you remember him, Annie? What was he after, hey? He said he could make me a jug of porter whenever the mood came over him."

Annie waited till her good friend fell asleep, her voice falling to the faintest of murmurs, the porter soothing her brain. Annie pulled the blankets up above her shoulders. Bríd's face was pale, her cheeks puffed and white patted with soft cotton buds. Her hair, once dyed, was an orangey-red; now natural grey looked white in the bad light. Bríd's breathing was deep and weak but every now and then she retained normality and reassured the room, which was adorned with all her belongings such as they were.

Annie noticed the hair brush face down on the dressing table. It was growing clumps of hair. The mirror, where it attempted to seek business, was cracked in the centre. The frame supporting it was stuck fast where it used to swivel. Annie sighed, leaving her friend and closing the door ever so gently least she roused her. Bríd's middle-aged niece who visited once a week sat drinking tea. She didn't speak but eyed Annie very peculiarly.

When Bríd died Annie didn't say too much. Thomas was heading to the secondary school in Clon, and Patrick, feeling the strains of age, didn't think much of it. Bríd was a good ten years older than Annie (more his own age,) and he never liked her or saw anything of interest in her. Annie attended the funeral alone and only the usual suspects from the village and her niece and husband were there. Patrick didn't want to take time from his job behind the counter in Neilands butchers. She was buried in Timoleague right up the back of the graveyard. It was a dour spot with no view over the estuary or the river. Annie placed a small bunch of wild flowers on the dark wet clay; she had collected them earlier, feeling the strain of the climb to the wood for the first time.

She was quiet that evening sitting by the fire, as Patrick busied himself with the Silvo at the kitchen table. Thomas was out and about, but it was rare for them to be alone by the fire in the evening. Patrick searched in the kitchen cupboard for the Brasso. He wanted to clean the old ornamental candlesticks that belonged originally to his grandfather and then his mother.

"Did she get a send off?" Patrick was back seated at the table; he used a discarded tea towel to clean the brass and a softer cloth for the shine.

"No. She didn't know many. In her last years she was never out, and most of the people she knew when she was young are gone from the parish or dead along with her. Father Breen said a few kind words about her, even if it wasn't true. He said she loved nature and wild flowers and the birds and plants and all the natural thing of the wood, but, sure, the world and its wife know why she went to the wood. It wasn't to see the flowers or the ferns or smell the sap of the trees."

"Priests say these things," Patrick said using the soft cloth. "They have to say something," he added carelessly.

"They do. I would say there weren't more than ten people there and when you take it that her niece and her husband were at it, nobody really turned out at all. A terrible end to a life when people aren't bothered to come out. Years ago people would pay their respects even if they couldn't stand the sight of you, but today everyone is so opinionated and judgmental."

"It wasn't a great day, Annie. People were put off, I'd say," Patrick said with empathy.

"Put off? It's not likely they can turn up tomorrow if the sun comes out, is it? It was the day that was in it. If the skies had opened, if there was a deluge, that was the last day above ground for Bríd Dargan, one last chance to pay their respects. People are funny about things, Patrick."

Annie picked up the poker to disturb the coals. She poked at the blackened sides, turning them upside down to burn. She stared at her completed work, feeling the heat from the coals warm against her calves and she turned to look at Patrick who was busy polishing. He was thorough; his work was on display, the brass gone from dull to bright, the silver reflecting random images.

"Is Thomas due home?" she asked.

Patrick lifted his head to look at her. Seeing she was tearful, he wanted to rise from his chair and go to her but he held back, saying calmly, "He is down the pier helping on the trawler. He won't be long now."

He looked at the old clock on the mantelpiece. "Finishes around eight usually, but he might drop by the Harbour Bar on the way for a lemonade. Thirsty work, lifting and scrubbing. It will strengthen his shoulders, fill him out."

Annie nodded, turning to gaze at the fire.

When Patrick got the diagnosis of lung cancer, Thomas ran from the house and was gone for hours. When he eventually returned, he sat in the corner of the kitchen drinking tea. He was quiet at first, but when the old man engaged him in conversation he spoke softly with a newly-found serenity. A week later, Annie started to drink again. He smelled it off her breath; it was the only way he could tell. Unlike before she didn't display anything in her behaviour, and there was no retiring to her room or wailing from the top of the stairs. He just knew by the smell.

Patrick was bearing up well. He sat by the fire most evenings talking to whoever might drop by to listen to him. Thomas didn't mention the drinking to him as he hoped the old man was unaware of it. Sitting with him was becoming a nightly ritual as Patrick held court. He told him stories of his youthful adventures—how they poached salmon out on the Bandon River and later on the Argideen. Every now and then the old man would cough, spluttering phlegm, his face as red as beetroot. He spat a mouthful into the fire, coughing into his handkerchief, wiping his lips, looking at his son embarrassed.

"Are you all right, Father?" Thomas asked.

"Be right in a minute when I can breathe."

Patrick coughed again, this time till Thomas went to help by clapping him on the back; this he hesitated to do it as the old man seemed so frail.

When Patrick recovered, he said hoarsely, "I am fucked, Thomas. No use in lying about it or trying to fool anyone."

He paused, using his handkerchief again, wiping his lips, which seemed to moisten mysteriously.

"I hear your sister is coming from Dublin. So be it. She never comes to Wood Point; only if some drama is afoot. She is coming to see the final end of her father."

"Don't be saying things like that; the doctors haven't said anything like that to you." Thomas forced a smile, but Patrick looked on at him coldly.

"It is the end. Don't fret, son. It comes calling on us all. Soon it will be my turn, and I need you to help me sort out my affairs, you get me? I don't want Eileen fixing anything up for me, Thomas, like nursing homes or the like. I don't want any priests around either. Once I am dead they can do what they like, but she terrifies me, son, because your mother will be incapable. You know she is back on the drink."

Thomas feigned surprise, but Patrick wasn't fooled.

"You can smell it from five yards, and she thinks we don't notice. That's often the way of it. They think cuteness is their right. You do smell it, don't you?"

Thomas nodded.

"Maybe she won't go as bad this time, Thomas, though I doubt it. I am just thinking with Bríd Dargan gone; she will have to do on her own. Maybe Eileen will have her locked up. It is a lousy thing I leave you with, boy!"

Thomas watched as he spluttered into the handkerchief once more, a lump of phlegm caught in his windpipe. He threw the lot into the fire, the handkerchief and all.

Patrick died three months later, and Annie stopped drinking for the funeral. She had been drinking heavily whilst her husband fought his illness, but in fairness she stayed out of the way and she was quiet. The house was strangely silent.

Eileen had returned to throw in her tuppence-worth. Her Englishman had the sense to stay in Dublin this time, as Thomas would have laid him out for sure. His father died at home in his own bed, and when he went it wasn't in the midst of a mad splutter but quietly in his sleep. The doctor had pleaded for him to go to the Mercy Hospital, but the old man was nothing if not stubborn to the last.

The day they buried him Thomas got mightily drunk for the first time, drinking whiskey and stout. Eileen labelled him a disgrace as he could barely talk to the visiting neighbours. Later in the evening, he sat in the corner of the kitchen watching as the fire died in the grate. All the visitors had gone. Annie and Eileen had gone to bed leaving him there.

He remembered things the old man used to say, the way he teased him and magnified certain things just to raise his goat.

"When will you ever get a girlfriend? When I was your age I had three girlfriends, and there were only four eligible girls in the parish. The other one was Anne Marie Sexton, and she was so big she couldn't fit out the garden gate."

Thomas didn't have a girlfriend. He didn't even know any girls. He was so shy around them. They were too fucking pretty, that was it. He got nervous when girls were around. He was a man's man, as they say.

Patrick was only ribbing him about it; he liked the ruggedness of his only son, the strength to stack fish boxes and the back to pick periwinkles down near Broadstrand. He was gone now. What a stupid thing to happen. One day a person is here with you—your own father—then he was gone. Why did you have to leave because the body is no longer working? Why hadn't they figured a way to store the spirit, to put it in a jar, keep it in the larder with the marmalade and the golden syrup?

Strangers came and they took his body away to bury it in the ground, this living breathing person who you were only chatting to yesterday. Why, if it was an old heater, we would get a new part. It was a question of mechanics or plumbing, my God, for the sake of a plumber! The old man said it was the best of trades these days, great work to be had with the County Council building houses all over West Cork.

Thomas lowered the last of the whiskey.

Whatever he said is useless. All I have now are words going round in my brain. Only his words spinning around come in to my mind, then slipping out again. He is gone. The living part of him is gone to rot in the ground like the spuds up the back garden, in a bad year bits of them missing, maggots in the core. How do we deserve this end? And why choose between people?

She is the one who should have gone, with her carrying on and the wailing and the shouting. The patience he showed sitting by the fire, his face red from the glow. "Go see to her, Thomas. She is in the wood with Bríd Dargan. Go see to her and bring her home." Patience…or was it pride? Maybe he didn't want them talking about him around the place. No fear of him going to get her himself. No, it was always, "Thomas, go get her."

Soon the fire started to wane, and he was suddenly cold and wanted his bed. Not to sleep but for the warmth of it.

Thomas went to the dark place between sleep and exhaustion. He stood again over his father's grave, noticing the grave next to it had collapsed, leaving gaping holes, the soil empty like the aftermath of an earthquake. He read the name in an effort to distract himself from the inane muttering of the tired grey-haired priest.

Mary Kane
Timoleague
Died April 5th 1961

That was it. A life in a few words. Who was she? Why did she walk the earth? Who did she speak to? Who loved her? Did anyone love her? There was no mention of a husband, or sons and daughters, not even brothers or sisters.

The priest continued the litany, and Annie started to weep, the tears running down the cold of her cheeks. Eileen, braving it, put her arm on her shoulder, but Annie moved away, moving closer to the gaping hole before her. As they lowered the coffin, Annie threw the single rose she carried on top of it and Eileen followed suit, pulling her coat tight at the collar as she stepped backwards. He noticed Bill Thornton standing expressionless by the back of the grave. Some women from the village gathered the wreaths.

The priest started to shake hands and went to Annie and Eileen. Lastly he shook hands with Thomas, his grip harsh and cold. Thomas nodded at him, taking in his eyes for only a second. The crowd dispersed, moved slowly but quickened, chatting among themselves as they neared the cemetery gates.

She surprised him when she approached, and he sensed her hesitancy.

"I am so sorry for you, Thomas," Kate Donovan said. "I know you loved walking up the point with him. Now he will be looking at the sea all the time, won't he, Thomas?"

Kate Donovan—what was she, twelve years old? She looked into his eyes. He felt the warm beat of her heart. It soothed his mind. Dancing off after her mother, he watched her catch up. She had left him soft instilling hope, and he wanted to smile but more relatives, female cousins of his father who he never had time for, came forward to hug and kiss him like they were the closest thing in his life. People he would see once every five years or so. Eileen led Annie, arms interlocked, to the waiting limousine, and Thomas followed slowly glancing back over his shoulder. Bill Thornton chatted with Michael Harrington, and beside him Madge Butler stood looking dark and lonesome wearing black.

Wood Point, Many years ago
14.

Night came to the estuary, a dark glove on the pale white of her hand. Soon the rolling hills and random trees were extinct, replaced by the glare of manmade light. Madeline felt the softness of it, refusing to pull the drapes. Cars rounding the bend coming from Ballinspittle spread giant torches to disturb dark birds staying out late. When they swirled she imagined these creatures ducking and diving, falling to the water as if they were shot, these fallen gulls breaking the surface only to rise once more, swirling to fade in the bad light beyond.

As a child she remembered seeing thirteen swans float by at the back bend, just before Timoleague. She had counted them twice in case she made a mistake, but she hadn't. Thirteen swans—odd, she thought. It means one of them is alone. Which one was it? The last one, detached, floating by, or was it the one in the middle, playing games, keeping the sunny side up? Or it could be the leader, swimming along, trying to prise a loyal partner to stray.

"Look at me! See how fast I can go?"

The swans stayed in Wood Point most of her childhood winters, and her father stopped the car to let her go have a look. Why thirteen an odd number?

Madeline felt the dog move. He had stretched out over her feet. She didn't mind it he was a rug. Bob sighed, opening his mouth to yawn, saliva dripping from his tongue.

"Oh, Bob, don't you slobber over me."

Bob, sensing her displeasure, struggled to his feet. Shaking himself clean, he made to the fire waning in the grate. Madeline wanted to tend to it, but she hardly had the will to move. Her glass was empty; she would have to stir for a refill. Grab a block from the pile of wood on the way.

Her father waited for her patiently. He had bought the
"London Times" ordered from the best news agents in Clon.
He read it cover to cover whilst she braved her swans,
deciding in the end it must be the last one because it was
detached. Mother took a dim view, fretting, save her daughter
should pick up pneumonia or worse, but her father, rolling
the tobacco for his pipe, spoke softly telling her not to worry.
These things she worried about didn't exist in the freezing
cold air, he said. Those warm wet places were far more
dangerous. Mother went quiet like she knew she was
chastised by somebody far wiser than she.

Madeline put a block on the fire and watched as it caught
flame. The flames were small at first, hugging the
underneath, the colours yellow and blue, the smoke dark at
first changing to white.

When father greeted her, he doused his pipe, placing it
under the dashboard, the aroma sweet but warm after the cold
air.

"I saw thirteen swans," Madeline said.

"Did you, sweetheart?" he replied incredulously.

"Six of them are married and one is a bachelor."

"Really?"

"Yeah, I think it is the last one."

Her father strained to look out the car window to see the
swans, but they had rounded the bend and were heading
towards the bridge.

The flames shot up, engulfing the complete block;
suddenly she felt the heat starting in her ankles and moving
to her calves as she turned her back on it. Bob, who was
stretched out on his side, wanted to re-adjust his position.
Now there was real heat. But she blocked his passage with
her left leg. He moaned, butting her with his head before
finally giving up and lying flat with an enormous sigh.

Her mother taught her how to be a wife. She started at a
young age, learning all the domestics. Even though they had

a cook and a lady to clean, she taught her sewing and knitting and how to hold herself when dressed in a nice dress. Mother even taught her how to take evasive action should she be surprised by the unwelcome arrival of body functions.

"Cough, dear. If that doesn't work look around you, like you heard the rude noise too, and if that fails look at your companion accusingly. That never fails. Of course, one should sit on them whenever possible."

Madeline thought it strange: both her parents were English, but she never got the accent. Her father's people were wealthy—not that her mother's weren't—just his were really wealthy. He was managing his grandfather's textile factory in Bandon; Mother came with him as a kind of accessory: "Wherever you go, I go."

They were in Cork ten years before Madeline danced on the earth. When she was old enough her mother taught her about sex and gave lots of instructions.

"A woman must stay neat and tidy for her man. Never allow yourself to wane, dear. A man likes a nice night dress, revealing but never vulgar, not like these modern women, you know, with pyjamas or sportswear. God help us, you need to remain desirable!"

God blesses indeed if she were around to see her now. Madeline helped herself to another drink, discovering a standing position by the fire. Bob was perplexed; he didn't know whether to move when she did or just laze it out. He chose to laze it out and sigh to show his indignation.

Imagine if she said those things to Georgina. What would she make of me? Her own mother was so incredibly old fashioned, lost in her books about secret Victorian love affairs. Funny, she came into her own when Father died, when she should have been rendered useless, devastated. But, no, she came into her own.

Her father died very suddenly at work. His secretary found him sitting in his chair, his pipe in his right hand, tobacco ready to roll on the desk, as dead as could be. The poor woman almost died herself of shock. Mother was a revelation. After the suitable mourning period of a year or so, she did things: learning to drive, getting a regular modern hairdo, and holidaying twice yearly in the south of France. She never brought another man to Wood Point, yet Madeline was sure there was somebody, judging by the regularity of the letters arriving. Mother would dismiss them in front of anyone present, but they were secreted to the bedroom for private reading.

Of course she was only fifty when Father died. Seemed ancient then, but so young now. She still had the spark of life in her all the same. Madeline felt tears swell. She was fifty-eight years old, yet her mother had lived a better life than she. Why, when life is the means to evolve, we are to better our parents. It is the essence of logic, and it underscores the very reason of existence.

In her later years her mother went back to England, giving the house to Madeline whilst always keeping her own name on the deeds. Two years now since Mother died. She suffered too, not like father. Her body rotted from the inside out. It was a desperate, painful end. Donal was still trying to sort out the tax implications. Leave it to him; isn't that what his snarling personality gets off on?

The vodka almost empty again. A refill. The dog in a dilemma. Lazy dog. What does Georgina think of it all, her mother spending her evenings alone in the drawing room? Drinking this foul stuff, talking to the goddamn dog. Funny, she doesn't say much about it one way or another.

Georgina was a quiet girl, but Madeline could tell by the way she looked at her. Sometimes she knew by the way her eyes sank and her head dropped whenever Madeline walked into the room. Sometimes when she was going out in the car she got very close by making sure to kiss her mother on the side of the cheek, but as she withdrew she sniffed deep intake smells. How much has mummy had today? Yet they say you

can't smell vodka. Madeline laughed out loud. Bob looked at
her puzzled.

"Are you talkin' to me?"

By God, she can smell it from five yards, but only once did
she stop her from going anywhere. Madeline stomped
upstairs in temper, missed the step, and fractured her ankle.
She cried like a baby whilst Georgina got Madge Butler to
come help.

How is Donal, her father? All he does is sit at that bloody
desk writing copious notes or making entries in his ledger.
You would think like all modern businesses he might invest
in a computer, but not Donal. It would register as an
unnecessary expense, one which no matter what could not be
justified. Either that or he was flying around the countryside
in his jeep, chatting with this fella or the other and arguing
with Peter or threatening Paul.

Of course he was even worse on the sauce, only it didn't
do for him to be drinking alone in the drawing room. No, he
had to go present his credentials to the entire parish of Wood
Point. Madeline was thinking. Did Edwina Edwards like
him? Like maybe really like him? He spent so much time
down there.

Freddy is a joke, pinching women's bottoms, finding it a
great laugh. Good for him. Laugh away. Glad somebody
finds it amusing.

Madeline was thinking that Donal made a holy show of
himself.

People will wonder what's got into him. His status won't
protect him forever. He will end up the laughing stock. How
can Georgina be his daughter? How did things end up like
this?

When she met him, Mother said he was a tosser.

"Why does he want to get his feet under your table, my
dear?"

But Madeline thought there was something wild and romantic about him. His people were all right. They owned a shoe shop in Clon. He was educated in a boarding school and did well in his exams. He started out running his father's business but then studied auctioneering before he went out on his own.

Things were good at first because they both liked a party and he was funny with drink and quick-witted. The dinner parties were exciting and whilst Donal was brash and confident, he sometimes lacked the finesse befitting to some of Madeline's guests. As time went on, Donal started to invite his own cronies—fellow golfers and builders, his drinking mates. Madeline was relieved he invited the Edwards. For all of Freddy Edwards' faults, at least they owned the best establishment in Wood Point, and that carried a little weight.

Madeline tried hard to dilute her husband's manners by inviting people she knew from Clon. Some of them were musical, and she often got Mr. Farrell, the vicar's son, to play the piano. His wife, Eilish, could sing too, and she sang songs from the Gilbert and Sullivan operas. Madeline thought it made a lovely sound, especially in summer when some of the guests retired to the garden with their drinks. They sat by the sycamore with their cocktails, the younger women dressed rudely in flimsy dresses and their young men standing tall, wearing suits most of them weren't used to. Donal used these occasions to talk business with whoever he could find to talk business with.

Wood Point so many years ago; it was difficult to remember, to still see those faces. When Madeline had enough to drink, she would sing a song her mother taught her from the musical "Oliver." She hadn't a bad voice, but it was a struggle.

"As long as he needs me..." Donal led the clapping and was the first to cheer, his friends all complimenting him on how lovely a singer his wife was.

Georgina came along, and it was a complete shock to the system as Donal had shown little interest in her since they married. He had taken to sleeping in the single bed opposite the widest double bed ever built, complaining about his sore back and his wish not to disturb her when he rose in the early hours to go down to his study and work. They had sex one night after they had partied till dawn, falling unto the widest bed in the world exhausted. After a few failed efforts at sleep, Madeline kissed him on the lips softly and, as if awakening, suddenly he responded. The sex was functional; she didn't have time to slip off her nightie.

Donal was a little tipsy, and he struggled to get himself ready. Eventually she gasped whilst he giggled.

"What on earth ails you, woman?"

Madeline moved beneath him. "You are too heavy, Donal!"

"Heavy?" he grunted.

Madeline longed for gentleness, some sense of softness and heat. She soothed herself, imagining her lover. She pictured the merging of their hearts. At once she saw her childhood dreams in action, her strong muscular lover kissing and fondling her till she collapsed in exhaustion.

Instead she lay awake after he fell asleep, listening to him moaning in his disturbed dreams. He tossed and turned and sighed before rolling over. She thought of how helpless she was, of how helpless they both were lying naked on the largest bed in the world, the intermittent moonlight making strange shadows through the open curtain. For a moment she sensed the heat from him, and she saw in him an innocence that she never knew existed. In his dark sleep he was vulnerable and childlike. For a split second she felt like reaching out to stroke the side of his cheek and whisper comforting words into his right ear.

But she resisted as she remembered how removed he had been and how he ignored her protestations, not out of any

malicious sense but out of something almost worse: his calm
and deliberate indifference to her and to the respect she
expected. After an age sleep caught up with her, and she
dreamed of the animals in the field.

She looked at the dog he once more seemed unsure as to
whether she was talking to him. So he rolled over on his
back, his paws lifting weights.
Wherever does he go? Sometimes he is gone for two,
maybe three days, no explanation. Perhaps he doesn't feel the
need to explain anything. It is like he lives and breathes in
another place. Somehow his body is here, but his spirit is
elsewhere.
From the time Georgina was little, he did his duty, no
more, no less. He might walk her round the garden holding
her hand, play peaky boo at the kitchen table. As soon as
Georgina tired, he was off and out again wheeling and
dealing. The child didn't notice. She would jump for joy
when his car splashed up the driveway. Donal picked her up,
giving her a hug, her curls brushing against the silk of his tie.
As she grew he took her down to the harbour to see the boats.
On occasions they might go to Broadstrand for a swim. The
sea was always cold, but the beach was a suntrap. Georgina
would get excited as they drove down the dark narrow road
shaded by trees, letting out a scream when the sea first came
into view. Donal would bring her into the cold water,
splashing around, picking her up on his shoulders, dropping
her head first over the side splash. "Do it again, Daddy!"

One more drink. It will help sleep. This time Bob followed
her across the room. She felt his nostrils' wet touch the back
of her right leg as she poured.
Now he lends money illegally and builds unwanted holiday
apartments in the middle of nowhere with the same old
mantra.

"I tell you, Madeline, the world is changing. This is the way forward. Property is the key, Madeline. Mark my words: property, property, property..."

But it was her mother's property, this house, where her husband might sometimes sleep in that stuffy study and then chat for ages with that tramp Madge Butler.

What has she with Donal Travers? He doesn't have a mistress. What does she do for him? Does she tell him all the gossip from the village? Is that it? She tells him what they're all up to, does she? All about Mr. Thornton and Mr. Harrington, and she probably does a line on the Edwards as well.

Bob made a soft whistling noise as she approached the fire as if sensing her excitement.

"I hate this house, Mother. I hate this place. I live in terror here on my own. There is nobody. Can't you see, Mother? He is solitary. He is emotionless and solitary."

Madeline drank the drains of her drink, watching as the fire tried its best to keep a flame. She sang, ''There were thirteen swans sitting on the wall, and if one little swan should accidently fall, there'll be twelve swans sitting on the wall...''

The cold grabbed by the wind fanned her face. From nowhere paint licked rosy little piggy cheeks. She looked back at Father, sucking his pipe, as he turned the page of his newspaper. He gave it a hard pull to settle the creases. Thirteen swans sailed by, turning the bend to face the bridge at Timoleague. She heard the naked cry of the river Argideen. It purifies the salt water, and the swans all drink. She is stoic, coming from a long line of strong women. Child Madeline follows the swans till they round the bend beyond the bridge. The red canyon is followed by lines of evergreen trees.

At the bridge she saw a man ride a dark horse, jumping real hedgerows. Her eyes lost in the glare, she is seduced to where the water disappears. In the distance the small swamp ends where lush grass is sown; she sees the last swan fall into the red canyon with the glitter of rock somehow reflecting the dull light.

Wood Point, A few years ago
15

Caw unfolded his wings flapping like mad, fanning the cold air beneath till it swirled warmer by his head. He stared at the wood pigeon walking nervously from the shadow of the tree. How does a creep like him get to live in such stately place like the sycamore?

The wood pigeon went about his business, pecking at tiny mites busy in the dust heaped among the debris of the loose chips of rotted wood. Finally he stopped where the overgrown grass resembled a small field of barley. Caw felt the draught of wind blast up through the hole in the slates. Once he had fallen through it by mistake. In his panic the white sheets covering the beds and the full length mirrors left him rigid with fright. He remembered the piano music from years ago. Listening intently with his wife, they sat together on the roof as the melody played and warmed them and Mrs. Caw got all romantic and silly. That dreadful day he was trapped in the room, eventually finding an exit through the broken bedroom window, glass shattered all over the wooden floor.

The wind was cold against his feathers now, the chill inside of him, shivering, his head bobbing uncontrollably. The wood pigeon spotted him, holding his head down pretending not to recognise him. He didn't want an exchange of pleasantries. What was pleasant about the common crow?

Caw cawed, and the pigeon decided to shut the front door. He disappeared into the shadow where the moss was damp and maggots hid just beneath the surface. Caw cawed once more. He blamed the likes of the pigeon for everything. It was the likes of him that upset Mrs. Caw, making her unhappy, discontent with her lot. If it weren't for the likes of him, she might have stayed even after the place fell to ruin.

The rats were as bad but in a different way. In fact it was almost the complete opposite. They were envious of Caw, thought he had something because he had saved up lots of nesting materials. And Mrs. Caw was ambitious, their nest cosy. They had taken their time building it, saving good twigs and straw. The rats were jealous, slithering by in the bad light making comments.

"You must be rotten with it!"

Caw cared so much he had begged the elders from the fields to help get him the best of stuff. He did jobs for them in return. How many times had he gone to the murder of crows for assistance? They were usually fairly good and patient, but they had their rules, and he spent hours scanning the hillsides for the sight of a farmer laying poison or the reporting of scarecrow locations. Miles of flying, hanging in the air, on really cold days too. Sometimes he worked in the rain and came home saturated and shivering so bad once Mrs. Caw thought he had pneumonia and was about to die.

Later when he became more acceptable to the murder, they allowed him to go on retrieval missions. This was gruesome as the work involved the retrieval of smashed body parts from the road. A team of crows was sent to return the bits and pieces of splattered crows to their loved ones for a proper burial. (Often this was done to deny the rats a midnight feast. It is a strong part of crow folklore and custom to deny the rat at any opportunity access to feast on the corpses of dead crows.)

This was the life of a good crow in Wood Point. Until, of course, the entire murder was poisoned and left in a pile in the corner of the lower field. Rats came from near and far to feast. It is even said that sewer rats from Clon and the nearby shoreline joined in to what became a three-day festival. So much for trying to better oneself. But didn't it keep herself happy for the duration? And he was also elected chief intelligence officer in the new murder.

*

I have to say I had mixed feelings about Caw and the house. For the life of me I could never figure out why he wanted to go back there as the place was full of sad memories, with the holes in the roof and the smashed windows. It could only lead to misery and sadness. How terribly lonely his life was now. It didn't do him a bit of good sitting up there watching the wood pigeon show off. Caw was like that, though. Misery was his middle name; life just couldn't be miserable enough. He had to pile on the agony. "Walk down the avenue."

He revisited the locations where once, even if it was only for a short time, he experienced some semblance of happiness, which was indeed "Bang, bang, choo, choo, yeah!"

He was the same when I sat on the fish boxes with him, as he eyed the dark gull skimming the water searching for fish, so full of grace. Caw watched his wings flap, fanning the air, stirring the water till he dived and was fed. It was at times like these that Caw regretted his crow lineage and wished he was something else.

Caw was still useful, though, for he always told a good story, and sitting with him on a freezing cold November day he could warm your heart with his stories of scandal from the village.

He went on about Jack Browne and how Kate called by unexpectedly and Jack was flapping because she had Sarah and Fiona with her, which meant Jack had to be on his toes, entertaining them and staying patient while minding his laptop. Caw said she was in good form, too, with lots of one liners like, "We will be the talk of the place, Jack. They will put us down for having an affair." Jack, not taking her up on it, made excuses, taking ornaments from the mantelpiece, making alchemy toys.

Jack makes her laugh, telling her about the goings on around the place. She laughs, asking him if she should fix him up with her Aunt Myrna. Jack is amused but doesn't comment. She tells him Ted is coming home. He ignores this offering to make some tea.

The children are noisy, especially Fiona; she is firing ornaments at the sofa. Kate shows her disapproval, but she is soft and it is not enough so Jack says, "I will have to take it back, Fiona. You see, it is not mine, it belongs to the lady that owns the house."

Fiona stares at him like it is the first time she has heard him speak. "Daddy, Daddy." Jack smiles at her.

Kate says, "She loves her daddy.'" But she doesn't say it to anyone in particular. It is like she is speaking to the inanimate room.

Then Caw hesitated. He was taken with the departing tide, the green patch of weed, and the small nest of rock at Burren. It sat where the road bends at Kilbrittain. Caw moved nervously, his head rocking forwards and backwards but when he turned he was like a superstar sticking his belly out.

Jack was showing his appetite for her, and she was showing her appetite for him. The way their eyes met as she dropped her keys on her lap. As she sat in the car, he leaned in the driver's window and she caught his stare.

"You would think I was drinking, Jack. My head is spinning. It has to be these two. They are full of excitement. Maybe it is you. I don't know. I better be going now."

Jack, withdrawing, stood upright. She glanced at him as she turned the car up the tiny hill.

"Ted is home next week, so I don't know when I will see you."

Jack was blasé; he said, "Whenever." And she was gone, and he stood for a full minute without moving.

Then Caw came back to me, perching on a load of damp pallets. They reeked of fish. Some of them were good on the bottom, but the top ones were older. They had their corner blocks missing on one side.

She came by another time. Somehow she talked him into going to the gravel garden. She sat on the garden bench. It was like a seesaw; if you got up the whole thing got up with you.

Jack had a beer and so did she. The girls played with Jack's alchemy toys. Sarah had a car and Fiona an airplane. Jack kicked at the gravel stones, pulling his shoe against their weight.

"Mind yourself," Kate said. Getting up, she spilled some of the beer on her jeans. "Sloppy me! I am always doing it. I tell you, Jack, be careful of that seat, or you will end up on the roof."

Kate sat back down, allowing the late evening sun to devour her face.

"Years ago I worked in finance. You wouldn't think it by looking at me, would you? I was married, but things weren't good then. If I got home early and the odd day I did, I would watch my daughter play out the back garden. We had a nice garden. It wasn't very big, Kate. A bit bigger than this, of course. We had a nice lawn, none of this."

He kicked the stones petulantly. "It was winter. I remember because it was really cold for November. Jane used to sneak out the back garden. She was about eight then. She always did the same thing, you know—the little coat, the wellies, the woollen hat, and out she would go to get the last of the day. It was like she wanted to smell the daylight, you know, and watch as it slowly faded away. Of course her mother shouted at her out the kitchen door. 'Jane, Jane, come on in, you will catch your death.' Soon I might walk to the door to see if I could spot her in the bad light.

"As I said it wasn't like we had a field or anything, just a normal little semi d. Down the end of the path I had a small wooden tool shed with a felted roof. A few rose bushes climbed into it. We had a number of other plants. Some were meant to be small trees. We planted them when we moved in—you know, they were supposed to grow with us. Anyhow we both started to call her. I was about to go get a flashlight. My wife was still calling, 'Jane! Jane!' till suddenly she appeared smiling. She had walked up the paving slabs not directly to us across the grass. She appeared from nowhere."

Jack paused for breath. "'There you are,' my wife said. 'Where were you hiding out there in the dark?' I said patting her back and supporting her up the step. 'I was leaning against the bottom wall underneath all the plants. I kept tearing my sleeve off those thorns, Dad.' Jane said."

Kate looked at him sort of bemused. She drank the last of her beer before saying, "Kids are funny, Jack. You want to see some of the things I got up to when I was eight? I drove my father demented. Watch it!"

She went to get up. Jack jumped up also. "When Anne and I were fighting things out—it was near the end—she did the same thing one evening. I was off all day. I took some time out. I watched her go through the ritual—the wellies, the hat, the coat, and off she traipsed. I don't know whatever possessed me. I went upstairs to my room—it overlooked the garden. I watched her. She was down by the shed like she was talking to someone. When she looked around, I stepped back in case she could see me. She didn't despite looking upwards. Her lips were moving. She was muttering words. Maybe she was singing. I dunno."

Jack went quiet as Kate broke his concentration by shouting to Sarah, "Get Jack's car and his plane. We have to go home."

Sarah looked at her good-humoredly like she was accepting the fun was over. Fiona gave a cry.

"The plane!"

Somehow it had gone over the small garden wall through the light hedgerows landing on the road. It was one of those funny walls, not smooth. It had pieces of stone set into it about six inches apart. Jack struggled over it, his chest scar wringing inside. He felt his left side go numb, but he didn't say anything, cursing under his breath as he retrieved the plane from the road. The return climb was just as difficult, and he landed on the gravel.

Kate, sensing his discomfort, said, "I'd have gone around, Jack. Give the plane and the car back to Jack," she commanded the girls. He watched as she walked the three wooden steps to the upper level with Sarah struggling after her and Jack lifting Fiona.

Caw looked at me funny, and I winced. It was getting really cold, and the wind had whipped up blowing southwesterly. In Wood Point that meant only one thing: cold air and plenty of wind. This day the wind ran over the water making it sprout wings, flying in different directions like it was out of control, the currents doing battle as the tide tried to go this way and that. But the spoon moved without any plan, and it was anarchy as strange creatures hugging the surface opened their ferocious mouths, gaping holes spitting white surf that closed just as quick allowing bare glimpses of the dark bodies beneath. It is what she said when she was leaving that surprised me.

Flapping his left wing only and bobbing his head exactly five times.

"I used to talk to myself all the time when I was a kid, Jack. I did it every day especially when there was nobody around to talk to or argue with. It is what lonely little girls do."

"Ah," said Jack. "I knew she was lonely. I knew by her way she had to be cold just standing there, but she wouldn't allow it hurt her!"

Jack stopped as he felt the tears climb behind his eyes. "Life is cruel isn't it?"

Kate sighed before calling the kids to come back from the green opposite, Sarah holding little Fiona's hand.

"What is she doing now? Is she working or she still at school or college?"

"She lives in an apartment with her friend. She was doing arts in Ucd, but she packed it in last year. She says she will go back, but, you know, I doubt it. I think she may have lost the habit of studying. She is working in a pub behind the bar, would you believe?"

Kate laughed as Fiona grabbed her by the leg, giving her a glue-like hug.

"Come on, you two, Jack is tired. You look tired, Jack. You might be better off getting a job, you know, where you can go meet people. You know, maybe there is a woman waiting for you out there!"

Kate laughed again getting the kids into the car, fixing Sarah's belt and pulling Fiona's car seat forward and back until the belts clicked. When she resurfaced Jack smiled at her, and she smiled back.

Wood Point, Many years ago
16.

George Whelton didn't like Donal Travers, but then George didn't like a lot of people. And those he didn't like were afraid of him. Fellas whispered about it over pints of stout whilst watching football matches on television, most of them imposing a strict policy of silence if George Whelton or any of his cronies were in earshot.

His trouble with Donal Travers went back years. It all started after Donal employed a few heavies from the city to claim his money from old Mrs. Whelton before she died. George Whelton was particularly pissed because his mother had softened up before she departed; she instructed George there was no need for revenge as she hadn't been roughed up. Indeed she had offered to make one of the goons a cup of tea, and he accepted before the other man refused for both of them. In the end they said they would call back when George was home, but to be sure and tell him Donal Travers needed to be paid and to have the money.

A few days later the men returned to find themselves outnumbered by George and some of his mates. The two city boys took a right bashing with the more polite of the two spending a week in hospital with two broken arms and a split lip. However Whelton did pay up, dropping the notes dramatically on the badly-injured man's chest saying, "Tell Travers to choke on it and to call here no more. We don't need his loans or his criminal interest. Tell him George Whelton can stand on his own two feet, not like the old days. Not anymore."

Ten years later George had changed physically. He suffered a stroke when he was only thirty-eight years old. It left him lame without the use of his left foot, so he used a stick to compensate. He suffered a second stroke when he was forty-four and nearly died, but he made a miraculous recovery, baffling his doctors.

Soon he was back on his feet. Once again the price he paid was a distorted jaw line, which now sort of caved in on the right side of his face. And when he looked at another person head on, his face angled to a point like a pared piece of wood. Probably as a result of his impairment, his teeth fell out till he was left with just two molars one each side. These were rotted green, and when he engaged people they often uncontrollably sighed and moved a step back. It was akin to addressing a living skull.

George lived for most of his life on welfare, and since his strokes he was classified as permanently disabled; however, he did make a few bob through what he termed as his activities. This ranged from burglary to car and bicycle theft, fencing stolen goods like electrical items and jewellery, but he never got involved in drugs or tobacco trading as he disapproved of these activities. Over a pint George would lament to his good friend Diamond Jim.

"One day, Jim, he was a fine boy, six foot tall and shoulders on him like this." He would point beyond the parameters of his own shoulders to indicate the size he was referring to. "Now look at him, Jim. He is only a shadow of himself. He is like the shadow on the wall, and his shoulders have sunk into his chest like some bastard smashed his crown with a mallet."

Diamond Jim agreed and smiled as he was pleased that his loyalty to George had never led him to sell drugs. What was it they said? A good honest crook making a few bob on the side getting one over on the guards but not killing the neighbours' children, thank God. Diamond Jim got his name from the small stud that decorated his right ear. It was like a shining star illuminating some sad grey stratosphere, surrounded as it was by planets of purple and yellow.

Diamond Jim had relentless blood pressure and several fat tissue growths on his neck and cheeks. Together they were some sight, but sitting on the high stool of the Salmon Leap Bar they commanded respect and the locals knew to greet them with courtesy, maybe share a quick joke or comment but never to infringe on their privacy as they discussed the current state of play.

"Jim, as long as I live I will never forgive her."

"Who?" Diamond Jim was distracted by the television news.

"My mother," George said ruefully. "I will never let it be," he went on.

Diamond Jim looked at his friend. He was so used to looking at him that he thought little of his disfigurement.

"Can't you let her be now? She is a long time dead. It is no use to you, hanging on to it all this time and she rotting in her coffin."

Jim was still a little distracted by the television news so George said, "You didn't grow up with it, not like me and Daniel. The best thing he ever did was fuck off to England as soon as he had the fare and the balls to do it. She would have stopped him, but he was gone before she could do anything about it. He never came back as you know, not even for her burial. Isn't that saying a lot?"

Diamond Jim, sensing the urgency and conviction in his friend's tone, turned his stool round to face him and blank out the noisy television.

"I remember Dan so well, George. He was one of the best. A scream. A right scream, always up to devilment. An honest rogue if there ever was one!"

"Never hear from him now, Jim. I sent him a letter when she died to the last address we had for him, but I didn't hear back and not a thing since. You wouldn't know, with Danny he might be smartened up, living with someone or married. Who knows?"

Diamond Jim laughed a little too loud before saying, "He could be locked away too. That would be Danny all right, just the fella to get caught up to his knees in crap."

George went quiet. He looked over the counter at the row of spirit dispensers neatly in line.

"I will never forgive her for making him go. She made us so miserable, always whining and moaning about her no-good sons. You know, when the old man went she actually laughed. She laughed calling him the biggest 'feckin eejit' to have ever hit the earth and how glad she was to be free of him. He was my old man, like. She was talking about my Da."

Diamond Jim saluted a fellow walking by to go to the toilets. The chap was about to stop for a natter but danced by once he saw George, who watched him until he disappeared.

"She is gone now, George. No need to worry about her. Not a thing you can do about any of it now. She is for the maggots. Her time has come. Some day it will happen to you and me, and where will it all be then? It won't matter, and all the trouble we have will count for nought either. So what's the use in holding on to stuff that won't matter? She is gone forever, George. She did what she did and now she is propping up the daisies, so let it pass, old friend."

Diamond Jim stopped to study his friend's reaction, only taking the tiniest sup of his pint.

George was lost in his own thoughts, his head bent forward slightly. He finally looked to his companion and said, "It was the old lads she brought back to the house with a feed of drink in them, and they thinking they owned the place and Danny and me were scum. One of them used to hit out at me and tell me to clear off when he wanted to be alone with her, and me and Danny would sit on the stairs while the horseplay was going on in the bedroom. The old fella, falling out of the room, would go pissing with his trousers stuck on his ankles. She was there inside, Jim, laughing her skull off yer man, shaking his fist down at us, telling us to clear off out of our own house. And there wasn't a loaf of bread in the kitchen either, not even a slice of stale bread."

Diamond Jim sighed and held his head low over his pint like he was in mourning. The fella passed by on his way back from the toilet; he didn't reckon either of them.

"She was on the game, George. That's what some oul wans were doing back then to make ends meet. I suppose when your old man went there was nothing coming in?"

"She didn't have to do that. Loads of oul wans lost their husbands. They either fucked off or died, but they didn't turn to that. Lying on your back, feeding dirty oul lads for a couple of pound a pop. No, that was her. She did it to show us she didn't give a rat's shit about either of us. I am sure of that!"

Jim didn't counter; such was the venom in his friend's voice. He knew better this time. He took a good slug of his pint.

Later as George poured his friend a cup of strong tea, his walking stick fell over from where he had it propped against the kitchen wall.

"Curses," he said, leaning over to get it. Diamond Jim made a move for it, but he was too slow and George had it in his right hand. Diamond Jim was enjoying the tea after the cold stout. His face flushing pink, he pointed to the photograph of Mrs. Whelton, old and faded on the sideboard near the door.

"She was a lovely looking doll all the same, George."

He was sorry he said anything, and more importantly he was sorry the way he said it. But George just grunted, sitting down, stirring his tea with a dis-coloured spoon.

"He wants it done on Saturday. I said Sunday would suit us better, but he insisted Saturday as that is his late night. He said we might drive out there on Sunday, and he wouldn't be out at all and we would be wasting our time and petrol."

George looked blankly at Diamond Jim, like he expected him to say something profound.

"It's gone a fierce price, isn't it? My God, I went into the city twice last week and I am on the dredges. It is like everything else these days. They are robbing us blind between petrol and everything else," was all that Diamond Jim could muster.

"Saturday he goes into the Harbour Bar. He stays till late, so you might want to bring a book or a newspaper," George said. "I won't want either. I will have you!"

Diamond Jim chuckled, shaking his cup as he lifted it. He drank most of it down.

"Has he decided what he wants done? Has he told you, George?"

"He wants us to give him a bath. The full treatments see how he takes it. We are just to cut his ankles off; you know what I mean, Jim? He has gone cocky again. We will show him once more what you can do and what you cannot do, so don't be drinking early. Stay dry. I will stay dry myself. It would be stupid if we were stopped by the guards."

Diamond Jim nodded his cup empty. He got up to get a dribble from the warm teapot.

"How much?" Diamond Jim asked pouring the tea. "Do you want a hot sup, George?"

George shook his head. "One fifty each. I said that was okay. A handy one fifty I was thinking. What you think, Jim?"

"Yeah, oh yeah, a handy one fifty that." He sat back down. There was a pause broken by George when he said, "We will bring the mallet and the wooden stakes. The only way to kill a vampire, eh, Jim?"

*

Diamond Jim was driving and the old battered escort van had to stop twice going through Old Chapel to allow traffic through before finally taking a left turn to the West Cork coastal route and towards Timoleague.

George was quiet, so Diamond Jim tried to cheer him up when saying, "Great stretch in the evenings now. God, it is great altogether. In a few months it will be bright beyond nine o' clock. It's the best time of year, George. You can go for a walk after your tea, and if the mind takes you can have a nice walk down by the river before nipping in for a nice pint."

"What was that we ran over?" George said sharply. "It was too big for a rat and too small for a cat. What you think it was?"

"Dunno," Jim said searching the side mirror on his left hand side. He could see nothing now rounding a sharp bend.

George, sounding disappointed, said, "It wouldn't be a stoat, you know. You don't see them very often. Or would it be a weasel maybe?"

"Stoats and weasels are the same thing, George. I studied them you know!"

"No, they are not," George said, looking out the window in a vain attempt to find samples of the little creatures to assist in the making of his point.

"Weasels don't live as long as the stoat," Jim said pointlessly.

"I know that, Jim. They only live a few years. The stoat lives far longer!"

Jim was quiet for a second, trying to remember all the stuff he had read on the subject: all about their hedgerow habitats; the fact that they lived near farms and could take chickens and eggs and game birds.

George went quiet also. He was also trying to retrieve information long lost and mostly forgotten. He was lost in the dark recesses of his stoat and weasel files when Jim said, "What's the difference between a stoat and a weasel?"

George, sensing a hint of fun in his voice, looked at his friend oddly. Jim, glancing at him, couldn't help the visceral pang of repulsion engaging his stomach muscles as George showed the full extent of his deformity.

"A weasel is weasily wecognised, and a stoat is stoataly different!" Jim kept his eyes firmly on the winding road ahead as the small van began to climb the bends, which came at him faster and sharper.

"Fuck you," George Whelton said, his spit forming a white scum in the crevices of his lips. "Maybe it was a small fox; would it have been?"

"No way, hose A, it wasn't a fox." Jim had to press hard on the accelerator to keep the momentum. He delivered his words with great authority. Coming down the hill the far side, the road twisted this way and that; small gaps in the hedgerow allowed sightings of the Argideen below. George was disappointed. It disappeared again as the road ran away from it by the disused quarry. He knew that when the river was in flood on the spring tide, it swallowed small sections of the surrounding fields. But on this day it had retreated to flow harmlessly within the parameters set out by man.

Crossing the bridge to Timoleague he noticed the tide coming in slowly, but the mouth of the river was sunken in soft mud. The Abbey stately watched over the birds and the small ducks that foraged fruitfully in the soft earth, and Diamond Jim pulled over so they could see.

"His body will sink in that, George. We won't get a stake in there. It will be swallowed whole and him with it!"

"It will not," George said. "The sand is much firmer further down. It's perfect around Burren pier."

Diamond Jim looked at him in disbelief. "I don't want to disappear myself. Are you sure of the facts?"

George, laughing, said, "I'm as sure as anything I have ever been sure of. Did you bring the thesaurus? You didn't forget, did you?"

"It is in the glove with the sandwiches, and the flask is behind your seat."

"What's in the sandwiches?"

"Egg and onion and a few ham and coleslaw."

"Good man. Did you put on the Hellman's?"

"What else?"

"Why did we come out so early, George? We will be bored out of our minds."

"Jim, I am overseer of operations. I have my reasons, and I want to enrich my word power. If you get bored, have a sleep. We need to see him go in, and then we need to pounce when he comes out."

"Sounds the hard way when we could just come out here at ten or eleven and, as you say, pounce."

"We need to identify our target and watch him go in. We will have our target under surveillance, right?"

Jim didn't seem too impressed. He looked once more over the estuary at the soft mud deep and dark warning of the mouth of the river.

"Do you want a sandwich now, George?" he said.

Wood Point, A few years ago
17.

Like I said, Caw wasn't always reliable and sometimes when he said things to me—well, to be honest, I took them with a grain of salt. I mean, who is going to place much credence in an emotionally wounded old crow? Caw was still going on about Jack and how miserable he was coming home from the Fisherman's late at night, pissed and full of self pity, Caw mimicked him falling about and waking up confused hours later as to how on earth he landed on the floor.

Sometimes he holds his belly like this. "Look," Caw said and he screams for ages: "Caweeeeee!"

Caw went on about Kate, also saying she was a right one messing about behind her husband's back and him off all around the world stuck on a ship. "God knows where."

She pranced around, dragging her poor kids behind her to see the likes of him who was over ten years her senior and him recovering from "God knows what." If she ran away with him, he might just keel over. It wouldn't be the first time, and maybe not the last. You might think a woman like her would be wise to it, but she is cute, though maybe not in that way. But she is cute enough. She always got a question for him and always about his plans for the future and money.

"That's women for you, Sean, always need to be minded."

I not sure I agree with Caw on that one, as Mammy Rosie never asked to be minded. She only ever spoke of love and how Michael Harrington didn't love her, and she felt he was paying far more attention to Madge Butler I wouldn't mind!

That was well before there was anything serious between them, but maybe Caw does have a point as Madge Butler had set her stall out on Michael Harrington long before Mammy Rosie died. Of course, she knew he was married, and, yes, he and Mammy Rosie had their problems. I am sure she wasn't easy to live with, but she was Michael Harrington's wife for all that.

It was well after Mammy Rosie died that I saw them together, and it was a funny thing to happen. I expected I might catch them having a cuddle or her sneaking about the place, trying to hide evidence of what they were up to, but, no. It was red-faced or should I say red-arsed as Michael and Madge frolicked on the sofa in the tiny living room.

They thought I was in bed sleeping and it was very late, long after they had cleared the bar. I don't know much about sex—after all whom have I got to teach me?—but there they were up and at it, his big hairy arse flying through the air. It's a little hazy now, but my only memory of her is how large her breasts were. They were humongous. When she stood up for a moment her buttocks were firm compared to the rest of her, and her skin was paler than milk.

The next day I heard them chatting, just ordinary idle stuff about going to the creamery in Barryroe and she debating whether to go down to Timoleague to get medicine for her mother. Michael Harrington offered to drive her, but she wouldn't hear of it. She was watching me sitting at the kitchen table, pushing my glass in circles and then along lines of railway track, a single line and a double line.

When she figured it was safe, she said to him, "You had a good time last night, Michael?"

He was fiddling about under the bar counter for a marker to advertise the music on Saturday night, but he had to do it blind as there was old stuff in the way. He moved the deep fat fryer that blew up one Friday evening at a twenty-first birthday; the place had to be evacuated because of the smoke.

"I did," he said, turning to her for only a second before he grappled once more.

"Maybe I could do with a bit more, my love. Would you consider that?" Either he wasn't really listening to her or didn't understand a word she was saying because he kept grappling away, and even took to cursing under his breath.

Madge glanced once more in my direction, and I continued to push the glass outgoing train. Then I pulled it to me till it was the incoming train choo choo.

"I want to go there, Michael. I want you to give me a lift there, not to Barryroe or Timoleague. I get to those places myself."

At last he recovered a small plastic bag with one used and one brand new marker. He stood to face her in triumph.

"So, you are driving yourself, Madge. Good for you. We just can't practise enough." Michael Harrington was off to turn on the television for me, and I had yet to decide between "Once Upon a Time in the West" and "A Fistful of Dynamite." I picked "A Fistful of Dynamite," banging the plastic cover so hard that Michael Harrington just had to respond. He did exactly as he always did: he watched the screen till the snow disappeared and the company logo came at us suddenly. Then he fiddled with the remote control until he was satisfied the sound was good, not too loud to annoy his customers yet not too low so as I couldn't hear it. If I couldn't I sulked, kicking over chairs, and if I got near a glass I might smash it all over the floor. This day he left it perfect. I could hear it perfectly, but to most people it was no more than background noise.

*

I sulked the day Mammy Rosie brought me to Burren. She gave me my fish net, opened the driver's door, and proceeded to sit there with her ulcerated leg dangling, scraping off the green algae stuck to the stone slabs. She expected me to sit on the dampest of rocks, stroking my little net through the edge of the tide made of tiny stones mixed with surf. Every time I think of that, I think of turf and surf and I wonder about the tiny mind that thought that one up. I have visions of a cow in a field being followed aimlessly by a salmon, and

the cow turning every so often and telling the bewildered fish
to go away.

Anyhow I needed Mammy Rosie to pull up my trousers
above the knee so I could wade in a bit and trawl for
minnows, but her foot touching the old flat stone was all she
could manage. It made me wonder why Michael Harrington
didn't bring me. Too busy I suppose. The pub opened at
lunchtime, and Madge Butler was mopping floors at half-past
ten.

Sulk I did, and I was good at it and Mammy Rosie knew it
as well. She looked away from me, avoiding eye contact. She
stared for a long time across the tide to the far side. Wood
Point was very quiet, just the occasional car and the odd
fellow walking the small pier to check on his boat or to chat
with the trawler boys who hadn't gone out for three days
because of the cold weather and the gales at sea. They
awaited the correct conditions to churn the seabed so they
could lift the prawns, as usual a game of patience.

She was staring like she was eyeing something, but for the
life of me I don't know what as everything was in miniature
as it was too far away. I mused she was looking at the beech
trees up beyond the village, eyeing the line of trees falling to
the old coast guard station. It was like a giant wave of green
crashing to sprinkle the village below.

I got fed up after a bit and I walked in myself, getting my
trousers wet almost to the knee, trawling with my net. No
minnows, but at least I was picking up some weed, soft green
lettuce. Mammy Rosie didn't notice. Every now and then she
would check on me, but she didn't say anything. The cars
and the vans coming from Kinsale passed by curiously, the
occupants checking on our car and me in the water.

Some of them stared so hard I was sure they wanted to
interrogate me. Name, rank, and serial number. I always
think it should read "Name, rank, and cereal number." I
would opt for Rice Krispies over Cornflakes. They hissed
when I poured the milk on, like the land cracking up in an

earthquake. I saw small people fall off my spoon, clinging to a crispy for dear life, screaming for help and shouting, "No, no, nooooo!"

I searched for them with my spoon but they were gone, dead, drowned in the milk, their bodies liquidised. I scraped the bowl to remove any trace of them. It was a lot of fun playing the cereal game because nobody else knew what I was up to. The watching world thought I was eating up my food with enthusiasm.

After a while I noticed Mammy Rosie was getting cold. She allowed the door close over a little, and she retracted her leg. To tell the truth, I was feeling the cold myself as the wind whipped up from the east. It blew hard into my neck and made my head feel cold. She called me, wanting me to put on my cap, but I was still sulking so I pretended not to hear her. And then I picked up a black stone from the seabed and threw it at her. Of course I missed, the stone striking the bonnet, but it shook Mammy Rosie into returning her leg to the fresh air. Glaring at me she raised her right arm, making a fist and shaking it at me.

"Don't take me on, boy! I am in no humour, Sean. You can come out of it now!"

I swished back to the water's edge, my feet stuck in the sinking pebbles. I waved my net at her furiously but she was gone again, staring over the tide. And then I forgot what I was doing, leaving the net perilously close to the breaking water. I walked over to examine a rusted paint tin wedged between two small rocks embedded in the earth. Mammy Rosie still stared her view partially blocked by the arrival of two row boats, which had popped up like corks aided and abetted by the incoming tide.

When it was time to go she stayed quiet about my wet trousers, and she watched over her shoulder as I fixed my safety belt. This was something I could do. She had taught me how to do it patiently, as it saved her so much trouble, heaving and breathless as she strained her diaphragm. But I could do it now slickly, and she watched and listened for the click in unison.

This is where it all gets a little sketchy as there are two worthy versions of it. One is that Mammy Rosie made a simple error, and we paid the price. The other of course is all mine, and I contend she meant it. It was the look in her eyes—that faraway look had stuck to her pupils. It was quite in character for her to insist on my belt for two good reasons: the first was that she had absolutely no wish to hurt me physically; the second was it made the whole process that much easier when we sank to the seabed.

Anyhow, we will go with the accidental version as a compromise to those who just don't see the world in the dark terms that I do. She turned round, turning on the engine, and it made its usual rattling sound. She held her foot firmly on the clutch, but as she fiddled with the gearstick her foot slipped off the pedal and the car bounced forward. It all happened too quickly.

Mammy Rosie just sat there like she had resigned herself to the inevitable, and that was that. I watched helplessly as we tumbled through the air, catching unusual glimpses of sky and earth. Then splash! And the sea sucked us downwards. I could still see light for a few seconds, but then suddenly it was dark. Then I could see nothing at all for a minute or so, until we finally came to rest on the sand, the light returning like we had emerged from the shadow of the pier.

Mammy Rosie hurt her head. Blood trickled down her right cheek. She tried to turn to me, but she was unable. I slipped off my belt, and I scrambled through the gap between the front seats. I was able to rest my knees on the passenger seat. The water filled the car through tiny gaps in the doors and through the foot pedals holes. Mammy Rosie turned her bloody face to me. She had no expression. Her eyes, without passion or hope, were devoid of light.

I remembered watching a documentary once about a submerged car and how the brave occupants allowed water in to fill the vehicle, thus equalising the pressure on both sides and allowing the passenger door to open. I wound the passenger window down a few inches till it got stuck. Mammy Rosie, her hands flailing, tried to stop me. I got into one of my sulks, and I fended her off with my left arm. All the while she screamed silently but like a wild animal. I heard her piercing voice. At once I saw her lost in a wood, and she was wounded, screaming in tortuous pain and scaring all the other creatures.

Now her face contorted, filling with air, making her features burn red. Her eyes expanded till they were almost too big for their sockets, the water filling till it reached my chin. I prised the door open. I moved across her, releasing her belt with surprising ease. All she did was flail her hands through the water like she had invented some new swimming stroke. The sea regurgitated her breath till it felt warm, the gulfstream flowing from her mouth. I went to swim out, deprived of air. I tried one more time to drag her with me, hoping the water may render her weightless and she might float. But she just sat there, staring at me, her eyes made of metal. I swam for the surface kicking my legs as fast as I could.

Wood Point, A few years ago
18.

Caw has told me of your ramblings, and sometimes when the television is off and I am too tired to watch my films I close my eyes and I watch you ramble, making my own movie as you go, film star that you are. Where is it you go, Jack Browne? To watch the dull birds play in the mud, and the sheep in Lyall's farm that are lambing the first day? Baa, baa, black sheep, two weeks later there are three more. One is only a few hours old weak legs, carrying no weight and when you pass again a few weeks later he is chatting to another, boasting about pride and how he belongs to a prize flock.

You think of the rhyme and suddenly you have another thought about "The little boy who lives down the lane." You imagine the lane and see his face. He is very small for twelve years old, and he stalks the lane up and down but no further. He was warned and he searches the crevices in trees and he deciphers the meanings of nursery rhymes. Then the lamb wants to play. He dances on the soft grass, and the ewe wants to play as well. She wiggles her rear end and the lamb jumps with delight.

One day not long ago, the wind grabbed the estuary. It was biting cold and you had to button the collar of your coat and fix the woollen hat over your ears, feeling them red and sore and the thick scarf covering the mouth, numb skin facial rigidity. The sheep knew, bringing the lambs. They moved ever so slowly to the top of the field, softly ensconced below a rich line of trees towering and thick with bushes like a parasitic hedge hugging everything.

Leaving them to walk the matted grass with regret, the sound came of a cow roaring somewhere, bellowing like it had been speared and it lay dying exhausted in the hills beyond. They breathed cold light and the wind forced its halo around your head till you, spinning, saw the worst of the sand

battle hardened, forcing you to imagine: what if Madeline
Travers rides out to greet the waves, you inventing her horse,
the brown foal? Further on horse goes clippity clop and she
moves to the ocean with grace. The only debate left now is
should she stay on or dismount before she goes in? Still it
beats the rat poison, but you change your mind thinking the
rat poison might be more effective.

Kate drives past and she beeps her little red car, creeps
around the bend. It is stuck to the road, and you want to
chase after her to sneak a better look but she is gone. As you
round the bend there he is having a bath, Caw washing in a
tiny pool of muddy water. You notice his head is bigger than
you first thought, and his chest is firm and strong. He sees
you but he ignores you. Walking the walk you quicken as the
seven heads post is the finish line. Caw races you; he is much
faster. He glides through the air, and then he tries to shit on
you. He misses and then the rumours start, for as you stared
after her she was lost in the dark place and Caw moved from
your house, such was the shame he felt.

His new place is the ruins at Abbeymahon, where he has
commanded a view of the estuary that is second to none. And
on cold days he could run across the hard sand to Burren,
avoiding the drain of the river with the railway track of fresh
water. It is full of iron and ducks stick to its sides like
currents in a bun. He gazes at sheep with the lamb—just one,
now three, now four. The black-faced little lamb hides
miserably in the dark. He sits and squats like a tiny puppy; he
scrapes the earth and hides in less than six inches of grass.

Caw hoots like an owl. He always wanted to be an owl as
they get to stay out late and they are well able for the dirty
rat. His new home is rustic but has a good feel to it, with old-
world charm and its own private entrance. His neighbours are
sheep and small birds nesting in the line of trees beyond. He
figures it a desperate line as it is full of vagrants who hobble
about the ditches. Emerging wet and mucky, they scamper
through the barest of fields and are frowned on by the passive

horse that lifts his tail to pee and surprisingly has buckets of it.

Caw spends the afternoon collecting small twigs from the lane way. He is unhappy. Getting his feet wet in the small pools, he is busy smelling the burnt-out wood that is sodden with moss and the wildness of nettles and the wasted seed of failed corn. Caw flies and Jack watches as he circles the lamb and the woolly back is frantic. Its permed head barks at him like a dog, and Caw retreats. The lamb looks at Jack walking and goes hiding beyond the ewe.

You are hand cooked and the hill fields are salted with the sun wrapped by clouds of cotton. Over by the farm with young horses a dark figure moves but the animals are unperturbed, knowing him, turning their heads, bored by his presence. Thud—a large truck comes up the causeway. He takes the branch off a pine tree, the only branch that extends across the narrow road. Bang! Just like Mrs. Caw, the branch falls on the roadway. Now you are sainted, salted, and the branch is heavier than you thought. Lift it heavy over the side, but the sea is gone. Nothing to wash it with; nothing on which to float. It sticks on the hard mud.

Further on you notice the reflection of clouds. You are staring into the snow white mirror. Soon her face will appear and speak to you. Cars pass hurriedly; people look small and funny seated at such speed. You are gathering what it is their bodies are at in warp speed five. The women have faint looks of delight. They look at you screaming, "I can go fast!" whilst the men are cool and in control. Even the older ones regard their cars as extensions of themselves.

The horse cantors by, and Madeline wears full riding regalia. Her boots are stiff burnt rubber. The chestnut steps down the gap in the wall. He is surprised to see himself on the sand. He looks forward to trotting out as far as he can, excited by his date with the Romans. Thud. Thud. Godzilla comes to eat you. He picks you up but spits you out unto the grass apron. He doesn't like the taste of you, Jack. Plod, plod,

thud, thud. He picks up a farmhouse in Kilbrittain, takes a
bite, and then breaks it in half. Then he thuds his way back
across, smoke coming from his mouth. He has just
swallowed the chimney.

The young horses neigh; such is their fear that they collide
with each other in the paddock. Madeline rides on regardless.
Godzilla picks you up and bites your head off, Jack's blood
spurting everywhere. You see the headline: "Writer's head
bitten off in West Cork." Nice headline; good monster. Till at
last the calming yellow claims you for itself, and it heads to
Caw's turret and the horse farm and the lane ways running to
the farmhouse. Honest corridors barely the width of a car
with ditches both sides. You wonder why you love ditches
full of water, sleek foxes, and giant rats.

Wood Point, A few years ago
19.

"You don't love me, Jack. It's just you, quirky you. It is true, Jack. You hardly even know me. You have these ideas in your head about me. I am married, Jack. I took my vows, and I'm going to stick to them. They have to mean something, right? I give you, things aren't perfect between me and Ted, but, sure, who is perfect? I wouldn't be cut out for this carrying on business."

"Carrying on—that's what you call it?"

Kate looked over his shoulder. She felt the breeze blow lightly on her face.

"I don't know why I agreed to meet you. This isn't me, you know? I made my vows. That has to count for something. And he loves me. Ted loves me and the girls. I know he is away most of the time, but that's what he has to do. He works in shipping. It's what he does!"

"Kate, I am not asking you to leave Ted. I just wanted you to know how I felt about you. I dunno, maybe I am just tired after the book. You know, it tired me out. I am not used to it, all the concentration, the editing, and the rewriting. I'm wrecked from it. Maybe I just don't get it. I am too bollixed to work anything out rationally. I dunno why, I just fell for you."

"You can't fall for me, Jack. That is your problem. The bare fact that I am married should tell you that I am out of bounds, but I would say that this is not the first time for you."

Jack inhaled deeply, the sea air hurting his nostrils with stinging salt.

"So I am divorced. So what? As you said, it isn't a perfect world."

Kate was quiet for a second before she said, "I have to go in a minute, Jack. The kids are with Myrna, and I don't want to leave them too long. It isn't fair. Why did I come here?"

Kate giggled the last sentence like she was suddenly aware of how bold she was.

"I came here when I was a kid on holiday," Jack said softly. "We had a little caravan on the other side up on the headland."

"Thank God you picked this side. Jesus, if anyone came along and saw me I would have to leave Wood Point. There would be no living here, and Ted would kill me and I don't blame him."

Kate paused. She moved her body to lean back against a protruding rock. The air was quiet as the gulls overhead had stopped screeching for a moment. They listened to the sounds of the sea.

"How old were you when you came here? Who was with you?"

The wind tossed her hair against her left cheek, and she threw her head back to look at the sky. A single drop of rain fell on her forehead. She wiped it lazily with her sleeve.

"I was thirteen," Jack said. "My brother was only eight, and my Mam and Dad of course. It was the year before he died. He was very ill when we were here, but we were too young to really notice."

Kate sighed, tugging the collar of her overcoat.

"I used to wade into the sea just off the shingle beach over there, he watching over me, lighting his pipe, you know, keeping an eye, one small boy standing in three feet of the Atlantic Ocean."

Jack looked at her sadly. He noticed her cheeks slightly red from the abrasive wind.

"I should have worn a hat but that might have made sense. Jack, I have to be going. The girls will be kicking up, and Fiona needs her dinner. She has to eat regularly. I told you about her little problem, didn't I?"

Jack nodded. He stepped awkwardly on the shale, his foot sinking, and he smiled at Kate saying, "Pity things weren't

different, Kate. We could climb up there and then walk to the
main road. It's lovely under the cliffs."

Kate, making to go, smiled at him. "You are a bloody eejit,
aren't you, full of romantic notions." Then she stopped in her
tracks. Turning to face him, she caught his gaze full on.
"Why does nothing ever work out, Jack? You know, nobody
around here wanted me. Myrna used to tease me. She said I
was going to be left behind whilst all the girls were settling
down and starting families. I was sure to be left behind, she
said. I was too boyish, lifting fish boxes with the best of
them, and that was it. Katie Donovan, a spinster. Can you
imagine? Then I met Ted, and after an age he wanted to
marry me. Now you come along after all this time. Why
didn't you come along back then? Why do things happen at
the wrong time?"

Jack could see tears in her eyes but she was brave, and he
could see she tried valiantly to stop them.

"I just can't take to carrying on, Jack. This is a small place.
You couldn't keep things private round here. I will be
amazed if we are not headline news around the village
already."

Studying the bleak look of realisation on Jack's face made
Kate giggle. He was too sad-looking to countenance, and he
did look tired.

"Best leave it, Kate. I just don't know if I can stay on here,
you know, seeing you with Ted around the village; I think it
might kill me off. No, it may be for the best if I made a fresh
start."

"Do what you have to, Jack," Kate interrupted. She started
to walk up the steep jetty to her car.

Jack followed but he allowed her stay a comfortable
distance ahead. "You know it was the same for me, don't
you?"

Kate was almost at her car, but she turned back, looking at
him inquisitively.

Jack walked right up to her till his face almost touched hers and said softly, "I wish I met you a long time ago. This is the wrong time for me as well. I only wish I knew you before my body caved in, before everything went wrong for me. If only you had met the old me, the vibrant me!"

Kate went to step away but she felt his hands touch her shoulders, and he moved his lips against hers so gently she had no time to protest. She warmed to his embrace and felt him explore her tongue. She pushed against him to feel his heat, allowing his hands drop to wrap round her hips and bottom and he pulled her close. Kate gasped and he kissed her neck, which she extended as he kissed the length of it, cradling her with the power of his lips.

Jack withdrew to inspect her like he wanted to examine her mood. Kate was shivering nervously, her lips wet from him. He saw her eyes moisten till at last he glimpsed the mortal soul of her, and she was terrified of what he had just done and also of how it made her feel. He stood watching as she opened the car door.

"I can't do this, Jack. I just can't. I can't go carrying on. I have to go. Myrna will think I have gone away. Be good."

Jack watched as she used the small entrance to a lonely summer house to turn her car. He watched as the little car made good its escape along the laneway divided by silly tufts of grass. He retreated to the warmth of his own car half-buried in a hedge back towards the jetty.

*

Kate said that Barry Cousins was getting older and uglier, but Jack was a little jealous of his good looks and the way the girls circled him whenever he went to the stage. It wasn't much of a stage, really—just a small area in the corner underneath the television. The DJ had set up, playing a few backing tracks before singing with his guitar himself. He sang "Nancy Spain," and then he sang "And I Love You So"

Barry Cousins brought him a pint of lager, which he placed safely on the shelf behind him. He was careful to make room for it and also not to disturb the array of rowing cups that lined the shelf. Jack liked them; they gave the place a successful gleam, and in fairness to Barry he kept them polished always as the Fisherman's sponsored the annual regatta.

Kate, leaning over, said, "I think Margaret might win. She has a much better chance now that she has ditched Pee Wee."

Jack could barely hear such was the noise. He just nodded his approval.

Kate looked closely at Barry, who was preparing to say a few words, and said, "Ted can sing you know, but he has no confidence in front of a crowd. He is hopeless, but at home in the bath he has a good voice."

Jack said, "This might be on live on the ship, via satellite."

Kate smiled, distracted by Barry Cousins who was speaking.

"I would like to welcome you all to the Fisherman's tonight for our heat of the inter-pub talent show. We really have some great acts this evening with a magnificent prize of three hundred euros for the overall winner. You will agree with me that it is well worth entering. As you know we have some names in already, but if anyone wants to enter tonight just come up to us here at the stage in the next few minutes, and we will take your name and details. Thank you."

"Very good," Jack said, laughing as an old drunk was staggering his way through the crowd with the intent to confront Barry regarding the possibility of him entering. Kate ordered a drink for herself and one for her Aunt Myrna who was seated at a nearby table. Jack looked on, he knew Kate's form. For the entire world she was with Myrna, but really she would spend most of the evening by his side.

"Our first contestant is Liz McCarthy representing the Harbour Bar, and Liz will sing, 'All Kinds of Everything.'"

There was a pause as the audience awaited Liz to make her way through the crowd, so Barry Cousins added, "Of course this song was made famous by Dana all those years ago."

Liz sang but there was some turbulence from the PA system with the DJ twisting buttons and grimacing before he eventually moved the microphone; the sound improved immediately. Liz had a sweet voice, and the audience clapped and shouted when she was finished. There were wolf whistles from the back, and her own pals screamed, "Liz! Liz!"

Kate had gone to pay her respects to Myrna who eyed Jack kindly, smiling at him like she was thinking, "Anyone who is a friend of Kate's is all right in my book." Barry Cousins introduced two more acts, a kid from Timoleague who played guitar and an old man from Ring who told funny stories. The kid had some talent. He played the guitar sitting down, and he didn't sing but rattled off an instrumental that made even the most hardened bar fly clap as he came to the finish. He received rapturous applause, and Barry Cousins told his patrons to remember his name as the kid was sure to make it big.

Jack forgot it thirty seconds later as he watched Kate in deep conversation with one of her new neighbours in the Anchorage. The old man didn't so much tell jokes, but he told stories with a funny twist in the tale. His agricultural voice sort of got on Jack's nerves, but one of his tales concerning a prize bull got a lot of laughs and he too was cheered vociferously back to his seat.

Barry Cousins had the microphone once more.

"Ladies and gentlemen, it is now my pleasure to introduce the young lady who represents us here in the Fisherman's: Margaret O' Neill. Everyone, a big hand..."

Barry's voice was drowned out as the locals lifted the roof and Kate was on her feet. Margaret was going to sing "After the Gold Rush" by Neil Young. There was a deafening silence followed by, "Well, I dreamed I saw the knight in armour coming..."

Jack saw Kate. She was silent, listening to the lyric, and the bodies around her moved in slow motion as the stray light from the back bar flushed against her face, fading. Once a body in front of her moved or raised their hands.

"All in a dream...the loading had begun...flying Mother Nature's silver seeds to a new home in the sun..."

The roof almost blew off the Fisherman's when Margaret finished with a soft smile. Kate loved it and cheered on even after most of the others had stopped.

"How do we follow that, folks?" Barry Cousins said. Then, realising he might be accused of bias, he added, "Sure, aren't they all great tonight? It will be some job for the judges to separate them."

Jack was staring at Kate who, noticing his gaze, locked eyes with him. It was a game of dare to see which one would unlock first, but it was Jack as Thomas Crowe, slapping him hard on the back, said, "Jesus Christ, hasn't she got a voice to die for? And her father was a great singer too. He won this competition three times in his day."

Jack agreed with him, but Thomas was taken with Kate. He smiled, placing his right hand on her shoulder in friendly fashion. The rest of the acts kept up the standard with one holiday-maker singing a little-known Elton John song that went down very well, and Helen Cashman representing Michael Harrington's gave a very emotive version of "Sweet Sixteen." Thomas loved that one and he told Kate it was one of his favourites and that he especially loved it when he was full of porter. He went out the back for a smoke when the judges were called out to the back bar to discuss the merits of the contestants.

Barry Cousins was doing what he does best back behind the bar: serving drinks. He was like a man possessed, speeding up and down, pouring spirits from two dispensers in unison whilst settling three pints of Guinness at the same time.

Kate ordered Jack a pint and said, "I will have to go after this, Jack. My mother's babysitting, and she doesn't like being too late."

Jack smiled at her, but secretly he felt his heart drop as he was hoping she might stay late and he could walk her up and have a chat and maybe...

"I hope Margaret goes through, but Helen Cashman is brilliant too, isn't she? Who do you think will go through, Jack?"

Jack saw Thomas Crowe smoking out the back. He turned his back to speak to someone, the smoke rising as if from the peak of his cap.

"Margaret will go through for sure. I thought the kid on guitar was very good. He will go through as well."

"The final is next Friday down in the hotel. Are you going, Jack?"

Kate was collecting her drink, and she waited till Jack got his pint.

"I hope to be there, Kate. Should do."

Kate went back to Myrna, who once more smiled at Jack. Barry Cousins was back at the microphone, beads of perspiration streaming down his forehead.

"Do you want to know who got through?" he shouted.

The audience responded with a loud, "Yeah!"

"John Friel from Padjo's bar with his guitar, and Helen Cashman from Michael Harrington's bar with her "Sweet Sixteen," and finally Margaret O' Neill from the Fisherman's with her rendition of "After the Gold Rush."

Another almighty roar, and Jack could see Thomas Crowe roaring in celebration on hearing that Margaret got through.

Kate said, "The kid with the guitar made it?"

Jack smiled to show he approved. Myrna shouted something to Kate, but she didn't hear and went closer to listen.

Barry Cousins said, "Don't forget, folks, next Friday in the hotel the grand finale. Everyone is welcome, and we hope to see you all there!"

Another great cheer, and Kate was getting her bag from the floor under the table. Myrna was readying herself also.

"Stay awhile, Kate," Jack said.

"I would love to, Jack, but it is getting late. My mother, you know?" She looked at him seeing the disappointment in his eyes.

"I will be going next week. Maybe she might stay up a bit later. I will see what I can do."

Kate went to go but she stopped, suddenly eyeing Myrna in the process.

"I am not free, Jack, you know?"

Jack watched her leave. She didn't hang about, and the crowd had thinned by about twenty-five percent. Suddenly stools were available, and Thomas Crowe sat himself on the one beside him. Jack ordered another pint, and Barry Cousins went to pull it dutifully.

Wood Point, Many years ago
20.

"You know, Kate, I am giving up on Barry Cousins. He is a big fool. I hear he is going to dances in Clon and getting into fights!"

"Trouble every place he goes. I hear he has stopped the hurling!"

"Has he?"

"So I hear," Kate said. "He hurt his hand bad-like, broke two fingers, but he is not back playing."

"Gees," Georgina said as she turned to lie flat on her tummy.

Kate smiled to herself as her friend lay under the smallest of branches, her head just missing a small pine cone. Kate was about to warn her but decided it wasn't really going to hurt her anyhow. She rested her elbows on the pine needles looking at the sea. It was abandoned on a day when the wind swirled and white horses gathered to lash against horse rock.

The fields above the Blind Strand became moving shadows with the seabirds resting in soft pockets of air and watching cattle move further inland for respite. They sheltered for twenty minutes as the wind brought rain showers from the Atlantic. For a while a deluge of rain lashed the ground, making dripping showers of trees. Kate had suggested the little oasis of pine. She was impressed as the pine needles stayed dry, the trees huddling close to protect themselves.

"I wonder, will I ever fall in love, Kate? You know, find a husband. Even then there is no being sure, is there? It might be the worst thing a girl ever did." Georgina had turned back to her to study her expression.

"I dunno," Kate said looking disappointed. "What is there to do? Isn't it what we are all about, Georgie? Kids and husbands, a nice little house? What else is there?"

Georgina came back to her, narrowly avoiding the small branch of the pine tree as she sat up.

"Some women go for careers," she said. "Now they're not bothered with kids or husbands. They can take it or leave it. Some of them sort of wait to see what's going to happen. They wait till they are old, like thirty-five, before they get married. You know, money made and nice hubby. They can still have kids, like one or two."

"I wouldn't like that," Kate said without explanation.

"I think I will go that way. I have plans, Kate, and I don't mean staying here all my life. The world is a big place, you know? I have relatives in England. I may go there. I like it here—it's nice and pretty—but what is there for me, you know? I am not going to marry any of the boys from Wood Point, that's a given."

Georgina laughed and she made Kate laugh too, such was her sense of disgust. The rain had ceased if only for a while. Kate walked to the edge of the oasis to get a better view of the sea.

"Will we go on, Georgie, or what do you want to do? Will we go back before it lashes rain again?"

Georgina was still sitting. She was lost somewhere in her own thoughts. After a gap she said lazily, "I don't mind, Kate. What do you want to do? I think my energy levels will only get me back to the village. The Fuchsia Walk, and I might die!"

"Might die," Kate giggled. "I wonder about you, my love, and your energy levels. You are always tired. Maybe you have something missing from your blood, or you might have the jaundice."

Ignoring her, Georgina said, "Come on, Katie, let's go back. It will be getting dark in an hour or so."

Kate agreed and they walked through the meadow over the stile into O' Regan's field, keeping a beady eye for the bull. But there was no sign of him. In the wood the rain had left a series of draining leaves. Some spat mouthfuls of water on the grass surrounds of the pathway; others were tired and only let the tiniest of trickles slide drop by drop.

Once they reached the clearing above the car park, Georgina said, "Do you want to come up to my place for a while? Mother's in Clon. I haven't a clue where my father is. Madge Butler goes at five on Wednesdays. It will be just ourselves, and I know what we can get up to."

"What's that?" Kate asked.

Georgina whispered into her left ear, and Kate spurted, "I will not! My father will kill me! Are you mad? He will kill me where I am standing."

Georgina laughed as Kate looked at her beseechingly. "I don't mind going up, but I won't be up for that!"

"Come on, then," Georgina shouted bouncing away.

Madge Butler left the kitchen spanking clean. The cooker top was shining and the table spruced up as well, the place mats piled up in the far corner by the shelf that held a selection of marmalades, jams, and spices. Bob was lying in his basket by the door to the small utility room. He looked bored and sad like he was miffed, having missed out on his walk earlier. Georgina was free and easy with no adults about. She put the kettle on, speaking harshly and then kindly to Bob. Kate sat at the table leaning back in her chair. Although she hadn't got wet she felt damp, but then the air was wet and the kitchen was cold.

"We can go into Father's study in a minute. He most likely won't be back till later. I think he likes to get drunk on Wednesdays, unlike mother who likes to get pissed every day."

Kate was a little taken aback. Georgina wasn't normally that honest, but she was in a giddy mood as she scooped three teaspoons of tea leaves into the pot. Then she added another for luck. She proceeded to fill the sugar bowl, shaking the bag to disturb the lumpy bits at the bottom.

"Two spoons for you, Kate, or do you want three if I let it draw for a while?"

"Two," Kate said, pushing the inquisitive Bob away with her leg. The dog had suddenly realised her presence like the great awakening. Kate knew he was in an annoying mode, and soon he would be slobbering all over her jeans and wetting her wrists and fingers with his snout.

"Go to your bed, Bob!" Georgina commanded and the dog, looking at her mournfully, obeyed. He sighed deeply and sneezed to show his displeasure.

"He missed his walk. He always gets like that, stupid Bob. If Mother was here he could annoy her upstairs, but he tends to be good for her. I think it is because she ignores him. You know she falls over him all the time like she forgets he is there, yet he is always with her like they have some sort of pact. 'Let's share the space, Madeline. You won't even know I am in the room!'"

Kate laughed at her friend who was pouring the tea.

"Wow, that looks strong," Kate said as Georgina's hand wavered slightly with the weight of the pot.

"Good," said Georgina. "It will put hairs on your chest."

Kate blushed slightly, embarrassed at Georgina's attempts to speak colloquially. When they finished their tea Georgina, changing her mind, insisted they go up to the drawing room.

"I must light the fire for Mother. She comes home in such a state. I just need to put a match to it. Madge Butler leaves it all ready, but at least it will be up and running by the time she gets in. This house is freezing at night. You know, Kate, you are as well off living where you do. It may be small, but at least you are warm!"

Kate stuck out her tongue at Georgina who plodded her way up the stairs with Bob nipping at her heels as he tried to get past and whining when she pressed her right leg against the wall to block him. Turning on both lamps, Georgina brought the room to life by pulling the drapes. She put a match to the fire, which was just ready to go and was set with good Polish coal and small blocks of wood.

"Now," Georgina said, "she will have little to complain about. The room will be roasting in an hour."

Kate sat in one of the armchairs close to the fire, enjoying the first visitation of heat. Bob sprawled on the flat rug, which was caught under the leg of the armchair opposite. Pushing the dog with her right foot Georgina sat in it. Bob had to make do with a corner, which was too small and left him flat out under Kate's feet. Kate stared at the fire. It was already glowing orange underneath, and the smallest of the blocks was crackling.

"Fancy a vodka, Katie?"

Kate looked at her friend in disbelief. "Are you mad, Georgie? My father would take my life."

"He won't know a thing. Vodka doesn't smell, not like wine or beer, so mother says. That's why she drinks it." Georgina was already at the drinks trolley. "We have ice, my dear. I can even give you a slice of lemon if madam so requires."

"Are you off your head, Georgie? We will be killed if anyone finds out!"

But Kate couldn't resist. She joined her friend out of nosiness just to see what she was doing. She watched her pour the vodka and then scoop three pieces of ice. She then poured some lime cordial. Lastly she placed a slice of lemon neatly to one side.

"We will only have the one, my dear, and nobody will be any the wiser. Mother will arrive home wondering why we are two such calm and collected young ladies, sitting elegantly, chatting by the fireside."

Kate had sipped a beer at Christmas and even tasted whiskey at her grandmother's funeral, but this tasted good. The lime was cold and refreshing, and when she swallowed some she felt new warmth inside.

"What do you think? Aren't we the right pair?" Georgina swallowed most of her drink down.

Kate went to swallow hers but only did got halfway.
Georgina, on her feet, took her glass anyhow and was back at
the drinks trolley. Bob was too lazy to follow. He raised his
head, stretching his neck. "I saw that awful fellow you talk to. What's his name?
Thomas. Oh, he is so sleazy. He was walking down Ramsey
Hill with a sack over his back like he was delivering coal."

"You don't know him. His family is very nice. He was
probably out at the strand collecting wrinkles."

"What?"

She returned handing Kate her glass. "Drink up, girl," she
said quietly. "Don't you know, wrinkles are periwinkles
round here."

"My God, what a horrible name! They could have called
them peris or winks. Bloody 'wrinkles.' What sort of a name
is that?"

Georgina was almost finished with her second glass; Kate
who was already feeling the effects had not started hers.

"He is so sleazy; he undresses me with his eyes. It is like
he is carrying a huge billboard with the words, 'I want to
ravage you' printed boldly on it."

"No, not at all. You have him all wrong, Georgie. He is
really nice, honest. He just looks at people funny. You know,
he spends most of his time on his own, so he just eyes people
funny like he is afraid of people, you know?"

Georgina replied, "I am afraid I don't know, Kate. I
certainly wouldn't like to be alone with him. Imagine his
grubby hands all over you. Did you ever see his hands, Kate?
Black as the ace of spades, like they never saw soap or
water!"

Georgina had lowered her glass. This time Kate restrained
her from taking her drink. Georgina shrugged and went to get
a refill.

"I don't mind older men as a rule, Kate, you know, but a
girl has to have standards. We should be careful who we
make friends with, you know? I wouldn't be happy

encouraging the likes of Thomas. He must stink as well, you
know, the fishy smell of those horrible winkles."

Kate laughed when she said the word. Georgina looked at
her puzzled.

"You said 'winkles', but it is wrinkles."

"Whatever." She made her way back to her seat, almost
tripping over Bob's front paws. The dog yelped bolting
upright, and then he looked around him like he was
wondering who had caused the fuss.

"Winkles or wrinkles I think it is a disgusting occupation.
Only a complete degenerate would contemplate it as a career,
like, 'What do you do, Mister?' 'I'm a 'winkle' picker,'" she
said with a purposeful lisp, and Kate laughed till the tears
rolled down her cheeks.

They had no time to react. Bob was up and over to the
door. He barked excitedly, and Madeline stepped into the
room unsteadily. She eyed the girls from a distance.

"Quite the laugh, Georgina, and you, missy, helping
yourself to alcohol. I did tell you, child, about drinking and
the dangers of drinking alcohol, did I not?"

Georgina stood and placed her empty glass on the
mantelpiece. Kate had left hers on the mat resting against the
marble surround.

"We only had the one, Mum; it was just a joke, look!"
Georgina said pointing at the half-full bottle on the drinks
trolley. Georgina burped and giggled at the sound she made.
Kate couldn't make any sound, her face rigid white.

"You are a disgrace, Georgina, after all the warnings I
gave you. And you, Kate Donovan. What ails you? And your
father only back home getting better. You, young lady, can
go home and make sure to tell your father why I sent you
packing. Stealing my drink! My personal supply of vodka
that I paid good money for! I don't expect to see you in this
house again. You are stealing from me, so good riddance to
you!"

"No, Mum, it was just a prank!"

This time her voice was shaky, and she looked pleadingly at her mother.

"It won't happen again, honest! It was just a bit of fun."

Georgina was looking at Kate who stood up to leave but stopped in her tracks as she had to pass Madeline to get out. Georgina reached over to retrieve Kate's glass but the bending over did for her when she stood straight again, and she spewed up unto the hearth.

Kate looked at Madeline, but she remained emotionless. "I better go, Georgie."

Georgina had recovered slightly, wiping her mouth with the sleeve of her blouse.

"Go, Kate. You go now."

Kate walked by Madeline without saying a word. She closed the door behind her, and as she reached the bottom of the stairwell she heard Madeline shout at the top of her voice, "Never again! I don't want her in here, do you hear me, Georgina?"

She waited a second to hear the reply, but she only heard a hoarse whimper, Georgina still pleading but her voice fading. Kate had to slam the front door as the lock didn't fit the receiver correctly. She hoped Madeline wouldn't think she did it out of temper. The walk down the drive was lazy as she tried to come to terms with all that happened. The evening was closing in a damp white mist, a halo over the gate, the hedges and the trees crying softly a small pool of tears at her feet.

Wood Point, A few years ago
21.

Caw thought of her, imagining she was still with him as she glided through the air and the lambs in the field below ran for cover. He watched her as she made her bed on pockets of thin air. How she would have loved this place, the ruins of the Abbey with its little nooks and crannies and her home with a front and back entrance with a view to die for! Caw imagined the boys below frolicking with the lambs, playing hide and seek with the young estuary grey crows. Here there was no foraging in dustbins but plenty of worms from the freshly-ploughed fields and mussels discarded by the adult grey crows.

Yet he was alone, and somehow the beauty was lost as something unshared. At times he longed so much to see Mrs. Caw and the boys again that his stomach ached, and to make matters worse Jack Browne walked by each day staring over the mud to the hills of Kilbrittain or stopped momentarily to survey the sheep and the big house. Lately he had taken to eyeing Caw in his new home. Caw, waiting till he was gone past, screeched, "Caw! Caw! Caw!" Jack would look back over his shoulder nervously, Caw flying and doing circles and flapping his wings heading purposely to the ditch on the far side by the lane.

Jack stares at a couple of sad horses. They are lost in the mist by the top field. Then Caw remembers him at the window, his face pressed against the glass and the boys huddled away in the corner. But he didn't see or take any notice of them. Later when Jack was gone, the urgency for revenge passing with him, Caw took to dreaming and staying warm within his little turret window. He got to thinking how he was so much better off now out here at Abbeymahon, alone save for the few sheep and the horses. His cousins flew

in and out, and nobody bothered him. He was now king of
the castle, that's for sure.

As time moved on he began to feel fatigued. It was the
same feelings he felt after Mrs. Caw and the boys passed
away, and he wondered whether he might ever defeat this
melancholy. Jack Browne—now there was one for
melancholy. Caw was sure he invented the term, sitting on
someone's roof day after day, night after night. You certainly
get to know them, and, by God, did the man suffer. But then
it was his own fault; nobody asked him to leave his wife and
kid. It was up to him to go seek out his daughter. After all
why should she put herself out for him?

But when you really got to know Jack you suddenly
realised how selfish and self-absorbed the man was. Caw
cringed as he heard the output of tears, sorrowful tears of
self-pity, as he sat alone on the corner of his bed after a hard
night in the Fisherman's. How much did the alcohol stir the
self-pity? Caw listened to him crib about his medications and
how the gods had robbed him of his wellness and how he
hated being alone and how he longed for someone. Anyone
would do; it was better than having nobody.

Sometimes his ranting and wailing would last till two or
three in the morning, and Caw often felt like flapping against
the window just to shut him up and give him something else
to think about. Then to try to make sense of it all, Caw made
a mental list of questions he would like to ask Jack Browne
like: why didn't you stay with Judith Tebbut when you had
the chance? Why treat her the way you did—just to go
pursue a married woman? It was a glaring problem for Jack,
one which he wouldn't confront save to talk deliriously about
passion and love like he was one of the romantic poets.

Of course Caw had his own opinion on romantic poets as
there wasn't any such thing in the crow kingdom. Crows are
very practical hands-on types; they basically believe that all
relationships between the sexes exist to procreate, and
romance has nothing to do with it. Hence when Caw misses

his wife, he is actually yearning for the years of ritualistic sex he is now denied. Judith Tebbut was much too good for him, Caw concluded. Anyway she was a lady, and he was only white trash!

Caw yawned, the spirit of the place raising his mood. Yes, the elders in the murder of crows gave him good advice to get out of the village and get into this wonderful development in this beautiful setting. Abbeymahon was a small complex with that rustic ruins appeal. Altogether there were ten apartments including his own penthouse suite. The site was unfinished, of course, with the next phase only half-built in the middle of Lyall's field. The apartment allows uninterrupted views of Kilbrittain and the centurion sea as its waves wash-white foam across the sand. Yes, indeed, the elders were right. It is indeed a splendid place. Below, the ruins of the abbey are adorned with graves marked by slate-like stones imbedded in the tough grass, within its walls a select few newer graves with readable names.

Of course Caw had to barter for this advice, and he agreed to attend the seminar entitled "Are Scarecrows for Real?" down on the roof of the hotel. The main speaker, a crow from Dublin four, contended that scarecrows were not in fact real people but instead were made of people's discarded clothes filled with straw. He also argued that the timely shotgun blasts, which caused twenty-six crow heart attacks last year, were not in fact shotguns but just what he said: a blast machine that in effect held no threat to the feeding crow population in general.

Caw was asked to disagree with this professor of crow folklore myth and legend. Yet the more he heard the more Caw agreed with, and in the end he found himself siding with the Dublin fourite, much to the displeasure of the murder of crow elders. Still, he redeemed himself greatly when he argued successfully against the amalgamation of the grey crow with the black crow on the grounds of evidence that the two ethnic groups co-habited a thousand years ago. Caw made his point strongly that there was very little evidence of this, and whilst he personally had no real problems with grey crows the evidence was insurmountable in favour of the common black crow as inheritors of the great crow traditions. Any dilution of this lineage would have a devastating effect on unborn crows; it could lead to anarchy, should it be encouraged.

The amalgamation proposal was defeated by majority of eighty-seven to twenty-eight. Now he found his new grey crow neighbours a great help, and to be fair they welcomed him with open wings. He appreciated how much trouble they went to, collecting mussels and having to do all the shell work. However there were things about them he didn't like. They were over familiar once they got to know you at all. It was like they knew you all your life, and they had this stealthy way of extracting information from a body.

It had happened that Caw covered his head with his wings to avoid embarrassment; their elders, of course, would go to great lengths to ingratiate themselves with him and by proxy to try to influence the murder of crows. Of course Caw saw through them straight off, making his displeasure apparent in no uncertain terms. The young grey crows were exuberant and cheeky, but to be fair they worked hard. One found it easy to turn a blind eye such was the vigour they brought to their work. Hundreds of journeys over the little road to roam the sands collecting small crabs and then watching in awe as the adults broke mussels on the narrow pathway.

Despite his prejudices he would have allowed the boys to play with them, but only after he enlightened them as to the difference as it was inherited down the ages. He often thought that he might have said the following: "It isn't the grey crows' fault, but it is a true fact that our lineage is better and we are the true bloods. They must be aware of it, boys. Believe me, but you have no need to mention it to them either as part of their condition is often to be cursed by

ignorance." Yes, he would love to see his boys below,
frolicking, dancing in between the sheep and the lamb.

Caw paused for a moment, his sadness tempered by the
temerity of the world around him. The sun, caught by a thick
white cloud, cast a dark shadow on the far side of the field
above. The house was still like nobody lived in it. When did
the owners come and go? The hills had borrowed the light.
The field bartered for shadows happily, making the grass a
deep green, the dark seeds perfectly stretched to inebriated
hedges sharing the boundary with old trees.

Caw wondered how even the barest seed finds a home and
the comfort of living. Many of his tiny cousins lived along
these battle lines, the borders which farmers protect and
reinforce. Small birds hide in nests of moss dark homes to
fend off the marauding rat. Still, Caw concluded, all was
going well now. He was safe in his penthouse, nobody to
bother him or to bother about. The days were long now. For
the next six or seven months he had food in plentiful supply.
As the crow said, "Sure, haven't you a grand set of feathers!"

Indeed he had four viewing choices—the front view for
which a rich American crow would pay millions just to gaze
across the estuary to Kilbrittain, and the side views over the
farms and the trees, the fields magnificent holding all of its
life serenely. The rear view offered the rising hills searching
divinity. Caw often sat there for hours, watching the wind stir
a small branch or to watch as the grey crows searched for the
shallows.. The two horses would stand rigid, bemused,
looking at a big black cow standing stately on the ridge. This
was his life now, and he was getting used to it. Thoughts of
revenge visited, but they didn't outstay there welcome.

*

When Jack Browne told the story of the statue, he told it
differently each time. As he read it aloud, Caw felt the
feathers stand on his head. At first he read it like he was

talking to himself, but then he read it like he was addressing the world. On and on he went. Caw was getting bored with it all until Jack finally went quiet.

Caw was nodding off when Jack started again. This time he read it, but he had added Kate to the story. Jack was always miserable with drink. Sometimes he might detour by the pier, staggering his way along at night. The water was dark green and the boats bobbled, welcoming the inebriated stranger, enticing boats in a dark green pool.

This night he walked lazily alongside of Kate. She was going on about the price of houses and how they would keep going up, so technically you could keep trading up and make a nice profit each time. Jack was walking her home from the Fisherman's. Kate was a little anxious as Aunt Myrna was babysitting.

After a long pause, Jack said, "How many houses do you need?"

Looking at him Kate said, "No harm in wanting the best for your family now is there, Jack?"

Jack didn't answer but stared into her eyes as was his habit, and it greatly unnerved her.

Kate turned away abruptly, but then Jack said, "A long time ago I just up and left. I left everyone. I just needed to get away for a while, sort things out in my head, so I headed south but it was late and I didn't get too far. The first hotel I came to was called 'The Seven Bends Hotel.' It isn't there now. They built a new road through it. I think it was on its last legs, to be honest. There was hardly anyone there, but I had a nice omelette and a few pints and went to bed watching TV till at last I went off to sleep. I slept soundly all night—not a sound."

Kate watched him as he moved his face closer to hers.

"The next morning when I woke up, the room was unusually bright like someone had sneaked in overnight with a bucket of white paint and glossed the ceiling and the walls. I was chirpy, feeling vindicated, having the guts to head off alone, shag the world. You know, Kate, it was probably the first time in my life I felt I was in control."

Kate made like she was tired, and Jack moved to one side so as not to smother her. She perked up as soon as he did this.

"I went down for breakfast. There was nobody there, just a little Polish waiter to take my order. He didn't speak a word of English, but he knew what a full Irish was!"

Kate laughed and Jack chuckled in unison.

"So I sat there eating, totally alone, when in walks this older man with longish grey hair and a young man in a striped suit. He wore thick framed glasses. They were followed by a young woman of around twenty-five. She was carrying a box, which she left on the floor beside her. They only ordered coffee, and she was nibbling on a complimentary biscuit.

"The older man was talking incessantly about products, and he seemed to be trying to convince the chap with the glasses that his product was brilliant and destined for millions of sales worldwide. The guy in the pinstriped suit listened to him intently, and the girl acted like it was all going over her head. The older man was looking around, but he only had me to check out, which he did as a matter of course. The waiter returned to their table to refill the coffee. He did it efficiently, but they all ignored him. The older man whispered something across the table, but the pin-stripe suit fellow struggled to hear him. Yet he pretended that he did and started laughing.

"I was near finished my breakfast, but I was captivated so I slowed down, helped myself to more tea, and I buttered more toast. The older man was waving his hands about, talking nineteen to the dozen. I only barely heard him. He was talking about refrigeration, measuring with his hands to show full then empty. Every now and then the pinstripe looked at me, grinning. The girl was quiet. She listened intently, but her expression spoke volumes. She didn't really get what she was hearing. Finally the older man gesticulated like he was giving up. In his surrender he whispered to the girl, who obeyed instantly!"

Kate moved away again, but she wasn't impatient. It was more like she was getting cold and needed to move to get warm.

Jack, drawing breath, continued. "She bent over, picking the box from the floor. She placed it on the table, moving the plate of complimentary biscuits. Pinstripe watched her closely as she removed the lid. I then saw it was in fact a white shoe box, and the lid was a perfect fit, the shoe manufacturer's logo initialled on the side. She separated the packing paper and removed a statue. It was about twelve inches long. It was the statue of a black crow, dull looking, no shine. The girl held it aloft, and the pinstripe stared at it for at least a minute, and the older man raised his voice and said, 'This is the brand, this is our logo.'

"The girl replaced the statue in the shoe box and covered it again with the packing paper. She then returned the box to the floor beside her. I saw it had more of the shoe manufacturer's logo on the lid."

Kate, smiling at him, started to giggle. "I don't get you, Jack. What are you saying to me? What's the point of the story? Come on, I have to go in. Myrna will smell a rat and go looking out the window soon."

"The point?" Jack said like he couldn't believe she didn't get it. He laughed himself, then sensing his own ridiculousness. "The point is, I went back to my room to get my stuff, and when I was checking out I saw them leave. The older man first, then the pinstripe with the glasses, and then the girl following behind lazily. They were in one of these SUVS. When they took off I noticed the girl had left the box on the bonnet of the car parked beside them. I walked over wondering, should I try to follow them?

"Then I guessed the best thing was to leave it at reception, and they would come back for it. But the man at the desk told me the place was closing the next day, and the whole building was scheduled for demolition at the weekend. So I wasn't sure what to do with it. So I brought it with me. The statue of the crow—the logo, the brand—it sits in the dark in the bottom drawer beside my bed."

Kate kissed him softly on the forehead. "Go home, Jack Browne. We are both a little drunk. You are acting the donkey keeping me out here in the cold, spouting nonsense. Go home with you."

Jack waited till Kate had gone in before he started his walk home. Caw flapped his wings excitedly as he tried to decipher what on earth Jack was on about. However, soon Jack was at it again, reading aloud.

"The walk from the Fisherman's by Michael Harrington's and on to the Harbour Bar, the stopper pulled, the green pool empties, leaving small boats buried in thick sand outside of the harbour wall. The sea is eaten by the night."

Wood Point, Many years ago
22.

"Cathartic," Diamond Jim said without warning, causing George's hand to shake and spill drops of tea on his jeans.

George gave Diamond Jim a filthy look. Resting his plastic cup on the dash, he wiped his knee with his right hand but it made no difference at all to the stain.

"Cathartic," Diamond Jim said again, this time with a sense of anticipation. George coughed politely using his left fist to cover his mouth.

"It means to flush out. You know like when you are having a shit, like, you know when it really hurts and you have to force it. But when it is out and swimming in the bowl, you feel the purification of the innards, which is called a catharsis. Bet I am right!"

George went for his tea again, making sure not to allow his hand wobble and spill it again. While Diamond Jim studied the thesaurus carefully, George said, "George Whelton is right!"

Diamond Jim, lifting his head slowly, looked at his friend with a wry smile. "Don't know how you do it, boy. But I will catch you. Don't you worry, we have all evening. Sure, he has only just gone in."

"He has," George said, winding the window down and empting the drains onto the pier. The smell of fish boxes invaded the space, and he wound it back up just as quick. "Erudite?"

Diamond Jim let the thesaurus fall face down on his lap.

"Come on, ask me a hard one, will you, Jim? That's too easy for a man of my knowledgeable ejeet a mation. Knowledge gained from scholarly reading one might say."

"Might one?" Diamond Jim imitated his West British accent and went on to say, "Of course, dear George, you are correct. But thou need not fret as I will catch you before the evening is out!"

George encouraged him to pick up the book once more; he looked across the road to the pub. It seemed deserted. There was Bill Thornton pulling the drapes bang on time at seven-forty-five. George wondered about the bar trade and how a fellow could make a dime from two or three customers.

"Sacer Vates?" Diamond Jim interrupted his thoughts.

"Say again," George asked seemingly unperturbed.

"Sacer Vates,"Jim said excitedly.

"Sounds like a football team from South America. Are you mad, Jim? The rules say the words have to be in everyday use. When's the last time anyone round here said Sacer Vates? I mean, give me a little, will you? Sacer Vates, indeed!" George pretended to be angry when he wasn't.

"Do you give up, George, then?"

George looked at him exasperated. "A new word, Jim, come on!"

Diamond Jim held the book aloft. It was closed barring a small space near the top, which housed his thumb.

"Do we have a countdown? Will George Whelton run out of time, and will he be defeated for the first time ever in tonight's 'You Got to Know the Word?'"

George didn't find his commentator voice in any way funny. He glared at Jim.

"It has to be a word in common usage, or at least a Dublin fourite must know it!"

Diamond Jim started to wave the tiny book through the air, much to George's annoyance.

"Give me a new word, and tell me what that other crap means!"

Jim returned the thesaurus to its correct position. He read the meaning of the word slowly.

"Sacred poet," he said with a distinct air of triumph.

George spluttered. "Sacred fucking poet. Did you ever hear the likes of it? Nah, it has to be a word we might know or at least should know. We can't have any old words, do you hear me, Jim, or it will be just plain stupid!"

"All right, so, boss, if you want to be childish about it, I
will try and find some words that are more in vogue."

He said "vogue" with great emphasis to highlight that his
own knowledge wasn't so bad either.

"Do you want another sandwich, George, or do you want
to wait? We will be here all night. Better not eat them all."

George, nodding said, "I will wait a while. If we ate any
more of them now, they will be all gone. We might starve
ourselves later."

"We might." Jim watched a small boat with an outboard
steal up the channel, trying to cheat the approaching
darkness. Soon the lights went on in the Harbour Bar and off
in Detta's shop. Nobody had entered either establishment for
at least a half-an-hour.

*

Bill didn't like the look of Donal, and it wasn't that he was
full of drink. His face was red and serious, and his silver
head had a damp look like he had used too much hair oil. The
tops of both his ears burned brightly like they were infected,
and his mood was no better either. He snarled for his pint and
a brandy sitting at the far end of the bar by the fire. He made
sure to keep at least two empty stools between him and the
wall. If anyone came close he would rest his right foot on one
and fiddle with his overcoat pocket as it rested untidily on the
other. A fellow would be forgiven for presuming that he was
in the company of three rather than a man alone.

Bill didn't like it; bad for business. Why book three stools
when there was just one person? It was the definition of
greed, bad manners, and downright bloody-mindedness.

"Were you down below?" Bill asked messing with the till
and then taking an age to count the change before depositing
it back where it came from, evidently satisfied.

Peering up at him, his eyes sunken in his head, Donal said,
"I didn't bother. To tell you the truth I was away in Clon

earlier. Had a skin full. We were organising the new tourist office. As I said, we had a skin full and the food was fabulous."

Donal spat out the last sentence to impress upon Bill both the size and quality of the fare on offer.

Bill, inquisitive, asked, "Was it well attended?"

"It was," Donal said before adding, "These things draw a crowd. Sure, if there is money to be made, you will always get a crowd. They were all there—Clancy and Bennett, Mary Hargan, some fellas from Dublin. You now, the ones that built out in Owenahinca."

"Byrne, that crowd?" Bill asked, picking up a rag and wiping the counter.

"No, not Byrne, those fellas. Their old man was from Cork. What's their fuckin' names?"

Bill stood patiently, waiting for Donal's memory to click. He was called to the far end of the bar as Thomas Crowe wanted another pint. Thomas sat, his head bowed over the counter, his woollen hat too high on his crown. He had nursed several Guinness, and now was counting his coppers for one more.

Donal waved his arms furiously at Bill to return to him, which Bill did as soon as he had served Thomas.

"Lucey! Fuckin' Terence Lucey. His sons. They built out in Owenahinca. They were there. A fine-looking bunch they are. Too prosperous, Bill. Put us to shame!"

Bill gave him a look that said, 'Speak for your good self my man,' before taking his brandy glass to refill. He turned his head as he topped up the brandy glass from the Hennessey wall dispenser.

"How are things?" Bill said softly as to make sure nobody overheard.

Accepting the brandy Donal said, "Things couldn't be worse, and favours can no longer be regarded as anything but a weakness. A fellow can't do anything without the proper capital. You know, Bill, there is no way I will give anyone

more rope. You know, tourists or no tourists, my season is
every day and cash is king. Companies go out of business
every day just through lack of cash. On paper they could be
raking it in, but cash is king. I need to call in all of my
favours. There you go. That is my contribution."

Donal handed him a twenty for his brandy, which Bill took
smartly, walking back to the till like he was analysing
Donal's words very seriously. Danny Murphy walked in
from the side door. He saluted Bill and ignored Donal. Going
to the far end of the bar where Thomas Crowe sat hunched,
he ordered a Murphy's. Donal Travers scowled at him but
somehow he managed to keep it within his skin.

After a gap Bill went back to speak to him. He was trying
to act cool, but his uneven voice betrayed him.

"It is still too early for me, Donal. I need the season. That
is the truth of it. Anything else and I would be lying, and
what good would that be? If I can just have the season I can
pay on the double if needs be. You know, Donal, you can't
get blood from a stone. Maybe you should talk to the
mortgage people again."

"No budging them," Donal said with venom. "You all
signed up to this, but when the chips are down you are
welchers, one and all. I can't be running my business like
this. I need the cash now, Bill. This week you will have to
sell the family silver!"

Bill walked away, visibly carrying the weight of Donal's
words. The bar was getting busier and Donal was becoming
frustrated, aided and abetted by the drink. Needing to relieve
himself, he passed the defeated figure of Thomas Crowe who
almost hid under his hat. Danny Murphy was talking rugby
with a decidedly uninterested Bill.

Thomas looked up as he brushed by. Catching his eye, he
said, "Hello, Mr. Travers."

"Hello there, Thomas," Donal said, forcing a smile. "Fit
and well you are looking. Are you still at sea?"

Thomas smiled at him. He knew the question was genuine, just way out of date.

"I go, lend a hand the odd the time. I am busy doing the wrinkles. It has my back broke but keeps me in this!" He lifted his pint in deference to his quip.

"Is there much demand for them? Donal asked, ignoring Danny Murphy who had turned back to face him.

"It is small, but we can ship them out to the market. It is keeping them fresh that's the problem. I can get a decent price if I can collect enough of them."

"Hard work," Donal said.

"Back breaking," Danny Murphy added, like he was somehow holding Donal responsible.

"Keep it going. You never know, some day you might have your own plant across the road, and you will be shipping them to the four corners of the world!"

Danny Murphy watched Donal step out into the hallway and head for the gents.

"That fella will never have to pick a periwinkle for a few bob, that's for sure, and he is so mean with it."

Danny ordered a pint of Guinness for Thomas and a Murphy's for himself. Thomas straightened his hat when Danny said, "That's on me, bucko."

*

"Visceral."

Diamond Jim had adjusted his seat to allow more leg room and stretched as he spoke. George watched a car drive slowly down the village. It made a strange sound, like it had lost its exhaust pipe.

Diamond Jim smiled. "Too easy, eh?"

"No, no, I wouldn't say that. It is a difficult word. Not many people know it or use it. They usually think it means something obscure, you know?

"So what does it mean?" Jim asked, resting the book on his lap.

"A physical reaction, like when you are scared and your body reacts. You know fight or flight."

"Spot on, my man."

George allowed a smile, pulling at his crotch in an effort to get more comfortable.

"I need a piss, George," Jim said. "What you think?"

"I am thinking wooden grates," George said smartly.

"All right." Jim got out, making a racket with the seat belt against the metal frame. "How do you hold it, George?"

Jim put the thesaurus upside down on his seat. "No peeking now!"

George wound the window to get some air. It was getting cold, the wind slight, just pinching his face. Beyond, the lights above Timoleague spread without order. The sky, anticipating a full moon later, allowed thick clouds to roll by. Some were white, others dark like they were stained with oil. When he rewound the window, the cold air stayed for a moment. He sighed, taking a deep breath, his concentration disturbed as Diamond Jim returned.

"Gone cold, George. Brass fucking monkeys for yer man. You know, I was thinkin' and pissin'. What do you think of him with the little boy?"

"What?" George wasn't sure what he was about but then realised what he meant. "You mean the little boy that lives down the lane?"

"Yeah, young Meade."

"I dunno what to think Jim. Any man that could do that to a boy. Just thinking of it makes me sick, the poor kid."

"I think she was really sorry later," Jim said sadly, before continuing. "She says she really didn't know what she was agreeing too and the money was for his education. He brought him into the city, buying him things—food and soft drinks and they went to the cinema. He gave her a lot of money."

"The mother could do with it. At least it was something. It beats me how she says she didn't know, though. Like, I mean, Jim, a grown man and a kid—what did she suspect?" George said, still not happy with his crotch. He was pulling at the material in his jeans once again.

"She owed him thousands, George and he wrote it off and still gave her money. Is it money with Thornton?" Diamond Jim had reopened the thesaurus but was only pretending to look at it.

"Money is right. He has an interest in the apartments they built over in Butlerstown. There was a few of them in on it, but most of them can't afford it. Travers is left with it. You know him, issuing threats, no patience. Thornton wants to put him out for a while, I suppose, buy some time..."

"Does he know about the little boy?" Jim asked.

"No, not many do besides us. Only his mother and us. She has nobody, has she?"

Diamond Jim resumed his reading. A man left the bar turning right to head towards Michael Harrington's.

"On tour," George said softly.

"I wonder, will Travers ever stand for election? He has the profile. Don't suppose there are many who would vote for him. He isn't liked, is he?" Jim commented.

"No," George said, and then went on. "But I dunno if you need to be liked. People go for the ones they are in awe of. You know, people they respect because of their wealth. Money power, boy!"

"Auspicious." This time Diamond Jim held his breath before commenting. "Sometimes it's the easy ones that will catch you out, the words we use every day. Isn't that right, George? Will this contestant get stuck on such a word? Oh my word, the boy is struggling!"

George raised his foot as high as he could towards the dashboard with Jim resting against the steering wheel, the thesaurus still in his hand. George went quiet, considering his options twice. He went to speak but the words didn't form. Diamond Jim sat back, unable to tame his excitement.

"Always the easy ones," George said watching a bulb blow in a street lamp just down the street. What was bright was now only dark shadows. "Our friend Mr. Travers, he is auspicious, am I right, Jim? Very auspicious!"

Jim closing the book over on his finger admitted defeat. "George, you are a right one. I thought I had you, but you know all—'prosperous, promising success, favoured by fortune.'"

"Makes you wonder about words, Jim, doesn't it? Like, we have so many words, some of them meaning the same thing. Did you ever wonder why some people use big words and some don't? Like, you hear intellectuals on TV using words that nobody you know ever uses. Even if they might understand them, do they use these words among themselves or do they only use them for effect when they know ordinary folk are listening?"

"Dunno," Diamond Jim offered. "I would murder another sandwich, what about you?"

George looked at Jim who was reaching into the cool bag behind his seat.

*

Danny Murphy was on his third pint and Thomas Crowe his sixth. Donal Travers was back at his stool, eyeing Bill Thornton oddly and occasionally slapping himself across the face in an effort to ward off a drunken stupor. The pub was a little busier, and Bill was outside the bar delivering drinks to Madge Butler who was entertaining her maiden aunt. Bill was hoping to have a quiet word with her regarding Michael Harrington, but the maiden aunt talked incessantly, making trite comments about the charm of the bar and indeed the village. Madge Butler paid not a blind bit of notice to Bill's prompting. She was very off-hand when Bill mentioned Michael and asked harmlessly how business was.

"Michael's business is his own now, Bill," she chastised, much to her maiden aunt's amusement.

"We are all struggling," Bill said, clearing away the empty glasses from the table beside them. "You would wonder, is there money to be made anymore?"

Then he was walking away when Madge said, "Those who adapt the best will survive, Bill. It is time for the people in your line of work to use their imaginations. Look at the Fisherman's with his food and music. People didn't give Barry Cousins much of a hope, but he is proving them all wrong. Get the bums on the seats and keep em' there!"

Bill grunted and left, leaving the maiden aunt laughing and then whispering into her niece's left ear.

Thomas Crowe was now warm from the drink, and Danny Murphy bought him another before moving on to join some of the yachting crowd who hogged the middle of the bar. Pee Wee Flynn came in the back door giving Donal Travers a wary eye before brushing past bodies to take Danny Murphy's stool.

"It's going to rain, Thomas. It's already spitting. How's that pint, is it good?"

Pee Wee lowered his voice so as Bill wouldn't hear him and went on. "They were shit here on Tuesday. I had to switch to Murphy's!"

Lowering his voice even further he said, "He doesn't clean the taps, that's what it is. He never does it. That is why the stout is shit!"

Thomas didn't reply. Things had been going so well with a couple of free pints and a chat. Now with the arrival of Pee Wee his chance of a little peace and quiet was gone.

"I will have a Heineken, Bill," said Pee Wee as he glanced up the bar once more, looking at the solitary figure of Donal Travers who was talking earnestly to himself.

"Been out lately?" Pee Wee asked.

Thomas was irritated by his English accent. "This and that," he said not really wanting to engage. Then he went on, "I am still collecting wrinkles, but it is hard sometimes in the bad weather!"

"I hate this weather. You can do nothing. Like, I would love to paint the old man's house, but you can't in this shit. As soon as you would put a coat of paint on the walls, the fuckin' rain will come lashing down and wash it all away."

Pee Wee chuckled like he had just made a very funny joke. Thomas allowed his head to sink over the counter. He pretended to be interested in the labels on the beer bottles stacked on the shelf opposite. Pee Wee, sensing his lack of enthusiasm, looked around for someone else to engage. Most people were locked in conversation. He noticed Madge Butler sitting in the corner with a lady he had never seen before.

Turning back to the still-distracted Thomas, he said, "That Madge Butler has some set of jugs on her, hey."

Thomas, unable to help himself, turned around, and as luck would have it Madge Butler was standing behind him waiting to order more drinks. Pee Wee leaned forward, sniggering.

"Hello, Madge," Thomas said.

She studied him for a second before she answered.

"Hello, Thomas. Hello, Peter," she addressed the back of Pee Wee's neck.

He turned to her smiling. "All right, Madge, here, do you want to get in?"

He moved to one side to allow her to order. Madge glanced up the bar. Donal was deep in thought, his left hand resting against his left cheek. He held his gaze when their eyes met, but he displayed no emotion nor did she.

Turning to Thomas she said, "Make sure and keep me a few wrinkles. I will use them at home."

Pee Wee interrupted, "How is your mother?"

Madge was surprised by the question. "She is still the same."

Pee Wee muttered something before saying, "What age is she now?"

Madge, sighing, said, "Eighty-nine."

"A great age, that eighty-nine."

Madge, picking up her drinks, said, "It is indeed, when you know who you are and where you are. Don't forget me, Thomas."

"All right," Thomas said to her back. "I won't, Madge," he added unnecessarily.

"I thought she was going to stab me with those balloons of hers. How does she carry them around with her? Everywhere she goes, they go. It is like carrying a stone of potatoes full time!" Pee Wee said.

Thomas felt a mist appearing to water his eyes. It made him blink so as he could see Pee Wee properly, and then he felt suddenly sad and alone

*

"Do you think it is true, Jim? What are you doing?"

George watched in amazement as Diamond Jim rubbed his hands vigorously. "Are you cold?"

Blowing on the tips of his fingers, Jim said, "I am stiff holding this book up like this. My fingers have gone stiff, George. Is what true?"

George, chuckling softly to himself, cast an eye out the window at nothing in particular. He was thinking of strolling around the pier to catch the late night air. Sometimes he found it calming to gaze at the moon water, seeing it reflect the heavens.

"Women, you know, when they say men only think with their dicks."

Jim was about to jump in with an answer, but he hesitated before saying, "Women say that, George, but don't they only think babies and security nice houses and good safe jobs? It isn't like they could teach us much!"

"True, very true..."

Before George could finish, Jim said loudly, "Very, very, very true, my good man."

George laughed and then Jim laughed with him.

"Of course, George, my good man, it is a truism. Men do only follow Sir Dick. Whatever Sir Dick says goes. There is no arguing with this merchant!"

George, digesting the information he had just received, lifted his head towards the roof of the van, coming face to face with the felt cover. His neck muscles relaxed.

"I am sorry, I never got married, Jim. I wasn't bothered when I was younger. You know what they're like in Bandon, and once you have the right address in Cork you won't starve, that is for sure. Most of them round our way will do you for free if the husband is gone or inside. No worries there, Jim. I just didn't want the hassle of a wife waiting for me when I got home, going on at me about my business. When you are socialising you have seen it many times, haven't you, Jim? The boys making up stories to tell the missus? 'I am not here; tell her I am not here!' It's all well and good, Jim, but there are bound to be small ones left at home waiting for their old man to appear. It just seems very complicated, but I suppose I could have done it. Jim, you remember Brida? She was a special one, bright and breezy. Never a dull moment with Brida. She had the measure of me, didn't she?"

Jim was at the thesaurus again, leafing through the pages, using his pencil torch so as not to run down the van's battery.

"Brida. Brings me back, George. A fine woman. Pity about her, poor thing, and she was so full of it. Especially around you, George. She really took off when she was around you. A great one for the old..."

Jim didn't finish what he was about to say. He coughed awkwardly instead.

George, lost in his own thoughts, hadn't taken offence. Instead he said, "She understood men, Brida. That's what comes with having a lot of brothers. She understood things about men that most women don't. Most women want to trade. You know, 'You give me this and I will give you that', but Brida knew how to give. She didn't need anything back."

"Terrible the way she went, though, George. She should never have gone into the city. She was safe here, but the city is an animal. She must have met an animal, the way she was killed and her body dumped in the river. Would you say it was a foreigner, one of those Eastern Europeans? They are all tricky with knives, and when they drink the sup they go crazy. George, they don't drink in the pubs like us, they drink at home, litres of firewater!"

George opened the passenger door just to let the cold air circulate. Jim, putting down his book, started blowing at his fingers again.

"I might have married Brida. I never met anyone else that interested in me. All too fussy for my liking. Sometimes I think all women have a bit of a tip about themselves, like they're special, you know, and we have to treat them special!"

"It must be the way God wants it, George, or it wouldn't be the way of the world. Anyway, to be honest with you I wouldn't mind a wife now. I am getting older, George. It's costly going visiting. You can't always expect a free one. You have to bring something at least, or go out for a bite. You know as well as I do you need someplace, to put it within limits I am saying."

"You are right, it is a pity that not everyone realises the limits, isn't it? I am not one for going on about queers, nor am I into bashing faggots. Let them alone as long as they keep it to themselves. But when it comes to children, that's a different kettle of fish."

"A whole different ball game, George. A shame they needed the money so badly, how could a..."

Jim stopped like he just couldn't bring himself to utter the words he wanted to say. George looked at his friend, his face barely visible from the light of the pen torch. Jim was still flicking through the thesaurus but not making much headway.

George was still debating if he should stretch his legs when Jim said calmly, "Did you ever think, George, we're all the same? The design is so fundamental. Each one of us has arms and legs, a head and a prick or a fanny. The prick goes into the fanny, and another copy is made, hey? In between we do all sorts of things to each other. We steal, beat up, murder, imprison, rape, and torture. Then we also have our birthdays. We fall in love and have parties, we shop and we buy and sell and we go to the hospitals to see our sick relatives."

George laughed when Jim said his piece. Then he added, "You are right, Jim, it is a funny business being alive."

*

Bill had cleared most of them out. There were only a few stragglers, including an extremely drunk Thomas Crowe and the erratic Donal Travers. What worried Bill was that he had all the looks of a fellow who was in for the night. He ordered another brandy before he had even started the one in front of him, and he was in one of his black humours too, scowling at everyone and contorting his face, slapping himself with his spare hand, the other one perpetually holding up his chin.

Soon Thomas Crowe slipped out the door with his hat tight on his head even for the short walk home. Bill decided to brave it. Putting the brandy up in front of Donal he said, "On the house, Mr. Travers."

Donal, slapping his left cheek sharply, said, "Buttering me up will do you no good, Bill. It is the colour of the notes over in your till that interests me. We cannot have a situation whereby a fellow in debt can make a deal with himself and then bind it on the very man he owes the money to. It is not known in economic terms as a profitable exercise, so when you have a moment grab a stool and we will thrash it out like men. Who knows, I might even toast your good health before I leave, once I am satisfied you are with me one and all and that you have an understanding of the gravity of our present situation."

Bill scoffed, shaking his head. He dragged his own bar stool till he sat face to face with his tormentor. Only the counter separated them. He was anxious to bring it to a point where Donal would just up and leave. Then he was sure events would turn in his favour. The annoyance, of course, was that on this night of all nights Donal procrastinated without explanation.

Suddenly a rush of panic: what if Donal was aware of his plans? Maybe he had secretly met the two boys, offering to pay them more money than he had offered and then persuaded them to turn the tables. He shivered as he realised the sudden truth, imagining the cold hard damp sand.

"I never really liked you, Bill." Donal sounded surprisingly sober for one that looked so drunk. "Not at any stage. You might as well know. It is better to tell a man to his face than spend hours and hours bad mouthing him behind his back. Not even when I met you first with Mrs. Edwards, and you were a favourite with that lovely lassie, Julia. How you messed that up, boy! Shows me the true Bill Thornton. Big man in talk and waffle but with the brains of a roaring ass. She was too good for you, Bill, and you probably know it, but people like you are stubborn. I won't compliment you by branding you cute. Instead I will insult you by classing you as a mere want-to-be-cute, bucko.

"You possess none of the acumen or the drive that it takes
to be a success. Me, I come up with the idea and the finance,
the location, the where-for-all and the imagination. Look at
you, big talker, big mouth but no money, not a dime for
nearly five months. The balls of you, expecting me to sub
you until you are ready to pay me, and then you want an
incremental profit in arrears, like you were always a partner
of mine."

Donal swallowed most of the first brandy looking steadily
at a stunned Bill, who showed nothing, not even anger or
fear.

"As I said before, you are not the only one who has tried to
fuck me. The others, they will get a visit soon. Don't worry, I
am not a registered charity. I have only one responsibility
and that is to me and those that feed off of me. You do see
where I am going with this, Bill."

Donal leaned over the counter till their noses almost
touched. Bill reacted by dragging his stool back by about an
inch but just enough to allow himself space to breathe again.
He thought, Betrayal! He is so aggressive.

Bill half expected the boys to burst in through the side
door, and then he imagined himself been dragged out with a
hood placed on his head and bundled into the back of a van.

"Here is the deal," Donal said cutting the air, causing Bill
to give him his full attention.

"I am not trying to say that I am reasonable, but I am
pragmatic and it is only to serve the cause of pragmatism that
I make this offer. Five months works out to three grand even,
right? Now, you give me one thousand by next Friday and
another five hundred by the end of the month, right, and I
will allow you to pay the other fifteen hundred when the deal
ends in five years' time so long as you keep up the normal
payments from next month. See what I am doing? See what I
am offering? A chance to suspend fifteen hundred for five
years. It isn't just a fair offer, Bill, it is charity because I have

already paid interest, and these are just the capital arrears we are discussing. What do you say, huh?"

Donal, swapping his hold-up hand, slapped his right cheek this time, and Bill watched it slowly redden.

"I don't know, Donal, it sounds like a very generous offer, it really does, and as you know in normal circumstances I would jump at it, but business is very slow yet, so I am still at my wits' end."

A voice was screaming internally. Why didn't he make this offer a month ago?? It was well within reach then. Also the postponed payment might never come to fruition as there is a good chance the investment would pass on by then and any profit divided. Yes, he argued the money would still fall due, but he wouldn't need to raise the whole lump sum.

"Donal, you are far more astute than me in these matters, yet I feel you are unfair to me at the same time. You come into my bar, I allow you to stay here till you can drink nothing more—not a sad drop—then you come up with propositions and proposals. 'This will make us a fortune!' and 'Bill, don't miss this one' kind of talk, till I feel I am railroaded, squashed up against the till here. I enter into the spirit of what it is you are suggesting, but I have no measure of backup should we hit problems or if things are slow. I think you want me to go out the yard and drill a hole in the concrete to recover the funds I have buried there.

"Donal, you are right, I am not like the fox. I don't have the patent on cuteness. I run a bar. I am a simple man. I will think about it and see if I can make up a grand by the end of the week. I know where you are coming from, Donal. You are not wrong to want to tidy things up, and in fairness you have shown remarkable restraint in a time when people are throwing money at property investments."

Bill searched his eyes to see if he was satisfied. Gone was that cold, dead-fish look. It was replaced by a more general look of contentment.

Wood Point, Many years ago
23.

When the night air hit him it brought with it an afflicting stagger, and twice in the first few yards he had to use his right arm to steady himself, cursing softly under his breath as the village at night echoed like a drum. It was an old habit. Donal stopped for a moment to pull the collar of his coat tighter round his throat, but once he relaxed his grip it sprang open, leaving him just as exposed to the breeze coming off the sea fanning over his skin. He took two tentative steps forward, dreading the walk home and the last punitive climb up Ramsey Hill. He decided to keep an eye out for a straggler. Should a car arrive, they might drop him off at his gate. It wouldn't be the first time.

Once he fell asleep in some stranger's car, only to be deposited at his front door and the doorbell rung. Georgina took him in and somehow managed to get him to his bed. To this day he had no clue as to the identity of the Good Samaritan. Safe to say it was someone he knew well.

Walking alone he was beginning to sense that vacant sureness of invincibility one acquires when walking in the dead of night. The street was empty as far as the eye could see, and there was no sound of cars or doors closing, windows banging shut. All was quiet; all was well.

He hadn't quite reached Michael Harrington's when he heard the soft sound of a car driving slowly behind him. Turning, he saw a dark vehicle with lights excessively bright, the white headlights trapping him like a cat, the beam search-lighting against the stone wall in front of him. Donal continued on the path ahead, his sense of power undiluted. The car most likely was crawling home illegally with fellas who were drinking down in Timoleague or Kilbrittain.

As it pulled alongside him, he saw it was in fact a dark escort van of dubious vintage. It parked in front of him awkwardly hitting the curb. He was half-expecting the window to roll down, so he turned to the road in an effort to see if he could recognise the driver but he was grabbed from behind and then from the front. He felt a strong hand cover his mouth, and his body buckled at the waist, snapping him like a folding deck chair. The back doors of the van opened. He was lifted inside till he was lying on his side midst hard things, like pots of paint and tools. He could taste iron, and when the hand on his mouth released he went to scream but a fist hit him so hard it broke two of his front teeth and the blood spewed down his chin.

The engine roared as the van did a U-turn. He tried to cry out as it hit the hard bumps on the road. Funny, he could tell how far they had travelled by the bumps in question, and he knew by the grating sound of manhole covers that they were leaving the village altogether. Heading out the sea road to Timoleague, he listened to the muffled voices as he swallowed blood. Soon the numbness wore off, and it left him feeling the exact pain. It hurt even more as he tried to spit out the remains of teeth that stuck in his gums like sprinkled grit.

The van was taking the bends, approaching the bridge at an alarming speed. From his lying position, he was sure it would turn over. He knew when it swung right that they were headed by the abbey, the road low. He imagined the silent water and the mud of the Argideen. The van took a hard right and on till it screeched right again. Trying to keep his wits about him, he wondered who his attackers could be and where on earth they were bringing him. What were they about to do to him? He had many enemies, but who would stoop to this? What great harm had he done to deserve this? And not a sinner came to his aid. He was abducted from his own place without a single person knowing.

*

George, his face hidden behind the balaclava, was enjoying his tunnel view through the slits. He could see Diamond Jim. His balaclava was poorly made. He had to adjust it twice so he could see.

He took a strong grip of Donal's hair which stuck to the sides of his head as the rest of his crown was bald. The blood draining down his chin was dark. His cheeks were squashed, bruised by the bumps and the hard floor of the van. Donal was trying to speak but his mouth was stuck, the blood forming a congealing adhesive. Diamond Jim pulled on his hair violently as Donal made each attempt, the strange combination forcing him to give up. He was on his knees gasping for breath.

"Welcome to Burren, a lovely place at this hour of the day, and thank God we have the moonlight so we won't need the torches, the very thing that concerned me most," George said.

"Needless to say," he continued, "we are mad at you, Donal, making us wait all evening and us with nothing to do, just kill the time. You know, Donal, it is probably the hardest thing a man has to do, don't you think? Kill time. Me, I spent so much of my life sitting around thinking, wondering what it is all about. You don't spend much time sitting around do you, Donal? Sitting around thinking isn't for the likes of you, Donal. You are too busy out making money and messing about with little boys aren't you? This thinking lark is for a poor asshole like me, would you agree?"

George didn't expect an answer, so it was Diamond Jim who agreed, nodding his head in an exaggerated fashion then pulling harder on Donal's clumps of hair. Donal tried to speak again, but he was unable to compose a proper sentence, his knees hard against the damp slabs of the pier.

"Who are you?" His voice was so dry the words were barely audible.

"Let's get him below before someone drives by," George said.

Jim responded by dragging Donal to the small beach
below, almost carrying him over the stones cemented in the
sand. George collected his equipment from the rear of the
van: it consisted of a rope, four long wooden stakes, and a
mallet. They were in one single sack, which allowed him to
sling it over his shoulder and keep hold of his walking stick.

Jim dragged Donal by his right arm and allowed him to use
his feet, taking him beyond the shale onto the hard sand
abandoned by the outgoing tide. From the darkness birds
screeched as if sensing an intrusion. On the far side a car
heading home lit the whole scene. As it turned the sharp
bends before arriving on the sea road proper, its illumination
dulled as it sped towards Wood Point.

Diamond Jim, slightly short of breath himself, let Donal
fall bottom first onto the wet sand. Donal was quiet, his head
falling forward occasionally as he tried to wipe the hard
blood from his lips with his sleeve, his breathing erratic.

"Get him to strip," George commanded as he arrived,
laboured by the uselessness of his stick in the sand.

Diamond Jim, keeping his voice calm, said, "Come on, big
boy, get them off you."

Donal looked up at him and muttered, "Fuckin' serious?"

Diamond Jim hit him hard again across the cheek, breaking
more teeth. Donal's head bounced back into the sand,

"No, no, that is too hard! We want to keep this baby alive.
Boy, if you keep hitting him so hard, we won't need this
stuff!"

George struggled to remove his implements from the sack.
Jim helped Donal to his feet, and then he took off his coat.
He watched Donal, dazed and uncertain, undressing slowly
till he was left standing shivering in his underwear. George
ordered him to remove his underpants also, and Donal
eventually did under threat of another fist.

George ordered him to lie down face first, which he did,
his face sinking in the sand. Diamond Jim used his left foot
to subdue the fragile body shivering before him. George

stared at his pale skin with tufts of hair growing in odd places; his buttocks, small and tight, were out of proportion to the rest of him. Diamond Jim tied the rope around his wrists, attaching each one to the stakes he had stolen from a site for sale out the road to Beal Na Blagh. Donal was mumbling, trying to muster his strength. Diamond Jim was making sure the rope was tight before moving to his ankles and hammering each stake into the sand.

When he was finished Jim stood upright, holding his back to ease the muscle just above his buttocks. He stretched to try and relieve his discomfort. George brushed past him, looking at the crucified body face down in the sand. He could see his victim holding his head sideways to avoid the water sifting through the grains of sand.

"You are looking well, Donal. In fact I haven't seen you looking so well in a long time. I bet you wish you were at home in bed nice and warm with that strange missus of yours. Bet she goes like a train, hey? But that wouldn't be your cup of tea, would it, Donal? I heard you prefer boys, isn't that right? Small boys like young Meade from Bandon? You know him, Donal, the little boy who lives down the lane."

George walked up to where Donal rested his chin. He was trying so hard to control his breathing, his shoulders moving up and down like clockwork, breathing in and out.

"The tide is turning, Mr. Travers. Give it about three hours, and where we are standing now will have about five feet of water. What are you in there now, my man? Two inches maybe? Try breathing in five feet. Look at you. Do you know what he is like?" George said, loosening his belt. He held it aloft and Diamond Jim could see the extent of it and the big steel buckle at one end. "He is like a baby frog. Remember how we just caught them as kids and we would stick a piece of straw up their arse and blow till they exploded? He is like a baby frog, my God, he is!"

Diamond Jim looked up. A car passed by Burren pier, its lights searching ten yards further on before its sound and its lights finally disappeared as it turned into a laneway to the dark countryside.

"Baa, baa, black sheep, have you any wool?" George went on.

Diamond Jim laughed. "Yes, sir, yes, sir, three bags full."

George pounded his belt between Donal's shoulder blades, causing him to wince with pain. It left a red mark that took the shape of the steel buckle.

"One for the master, and one for the maid..." George hit him again, this time a little harder and on the bone of his right shoulder blade. This time Donal screamed. It came from the animal within wounded.

"...and one for the little boy..." George hesitated, his victim still wincing in pain from the last blow. He struck again, this time with even more menace.

"...who lives down the lane."

Donal fainted, his head falling into the sand, water rising to touch his nose.

"Let's go," Diamond Jim said fretfully.

"Bring the mallet. We might need it again sometime," George said, and they plodded their way across the dark sand to the shale, the pebbles sinking beneath the weight of their feet.

*

When Donal woke he felt the water rinse the insides of his nostrils. Instinctively he moved away trying to take in air. Distracted by the pain in his back, he tried to place his two abductors. He thought he knew one of the voices, but he wasn't sure. The bigger man who punched him wasn't familiar at all. It was pointless, he concluded. What does it matter who they were? It won't make any difference. Now, how to get out of this?

His mind suddenly raced. People would be passing in the first light—someone was bound to find him. He could shout. For all their thoroughness they hadn't gagged him. But when he tried to shout out, he could see why. His voice was muffled by the sand beneath. He had no room to move, get his lips at the air, and he was shivering now as the morning was only set to be rubbed down. A car passing on the road kept going, the driver braking hard as the road narrowed.

He thought of Madeline and Georgina. Would they miss him from his bed? Probably not, as he rarely surfaced from his bed before Sunday lunch and most times he took his food alone in his study. Madeline would be doing what she does—sitting alone in the drawing room, the dog at her feet, while Georgina would go horse-riding in Kilbrittain. Nobody would notice he didn't come home.

Then it came to him in a flash, the thought somehow warming in its clarity. That's who the smaller one was—George fucking Whelton, of all people! Gorgeous George! He tried to disguise himself but it was him. George knew the people from Bandon. She must have told him, despite the money he paid her. She broke the silence and told Gorgeous George. Why pick him up for that? No, there was someone else. Who would do this to him?

Donal drifted in and out of consciousness. Images came to visit. All sorts of stuff. He was trying hard to put the images away as he concentrated on his breathing, his body functioning as normal. He peed into the sand and was inexplicably relieved. They had removed his pants. The boy, a grand day out in Cork, shops and sweets, a McDonald's—it wasn't like she hadn't agreed to it, taking the money and then some more. Then she told Gorgeous George, and he had punished him, flogging his bare back. Tears ran down his cheeks as soon he heard the water break, and he knew it was coming to Burren pier. He realised he had perhaps an hour at most; it was starting to brighten.

He saw the first birds landing close by, picking at the sand. Staring into the dark sand, he wanted to talk to them, call them over. If it were a movie, one of them would fly away and get help, but in truth he could picture Madeline. He saw her face as she sat, contented, in her bed. Later she might look at his bedroom door sadly and then go on sourly to the kitchen. Bill Thornton, accepting his offer of appeasement. What a sudden turn.

It was him. It was Thornton. He wanted him gone away, removed so he could keep his money. That was it—Thornton did it. Ever since Julia and the way he treated her, his mauling hands all over her. Julia. The only woman he ever cared for, and Thornton got her. And then he ruined her till she left and never came back.

Donal felt the water swish round his feet. It was cold at first, but after a bit it got warmer. Soon it came under his knee caps and into his groin. It was cold now, sloshing its way over his buttocks. He remembered the long chats with her on damp afternoons when the fire was blazing in the grate. She made him hot whiskeys and listened intently to his yarns. Then Thornton came in, and Donal could see she was taken with him because he was giving her the line that she could be the lady of the house, the proprietor of the Harbour Bar, his good wife, overseer of food and drinks, the purveyor of quality. The water was rushing now, and he tried to scream, barely able to lift his head from the sand filling below. Cold, the water over his wounds stung. And then it came over the back of his head, and suddenly he was unable to breathe.

*

In Bandon Diamond Jim drank the last of his tea. He was disappointed as the dregs were cold, and he was annoyed he had left it lie so long.

"A good day's work went without a hitch." George was washing his mug at the sink, and Diamond Jim deposited his mug into the suds without apology. George sighed before picking the mug out of the wash and proceeded to wipe it thoroughly with a J cloth, especially round the rim.

"What's the worst thing you have ever done, Jim? Like, if you met St. Peter, what would you have to apologise for at the Pearly Gates?"

Jim, looking tired, sighed. "I don't know, George. Lots of stuff. I regret things I should have done but didn't and things I did I shouldn't. Maybe the time the old man wouldn't give up on the notes in his drawer. Jesus, I pleaded with him, you know? I tried to be rational, like, what good is it to you? I said, 'If I box you and kill you, what use would that money be then?'"

"I think I remember that. Was it the time the old man tried to get you with the shot gun?"

"No, George, that was over in East Ferry. No, you are mixing it up."

Diamond Jim was displaying fatigue, so George said, "Go on then."

"This was in Dunmanway, and I begged him to give me over the cash so as I wouldn't have to box him. He was a stubborn old fecker, and I had to give him a good hiding in the end before he gave me the few bob mercifully."

George looked at his friend oddly. "You should be getting to your bed, Jim. You look shook. It is probably the cold out in the estuary. It is always cold down low like that, and there is always a wind, it is so open, you know."

Diamond Jim nodded before lazily getting up to go. Dragging his chair across the hard kitchen tiles, it made such a noise that George looked at the floor to see if there was a mark.

"The worst thing I ever did myself," George began as he stood back, leaning against the kitchen sink. Jim stopped in his tracks as he awaited George's confession.

"Years back I was sent to the corner shop off Main Street. I had just enough for what I needed. I think I had a half-a-crown. Anyway, old Mrs. Seery she was getting on. She was helping her son, Mick, the way older people do, but she was more getting in the way."

George looked towards the ceiling, his face fallen in the light casting shadows across his chin to make him even more grotesque. Jim sat down again. The story was lasting longer than expected.

"I was buying a sliced pan and some cabbage for the mother. Anyhow, I gave her the half-a-crown, and Mick was busy carrying a sack of spuds outside. She took my money and off she went. She diddled about at the till, which in those days, Jim, was just a big old biscuit tin. So she comes back, and she counts out my change—one shilling, two shillings, she says, but doesn't she give me a shilling too many.

"I was just about to say it to her when she got distracted by someone she knew, and I lost her attention. It was someone important because she just blanked me and started to converse with whoever it was that had walked in; off I went home a shilling richer with my sliced pan. Bad, wasn't it? The old woman died later that year. Often felt bad about it!" George looked at the floor sadly.

Jim, rising again, said, "Best be off, George. I am fucked. I will sleep this morning, hey?" He put his left hand on George's shoulder.

"Do you think someone came by to free him?"

George turned back to the sink. Picking the mugs from the draining board, he rinsed them again under the cold tap.

"You wouldn't know, Jim. What do we care? Wasn't he a scum bag always?

Wood Point, Many years ago
24.

"I thought I might put them back. Hardly good to leave them lying around," Madge said.

"You should have checked with me. These are his personal papers, private things concerning his business. Just because he is gone doesn't mean he shouldn't get respect," Madeline said sternly.

Madge stood up and walked to the window. It was a dull grey day, and the sycamore looked tired and sad.

"Don't suppose there is any news?" she asked, trying to be conciliatory.

"No news. Nothing. They just returned all his papers. I doubt if there will be anything. It has been over a month now."

Madge, getting braver, said, "I see the lifeboat was out again yesterday. Christy McCarthy said they searched high and low. They had people checking the beaches but not a sign of anything. Not even a shoe." Madge went to pick up a dust pan, which had sat under the window frame for an age. She searched for the brush, but it was nowhere to be seen.

"I have been hearing gossip, Madge. Nothing much, you know. Not enough for me to tell the police. You wouldn't know of anyone who might have had it in for him, do you?"

"What sort of gossip?" Madge looked comical holding the dustpan without the brush. Noticing herself, she let it drop tamely by her side. It dangled in her left hand.

"My husband had his faults, Madge. I am sure you are aware of that. You have been coming to this house long enough, but this gossip paints him as a monster. I have to consider Georgina. Our name is already mud around here, but these rumours about her father…

"I was just wondering, seeing that you like to be privy to his papers and stuff, would you possibly have any idea who could be responsible for spreading these vicious lies? And maybe you may know what on earth they are referring to? Before you answer, Madge, we all know Donal's sexual problems, but it amounted to little to the best of my knowledge. Unless you can tell me something different."

Madge was stunned. She had no idea Madeline knew about her husband's secret life, nor did Donal suspect it either.

Thinking on her feet, she blurted, "I don't know what you mean. I wasn't aware that Mr. Travers had secrets in that area. To be honest I always thought his secrets were tied up in his business dealings. You're coming to the wrong lady, Mrs. Travers. I do my job thoroughly but I don't pry, and people are entitled to their privacy, I believe that."

Madeline looked her up and down. She walked by Madge to go open the window. Although it was a horrible day, the room was getting stuffy.

When she opened the side window, she said, "Everything has changed now, Madge. Things can never be the same anymore, so I have made a few decisions. I am closing the house at the end of the year. Georgina is going to England to relatives. I think I will follow her later, as soon as things with Donal are sorted. I will probably go stay with a friend in Cork. In the meantime we will find a home for Bob. I am sure someone in the village will take him."

"Are you giving me notice?"

"No," Madeline said tersely. "No, you can go right now. I left an envelope on the kitchen table. It pays you till the end of the month, and that will be it. You can leave the key for me."

Madeline left the room and Madge stood silent, eyeing the papers she had been sorting, strewn across the desk. It was a desperate end and not of her making.

*

Bill Thornton heard many versions of what became known as the Donal Travers mystery. Many said his body had been washed far out to sea, never to be seen again. Others said he was eaten by crabs inside a couple of days. The word was that he decided to end it all out of the fear of revelations concerning his sex life. Rumours also abounded that he was indeed murdered and forcibly drowned, restrained by a concrete block or by wooden stakes. The wooden stakes came from local folklore going back to smugglers and poachers and the way they settled disputes. Perhaps the most bizarre story doing the rounds was that an early morning angler checking the tides saw what he thought was a body on the sands, but he was confused whether it was a dead otter or a seal. The police of course found Donal's coat washed harmlessly on the pebble beach, but they found nothing else.

As rural legends go the one that comes with his own sworn testimony is the claim by Thomas Crowe that he came across two wooden stakes, rope attached, when he was picking wrinkles out near the Blind strand. His offer to come view them is constant as he is using them to fence spuds in his back garden.

Bill was in turmoil. They had gone too far. It was only meant to shake him up, not kill him. The news came to him as a great shock and a major source of worry. Time and time again he sought solace by locking himself away from the torment of: what if the guards discovered he was involved in what was now a conspiracy to murder? Who would believe him? He had visions of himself pleading in court that it was only meant to put the frighteners on Donal Travers.

However as time passed and the body was not recovered, he regained his equilibrium. The guards had parked the case, and the reported sightings of a dark green van in the area had led up a blind alley. Some witnesses said it was red, others blue. Some said two male occupants, another said it was a man and a woman. Soon what was the topic of conversation everywhere you went faded, and something new replaced it.

It was carried in the Southern Star, and the Examiner did a feature. Even the Bandon Opinion carried a photograph of Donal Travers, appealing for anyone who might know of his whereabouts to come forward.

The Examiner's feature took up two full pages with the headline, "What really happened to Donal Travers?" The article referred to his business dealings and some controversy in relation to money lending, and it scratched the surface of a possible blackmail. But the core of the piece was more a biography than a proper analysis. It did create a bit of a stir, but it all soon died down to be buried in the ashes.

Three months later Donal Travers was rarely mentioned, save for in jest when a fellow slagging his pal might say, "Be careful now, boy, or you will be sleeping with Donal Travers tonight!"

For Bill life returned to normal, even if he had to warn his accomplices that it would be never safe to return to Wood Point. They reassured him that all the tracks had been covered, the van got rid of, and their alibis were nailed on. Madeline Travers had her solicitor call by. All the properties were sold off, and the investors paid their interest. A small profit was made, and at least Bill's capital was returned and he no longer had the drain on his resources. All in all he was very satisfied with the outcome.

The locals rarely mentioned Donal, and even though this smart journalist fellow from Dublin arrived snooping around and asking questions he eventually left after he found nothing. There was just nothing to find. The man was gone. That was the end of it. As the weeks and months passed, the chances of ever finding his body receded. There were nights when Bill awoke with a start, flying upwards in bed, sweat running from his face unto his neck, his breathing erratic. It would take a full minute to realise and note it was in fact just a dream.

Still, as he recovered, praying desperately for sleep, the stain of guilt stalked his mind. The pictures of Donal Travers lying face down in the sand. His naked body torn apart by feasting crustaceans, slowly piling on top of each other for an orgy of flesh eating. What remains of him floats like a seawater balloon aimlessly, from rock to rock, from cavern to cavern. Bits of bone ripped off by passing fish, the bone falling to the soft sand below. Donal Travers. His eyes gone, his tongue and brains stolen. Where was he now? Where was the opinionated so-and-so? Little use his smart ways and filthy tongue now, or the way he had of belittling people.

Sleep was a difficult chore, but he hadn't been sleeping right for years so it was a matter of being used to it, finding ways of distracting himself, using the small entertainments of the body. He thought of Julia, as he still found her alluring, and yet it was such a long time ago. And for all that she was hardly a stunner. But she had the perfect womanly shape for him. For some time she allowed him to caress her nipples. With both his hands up her blouse he brushed her with the tips of his fingers, barely touching her nipple thorns till they went hard. He found the weight of her pressed up close as sensuous as anything else.

Sometimes he nibbled on her ear and she would ask him to stop like it was the start of a flood, weakening her defences till passion flooded the core of her. At one stage she promised him it would be soon, she was almost ready, she only needed a little more time. Things were almost perfect. Best not rush it as it would become cumbersome, and it might raise issues between them.

Then came the announcement she wanted him to take Madge Butler in for a few days so they could drive to Belmullet to see her mother. Bill was disturbed by it. Madge Butler was all right in small doses. Would he want her controlling the till for two whole days, and her as thick with Michael Harrington as one could get? Yet she had promised him, and she made him feel betrothed to that promise.

Her mother was a sour old woman who had little to say. She dressed like a widow but had the look of a woman who had always been dour. She was sitting in the corner, nervously playing with her fingers, her head bent over as she spoke in riddles. Her accent was thick. She spoke English like she was directly translating from Irish as the words left her mouth. She loved Julia. He could tell by the way she spoke to her daughter, a dancing sound arriving from nowhere at the mention of her name. Yet she eyed Bill with suspicion and made him feel like an outsider.

They arrived in the early morning, and it was a windy day with the skies clearing before dark clouds ran in from the Atlantic to give spits of rain. They ate breakfast with the mother supplying too many sausages, with rashers and eggs. Bill had to leave some on his plate. He washed away the residue of grease with the strongest of tea. The mother watched the way he ate his food and kept up her incessant questioning of her daughter like Bill wasn't in the room.

"How's the weather in Wood Point? You don't get the rain like we do here. It rained every day from Christmas, and it did not to stop by Easter."

"Mother, the farmers in Barryroe are complaining of drought," Julia would answer politely prefacing each statement with "Mother." Bill excused himself to visit the bathroom, and when he returned there was a dead silence. He wasn't sure if some kind of argument had taken place or whether the two women had run out of things to chatter about.

He jumped slightly when Julia banged her spoon off the table cloth and said, "Bill is taking me for a drive out to the Atlantic beach."

It was news to Bill, but anything to get out of the stuffy house and the equally stuffy mother.

The beach took his breath away. They had driven out through Binghamstown and on by Elly Bay. The roads were very narrow but the surface was surprisingly good. Julia got

him to park down a sandy entrance facing the dunes, each
side flat fields with weeds growing, fenced by rusted barbed
wire. Tough looking cattle stood idling their hooves, sinking
in muck.

Once they reached the dunes the world opened and the sky
touched the earth as the waves rolled in hard against the
shoreline, these waves born on the east coast of America. Bill
sucked in the Atlantic air. Julia, running ahead, her hair
blowing like the sea, had caught hold and was dragging her
in. She kicked off her sandals, wetting the soles of her feet,
the white water hiding her toes. Later they sat side by side
between dunes to shelter from the wind. It was warm and
moist but it was still blowing her hair, the noise discouraging
conversation. Bill snuggled close to her, admiring her frock
as it withdrew up above the knee. It became see-through in
the light, and he was excited by the view of her thighs.

"Julia," he said putting his arm around her shoulder and
squeezing her, "I really want you. It is driving me crazy, my
love."

Julia, smiling, started picking bare straw from the sandy
soil in front of her.

"We used to come here as kids, me and my two brothers
and my older sister, Cáit. Of course we just horsed around in
the surf, you know. We didn't have boards or anything. We
just lifted each other up and over the waves. It was just as
good as anything else. Sometimes we would race along there,
you know. It was done like a handicap, with me the smallest
going off ahead of the others. Then they came after me, you
know, each one in order by age. It was fun." Julia threw the
straw away. It floated on the wind before a gust carried it
away.

After some consideration Bill turned on his side, letting his
hand slip up the inside of her frock. He tried her right leg, but
he found that too awkward so he switched to her left and that
was better. She didn't seem to care about it. He thought of
French kissing her, but her head was in the wrong place. He

thought about her breasts, but then figured he might run a risk whereas she seemed happy enough with what he was doing.

Julia was preoccupied, her head resting against the soft grass caked in sand. Beyond small sections of barbed wire fencing, cattle moved slowly to investigate. Bill was taken by their dark coats, their skin sleek and black. They stared on without feeling, eyes dead in their heads.

As his hand slipped up her thigh, at first she resisted by closing her legs. But then she relented and he rubbed her skin gently.

"What are you at?" she said playfully.

Bill, sighing, replied carelessly, "Nothing. Just wondering, will the sun come out? I could make my bed here and fall asleep."

"I see we have an audience." Julia referred to the cattle who were now brushing their noses against the barbed wire as if in anticipation of some great event. Bill rested the palm of his hand against her thigh, still lying on his side, sighing once more like he was oblivious to anything sensual. Julia went to sit up, but he held her hand fast and covered her with his right leg. She turned towards him, the wind catching her hair, making it stand up and then falling incorrectly and blinding her temporarily.

"What are you at?" She tried to move again, but he had her pinned under his leg.

Withdrawing his hand he lifted himself till he was upon her. Julia, still not sensing any real effort on his part, laughingly pleaded.

"Get off me, you brute. Unhand me, you beast."

Bills giggling, made her relax, his body weight distributed fairly as his weight fell mainly on the sand and grass between her legs. He was happy to allow his body to rest on the soft ground while still feeling her soft middle. He wrestled playfully, using most of his strength, and he pinned her wrist flat. She moved her head hard to the right and then the left.

He stared at her, catching her eyes, which were trusting. He tried to kiss her but she resisted playfully.

"We have to go, boy. My mother will be wondering where the hell we have got to."

Bill started to kiss her neck in the hope that his licking would arouse her. He caught her skin in a suction-like grip.

Julia started to get uncomfortable and said, "Leave it, Bill, I need to get up. Let me up, will you?"

Bill grappled beneath the light fabric that barely covered her, and he found the elastic of the small pants she wore. Her legs lifted in defence. Tearing the fabric he ripped off the pants. They wrapped around his left hand, and he discarded them somewhere beneath him.

With her right arm free, Julia tried to push him off but he warned her, "Don't. Not now."

His voice held such a desperate chill, Julia did as he commanded. She lay still, watching his face redden. She noticed his eyes change like they were no longer his. Somehow they lost all contact with her, looking over her head at some tiny speck in the sand. She watched as he let go temporarily to open the catch of his trousers. He slipped them off below his knees in unison with his underpants. Soon his skin sparkled as the wind rushed up his body, and the arrival of the sun brought a dead heat on her face.

"No, Bill," she said fast and furiously. "I can't, I tell you. Bill, I can't!"

She felt the open palm of his right hand slap against her left cheek.

"Not this time," he muttered, sucking once more on the soft skin of her neck. Then he licked her till she was wet from his spit. Lifting her legs she felt him probe her, his first attempts awkward and failing. She was sensing anger and frustration building within him. The wind was blowing hard, pushing her frock backwards. It was flapping against her thighs like a flag. She helped him as it might save her another slap, but she failed as well. She was unready and she could feel the pulsating manhood of him bitter and fraught with frustration.

Bill slapped her hard again with his open hand. "Put it in," he commanded. This time he shoved, and it slipped inside her. She felt it, huge and unnatural. He was prising her mouth open with the fingers of his right hand before inserting his ugly tongue. Julia, her mind racing, tried to respond, but her body disobeyed. He slapped her once more. The cattle were moving slowly away like they were either bored or disgusted by the events before them. He thrust hard inside her, releasing his grip on her right wrist till at last in his excitement she felt his action quicken and his breathing increase, his face contorting like some huge pain was releasing from him. At last he was done, and he collapsed on her. They both lay still.

She explained away the marks on her cheek by mocking herself and her awkwardness in getting out of the car. Her mother gave her a damp cloth cooled with tap water to try and stop the swelling. Bill had said nothing as they left the beach or on the journey back through Binghamstown.

When they turned right for American Street he offered softly, "Best to get it done, and now it is done and out of the way."

Julia didn't answer, and she rarely spoke to him again. The long drive back to Wood Point passed in relative silence, save when they needed to stop for the toilet. When they had lunch she thanked him for passing the milk and she nodded when he asked her was her food all right. Back in Wood Point Bill acted like nothing had happened between them, still dropping by the hotel to see her. Julia was civil but offered him nothing more than that, making sure they were never alone together. One day when he called by, Mrs. Edwards informed him that she left the previous night. Julia had given notice on her return from Belmullet and whatever had happened with her mother up there must have disturbed the poor child, as she was never the same after her visit.

Wood Point, Many years ago
25.

Edwina Edwards wasn't the most charitable person in the world, but she had her moments. In general she held a steadfast disposition, believing that the world gave back to us what we strived for through hard work and endeavour, and that luck had very little to do with anyone's plight. This, despite the fact she was born into money herself. Yet in a way it was that very fact that most served her thesis. She talked so proudly of her father, his father, and her grandmother on her paternal side as they were all successful in various businesses, with her paternal grandmother having cleaned up buying up mineral rights in darkest Africa. Edwina was nothing if not loyal, and her loyalty became patriotic if any of what she deemed to be the chosen ones fell on hard times or met with catastrophe.

Thus Madeline wasn't surprised when Georgina announced her into the drawing room late one evening. Edwina wasn't one to mince her words, and she carried a quiet speaking voice that was laced with sharp edges. Refusing a drink she sat down in the furthest seat away from the fire. Twice she stared at the hearth in utter bewilderment as to why the fire was lit on such a fine evening. The dog stretched out before it, his head perilously close to the flame. Perhaps it was lit for his comfort?

"I think I will take my coat off, Madeline. It is wickedly hot in here."

Madeline went to take her coat, but before she could collect it Edwina let it drape over the arm of the settee.

"I was debating as to whether to wear it; I was thinking more of my return journey. It does get cold after dark. It is bad enough to have arthritis in both legs without catching a cold. I think you will agree."

Madeline, nodding, said, "Are you sure you won't have a drink, Edwina? I have Scotch. Donal got it from a friend of his..."

Madeline was pouring vodka. After a pause Edwina said, "I am trying very hard to cut down, Madeline. You know it comes at you very easily when you are running a licensed premises, and people stay late and buy you little drinks as peace offerings so you will keep the bar open. You know, if I can cut down for a month, I might even consider giving it up completely. They will all fall off their seats if I announced I was a teetotaler, wouldn't they?"

Edwina eyed the measure Madeline had poured, but as Madeline was taking notice she diverted her eyes back to the fire and the lazy dog. Madeline went to sit in her armchair, but she dragged it away from the fire, feeling the heat fierce against her thigh. She turned it to face her companion who was smiling at her. Eventually she settled.

"I don't suppose you will ever get over it, will you? Hardly. I can't ever see the people of Wood Point get over it, can you?"

Madeline allowed her head to drop. She stared at the fire flicker in the wooden legs of the armchair opposite.

"It is no secret we couldn't stand each other, Edwina. You are well aware of it. So is most of the village. But I didn't want anything to happen to him, and now he is gone. There is nothing left is there."

Madeline gave a gentle laugh before searching Edwina's reaction.

"I don't have that someone to detest or hate so as I can vent all my frustrations. It is almost like he did this to me to remove my anger once and for all."

Edwina, raising her eyes to heaven, smiled at the dark humour. Madeline watched the soft light that waded by the sycamore. It clung to the small panels of window glass, lighting her friend benignly, for Mrs. Edwards had once been very presentable.

"I am glad you said it, Madeline, because around the hotel it is a pure gift to be able to get things done without the worry of him coming in and laying down the law. Donal was so rude to my staff even when he was sober, and he was forever corrupting Fred with his silly fly-by-night schemes. You know, what was once a pleasure Madeline, turned into a bloody mess, and to be perfectly honest with you I think his days were numbered anyhow. His body was giving up. Not that I wish to comment too much, especially with Fred's health issues. But Donal was collapsing from within. He was bloated like a whale, yet from the waist down he was no more than a matchstick, and that was just the physical him. His paranoia about the syndicate and his money, and God knows what was not worrying him."

Edwina paused to take a breath, and Madeline sank back in her chair surprised by her outburst.

"How is Georgina managing?" Edwina asked softly.

Without hesitation Madeline replied, "She is good, but you know what people are like, quizzing her every time she puts her foot in the village. People are very rude, Edwina, dying to satisfy their crude desire for information. Georgina says she has heard everything—like, that Donal drowned himself, or that I killed him and put his corpse in water, or that we both poisoned him and then dumped his body. Yes, and the best one is that someone from the village put a hit out on him."

Edwina gasped, shivering like the very idea was beyond endurance.

"They were never close, Edwina, but your father is your father, you know? So she is sad at times. She goes into herself. She keeps talking of England and my family."

Madeline got up to fix another vodka. She was about to offer Edwina a Scotch, but she changed her mind. A shadow crawled along the wooden floor, and over by the window dust that she had failed to notice gathered. Edwina had grown darker. She was unable to see her eyes clearly. Soon she would need to put on the reading lamp on the sideboard at least to provide atmosphere.

"England will suit her. She was always a little lady. There isn't much demand for ladies round here. It might do her good, Madeline, to see a bit of the world. It is the one thing I always say to Fred. He disagrees of course, but the people here don't travel, and I don't mean two weeks in the Canaries..."

Sipping her drink Madeline said sheepishly, "They say it broadens the mind." She hesitated before adding, "But I see what you mean."

Madeline stood and turned on the side lamp. It presented a glow rather than offered any real improvement in the light. Outside the folds of darkness swept across the estuary. She could no longer see the top branches of the tree, or the sky clearly, beyond a dark blanket now interrupted only by artificial light.

"I am absolutely bored, of course, Madeline, and I was only thinking of you the other morning when I was riding out. I am opening the riding school for the season, and I was thinking I might just need someone to ride out with kids the odd time. You know when these legs give in, all in all I am just not reliable, I am afraid. I was wondering if you can fill in for me the odd day. You need not commit to anything, but it is a thought. Wouldn't it do you wonders to get out, all that fresh air? Dust yourself down, woman, beat off the cobwebs. You never know, Madeline, you might get the bug again just like in the old days. We have a couple of lovely horses, nice and mature, and Old Chapel Boy, he is a saint!"

"Isn't, or, should I say, wasn't he a pointer?"

"Ah, that was years ago. Must be five years ago now. He was a great jumper, but he was a bit small. They tried racing him. He had a super turn of speed, and he won twice over hurdles. But once they put the weight on him he just couldn't carry it. He went show jumping for a year before we bought him, but, sure, he loves life. Has them all following him.

When we take them out he takes charge. Madeline, he would be perfect for you, who hasn't sat on one for a while."

"Five years," Madeline said.

"Is it that long?" Edwina stopped suddenly to consider something she just couldn't countenance. "Five years. My God."

"It's been so long I would most likely fall off. I really don't know, Edwina. Maybe I will give it a go. What harm could it do? I will have to ride out for a while to see if I still have what it takes."

Madeline finished her drink and was about to refill before suddenly remembering herself and her company.

She said, "God, Edwina, I never even offered you a cup of tea!"

Smiling, Mrs. Edwards said, "Tea is for those who have easy lives, Madeline. I will have a Scotch. One of your famous ones. It will warm me for the walk back down."

Madeline obliged, delighted and relieved. She helped herself to vodka and made Edwina one of her renowned measures of Scotch.

"I hear you let Madge Butler go."

"Indeed, Edwina, you heard right. Isn't she busy enough with Michael Harrington? To be honest her position here was becoming a bit of a luxury. I mean it was all right when Georgina was younger."

She handed Edwina her drink, and Edwina accepted it gratefully, sipping it slowly to begin with, then drinking a mouthful. She shuddered. Madeline made them strong.

"She is a wily one. I met her recently. She was at the lifeboat dinner with Himself. She has put on weight, but it hasn't slowed her down or eased her at all. Still the sharp tongue. He ignores her, and she runs after him like he is a celebrity. She orders his food for him, starters and everything. He sits back allowing her, and she flashes her jewellery. Michael Harrington tells whoever will listen that he didn't buy it, joking that she robbed a bank and has the money hidden."

Madeline was silent for a minute before rising to pull the curtains. Outside was the sycamore, a dark shadow standing sentry; the moon was resting beyond a thick cloud with sharp bursts of light striking tiny areas of water. Glaring headlights burning the edges of field's dark ditches were illuminated suddenly before the pleasure was withdrawn and darkness reborn.

"I often wonder about her, Edwina. She lives a great life, you know, for a woman of her background. I mean, her mother lived in poverty most of her life, and she hardly gave her daughter an education. For a girl who is a housekeeper and a bar worker, she does very well."

Edwina, stirred by the whiskey, replied, "Rumour has it that she has bailed him out. That is why he is so close to her. The business in the village is gone. There is barely enough for one bar, never mind three. If you open all year round, with a few stragglers during the week you are depending on the weekends. The summer is good, but, by God, my dear, the winters are dreary and quiet."

"She got in with him after the tragedy. I thought that was it; she comforted him then."

Madeline awaited Edwina's reply.

"Perhaps she did." Then Edwina, lowering her voice unnecessarily, said, "Some say she was comforting him for a long time before the tragedy. Take that as you will, but she is a dark horse, and if she has bailed him out where did the money come from?"

Madeline swallowed the last of her vodka, unsure whether to refill immediately or to wait for a minute acting like it was unimportant. To her surprise Edwina agreed to another. She made this one a little weaker, as experience told her that Edwina was a lightweight. Over-indulgence could lead to her staying the night, or, worse, still needing a lift home.

"I wonder, will they ever find him? Doubt it, Madeline. Don't suppose there will be much left at this stage. Isn't it a funny thing? You know, there you go living your life and everything makes sense. You get up each morning, start the day with vigour, and you meet people and they meet you in the daylight hours. Little do you know what lies in wait for you around the corner. All those years Donal came into the hotel. Love him or hate him, there he was with his dirty suits and the dandruff caked on his shoulders.

"He could be funny, too, in a sarcastic fashion, and I stood behind the bar serving him drink, watching him descend into hell when he had too much. The anger in him was stunning, and he insulted me and the rest of the clientele. You would see him in all his different guises. If memory serves me correctly, for a few years when he first started the auctioneering he wasn't so bad. But he had a few regular cronies. Then Johnny Hartnett—remember him? God, he is dead years—they had some great arguments."

Edwina stopped in her tracks like she wanted to hold the image in her head.

"Wasn't he a solicitor?"

Madeline looked directly at Edwina who was succumbing to the effects of drink. She held her glass lazily. Madeline worried if she loosened her grip any further it would fall unto the floor.

Edwina confirmed by a nod of the head. "People are funny, you know, and time—it just sails by, Madeline, and none of us knows what's going to happen to us. You know, there is something I have always wanted to ask you, but I have never had the courage. I suppose, with the night that's in it, maybe this is the right time? Maybe it isn't, but, sure, I will ask you anyway. What the hell did you see in him, and how in the name of God, my dear, did you put up with him?"

Madeline, still eyeing the whiskey glass, wasn't prepared for the question. At first she was flustered.

"He was different when I first met him. You won't believe me when I tell you he was shy in his own way, if a little arrogant like his father. When it came to knowing things—anything to do with business or politics he was a real expert—but he was shy, for a man, you know."

Edwina indicated that she didn't know by smartly emptying her whiskey, holding her glass out for a refill. Madeline resisted the temptation to bring the whiskey bottle over. She collected the empty glass calmly and resumed speaking as she poured Edwina's first.

"He wasn't amorous or vulgar like some men, you know. His people had money from their shoe shops, but they were ordinary in comparison to my family. The money was made. It didn't travel through time like ours, so I suspect he always saw himself at a disadvantage. I think it made him insecure and shy sometimes."

Madeline poured her own, making it a neat double. Edwina took a tidy sup when her drink arrived, her taste buds activated by her previous efforts.

"Revisionism is so unhealthy, Edwina. What I would do today I may regret next week. Surely all our efforts are made in one complete moment, influenced by the ready information we have available. Unfortunately the gods give us no clear view of the future. I guess we may never bother to do anything if they did. I mean, if you met Freddie for the first time this morning, would you marry him?"

Edwina shifted in her seat. For a moment she was insulted, but then soft tears filled her eyes and she said, "I love Freddie, Madeline. I always have, and I always will."

Madeline, stirred by the sight of tears, went to her and sat close, patting the back of Edwina's head like a child. Taking the almost-empty glass of whiskey, she placed it safely on the table.

"Now, Mrs. Edwards, I shall walk you home. It is a beautiful night, and I can bring Bob for company on the way back. Now how is that?"

Edwina, wiping her eyes with the back of her left hand, half laughed. "Forgive me, dear, it has been a while since I drank whiskey. You know I nearly lost Freddie last year."

"Come on, Bob. Stop with your nonsense, Edwina. We all need a good cry every now and then. It doesn't do us any harm."

Bob, who had been lying under the window sill to escape the oppressive heat of the fire, was on his feet barking loudly.

"He is so excited," Mrs. Edwards said. "Mummy is taking you for walkies."

Bob barked even louder his feet, skidding on the wooden floor as he tried to burst through the door.

"Don't let me forget my jacket. It's hanging on the hall stand. I will need it coming back!"

"Yes, you will," Edwina said.

"It is to be very cold later on, isn't it?" Madeline said.

Wood Point, A few years ago
26.

Kate was tired thinking of him. She was waking night after night without proper sleep. The room always seemed different from the one that she fell asleep in—a jolt, then a frightening twenty seconds until the room was restored, coming slowly back to itself. The dreams were vivid, the battle never won. It just raged and she endured it. Soon she would have to get up and get the kids dressed and ready for Myrna. It had been a dreadful night with the wind lashing against the window, and someone had left a bin out. It rolled from one side of the path to the other, making a constant rattle.

Kate wondered, Did he sleep through it? He says he doesn't sleep much. He tends to sit up all night working. If not working, thinking. Jack is in danger of thinking himself away. It is not good to be always thinking. The mind needs to slow down, turn off. Anyhow, he is gone ridiculous and fanciful in truth. He is probably half mad.

The last time he was on about the field on the far side, the one with the single tree. He was on about it as he imagined a scene from a Mills and Boon historical romance, with him as the gamekeeper and her as the heroine, a posh lady who normally wouldn't look twice at the help. One day their eyes meet whilst she is shooting pheasant with a suitor—a nephew of the Lord Shannon, no less.

Secretly they ride out to the field with the single tree frolicking in the shade. The horses, standing by aimlessly, await their riders who are now making love. He caresses her breasts, which are falling from the bodice of her velvet dress. She lies naked with him, the gamekeeper. He kisses her violently but then softly. The coarse lips of him cover her mouth, their lips meeting. She stares over his shoulder at the vast sky. She screams through the bare branches of the tree. Digging her long nails into his shoulders, she draws blood.

Such nonsense for a grown man! You would think a man would have better things to be doing with his day than nonsense of that sort. Then of course he starts going on about the walkway and how it brings him ideas, clears his mind. Allows him to imagine, gives him room to create. If only she had room to create with dirty nappies and screaming kids. Jack Browne loves himself and he is so self-indulgent. The text messages, declaring his undying love. Now, if it were a young fellow from the village who was smitten... But Jack Browne was a seasoned campaigner and cynic. This same man had lost his marriage and his daughter was gone. She never visits Wood Point.

If Ted O' Reilly could see her now, unable to move with the weight of the world on her shoulders. Didn't he say it? When they first met he was stealing her, for the men in Wood Point are blind, they must be to allow such a beauty slip through their fingers. Only palaver men would say anything to pacify you, have you thinking you're gorgeous. Sure, she was never gorgeous. The only man who ever took a shine to her was Thomas Crowe.

Kate heard Fiona cry. It was gentle, like the first sound of the day. She was calling for company. She was always lonely when she woke. No sound from Sarah. Like her father, scheming, thinking, or maybe still sound asleep, another two minutes and up.

"Jesus Christ, I will be late for work if I leave it any longer," Kate said loudly to remind herself of the time. But her mind was still racing on.

He says very little about his daughter. He goes on about dreams, always dreams, like his world is made of dreams. He was remarking how her childhood flew by, like she was only a child and then suddenly he looked one day and she was a woman. Are all fathers like that? Do they see a whole childhood whistle by in a flash? Keeping the wind chime on the wall. It was hers and he keeps it by the window with the cross.

Jack sits there all day, a grown man tapping and typing, and every now and then he paces the room to give his fingers and eyes a rest. What a way for a man to live. It is so solitary. He is always alone, just him looking out the bay window at people walking dogs—'the joggers and the plodders,' as he likes to say—traipsing by day after day, hour after hour. He sits there watching them.

Kate wondered. Is he a pervert? Is he spying on women? All writers are perverts, she thought. You would have to be a pervert to think up the rubbish. You know, he frightens himself with his thoughts. Imagine doing that, thinking something for yourself and then getting scared. He said it's visceral, whatever that means. His mind races all the time, and he gets exhausted by it. He goes down by Lyall's farm and talks to horses. Only horses would want to talk to him. I suppose they don't even want to listen to him! Horse talk—horse shit!

He says if Ted O' Reilly doesn't want to look after me, then he will; imagine that! I would be mortified for my mother, and Myrna has him sussed. 'You wouldn't know what he was about to come out with,' she says. 'Anyway I wouldn't trust him as far as I would throw him. He would sleep with anyone. All those Dublin arty types are the same. I would say he is one of those hedonists.'

Kate slipped out of bed. Her feet were cold against the wooden floor. She drew the curtains and the light hurt her eyes.

Enough of him, she mused. She couldn't take any more of him.

Anyhow he is miles too old, and how would he support us? Ted O' Reilly isn't blessed but he is steady, and steady is what we need. Myrna can have him. He is closer to her in age.

Fiona cried louder, and this time Kate went to her. "All right, chicken."

Fiona stood in the cot, her eyes wet, trying to smile through her sad face, her lip dropping.

"It's okay, chicken, Mammy's here."

Fiona reached for her, and Kate picked her up cuddling her to her breasts. She walked into Sarah's room. She was almost out of the cot. Much too big for it now. She had to tell Ted O' Reilly that she needed a bigger cot. Maybe they do grow too fast?

Sarah was cross in the mornings. It was taking an age for her to eat her breakfast. Fiona flicked her food as far as possible, shaking her spoon. The further it went the better. A look of glee crossed her face when it landed in Sarah's hair. Kate ran warm water in the sink to wipe Sarah's face, using the corner of a J cloth. Fiona took longer. She wetted some kitchen towel, getting frustrated when it started to break apart. Sarah had an inkling of how to dress herself, but there wasn't time and Fiona threw a tantrum getting a clean vest over her head. For a second Kate was afraid to tug at it, save it might hurt her. But one last pull over her nose removed the soiled one to be replaced with a bright clean one.

Blue whiteness, Kate thought. Now what is that?

When she had them in the car she laughed at their expectant faces. She could be bringing them anywhere, yet with their shining skins and bright eyes they trusted her.

"Come on, we will go to Auntie Myrna's."

Both girls smiled at the mention of her name. Kate drove up the main street, the village deserted. A car pulled into the pier followed by a jeep.

Only for the fishing we would die altogether, she thought, and then Jack came back spinning around in her head.

"I don't know which pier you should dive from Kate. Maybe Burren. What do you say?"

Mad is what she would say. Diving into the tide—is he mad? I'd let him drown. It is as sad as talking to horses, and he tried to explain that but it made little sense either.

"You understand loneliness, Kate, what it is like to be completely isolated. That is what I really like about you!"

"Nonsense. Me, speaking fluent horse. If I told that to Ted O' Reilly, he'd throw me out on my ear for God's sake."

Fiona was getting heavier and Sarah more of a madam. Myrna made such a fuss of them, and the girls responding by acting extra good.

"Kiss Mammy goodbye."

They did, each kiss soft and wet, and she loved the smell of their skin.

"Bye," Sarah said, and Fiona tried to speak but it was more of a screech.

The road out to Timoleague was busy with a van and two cars ahead most of the way. She was late again and she couldn't make up time. Maybe on the main road but sometimes that was worse. Across the estuary she saw the hill and the single tree.

"He is nuts. I wouldn't be doing anything in that field with the world looking on. You could be seen from here."

Concentrating on the series of left-turning bends, the car bumping over manholes, the road layout made you hug the left-hand verge. She twisted her way to the bridge. A single swan gaped at the mouth of the river.

The last time she saw him he was sad, and he spoke about all these dream sequences from his book. He went on about the tree and the couple in costume. Kate found herself screaming at the kids not to touch his laptop, which as usual was open on the small table by the window. From nowhere Jack produced the cardboard box his new printer had arrived in. The girls thought it was heaven.

Kate refused his offer of tea or a beer. He closed off the computer, shutting it down. Turning to face her he said, "All of the things I say to you, I see them through this bay window."

Kate laughed nervously. "You're like the woman on the television years ago. Remember her? She used to hold up the hand mirror and say, 'I can see Kate and Sarah and Fiona, and I can see Jack.' I never knew how she did it. Well, not till much later!"

Jack laughed. "No, I don't mean it like that. It is just when I pause and look out I imagine those things in my mind's eye. They don't really exist in here. I guess they belong to a world that's out there someplace."

Kate smiled at him. She wanted to tell him he was really mad but she hadn't the heart.

"I was thinking of you," he said.

"You were?"

"Yeah, I was thinking about you, what you were like growing up. I imagined you sitting under the pines—you know, out the point before the Fuchsia Walk. You were looking out over the sea, and you were so at ease with the huge world around you. And then I could see you running through the wood and you were dreaming of fairies. You thought they lived in the holes in the tree trunks and there you were, sweet innocent Kate..."

The road to Clonakility was quiet but it demanded concentration. It narrowed in the most unimaginable places, and there were lots of side roads and boreens. A tractor could pull out in front of you at the last minute. As it was she made good time until a cattle truck pulled out of the road that leads to the agricultural college. She was already ten minutes late. He was so quirky, but did she need quirky? And him older quirky. Would he be too much? All this talk of fairies and beauty, the landscape and people's true feelings. His arguments for honesty she could live with, but honesty can hold a price. You wouldn't want to be that honest. Hardly do you good.

Then Kate did the age thing. What age will he be when I am fifty? That's very old and if he was sick again, I will be a

nurse. So many things to weigh up, girl. See, he thinks that
he is a smart man from Dublin, but they don't understand the
rules of village life. The people round here have known me
all my life, and if I change they will know and they will want
to know why and who is calling to see me, and the scandal
will affect the girls and my mother.

Kate braked hard as she reached the T-junction, turning
left for Clon. Two minutes and she would be there suitably
chastised. Yet Mick the supervisor wouldn't say a word. He
loved her dearly like a father. He'd be making excuses
already.

It is very fine for Jack to say, 'Grab the moment, don't let
it slip. How often in life do you find love?'

Well maybe he had found it, but Kate was not so sure.

He doesn't see the fallout of his actions. Whatever
happened to him first time round is still coming at him,
stabbing him in the chest, and now he wants to brave another
knife attack. People who live in cities can hide, but there is
no hiding in Wood Point. Where do you go for a walk or a
drink? What will people say when I turn up at mass? The
girls will grow up with the stigma. 'The mother left her
marriage for an older Dublin fellow, some sort of a writer but
I never read anything by him.' That is exactly what they will
be saying. Jack Browne, you have not thought it through,
living as you do staring out the window. The world you see is
distorted, unreal. The actions are based on emotions. These
emotions, Jack, how real are they? Do you live in a happily-
ever-after movie?

She found a space. Gathering her bag she went flying. It
was starting to rain, a few drops to wet her head. No time to
dry off. She stood for an hour making sausage rolls in pastry.
The sausage mix was thick and the pastry was good quality,
nice and light. People moved about her serving, and some of
the customers had loud voices. Funny how the women were
shrill and the men deep base. Each and every one out and
about the normal day.

She thought of Jack cajoling her at the rocks in Ballinglanna. She was so scared she might be seen from the road, but it was late in the evening and the road was quiet, most of the time anyway. The sea was dark on one side, like a giant tried to throw his coat over it but only half did it. The clouds gathered high in the sky over Galley head but beyond that she saw a deep blue. Lines of sunlight rode the waves, the sea rolling in, churning. It made faces in the froth. Each time it hit the sand the wash covered a different distance till she had to jump backwards to avoid getting her feet wet. Large waves full of foam sprang without explanation, splashing the rocks at the foot of the cliff below the summer cottages. Swirling, it funnelled round the bend to Simon's Cove.

"I don't believe you. You can't see it, Kate. Maybe it's what happens when you have a near-death experience, and you just live on in a new intensity!"

His words were hushed by the wind. She looked up at the road like she expected a crowd to have gathered at the wall, some of them cheering, others shaking their fists.

"Are you saying I missed out, Jack? Like you are recommending it? I find life intense enough with two little ones and Ted O' Reilly away for so long."

Jack always went quiet when she mentioned Ted, but he made sure never to put him down in anyway. Jack smiled at her when the wash almost ran over her shoes. Once more she stepped back, her feet sinking in the tiny stones.

"I am not making my point properly, Kate, or you are just teasing me. I know we have to live, work, go to the toilet, mind children, get toothaches. I know all of that, but what you are saying to me is there is nothing else. No feeling, no intensity, nothing more than the humdrum of everyday existence with the odd treat thrown in. You are the model citizen: I am born, I live, I marry, I procreate, then I die. Job done!"

Jack had an air of excitement in his voice that unnerved her. She was silent for a moment, looking up at the road. A small truck was coming down the hill by the Marian Statue. It reached the flat turning left and then slightly uphill, passing the wall. She turned her back on it, facing out to sea Jack shielded her with his body till the small truck disappeared.

"Was it up there you had the caravan?" Kate pointed to the cluster of summer homes.

"No," Jack said. "That was just a headland. Nothing on it, only a field. It was up there. Just us. One little caravan in that small field."

He pointed to the small field falling to the cliffs behind them. Kate smiled thinking it cute.

"Jack, don't get me wrong. I know what you mean. You know, in my job I see people running around, fussing over nothing, and all sorts come to the counter, you know? Fat people, skinny ones. Some people are so old and frail they can hardly carry their shopping bags. Little kids with notes, Mammy's orders written down. People just do their best. The world is theirs. As well they might not see it or smell it like you, but it belongs to them just as much.

"You know, you can see what you want to see too. Those clouds over the headland, they are full of shapes and images just like wallpaper. And when you peel it off the wall, you get maps of the world. At the end of the day we have to live in the reality we make. You confuse me, Jack, showing me things and saying stuff that's quirky and off-the-wall. I don't know if it is the way I was brought up or just this place, but life is very simple Jack."

As they climbed the rocks back to his secret slipway he was quiet, and she was sorry she had taken him the way she did as it was all very beautiful and romantic. Yet the wind on her face and the sun on the water didn't strike away the fear that was in her. It was a strange fear in that Jack didn't present a threat in himself, but everything he said or joked about did.

When they reached the cars he said softly, "Kate, you think I don't know about mundane and every day, like I live in bubble wrap. I did my years of normality: following the rules, never going with my gut instinct. Where did it get me? I lost my marriage. I ended up in a hospital bed. My daughter is a stranger. So what would you do? It might never come round again to find a person you love."

Kate felt it was her turn to be angry. "You keep saying that word, love. What do you mean by love, Jack? I will leave Ted and move in with you and you will take his kids on and me. We will all live happy ever after in Wood Point. Where do you want us to go, Jack? Do you want us to leave here forever? What about my family? You know, I love the fact that you love me, but what is this love? Where does it come from? I mean, did you love your wife when you met her? Did you? When you married her, did you really love her, Jack?"

She opened the door to her car, letting it go. It creaked as it swung twice on its own.

"You are too intense, Jack, too wound up. It is like I couldn't call round to see you, just drop by with the kids, chat and walk together on the walkway. I didn't even mind if Ted O' Reilly saw us. But you couldn't leave it at that. There are times when all I want is what you want. Don't think I don't daydream. I love walking the beach with you, sipping beer in the garden. I love the sound of your voice, and those eyes. You are such a gentle person. But I can't have you, Jack. Let it go, will you? For me? Just let it go."

He looked at her sadly as she went to close the door. Kate went to speak but he interrupted her. "You stay in this life, Kate, and you will do the same things for the rest of your days. I am not offering you anything, save that I love you. Do you know what that means, for someone to actually love you? Think about it, for God's sake. How many people actually love each other? The girls will grow and leave you, and in twenty-five years you will still be going to the Fisherman's with Ted. Or worse, you will be sitting up nights waiting for him to come home to you, rueing the life you could have had..."

This time Kate cut in. "Jack that is my choice. Maybe that is what I want. Have you even considered that? You know, you are a decent man, but you are arrogant. You think the only life I can have is with you. Don't you worry, I can be happy without you. Maybe it is something you have to learn, my man: self-reliance."

As she was about to leave she got angry with herself for what she had said because a part of her still believed in him.

"Then why do you look at me the way you do, Kate?"

Kate stared at him, shocked, his words stuck somewhere within.

"Why, Kate? Why? The longing glances and the emotive expression. Everything you don't say says, 'I love you too, Jack.' So I go away from you feeling so loved, and then I don't hear from you or you say stuff like you have just said to me. I dunno, Kate, it is like you are saving a drowning man, but then, heck, you decide to let him drown anyway."

"I am with Ted O' Reilly, Jack. That is it."

Kate left without looking back at Jack's forlorn figure.

She carried the baking tray to the oven, joking with Mick who was carving ham at the counter. The shop was busy with people looking damp and tired. For a moment she saw the world as painted grey, and she felt a sudden pang in her stomach as she was frightened by that single thought.

Wood Point, Many years ago
27.

Michael Harrington was a free man, as they say. I guess he only did what free men do. There he was, him on one side, and Madge Butler on the other, and me stuck right in the middle. For the most part she was decent enough without being all over me. She helped me get dressed in the mornings, picking out my clothes, and she put on my breakfast most days. And even when the weather was warm she made my favourite "ready brek." How bad?

She was good about my movies. When Michael Harrington might be cross or irritable, she would stick the movies on and sit me down, turning the sound up where he might turn it down. Needless to say, but after a sensible time, she all but moved in. I often caught glimpses of her coming and going from the bathroom. She was a hefty woman, but there was a pleasure in her that Michael Harrington could see and I suppose it wasn't my place to deny him.

Word in Wood Point spreads very fast, and the word was they were getting on great. Some of the gossip talked of marriage. Others whispered, "Why should she? It is she that has the money."

In my short life it was this kind of logic that baffled me; it was akin to the mystery of distance and of numbers, the interior of a grand piano, the motivation of the chap that piles six-inch nails into a homemade bomb. Why? I ask myself this and so many other questions. It is easier for me to file it under world wonders. Then I get to thinking: do we wonder collectively, or is there a guy who sits in a small room someplace that does all of our wondering for us? He gets up each morning with a list of wonders, and he spends his day wondering. I'd bet they use him to compile boys' own annuals and children's encyclopedias'.

I often meant to get Michael Harrington to write him a letter for me, basically asking him why anyone would marry for money. Why are people valued for money? I might even stretch to other questions about the universe, like why it is so important we know the exact distance between two points. It seems to be immeasurably important. The footballer scores from twenty yards in the fifty-fifth minute, so we can marry for money, have kids for luck. Not that I was lucky, you understand.

As far as I could see Michael Harrington was playing it cool. Why should he change the situation? He had what he wanted without the certificate. Yet despite her size Madge Butler was a real one to go, judging by the sounds reverberating from their room on Sunday mornings in particular. It always started with her laughing followed by a deafening silence. After a bit she wailed like she was standing on something sharp or she just suddenly got a cramp. He was always quiet; it was she who made all the noise.

Later when she made me my "Ready Brek" I could see the joy dancing in her. She was light on her feet for such a big woman. She made my cereal kind of crusty with some of the lumpy bits still powdery like they needed more milk.

The customers really took to Madge. As time went on she became the face of the pub, or, as others cruelly put it, the jugs of the pub. I suppose it is only fair to say that Michael Harrington was the happiest I have ever seen him, and that's including when Mammy Rosie was around. He was rarely happy back then, a tragic relationship of which I was the rotten fruit.

Jack Browne dropped in the odd time to drink his pint and listen to Pee Wee Flynn spoof about the hurling. I would sit watching my films, and he would always check and see which one I had on. No matter which one it was, he always said the same thing: "Nice one Sean." Sometimes if I left the box on the table, he would pick it up and read the blurb. I noticed he read everything like who directed the film or who wrote the music, the cinematographer, etc. till he got right down to the small writing at the end, stuff I could barely see, never mind read.

He might glance at the screen and watch intently as Jason Robards tried to hide his wound from Charles Bronson. He would watch as Margaret came by for her crisps and Coke. He would be back at the bar. When she would go to the microphone and the music from "Once Upon a Time in the West" filled the air, he would see the lines of dust rise from the half-open door and he would catch my stare as she would go, "Di da di da...da da...dah dah dah dahh, di a dah da dadada." I could see him dreaming as Margaret would make the wonderful sound, and I knew he was thinking of me and Caw and Kate.

*

Suddenly Caw found himself once again. He was reborn, finding energy he thought was lost now. His waking thoughts were bright, feeling an excitement he last felt way back when he was a young crow. He met her over in Barryroe by accident. He was hanging around the skip, not out of any particular need but more out of habit. She was with two old crows from Lislee. They were walking around the skip looking for cheap stuff dropped by younger birds. Caw watched her and liked the way she held her head up high.

She was proud; he could see that. She nodded at him politely when their eyes met and she picked up a full slice of mouldy bread with dignity. The old crows flapped and she gave the piece over to them without fuss.

Later Caw made some enquires regarding her, but little seemed to be known. It was only afterwards when he had bumped into a couple of secret service guys down the village that he found anything out. The young crow dressed immaculately, complete with tuxedo, said she was originally from Enniskeane but her people were from Barryroe, and after her abusive partner took a grain or two of farmers poison she came back here. His friend, an older crow also dressed in tuxedo, remarked that despite her partner's reputation she was well-liked, and evidently despite the awful life she had led she remained upbeat and full of joy.

So Caw came to meet her, once more by accident as he stopped by Lislee Church for a rest and another time by design when she told him she was a regular at the creamery skip on Fridays as that was a good day for a bargain. Over time of course, Caw, being Caw, fell in love with her, and after a gracious amount of time she came to the abbey for a visit.

Caw knew she was mightily impressed with his set up, and he was sure that she thought him a great catch with his penthouse apartment, the grass roof garden, and the magnificent view over the estuary. She soon took to calling by unannounced, and he found her easy and full of fun. She took to flying off suddenly and without warning, forcing Caw to chase her over the adjacent fields. She would fly low, skimming the rear of the two horses at the hill top they were not impressed by the aerodynamics. She would go fast, Caw following and almost hitting the darker horse. He surged high to catch her as she drew breath in a chestnut tree.

Soon she took to staying overnight where they would huddle from the cold the old turret window barely shielding the east wind. In the mornings Caw, with a burst of energy, flew low over the algae searching out the barren sand, looking for fat worms for breakfast. He skidded to a halt in a clearing, finding broken mussel shells discarded by fat grey crows. This was heaven, and she would love her breakfast. When she moved in it was his duty to give her a name, as female crows are named by their male partners. He chose to call her Troya whereas his first wife had been Susa. In crow Troya meant "new and unblemished"; Susa just meant "good" or "well-intentioned."

Late at night when the full moon washed the ancient abbey walls, and the fields were stirring only with the brush of the wind, Caw felt her cosy against him and she stroked his feathers like a mother does to a young chick. He could sense the pain leave him as his mind cleared with each stroke, and the heaviness that had engulfed him for so long dissipated in these soft moments. He was no longer angry. He no longer wanted to exact revenge on Jack Browne.

She told him of her misery and the awful death that befell the crow she had once loved and had given her three sons and two daughters, of which only three survived. How he had got very fond of the farmer's grain, and despite her warnings he kept returning to the same place, the same field, till one day when he came home he looked wretched, foaming at the mouth, his eyes red in his head. In her panic she wanted to fly off, but he fell over right in front of her, blood oozing from his eye sockets and his torso rigid. He lay there for hours, unable to move or make a sound. She watched him as the life left him slowly, his mouth opening and closing desperate sighs. Troya went to a nearby stream to get water. She passed it to him, cupping his beak, but most of it was lost on the short journey, and even the purest of water sickened him further till it was no longer any use and his eyes went dead.

*

I don't know how much of Troya is wishful thinking by Caw? Sometimes when Michael Harrington walked with me I would look up at his turret, but I only ever saw him alone. But in fairness he did chill out over Jack Browne, which came as a relief to me, seeing that I had much in common with the writer whom nobody knew because he wasn't famous. Once when Caw spotted us walking past he sort of made himself scarce, flying low across the weed. Skimming the hard sand beyond, I thought he was trying to show off his prowess, his natural windsurfing agility. But maybe he just got excited and wanted to distract me from looking at the turret more closely.

However Jack Browne swears he saw the two of them frolicking in Lyall's field both before and after the sheep were there. He says she sat idling on the top of the old ruin standing alone in the main field, whilst Caw did all sorts of acrobatic aerodynamics to impress her. Often when he walked by they would sail through the air up sides and down sides, landing on the grass veranda of the penthouse. He had tried valiantly to get a photograph, but each time he primed the camera they flew off becoming lost in the network of trees that divided the fields. Jack Browne of course fancies himself as a photographer, but, alas, he is better known for his writing, which says it all in a way.

Michael Harrington turned at the white gates and for whatever reason I walked alongside of him, although I usually traipsed along a few yards after him so I could stick my tongue out at the passing cars. We came by the sloping fields of young horses dancing across their paddocks, their mothers scolding them. In another paddock two horses had their first kiss and the mare ran away to stand still by the fence. The sunlight washed the hills in deep green and like marauding Indians cattle gathered, preparing to attack. The fields I liked because whoever was sent out to measure them was a drunk or an idiot, his divisions bordered by insignificant hedgerows mocking the small dark trees bred for purpose. The water to my left became dark with the sun, trapped somewhere, fighting a lonely battle.

Michael Harrington stopped to look across at what was now just a swirling pool of current and counter current. It was like the milk in the saucer swishing as you tried to bring it across the kitchen to leave on the back step for the cat. He stared at Burren pier long and hard. I stood by him and wanted to tug at his sleeve but was unable to do so. With the sun lost, the east wind raided long shadows from

Garrettstown. Millions of insects gathered; they rolled
abrasive against the sea in tiny beads of steel. Behind, the
hills rolled and the guy who made these knew how to make
hills. I could see how he drew them in giant crayon. I didn't
like his cattle, though; I wondered how they could stand
straight. Michael Harrington and I stood together in awe as
the saucer swirled and drops fell on the lino. Wipe the floor,
and I guess I knew why my man in the room made up the
crap about not crying over spilled milk.

After a while of staring and saying nothing Michael
Harrington moved on. For probably the first time in years I
saw his face. How old he looked. Age was eating into him.
He was putting on weight. Not too obvious, mind, but around
his chin and his upper arms and his behind. He surprised me,
placing his hand on my shoulder, more to keep me from
wandering than out of any obvious sign of affection. He told
me that we are here alone, always alone. He told me to
continue on my own, to get used to it. Despite what people
tried to get you to believe, loneliness was a good thing, a
natural state. This way we make all of our important journeys
and we will be judged by how we handle it. Our futures
depended on how we manage it. He said he thought I was
particularly good at being alone.

Afterwards I sat in the kitchen drawing, and he poked his
head in to see what I was up to. I was drawing figures
standing by the water looking over the estuary. It was so far
to the other side that I included the red Dutch barn and the
field with the single tree. I dotted silly cattle here and there,
some lying on their sides where they fell over. Michael
Harrington looked at the picture for a while before placing
his hand on my shoulder once more.

"Why do you do that?" he said to me. "Why do you distort
everything, Sean? It doesn't look like that look in the
photograph." He pointed to the framed sea view picture on
the wall over the fireplace. He removed his hand just as
quick. I didn't mind; I just missed the warmth of it.

Wood Point, A few years ago
28.

Ted came home. He spent a week acclimatising, which meant long visits to the Harbour Bar, before he went into himself in the second week because it was nearly time to go back. He spent time with the children, knocking great fun out of Sarah who walked with him around the green holding his hand. The look of delight on both their faces made Kate feel guilty, and he was good with Fiona who was sick with an ear infection. He held her in his arms for hours rocking her to sleep and whispering into her ear.

Kate tried to talk to him, asking him about how he felt about things, did he miss the children, did he miss her?

Ted would sit back, lazily stretching in his armchair. His stock answer was, "Of course I do, and it won't be forever."

Sometimes when he came back from the pub feeling amorous, he would grab her waist when she was cooking supper.

"When I come home, I am thinking of going fishing, getting my own boat. It is a hard life, Kate, but there is money to be made."

Kate leaned back into him to show him affection. She could smell the drink off of him, but he was only in good form. He wasn't fully drunk.

"I want to see the girls do well, school and all. Girls need to be one step ahead, don't they?"

By bedtime he was sleepy, having helped himself to beer from the fridge. Kate lay awake beside him listening to him snore. He turned on his side and the snoring ceased, his breathing a little heavy. When it was time for him to leave, she made him a good breakfast as it was the last decent sausage he would have for ages. She did him two fried eggs

and three rashers; he smiled when she added the black and
white Clonakility pudding to his plate.

"This is grand," he said breaking up a tiny piece of sausage
for Sarah. He had a game where he pretended he was going
to eat it himself, yet he let his hand fall in such a way that the
fork appeared right in front of her mouth. She would take the
morsel of sausage, and Ted would feign shock and surprise to
find his fork empty when he went to take a bite. Sarah
thought the game was hilarious looking at Kate each time he
did it. Fiona, looking on from the high chair, was laughing
too, even if she was just amused by the general banter of
those around her.

When Ted left Kate made up her mind to tell Jack Browne
once and for all that there was nothing happening or indeed
that nothing was going to happen. She was determined he
should know that her marriage was more important than
anything. She believed Ted. Eventually he would come home
to Wood Point for good and set up on his own fishing. The
money was better in fishing now, even if it was hard going.
There was no time for carrying on, and the girls needed
stability.

Yet when she saw him on the walkway she avoided him,
passing by unobtrusively, hoping he wouldn't notice her car.
He was looking out over the estuary, stopping at the disused
jetty before Seaview. Kate decided she should just not see
him at all. It was for the best. She would make no contact and
Ted O' Reilly would come home and that would be the end
of that.

It was getting late on a Friday night a week later when she
drank a whole bottle of wine and was starting on another. It
had been a hard day at work. The shop was really busy. The
people seemed exasperated by the cold weather. They wore
too many clothes, and the false heat of the store rendered
them cross. She saw customers argue with the counter staff
about the quality of hams and the freshness of breads. She
was busy making take-home dinners and filling trays made of

foil. The day dragged and somewhere mid-morning she felt sad. Ted hadn't rang the previous day when he said he would, and Fiona had another ear infection.

The weekend beckoned, but what of it? The same as it ever was—cooking, washing, and watching the television. The rest of people her age might be treated to a meal out or a few drinks in the Fisherman's. Not her. The long dark nights were alone.

When she collected the kids from Myrna's, Fiona had a high temperature. She was thinking of calling the South doc, but it went down fast after Calpol. Still, she was extra tired and Kate managed to have both of them down by half-past-seven, which allowed her to relax. She put on the TV. Keeping the sound low she sleepily raised her glass of red to toast herself. Soon her mind's wanderings started to make sense and the brick walls she had built began to crumble.

She didn't love Ted. That was the whole problem. She most likely had never loved him. She reached an age where the expectation weighed her down. Marriage or spinsterhood: no brainer. Along came Ted. He had reached the same point but along a different path. After a few awkward nights out came that one night down in Broadstrand. She gave him what he really craved and that was it. He was smitten. If this was to be his life's pleasure, she only had to repeat it for him.

A year later they were married. A photograph of their wedding sat high on the shelf in the corner. She looked at it gathering dust up there with the old books nobody wanted to read. She thought he looked well, but she was very thin. She didn't eat for a year beforehand, and that dress was swimming on her. She didn't like her hair either, thinking she should have got highlights at her fringe. Kate thought how men get away with it. A nice haircut, a shave, and a shower, and just turn up. All will be fine.

She didn't like his suit either. He looked well in it, but the jackets weren't nice. They didn't slim him down. He started the day well, and in his own quiet way he hid his nerves and just got on with it. It was a while since she got the photographs out and looked through them. Once upon a time it had been a regular occurrence, inviting the girls around, lots of wine, looking at photos, laughing at how they looked all those years ago, their stupid hairstyles and the like.

Jack doesn't have any photos, not even of his daughter. Of course men are like that, especially if they get to do the decorating. Why do they bother having families if they don't want to celebrate them? She imagined his room and him sitting in the dark, banging away on the laptop, drinking his Rose wine. How solitary he is.

She went up to check on the children before descending the stairs. Slowly she opened the second bottle of wine, having trouble with the cork and wondering why they don't just go with the twist caps. It wasn't as if the wine was expensive. When she texted him she did it on a whim. Her words didn't come naturally. She had to stop twice, checking her words carefully.

"What are you up to? Are you around?" Settling for just one line she lazed back in the armchair, thinking it was really time for bed. He could be anywhere. Maybe he was in Dublin or down in the Fisherman's. Friday night. Maybe there was a party in the hotel.

She drank more wine. Then the phone beeped.

"Working away at home. X"

She loved his little Xs, so nice and so romantic in a man. Half-an-hour later she greeted him at the front door. He had a shopping bag containing six cans of Budweiser.

"Have these ages," he said making himself comfortable on a kitchen stool.

Kate was still drinking her wine. "I would love a fag. I wonder, are there any around?"

"You gave them up," Jack said softly.

"I know," she said laughing. "But my mother usually leaves a half-pack behind her when she's babysitting.

Sometimes I throw them in the press for the next time, and then I forget."

"Be careful on the chair, Kate," Jack said standing in case he had to make a mad dash to save her. She fumbled and fiddled lifting plates and brushing against the cups with her sleeve.

"Aha!" she exclaimed, producing a packet that had two cigarettes inside. Getting down off her chair she walked unsteadily to the counter top. "Now, a light?"

"You needn't look at me. I am off them five years."

"Sssh! I think I hear Fiona."

After a pause for silence, she resumed lighting a piece of paper off the cooker ring and burning the top of her cigarette with it.

"Jesus, the smell!" She held the fag at arm's length before returning it to her mouth. Taking a small puff she exhaled immediately. Jack was laughing at her.

"What?"

"I think you are better off without them, Kate. You have forgotten how to even hold one properly. Where will I find a glass?"

Kate put the cigarette safely in the ash tray. The smoke bellowing upwards was disproportionate to what was left of the cigarette. She got a Jack a pint glass.

"I am going to bed soon. Early start in the morning. Don't get too comfortable."

Jack winced like she had suddenly pulled a rug from under him. Kate tried smoking again, but she gave up eventually, stubbing it out.

"I gave them up after Fiona, but, sure, I was never a good smoker anyway. I loved them, you know, but I was never good at holding them or inhaling. Some people are very cool smoking, aren't they, Jack? I'd bet you were a cool smoker."

"The madness is that I didn't start smoking till I was twenty-one. Then I went mad on them." He stopped for a moment in reflection. "I smoked for Ireland. Afterwards we

would go to the pub on a Saturday, and I might smoke twenty
Major and a couple of Hamlet cigars. God knows how many
pints. It might have been quicker injecting morphine."

He didn't like the taste of his Budweiser; it wasn't cold
enough, so he put the pint glass down.

"You look wrecked, Kate. What are you doing to
yourself?"

Kate, surprised, said, "You don't look too great either. Try
looking after two small children, getting up early every day,
and work—it has me worn out." She was looking around for
her wine glass but there was only a tiny drain. "I will have
one of these, and then I am going to bed and you can go
home."

Jack smiled but he was uncomfortable with her tone. She
brushed past him to get a can. He felt the heat of her against
him as she took a phantom step. He instinctively threw his
arms out to save her stumble. Then he felt her lips curve
around his and her body press against him. He somehow
managed to settle his feet to feel the whole mass of her. A
softness crept into his being. He gently rubbed her hair with
his right hand, and she threw her head back taking air. Jack
kissed the nape of her neck, drawing her soft skin, his tongue
a vacuum, till she sighed and her breathing was heavy. He
got the impression she was somewhere far away and she was
leading him there.

"Hold on," Jack said kindly. "What are we doing?"

He longed for her so much but he wanted to make sure it
just wasn't the drink and she knew what she was doing. He
wasn't sure because her eyes were glazed, a mixture of
tiredness and drink, she rested against his leg.

"Mammy," Sarah said standing at the kitchen door she had
pushed open; the child stared at her mother, ignoring Jack.
Kate stood to attention.

"Sarah, what's the matter, did you wake up?" She went to
the child, but rather than lift her into her arms and return her

to bed, Kate brought her to a little armchair in the corner of the room.

"Mammy will put on some cartoons. Should I?"

The child nodded and a video of cartoons came on flashing colours.

Jack, totally perplexed, said, "Hi, Sarah. Is that your favourite?"

The child looked at him but didn't speak.

"She misses her daddy, don't you, my love?" Kate said like she had an audience and felt they needed an explanation.

"I will go," Jack said reaching for his jacket, which was draped carelessly over the stool.

"Daddy will be back home soon." Kate again spoke too loudly, following Jack into the hall.

He leaned forward, kissing her once softly on the lips. She made no effort to avoid him.

"Best get her back to bed."

Kate smiled at him. She looked fresher now, like the arrival of Sarah had woken her and the effects of the drink had dissipated.

"Thanks for dropping round," she said blandly like she was speaking to a tradesman. Jack walked out into the dead of night.

Wood Point, Many years ago
29.

The news that old Chapel Boy was ill didn't deter her as
Mrs. Edwards allowed her take River Boatman, her own
horse. He was a seasoned campaigner and he led the trek of
teenagers up the village passing the harbour. The day was
warm and bright for April with the temperature well up in the
mid-teens. Madeline was sorry she wore her riding jacket as
it was very warm, but she knew she would be glad of it on
the way back.

The teenagers—three girls and a quiet chap from out
towards Barryroe—sat on their horses. The animals walked
lazily, allowing them to chat intermittently, their voices
drowned by the southwesterly wind. She brought them left up
the hill by the farm that corralled a mare with her foal. The
road narrowed, bending right, till they were surrounded by
fields. She saw the lush green hills divided childishly by a
maze of hedge. The original designer was a right joker, she
mused.

She took her charges down the gallops. The land was
owned by an old friend of Edwina's who spent her time in
Spain and Jersey. The farm was leased to a grumpy chap who
hailed from the north of Ireland, but his people had settled in
Bandon years before. Edwina still held the rights to gallop
her horses despite the tenant farmer's disapproval. He just
tended not to cooperate, running his tractor over the lush
grass, leaving tyre marks that filled with water after rain. But
on this day the track was perfect and the horses bounced off
the dry earth.

One of the young girls who was very experienced matched
Madeline stride for stride, hands and heels. Both horses went
flat out till they slowed as the gallops eased into the farm
properly, and the bored buffalo-like cattle stared on with a

worried demeanour. At first Madeline thought them black, but on closer inspection she realised they were in fact a deep brown. It was the glittering sunlight that lent them their sheen.

The boy from near Barryroe followed nervously; it was new to him, and his horse, an experienced old chestnut, did the thinking for him. Madeline restored order and they cantered back to the road in an orderly fashion. She stayed close to the boy in case he needed assistance but he didn't. She patted the mane of the old chestnut when they were stationary to allow a noisy tractor pass.

Following the road downhill, eventually coming out at the bridge at Timoleague, it was time to rest and water the horses. The water was supplied in a series of buckets from Mrs. O' Brien's. She lived in the corner house part hidden by cherry blossoms and white lilac. She was another of Edwina's friends, and although she was out she always left two clean buckets by the outdoor tap. The water was ice cold, and she filled a plastic bottle for herself, the horses resting. She held River Boatman's rein as she sat on the grass overlooking the Argideen.

Memories of her childhood sailed into her consciousness as she remembered the swans and how she and her father would stroll round the bends to see the ducks. She prised him away from the London Times to inhale the fresh breeze, the water at low tide, the mud soft and the birds idling, flapping their wings like they needed practise. Two swans set to flight, their necks stretched erect, gliding through the air with purpose. And this day there were more swans; yet many years separated their flight.

She thought of her husband; his remains may well be buried, sunken in the muddy riverbank. Once he had walked here with her. It was on an Easter Sunday before Georgina was born, and he walked with her reluctantly as it wasn't his scene to walk with his wife. The passersby who beeped only served to embarrass him. He nodded or waved politely but she could tell he was mortified and would have preferred to be anywhere else. She pointed at the plovers and the terns who sat like corks on the water. She asked him to smell the fresh air and the scent sapping from the trees that shadowed the road. She showed him the ladder shapes that ran the length of the grass on the hill on the opposite side, yet he walked with her emotionless without uttering a word while she marvelled at the world around her.

Eventually they ended up sitting at the very spot she sat in now. Donal was quiet; he gazed over to the bridge where young crows learning to fly jumped from the small arch. After a time he spoke and when he spoke he said very little, and yet as she stood and pulled River Boatman by the bit to steady him she now realised that what he actually said explained so much. So much about him—why he became the man he was. He didn't see things like she saw them. For him there was no difference should he find himself staring at a brick wall rather than the beauty before him.

"When I was in boarding school there was a fella there from Timoleague. He was a soft boy. His name was James Burke. One night when we settled down for our sleep, he started to sob. Like, he literally sobbed for ages. The other lads got fed up with him because he was disturbing our sleep, you know, with an early start the next morning. So after an hour of this I asked him to stop. He tried, like, for a minute or two, but he couldn't help it and he started up again worse than before.

"I asked him if there was anything I could do for him to help him settle down, and eventually he stopped crying and he turned in his bed and he looked at me. 'I am all mixed up in my head, Donal,' he said. 'I don't know what I am anymore. You know, when the priest comes and he runs his cane along the bars at the end of the bed, it will be your turn soon. And he did it to me last night. He has his eye out for me, Donal, and I can't stand it. Do you hear me?' He was crying again. His sobbing got so intense he cried himself to sleep.

"A week later Father Madigan picked him out and he took him away—I would say they were gone about an hour—and when he came back Burke was all bent over staring at the floor. He never sobbed again after that. Don't know whatever happened to him after we finished school. He didn't come back to Timoleague, although his family still live up beyond the church. Never heard what happened to him afterwards. Funny nobody ever mentions him around here."

Madeline remembered walking back across the bridge and around by the abbey to where they had parked the car. She was looking back to where they had come from; how different everything looked from the other side. River Boatman was fresh and he wanted to go faster than was safe on the narrow road. Madeline had a job holding him up but she had dealt with the likes of him before. She turned from the front and paced slowly to the rear of the small group. The horse bowed his head in behind the grey in front of him. Madeline relaxed as the horse had his attention distracted.

They marched in single file, the estuary drying out, and as the water receded small clumps of grass became cactus in this sea desert. Madeline ordered the lead horse to return to the back roads to avoid the traffic leaving the estuary behind them. The horses pulled up the hill and the warmth of the sun made them sweat. Retracing their steps by the gallops once more, she caught the sunlight on the hills, the hedgerows strangled by small trees and spiked bushes. There was no rhyme or reason to it she thought as she watched the cattle move in miniature. At one point she was surrounded by midgets hovering around the horses' heads and then their rear ends swiping at them with her left hand. They dispersed as quickly as they arrived, disappearing to nowhere.

She remembered how Donal spoke of the priest the one and only time he did. Yet he had many priest friends. He used to invite them over for the musical evenings. He wasn't religious, Donal, but he knew where the power lay and how important it was to be close to it. She had wanted to talk to him about those school days spent far away on the east coast. How hard it was to be away from his family? And did it shape him for the rest of his life? The horror with that priest, Father Madigan—did it scar him for life? They say many abuse victims go on to abuse others.

The small party headed down the hill and back to the walkway, the sketchy paddock mare hiding her foal from the world. The estuary was barren, save for a trickle in the channel that promised more than it delivered.

What drove Donal to like boys? Was it all this stuff from his childhood? Abusive priests, the never-ending company of boys? He would never speak of it and when she did try to bring it up, he would go red in the face and snarl at her like a rabid dog. She would never know what drove him to do anything. He reminded her of the fox sleeking around the countryside, willing to devour anything that was weaker than it. He perpetually sought out the sick lamb or the unguarded chick.

Imagine, that was a part of him always, even when they met first. He seemed so normal; there were no signs. He was amorous and interested in her, whispering things into her ear and touching her provocatively when she wasn't expecting it. Sometimes she might rest back into him if they were at a party and ended up standing in the kitchen. He would blow softly on the back of her neck. Involuntarily she would ease her bottom against him, and if this happened often enough she could feel him go hard and the rock she rested on was comforting.

What happens? Do the years just take from you? His life became more singular when Georgina was born. He changed. It was like his only duty from there on was to provide for her. Was it that he didn't own the house? Did this make him insecure? Maybe that is why he was dashing about, his fingers stuck in so many pies. Madeline felt the tears trickle down her cheeks. She had not only lost her husband inexplicably all those years before, but she also lost her lover and all the heat and tenderness that go with it.

Madeline was lazy and River Boatman responded to her lethargy. The others had trotted ahead; they were almost at Seaview. It was instinctive. She allowed her charge look over the estuary. She was the general looking over the hordes. A voice within screamed at her to get a grip and ride on home and soon a nice stiff vodka. She kicked with her heels, and River Boatman responded. He trotted down the old jetty through the rubble of broken concrete onto the sand. She steered him through the first of the tiny rivers the sea had carelessly abandoned. Small birds and ducks moved fast as the horse splashed his way through, and he mounted the sand bank. Madeline roared at him, squatting, and the horse sensing her excitement moved faster, his feet sinking in the softer areas. He kicked back mud splattering through the air. She kept the gallop up relentlessly till she slowed to wade through a small lake, trapped water, swish, the wash, the horse making white water as he waded through.

Soon she was back on the sand and heading to the sea. It was forming cliff-like surf, the wind blowing south-westerly away from the point, to reaching force four in places before it defused to fall harmlessly on the beach at Kilbrittain. Madeline watched it seek out the land. It was searching for someone down the innocent channels of swamp, conquered territory where the land imitated the sea and grass grew instead of seaweed. The sea kept its mighty waves just for the moment, antagonising the shoreline, a new wind whistling through the green buoy that marked the channel. The trees on the headland swayed and shuddered. Soon the clouds gathered for a meeting beyond horse rock with the heat of the day suspended.

The horse grunted as she patrolled the water's edge up and down, all her old skill returning. River Boatman in dressage, the sky changed again just as quickly with the sun bursting through, scattering the darkness, leaving it to fall over Broadstrand. Throwing her riding hat on the sand she kicked again with her heels and the horse ran forward, his dark leather body washed white. She pushed till the horse swam, a giant wet suit floating. Madeline grabbed him tight round the neck hugging him close, the horse losing his feet, kicking hard, treading water.

A weariness descended upon her, the sky becoming the earth, the sea turning to wood, the world a bobble. Behind her the channel ran like a river to the harbour, and the trawler awaited the changing tide. Alongside sat small craft in the mud. They were so sad, awaiting the returning sea to give them life.

A sudden fatigue, and she slipped from her mount, her head immersing in the cold sea. But rather than frighten her it allowed her to drift ever so slowly, falling through the cold sapping against her skin. Falling still till she touched the bottom, the sea moving as the horse retreated, disturbing the current. An arm floated towards her, all chewed and beaten, on the finger the ring, the one Georgina had bought for his fiftieth birthday. The arm stuck to her thigh. She grabbed it ripping it away and thrusting upwards to take air. She held it aloft above the tide. The sea gurgled round her neck and chin as she struggled to find her feet. The trees their branches onlookers, the green buoy gyrating within a sudden wind and the arm flailing.

She screamed at the elements, her voice carrying across the sound. She swung the arm like a hammer thrower, hurtling it through the air. It danced, skimming on a vagrant dark wave before it sunk. River Boatman waited for her to return, retrieving her riding hat she mounted him and he set off in a canter like nothing had happened. His dark sleek leather dried as they went and he tasted of salt.

Madeline was drunk but for once Edwina didn't mind and she repeated, "Are you certain it is what you really want to do? It is a big move. Like, I know you have relations there as I have myself, but it's so different round here. Everyone knows everyone. It's often a curse to find Biddy knows more about yourself than you do. But this is God's own country, Madeline. What will you do away from us all? You will die of loneliness. It is one thing for Georgina. She is young; she might enjoy the fast life. But you, my dear, I expect you will go mad!"

Madeline smiled when Edwina said that, her eyes filling with tears once again. "It is a done deal now, Edwina. I spoke with John Riordan this morning about the house and all our affairs. There isn't much left in the way of cash, but there is enough to start over. I have decided to board up this house. You know Donal always said there will be a huge property boom, so I await it. When it comes I will sell up. If not and he was wrong, what of it? I can always come back. It will all still be here. Fleming from the village will tend to the place. I know he is as old as the hills, but he is still handy and he won't cost me much. But there is a favour I need, Edwina. I hate to ask but really I can't think of anyone else."

Edwina listened, her ears pricked. She was drinking coffee having felt extremely queasy after her last visit.

"I was wondering would you take Bob? He is such an angel and he knows you so well. I have racked my brains but he was born here and I don't think..." Madeline allowed the tears to flow.

"There, there," Edwina said making heavy weather of it. She left her armchair to comfort her friend. Madeline cried from the heart and she was inconsolable.

"Now, now," Edwina chided, "all will be fine, dear. It will work out. Wait till you see, it will. Don't you worry, my dear, you have been through the wringer. Soon you will come out the other side. You will see the daylight, believe me!"

Edwina, rubbing Madeline's shoulder, was less convinced as she gazed at the dog lying by the hearth.

"He will have to live in the yard by the horses. He can sleep in the outhouse with the cats."

And then she remembered that old Fleming had terminal cancer. The last she heard was that he would be lucky to last the month. Still, this wasn't the time to discuss such matters. Plenty of time for that.

"Perhaps if I go down to the kitchen and make a pot of tea, you might perk up." Anticipating protest she continued, "Have another drink, by all means, my dear, whatever gets you through the night as they say. But I wonder, would a drop of tea help?"

Edwina pitched her voice high so as to sound funny, and Madeline laughed through her tears. Mrs. Edwards always made her laugh even if their friendship had become lukewarm over the years. But that was mainly due to Donal who had scourged her with his behaviour. She was on her feet over by the door. Bob raised his head, wondering whether he should follow but seeing Madeline still sitting he chose to stay put.

"A cup of tea, my girl, in times of crisis."

Madeline smiled once more at her friends stoic efforts.

Wood Point, A few years ago
3o.

It was Bill Thornton who mentioned it, yet it was Pee Wee Flynn who seized the moment when he said, "It's a disgrace, you know. The man's away workin'. It's not his fault, is it? He is doing his best trying to feed his kids, and this fella's moving in. It isn't right, Bill. That's what I say and I know there are other people in the village think the same. Brazen, like, out the walkway. He doesn't even try to hide it, like!"

Pee Wee paused to take a breath, and Bill cut in with, "What is he? If he is a writer it is news to me. I never read anything by him or saw him in the papers. Is he a chancer from Dublin? Chancing his arm. Maybe he is giving her a big story, you know, money and security. What you think? I would bet he is giving her a line. He has to be saying something to turn her head."

Pee Wee, now recovered from his break, said, "Ted O' Reilly will have his head if he gets wind of it. I was wondering if I should say something to Myrna. I know her for years; she used to babysit us when we were kids!"

Bill looked at him incredulously, instinctively moving to pull another pint of Bulmer's. "You don't want to be talking to Myrna. She most likely would approve. She is an unusual woman with a sharp tongue. I wouldn't want to be on the wrong side of her. When is Teddy home?"

Pee Wee took a second as if he was trying to work out who the hell Teddy was. "Ted won't be home for months. He is not long gone back. I wouldn't know what to say to him anyhow. I would be afraid he wouldn't like me mentioning it. You know what he is like. With a few Jameson's he might want to chin me for mentioning her name."

Bill put up the pint of cider and Pee Wee drank a little before retiring to his thoughts. Bill went to say something but changed his mind. He cast an eye out the window. The pier was quiet. The small vans used for transferring fish boxes were idle and lonely. The day hadn't taken off. The sun had offered to warm things up, but a thick cloud from the east put paid to that. Every so often a soft drizzle threw itself against the window.

Thomas Crowe came in, his woollen hat not fitted properly. He looked the worse for wear. He ordered a Guinness. Bill didn't know if he was glad to see him or not.

"It is soft, but I hear we will have wind and thunder later."

Thomas sitting on the high stool didn't answer him directly. Instead he amused himself by eyeing Pee Wee contemptuously.

Pee Wee smiling said, "We were just chatting about Katie Donovan and that fella."

Thomas, perking up from his stupor, said, "What is that?"

Bill intervening said, "Carrying on, that's what it is. All around the village."

Pee Wee gleefully added, "They are not trying to hide it none, are they, Bill?"

Thomas looked hard at his freshly-pulled stout and nodded before saying, "She is a married woman. He is all right himself. I never fought with him. Likes a pint and a chat. She is a fine girl, Bill. I know her all my life. She isn't the type to be carrying on, I tell you that."

Bill was a little surprised by Thomas. He didn't usually say much especially in commenting on others, but his musings were interrupted by Pee Wee who said loudly, "I tell you, Thomas, someone will have to have a word; we need to stamp this out. Like, Ted O' Reilly is one of our own, you know!"

Thomas fixed his cap and checked out its position in the wall mirror. He didn't like Pee Wee or his accent, and he waited a few seconds before replying.

"Kate knows what she is doing. She was always a fine girl, and what business is it of anyone's who she talks to or is friends with? It is a free country, Pee Wee."

Pee Wee looked at Bill. It wasn't what he expected to hear. Bill sighed and moved away to tend to some glasses. Pee Wee was searching for something to say but Danny Murphy came in the side door.

Bill, distracted, went to pull him a Murphy's.

"How is herself?" Bill asked picking up a dirty drying towel.

"She is prancing around the beach as we speak. God knows it will keep her quiet. I am turning off the phone," Danny said putting his mobile on the counter. He glanced down the bar at Pee Wee and Thomas.

"How are the men?" they replied in unison, but Thomas was inaudible.

"Who is she with?" Bill asked handing over the pint, the head spilling down the glass.

"My beautiful sister-in-law, who else?" Danny lifted his head to stare at the ceiling Bill laughed at his mocking antics. "I pay a fucking fortune for that bitch to sun her arse at my expense, and when I wake up in the morning I ask God to spare me and forgive me for my sins."

Danny drank half his pint down, Bill, looked on rubbing his right ear.

"She is an indulgence and St. Peter will give you great credit for your patience, Danny." Bill went back to the till pleased with himself, whilst Danny Murphy twisted his neck and rubbed his left shoulder with his right hand in an effort to ease a trapped nerve.

Later Pee Wee, a little worse for wear, landed beside Danny. His Bulmer's beside him warned Danny that a long stay was imminent. Thomas was ignoring Pee Wee but he now ignored both of them, so Pee Wee was seeking refuge as much as company.

"You've heard the scandal, Dan?"

Danny towering over him said, "I have no time for it. My sister-in-law is cleaning me out. It is all my mind can take."

"It's a good one," Pee Wee said. "That writer chap, Jack Browne, he is chasing Ted O' Reilly's missus all over the village, the two of them brazen as you like out the walkway, and someone said they were seen on the beach out in Ballinglanna. Poor Ted, away at sea in all weathers, you know?"

Bill, sensing excitement, posted himself close by. Danny shrugged; his whole demeanour smacked of not interested.

"It's not right, Bill, is it?" Pee Wee looked for support.

Bill didn't answer but Danny said, "He is a brave man. I wouldn't annoy Ted O' Reilly, but it is no business of mine." Danny, disgusted, drank his pint down shaking his head as Bill went for a fresh glass.

"I hope he doesn't end up like Donal Travers," Danny said on his way to the door.

"Are you gone?" Bill shouted after him nervously.

"See you later...," Danny said, his voice drowned by the closing door. A silence descended after Danny left so abruptly. Pee Wee went to say something and he looked to see if Thomas was listening, but Thomas sat sleepily bent over his pint at the far end. Bill fiddled with the dish cloth putting it down and picking it up again.

Pee Wee, smiling, said, "Maybe Danny Murphy is right. He needs a warning, a good fright, don't he?"

Bill cast a quick eye to Thomas and snarled, "Who will do the frightening?"

He threw the dish cloth hard on the counter, making a whipping sound and startling Pee Wee who instinctively grabbed his pint in case it should topple over. Thomas went into the hallway, standing on the doorstep overlooking the harbour. His roll-up was bent from his shirt pocket, and he placed it on the flat window frame massaging it to retain its shape, doing the best he could. It resembled a pipe cleaner; however, the smoke was satisfying. He exhaled clouds, which were swallowed by the mild air.

The pier was quiet, old pallets stacked high with broken ones discarded to one side. The small trawler alongside the mast disappeared when the sea inhaled; soon the whole place would fill with small cruisers and yachts. Some would stay on their moorings all summer. The wealthy owners would have announced their prosperity to the world.

Thomas looked onto the deserted street before him, but then a jeep rolled along coming from the Ramsey Hill direction. He searched it in the hope of reckoning the driver, but he didn't know the middle-aged woman from Adam. She gave him a serious glance but she never succumbed to the customary wave.

He pulled hard on his roll-up in exasperation. What was that Pee Wee Flynn on about, talking about Kate like that? He didn't know Kate. Typical, fucking Brit can't mind his nose. She was fond of him all right, her and Jack Browne, but what about it? That changed nothing; it was just the same as seeing her with Ted O' Reilly. No different; maybe not quite as bad.

Kate played a role when she was with Ted—all respectable like she was announcing to the world this was her family unit. This is my husband, Ted, look at the respectable us. At least with your man she looked girlish and a bit lost, like she wasn't sure as to what it was she was up to. She looked like she was ashamed of herself but unable to help herself, no bad way to be. Not for her anyway.

He always thought that she and Ted were not suited. It wasn't so much that Ted was wrong for her but that she wasn't right for him. A child walked out of Detta's with a carry bag. She was sucking a lollipop. She passed him nervously, her eyes staring at the pathway. Thomas wanted to say hello but he didn't; you had to be careful these days with people talking and they are very wary of single men, even in the middle of the evening standing on the doorstep of the Harbour Bar.

What was it about Kate Donovan? When she used to lift the fish boxes better than any boy, when she wasn't much more than a child herself at his father's funeral, she had stunning eyes that took the grey of the day and swallowed it whole. And when she danced with him one night in the Fisherman's in full view of Jack Browne, it was the only time for many years he felt human. Pee Wee wanted him to hate Jack Browne, but he didn't hate him. The man spoke to him and respected his intellect, unlike some of the others. All right, he had an eye for Kate, but, sure, who could blame him for that?

When dancing with her, Thomas imagined a camp fire with a big party taking place; all the girls and boys of his youth were there. Kate chose him to dance by the camp fire, her face aglow. She lifts his arms. He searched her eyes midst the giant flicker of light. This is the fertility rite; she is suddenly against him shivering with delight and expectation. He wanted to take her away from the crowd to a quiet place where she could touch his skin and see he was the same as everyone else. He wanted to look steely into her eyes and kiss the full red of her lips, strong lips sucking his skin for a moment. His humanity deserts him, and he has no longer fear. His body would be immortal as she coils before him. The romance is no better than the creatures in the field, they dark at one end, like with like, and Kate engages his brutishness for she is the harvest goddess. She is the one he adores and loves; he falls at her feet, sleeps with her in dreams.

"You might just have a word with Ted when he comes home. I can't see him standing for it especially with a few on board," Bill said, walking away just as quick in an effort to disassociate himself with his own words. Two older women came through the side door looking for coffee but settled for spring waters when Bill informed them the coffee was off.

"He needs to know, Bill, you know. It is going to be hard to tell him but someone's got to do it, or it will be still going on under his nose."

Thomas who had walked back in went to Pee Wee. Looking down on his drunken face, he said, "So you will be telling him, Pee Wee. Rather you than me. To tell a man his wife is carrying on carries risks. He may not thank you for it. Especially if you don't have the proof. I would be careful about what I say, boy."

Bill fixed on Pee Wee's eyes. Pee Wee tried to smile but his face didn't allow it. Instead he pushed back his stool signalling that he had drank enough at least for now.

"I won't have any bother. Ted and me, we grew up together, next-door neighbours. Well, not next door but very close. I looked out for him, he looked out for me. No bother between me and Ted. I can say what I like to Ted. He knows me."

Thomas threw his eyes to heaven. Bill didn't show any sign of acknowledgement even though he saw him do it. Pee Wee left through the front door, walking past the bay window with purpose. Bill, collecting his empty glass, sighed.

"I suppose she isn't the only slut in this village."

Thomas saw red and stood immediately. "Katie Donovan is no slut!"

Bill, unaware he had caused offence, stopped before he dropped the bottle into the container. He stared at Thomas whose cheeks were rose red, and he leaned as far as he could over the bar counter.

"I was only joking. God, can a man not say a joke? What is wrong with everyone around here, getting all excited and upset about nothing? God, I will be careful going forward. Sit down, will you, and I will get you a pint."

Bill checked on the two older women who sat by the window, oblivious to any fuss. Putting the pint in front of Thomas, Bill said, "Have it on me, Thomas boy, then go on

home for a bite." He walked back across the bar and out
through the hatch before Thomas could reply. He stoked the
fire and flicked on the television, but he didn't turn up the
sound as it wasn't news time yet.

Thomas saw her again, her eyes burning. He felt her heat
when he was cold. She cleansed his soul, her skin against his.
Kate gave him life, the light of his life. She ran away from
him. All through the different stages of her existence she ran
away from him. What had Ted O' Reilly got that he hadn't?
He had a half-decent family, maybe, but what fault is it to
have a deranged mother? It was the age difference. Ted was
her age. The truth was she was hardly likely to take up with a
roaring drunk like himself no matter what.

The day he met her on Ramsey Hill and she walked on her
own in the height of summer, he was carrying a sack of
wrinkles and she spoke to him at length. She was leaning
against the hedge and her breasts were hard. They hadn't
fully formed but he could see them, ball-shaped, push
through her top. She looked directly into him, her voice
lyrical, and she wore not a screed of makeup and the late
evening sun caught her making shadows till her skin glowed
in the fading light. The ease of her conversation ate at every
organ in his body. Three times he wanted to and almost told
her that he loved her and that he would always love her.

From the day of his father's funeral it was like the old man
left his world, and she came into it at the moment. But he
couldn't speak; he hadn't got it in him and when she waved
goodbye and walked on up the hill he missed her. He walked
home, alone and miserable. Nothing. There was nothing that
could match looking at her face, listening to her speak. No
amount of experience could replace her, and when he visited
his lady in Bandon she would often stop and ask him what
was wrong, why he was silent and sullen. He never found the
balls to tell her about Kate as he felt somehow he would be
betraying her, just to mention her name in such company, and

anyway how could he explain to anyone what even he himself failed to understand?

His lady was calm with him and she coaxed him along. Sometimes they would stop all together and just drink and chat. Eventually she would give up and conk out cold on the bed, and he listened to her breathing slow and then fast with a ladylike snore as she had drunken dreams. Thomas fixed the pillow for her so she wouldn't hurt her neck and end up stiff, but he would stay awake as sometimes that is what the drink did to him. He thought of Kate and drank whiskey till the image of her didn't hurt anymore. Later he left before his lady woke. Sometimes if he was flush he might leave her a twenty, but if he was broke he left her nothing. But either way he kissed her gently on the forehead.

Looking back at her in the dim light of the room, she was overweight, her cheeks puffed, and her chin had folding skin beneath. But he could see where she had once been pretty. How she still retained her kindness and good humour; good enough for him. He left, closing the door gently, walking the early morning streets slightly drunk, his shoulders brushing needlessly against walls.

Wood Point, A few years ago
31.

The tide was turning and the mullet knew about it before anyone else. They were flapping silver beasts beating the water, dark shadows invading the murky shallows. Jack stood watching from the ruins at Abbeymahon. The Cistercians were good builders. He had an old rustic view from rabble ruins.

He had wandered through it listening to Caw, relaxing, sheltering from the wind by the roof garden. From one angle his beak like a Roman nose tilted from the shadows. From another his tail fell almightily, lots of fresh air in his toilet. What a view he enjoyed! Lord Caw, ruler of the estuary, his stare on the hard brown cattle at the top of the field falling slowly to reach the docile sheep lazy near the road.

He lords over his cousins out on the sand, and as the water creeps in the egrets and the plover dance before him. He watches the tide reclaim the sands at Burren, swish washes the slime green stone. Small boats discarded are lifted to bobble like corks and hard orange balloons float with the hedges beyond defining boundaries more distance. Jack measured the afternoon and he strolled on evaluating his options: thinking of staying, thinking of moving on. How he would miss this dark place. Clouds settled over the hills of Kilbrittain and a small boat with an outboard moved purposely, one man and one boat alone to an unsighted slipway on the other side.

She is restless, he concluded. She can't make her mind up and maybe it is better that she doesn't. What good would come of it? Been down the road before, and it is no time to be thinking of small children. He found something, but what of it? Most likely just a romantic dream. Infatuation. The novelty will wear off after a week. It always ends up like that. At the start the newness of it, the glory position not found out yet, it is full of mystique. A man can paint his own

picture, add on to it whatever it is he likes, but that is not
reality. No, it will go stale no matter what. The daughters
would complicate things, for a man might forgo his wife but
not his children. A fellow will fight for his kids.

It might be different ten years back, but now he couldn't
raise a gallop or a fist to fight. Wouldn't last long with Jack
Browne ending up on the ground. Best be gone, move on.
There was a whole world waiting beyond the hills. Where to
go? He didn't know. Italy or Dublin, who knows? She
wanted to go to Italy with him when he told her about the
villages and the mountains and the glorious sea and beaches.
But mostly she longed for the sun, like she never really saw it
or experienced it for long enough.

"Take me to the sun, Jack." The villa of peace with her
beside him and the children playing in the pool, cold drinks
to cool the body down. In the evenings the children would
stay with the nanny while they went to the village for a meal.
She wears a savage white strapless dress, and as he drinks his
red wine she is sparkling. Jack stares into her eyes. He's
falling in love over and over again.

Later she would run her finger down the line of his wound
and whisper into his right ear, speaking of this place and all
the rugged beauty—the sand and the stone, the sea, and those
hills that invite gladiators—until soon he is drifting into a
warm sleep. She reminds him of the cold he leaves behind,
and the screaming noise, as he watches the crow mount then
dismount his perch. The tide comes in, then goes out, then
comes in once again, and she whispers just when he is on the
cusp of sleep. "I love you, Jack. I love you, Jack...You will
never be alone again, Jack...Never. Do you hear me, my
love? My precious boy...You will never be alone, do you
hear?"

He started to walk back towards Wood Point crossing the
matted grass just before the road bends, his head brushing
against the falling daggers of the exotic tree. The night he
called his daughter once, twice, three times, yet she came to

him the roundabout way, her sitting in her magic tree speaking to herself in riddles. He left her also. Why, Jack Browne, why are you always leaving? The wind crushed his face as he passed the low fields. Catching his breath the east wind forced him upwards to view the hills with Indian cattle and Sioux-like ridges. He watched her sing to herself for an hour once. Where was he to go with all this pent-up anger and hurt? Maybe to that pent-up anger-and-hurt place.

The world will hardly lose sleep over Jack Browne and Kate Donovan. Time to move on before it becomes a tragedy, and she gets implicated and some people in the village won't reckon her, especially other women. They can hurt. Kate ostracised, her kids too maybe. Most people won't give a damn, but it only takes one or two. He passed the jetty and on to Seaview. By now his face was numb with the cold and his calf muscles ached.

*

A month later Ted O' Reilly arrived home a week before he was due. Kate was surprised when she received the call from London. He was in good spirits, laughing and joking, excited to be so close to home.

"We put into dry dock for repairs. We could be out for three weeks depending how long it takes to get the replacement parts sent up from Spain. Stand by, they told us."

He was home later that day. Jack was surprised to bump into him in the Fisherman's. Ted was calm. He nodded politely, drinking straight whiskey. He was with Pee Wee Flynn who went out to the toilet when he saw Jack come in.

"How is the book coming on?" Ted asked softly.

Jack lifting his pint said, "Getting there, Ted. Nearer the end than the beginning."

"You would be wanting that, and you at it this long." Ted laughed.

Jack sighed. "I know."

Pee Wee returned with a gleeful look in his eye. Thomas Crowe came in, but on seeing the company he chose to stay at the far end of the counter. Jack looked around at a few of the faces occupying stools. Martin Kingston from up near Broadstrand was there nursing a pint of Beamish, while Billy Dwyer, the postman, was having a quiet one before bed. He had the look of a fellow who had hit the road early. He nodded and waved and Jack was wondering whether he should join him and get a few racing tips or leave it and stay where he was. He didn't want to appear to be avoiding the company either. Then a text message came. Jack deleted it straight away under the watchful gaze of Pee Wee who almost climbed the counter in order to get a view.

"Get a text?" Pee Wee asked stupidly as Jack put down his phone.

"My stock broker," Jack said smartly. Ted laughed and when he did his cheeks filled purple.

Pee Wee didn't get the joke. He said blandly, "People can't manage without them. A bloody necessity now and a shocking price they are too."

Ted, grinning, took more whiskey but didn't say anything. Jack really wanted to move as Pee Wee did his head in at the best of times, but right now he was out of sorts and he had no patience for him.

"What sort of phone have you? Give us a look," Pee Wee said with his hand outstretched.

Jack looked at him coldly. "And see all the texts from my girlfriends; not likely."

Ted laughed loudly whilst Pee Wee somehow retracted into his bar stool. Jack slipped the phone into his trousers pocket out of sight, and Pee Wee still looked at him and pushed his head forward in a sulk rocking slightly like an overactive child. Jack busied himself, talking with fellow waifs and stragglers. He was hoping they would leave before him, but Pee Wee was in an excitable drinking mood and

even gone the time he got another bottle of cider from Barry
Cousins.

Jack thought of the text she sent, short and sweet: "Ted is
home." At times he expected to see anger or resentment in
Ted's eyes, but he was his usual quiet self. Not engaging Pee
Wee, he acted like he was happy out with just himself and his
whiskey.

Thomas Crowe was talking to Sean Finn from Timoleague.
Sean went shooting at the weekends, and between the two of
them they shot just about everyone in the pub. Thomas aimed
at the baby bottles of spirits high on the shelf, whereas Sean
just aimed carelessly at the customers. Eventually he noticed
Pee Wee leave through the centre door with Ted following
behind, catching a glimpse of Thomas Crowe biting on a roll-
up before the door shut; he finished his pint, more relaxed
now. Then he asked himself was all this worth it and chided
himself for allowing his heart rule his head, perhaps it was all
in his imagination, till the text went once more and this time
it simply said, "Are you okay?" To which he replied that he
was.

When he hit the air the drink took effect. He could smell
the sea and the breeze. What was left of it came from behind.
Ahead the street was deserted, which served as a comfort,
and when he passed Michael Harrington's it was quiet also,
Harrington having bedded down for the night. A cat slithered
across the road at the pier, and he noticed the only light go
out in the upstairs of the Harbour Bar. The tide was full out
and the small boats resting on the sand within the harbour
walls looked naked.

Jack thought as he passed by, The sooner I am gone the
better. No future here for me anymore. I will finish the book
and go.

When the car pulled up he didn't recognise Pee Wee at
first, but when Pee Wee wound the window down and spoke
there was no mistaking him.

"Ted is dropping us up," Pee Wee said slurring his words. Jack was surprised to see Ted at the wheel as he was full of whiskey. Thomas Crowe sat quietly on the far side in the rear. "Hop in, mate, we will drop you off."

Jack was uncertain as to what to do. He didn't want to insult Ted. "I am all right. I need to sober up; the walk will do me good."

Pee Wee, smiling, said, "Hop in, mate, you're okay. We will drop you home. Come on!"

Against his better judgement Jack got into the car. Thomas shifted uncomfortably as Jack closed the door behind him.

Pee Wee did all the talking. Ted did the driving; he didn't say anything. Thomas brought the stakes. He confirmed it each time that Pee Wee asked him.

"You will have the honour and the privilege. He has two of the actual stakes in his possession that were used on Donal Travers all those years ago!" Pee Wee sounded proud. "You see, Jack, in a small village like Wood Point we look out for each other like. We don't want strangers coming in and messing our women about. You know, it is not on, and a fella like Ted here away all the time, he can't keep an eye, can he? So it is down to the local people to keep an eye for him."

Thomas moved his arm allowing the plastic bag carrying the stakes to fall between himself and Jack. The point of one of them was digging into Jack's right thigh. He lifted it away. It fell against Thomas but he didn't seem to notice.

"We wouldn't like anything to happen, you know, Jack? In a small place like this we wouldn't want someone just to come here and wreck a marriage, you know?"

Jack wanted to say something, but Thomas gave him a friendly pat on the leg as if to say, "Hush, you will only make it worse."

*

Kate was wide awake. She listened to the wind blow up the tunnel of the back lane. It whistled, leaving gaps in its wake.

She knew something was up. Where was Ted? He had only gone to the Fisherman's for an hour. She had sent him three texts but he didn't reply, so she texted Jack. He said he was okay but something was up. What could be happening? The children had gone off to sleep without a whimper, and the television was very poor so she decided to grab an early night. When her head hit the pillow sleep descended like a huge cloak over her face.

She woke thinking her sleep had lasted a long time and her dreams had been endless. She was shocked to see she had only slept for an hour. She picked up her phone this time ringing Ted, but the phone was powered off. She went to ring Jack but stopped as she dialled, thinking "What if?" and if someone took his phone from him and her number came up. The proof they may need to incriminate him would be there. She thought of getting dressed, ringing Myrna to come over. She would trawl the village till she found them all of them. But maybe they were not together. What if Ted was in the Fisherman's? Maybe there was a lock-in? Jack could be at home asleep.

Her mind was running riot, imagining all sorts of daft things. Sure, maybe they were down in the hotel. Wasn't Robbie Edwards getting married soon? Maybe it was his stag night and Ted had joined in.

She tried in vain to find sleep as she lay there cold, her mind racing up and down the main street. She was a bird flying over the estuary. It was day and the sea was a deep blue. Then all of a sudden it was night, and all she could see was dark sand.

Wood Point, A few years ago
32.

Jack has asked me to fill you in on a few of the details of what really happened on the night in question, which I have agreed to do so long as I can reach the conclusion of my tale of Sean Harrington, Madge Butler and most of all of me and Mammy Rosie. He has agreed for now, but, God knows how this will all pan out. I suppose at some stage of the proceedings I will just have to row in with him and trust him, even if that flies in the face of my nature.

When Ted O' Reilly, Pee Wee Flynn, and Thomas Crowe stood outside the Fisherman's, it was decided that something had to be done. Not that Thomas agreed with the proposal; he was more or less duped into it by the promise of a free late one in the Harbour Bar. And to be fair, his curiosity was aroused by Ted's promise of a tactical discussion.

Bill Thornton was locking the front door when they happened upon him.

"Men," he said, surprised.

"Any chance of a few shorts, Bill? A late one? We have a bit of business to discuss." Ted was convincing, for he didn't say much. So when he spoke people tended to listen.

"A quick one, so," Bill said sort of happy, because he hadn't had a busy night and three whiskeys is three whiskeys.

"Make them doubles," Ted said handing over a fifty, which Bill stretched out before depositing it in the till. He then leaned on the counter close by so as he could hear the conversation.

Pee Wee went to speak but Ted cut him short. "He will be coming up the street in the next few minutes, so we can't be arsing around. I left the car outside earlier. I intended walking home and collecting it in the morning, but needs be I will be taking my chances. I will be giving a certain person a lift, and it won't be to his home either. What we need now is a fine bit of strong rope and a few nice wooden stakes, and we shall deal with this the Wood Point way and give this fella the fright of his life."

He swallowed the whiskey in one take leaving the other fellas, including a seasoned drinker like Thomas Crowe, aghast. Bill Thornton filled him up again but the others were not ready.

"I have lots of rope out the back," Bill said. "I don't have stakes but there are a few metal stakes from the hurling goalposts."

Thomas Crowe added, "I have two fine stakes next door washed up on the Blind Strand. I found them when I was picking wrinkles not long after Donal Travers disappeared. They could be his; I dunno. Washed up by my feet."

Ted instructed Thomas to go get them, and Bill went out the back to get his bits and pieces.

*

Jack walked up the street slowly like he was in no hurry to be home. They watched as he studied the harbour, like he was counting the debris of pots strewn around. When Ted pulled alongside, he didn't really protest. More, he made excuses, and they had little difficulty persuading Jack to get in the car. Ted O' Reilly drove the car steady for a man full of whiskey, but there was nothing unusual in that as Ted was better at everything when full of drink. It was like the real Ted came out and the quiet shy person disappeared.

There are a few different versions of the events that followed, and, really, I suppose it is down to whom you believe. I like Thomas Crowe's version the best, but probably Ted's version is the most accurate. Yet for sheer entertainment, I think I will run with Pee Wee's account. He spares nothing on the entertainment and he also paints himself as the real hero, the brains behind the operation, as they say.

When they made Jack strip, Pee Wee says he looked away out of respect and that he allowed Ted do all the talking, as after all the whole sad matter surrounded him and his wife. He also claimed the credit for pleading with Ted O' Reilly that Jack should keep his underpants on, and, according to Pee Wee, Thomas was sobering up and was expressing remorse for the course of action they had taken, so much so that Ted had to chide him on at least three occasions.

Pee Wee himself was rock solid. He held Jack's wrists steady while Ted hammered the wooden stakes into the hard sand. They used the metal hurling stakes for his feet, and Pee Wee also stated that he would have offered Jack a smoke had he in fact been a smoker. But seeing that he wasn't there was very little a chap could do out of decency, so he just let Ted get on with it. Ted ran the rope over Jack's shoulder and across his chest to secure him properly. When he was satisfied that Jack was secured tightly Ted stood over Jack's shivering body.

"Did you sleep with her?" Ted asked him.

The first light of the day was crawling up the estuary like a mist, and Jack said, "I didn't, Ted! She didn't want anything like that!"

Ted seemed to accept his word for it. Then after a pause Ted got a little angry, and standing over Jack's head he said, "When I was a kid the oul fella would bring me down the Argideen sometimes. He would wake me in the middle of the night with a sort of puck in the side."

Ted clenching his fist mocked a polite punch in his right side. "My oul fella was handy with his fists. There is many a fella around here that will testify to that. So off he would take me to fish one of the pools, and at first light he would pour us tea from his flask and he might have made up a few sandwiches from a few crusts of bread. I would ate whatever he gave me. Fishing is a hungry business.

"Sometimes the fishing would be good, and we would bring home a few trout or salmon. When we did you could sense it in him. His whole mood improved, which was good, because if we had a poor time of it he could get miserable and tetchy and want to use his fists. He would curse the cormorants. 'Big black bastards,' he would say, 'standing on the sand like a vampire spreading his cape.'

"You know, Jack, they must ate twice their body weight every day, so you can see why fishermen don't like them. They have these worms inside of them, and the worms need the food, and if the cormorants don't feed the worms turn on them from the inside and eat their organs until the big black bird dies. So they eat, boy. They make sure they fucking eat. If you ever cut open a cormorant you will see the worms crawl out of them."

Jack, spread out like Jesus on the cross, didn't say anything at first. Ted walked away to the waiting Pee Wee who said, "The fucking boy will get his end, Ted. Maybe we should cover him with his clothes."

Ted was eyeing the shivering Thomas, who by then was crossing the sand to the car. "Leave him be; it won't be the cold that kills him."

Jack shouted after him, "Ted, you know the difference, don't you, between the cormorant and the fisherman?"

Ted stopped in his tracks. He turned to stay within earshot of Jack, who was testing the strength of his restraints. He was trying to raise himself, but they had done a good job and the stakes didn't budge.

"The cormorant is driven by passion. His passion to feed the worms. He lives to feed the parasites. At least it is a reason!"

Ted went to go back but stopped dead. "Enjoy the swim. You know what I hate about you people, Jack? You are arrogant. You are all high and mighty. You think the likes of me to be simple because I speak like I do. You are full of all of this crap thinking you are an artist. Some writer you are, 'cause I never heard of you before you set foot here. You are so full of it."

Ted walked back to the car with Pee Wee. The early light made them nervous, for soon there would be traffic passing coming from Kilbrittain.

*

It was a long time since I heard Michael Harrington raise his voice, but on this day he made up for it shouting his lungs out whilst Madge was at him in a much lower pleading voice. They were in the kitchen just like they were any normal Sunday morning before opening, and I was watching "Once Upon a Time in the West." I was thankful Michael Harrington put it on when he did, as I would not have stood a chance a half-an-hour later.

"I tell you, Michael, with my mother and what else going on, what choice did I have? Go on, you tell me."

Madge put it up to him, but Michael was having none of it. "I would have starved first, and didn't things turn around in the end? All these years, and you have kept it all from me!"

Michael's voice took a wounded tone; he went from shouting to talking normal, like he just scrambled to his feet having been knocked out.

"How much money did you get?"

Madge walked to the kitchen door checking around to make sure there was nobody about.

"I think over all he gave me twenty thousand."

"Twenty thousand. That is criminal. What were you thinking of? I can't benefit from that. Sure I might as well gone and stole it from him myself. All the work we did here, and you said the money came down the family. I will never live this down, Madge, never; this is a step too far!"

Madge was quiet for a second. I could see her profile through the line of dust falling in a beam to the floor.

"We were glad of it when it came, Michael, and you just over Rosie and all the tragedy. It wasn't like I spent it on myself, was it? Now I am sorry I told you about it at all, but the guilt was eating me up. I could hardly sleep with it waking me up, the thoughts filling my head. He wasn't a good man, Michael. He had lots of problems with people. He was ruthless and cruel. In the end he gave in to me like he accepted it almost as part of his business life. He would chat to me while I cleaned his study. I think in the end he was content with it all. He left the money for me in the drawer every month. I never had to ask him about it. He never forgot."

Michael Harrington still wasn't happy. He was up on his feet, restless, going to the sink. He lifted the kettle, testing its weight before pressing the switch. Madge followed him like she was besotted with his movement. She watched him from behind, unable to gauge his mood. She had a sense his violent anger had abated. He was still mad but he was deliberating now, like when one suddenly finds the impossible was possible after all.

"I am telling you, Madge, if the people in the village ever get wind of this, I am screwed. I may as well pack up and be gone, taking all my belongings with me. They will massacre me if they get wind of it. You might even face charges yourself. What do they call it? Extortion with menace. A very serious crime, and they will implicate me saying I knew about it all this time but said nothing!"

Michael had turned round to face her, as he leaned against the old cooker. Madge, as if realising the validity of his words, bowed over the table her face in her hands. I could tell she wasn't crying by the movement of her head, but she was mortally embarrassed and offended by the passion Michael had shown.

Eventually she removed the hands from her face, and, composing herself, she said, "I don't have any money now, Michael, and even if I had it is gone years and the house is in ruins, as you know. So who would I pay it back to? You are right about it, though. I did a bad thing, and I will be punished for it, but who knows what it was like? What he was like? What with Mammy ill and you in trouble, I thought it was fair. I dunno, I just wasn't right, was I? My head told me something, my heart another, but I did what I did."

Michael made tea, spilling some boiling water on the draining board. He cursed as it splashed on his right wrist. He brought the cups over to the table, placing hers in front of her. He sipped slowly on his own. It was too hot to swallow, so he left it for a moment. She went to take his hand but he refused her. She noticed his face was still red from anger.

"What are we to do?" she said eventually.

Michael could finally drink his tea. She hadn't touched hers, fiddling about with the handle, slurping drops running randomly down the side of her cup.

"It won't work anymore, Madge. Even if they never find out, you will have to go. It is the only sensible solution."

Madge looked stunned. She stopped playing with the cup and dragged her chair away, scraping on the stone floor.

"Have you lost your mind, Michael? After all we have done here, you want to throw it all away? For what? To protect your reputation around here? Well, I have news for you, boy. They fucking hate you as is, because you talk down to them and you patronise them. Without me you would never have kept it going with the few lousy pints you might pull on a winter's afternoon. Who would have paid for the modernisation, eh? The extension and the decorating of the back lounge? Who, Michael? I helped you survive after Rosie! You fucking owe me, my boy, and I tell you—I swear to you—if you make me go, I will tell the whole village about Donal Travers and the money and, what's more, they have more time for me than for you, so they will believe me!"

Madge went to go but was unsure as to walk out to the bar with me sitting there like a gobdaw or to slam the parlour door in his face. She chose the latter. After a while he poked his head in to see if I was all right, and I paid him no notice, as was normal, so he went to the window, pulling the drape back a fraction to see was there any stragglers outside. Pleased there was nobody as yet, he walked by me glancing at the screen and blocking my light.

The man with the harmonica played and Michael looked anxiously at the screen. I could see he had tears running down his cheeks as he sat beside me.

*

When I freed myself and got nearer the surface, the car became small. The further I swam the darker it became until it was a miniature, like one of the matchbox cars Michael Harrington bought me one Christmas. Finally I could breathe, sucking the air into my lungs at a great rate, my shoulders heaving; my head floating on the water bobbing up and down like a football. The world looked funny from where I was, the water sapping cold against my skin. I felt I was a camera and the swish of the water was covering my lens. I felt that any minute a giant hand would appear with a cloth to wipe my face. In my unstable world the sun shot a ruler of light from Timoleague. It speared through me till it warmed the green moss on Burren. For the first time I heard Jack read aloud his memories of his holiday in Ballinglanna, and it was so long ago.

I stood in three feet of the Atlantic Ocean, and he stood for a long time watching me. I wanted to climb the hill by the place that should have been a church. I wanted to pray by the Marian shrine; after all 1954 was Marian year, and a good year it was too.

*

It reminded me of one evening when Michael Harrington brought me walking through the village, and it was getting late, about an hour before dark. I always knew when the world was ready for night because the birds would get excited talking loudly to each other. The golden plovers would mass on the far side, and the swans would take off to sail back to the mouth of the river.

As they pass, their heads pointed stiff, they make a generating sound like you might hear from the fuse box in the house. I am passing the harbour. The trawler stands tall with the iron mast, and then suddenly the ground shakes as a convoy of tractors pass by over at Burren. They will do the circuit to Broadstrand, collecting silage to feed the cattle in the winter, and Michael Harrington has lost me. He steals ahead. I tag along behind him, tied on a lead like an old dog.

We passed a grassy area with overgrown thorns and dense bushes, and I remembered how I used to tug his arm to go in there but this evening he kept going on and on. He walked till the wind attacked us as we passed Seaview. Jack Browne who sat at his window waved amicably at my father. His head went back down again for a moment, but when I passed he raised his hand to wave at me before dropping it again. Obviously deeming it a waste of time, he was soon back tap-tapping.

Then as the light began to drop, leaving before me only the shallows the sea had discarded, I saw three distinctive roadways across the estuary. A crossroads of dark water, which flowed the wrong way as the tide receded, appeared to counter flow. I was at the crossroads and Michael Harrington walked too far ahead of me, the leash stretching to its limits. What was I to do? Which dark road should I take?

*

So the world bobbled. I floated, my world searching channels up and down, snow then static. I could see the pier at Wood Point and the old parish hall, and I could see a car slip into a space at Detta's. Above, the dark trees threw old light on the village below, and I suddenly thought of how I would love to get lost there. Up there fairies live in tree trunks full of holes, mushrooms grow savagely in the damp moss, and ferns aggressively mark the tracks made in the secret of the night. Michael Harrington never let me go there alone.

*

I wanted to take the darkest of roads as it seemed to lead all the way up the estuary to where the sea had dried to a desert beyond Abbeymahon. Around the bends it sprawled with buried dunes piled below the earth, pushing to the road on the far side. I think of how Caw listened to Jack as he read aloud, and I wondered about Jack and then I wondered about me.

*

The ancient stopper, an underground channel to the tide, you spoke of cars gently sailing the narrow bridge. The old railway signal. Some asshole signed away in the sixties to save money. Choo choo. A small group of children threw soft bread. Ripples across the pond. The duck must be fed by a relation of Mrs. Peeping Tom. She stops, leaning her bicycle against the bridge wall. The ducks are her children and fresh-faced gulls join in. They land among the excited quacks. In the Argideen, mud banks form. White duck uses stray wood as a raft. It sinks as you see the old stone wall of the abbey. The visitor's book buried now in the parish register with comments on marriages and deaths and knee this and knee that.

*

When Madge Butler walked in she stood opposite him, her make up running like yogurt down her cheeks. She was rigid as she tried to gauge his mood in the low light. Michael had stopped weeping. He just stared at the door of the pub, wondering if he had the strength to go over and open it. Already a straggler had hit the door twice, the second time quite hard with his fist.

"I will just throw water on my face before I open. Michael, I was having a think in the parlour. If you still want me to go I will go, and there will be no more said about it. But it is foolish, for we have a good thing going now, no matter what happened in the past." She spoke like she was trying to convince herself.

The film was nearly over and Jason Robards and Charles Bronson were departing. Unknown to the audience Robards is fatally injured. They leave Claudia Cardinale to run her new town where the train stops for water. The music starts: Da di da do da da da do do da doo...Margaret walks in and goes through the beam of light to the microphone; she sings intensely.

When we went uphill my brother stood at the base of a lonely tree. It grew out of thick gorse, and its roots were embedded in the bank of the ditch. The wood pigeon cooed and my brother stood watching him for an age, until I reminded him of the real purpose of our journey.

Beyond on the right was the farm gate, where we were greeted by the excited sheep dog he ran backwards and forwards barking madly. He was the sentry, and all he guarded were small lofts with cackling hens and old straw, half-full buckets of water, and some rusted tools—the only clue to the living. And when she met us at the door she smiled.

The women had rose cheeks painted like she was just about to enter in some very important stage play, her grey hair clipped to her head, which was the fashion at the time. She was perfect in her wig. He sat behind her at the kitchen table inspecting the largest basin of spuds I have ever seen.

Good-humouredly standing at the kitchen door, I took my little black-and-white camera. Gentle smiles. Click—saved forever the story of the brother and sister who shared the little farmhouse on the edge of a cliff.

As we trotted back down the hill with our eggs and milk, Mrs. Peeping Tom passed us. She went five yards before stopping and looking back at us intently, then a yard, maybe two yards, before stopping and looking back at us once again.

We laughed as we entered our field. I christened her and the name kind of stuck.

*

I am bobbling, just my head. Above the waterline the village comes into frame then disappears. The sea corrodes my chin. I watch the old coast guard station. It is protected by the dark trees that watch over Wood Point. Sentries high on the hill sense danger.

*

Michael Harrington walks ahead. The three dark roads become more distinct. With shelduck and widgeon taking to the sky, organised chaos tries to hoodwink the falcon who in turn is disturbed by the black and white oyster catchers. Somewhere beyond that, mullet hide at the bottom of dish water. Which road? Michael Harrington walks on alone. Caw watches from his roof garden. The silage tractors are on the move, flashing lights on the Kilbrittain side. Michael stops in his tracks and searches the half-mile to Burren pier.

Wood Point, A few years ago
33.

Caw was lazy and Froya had gone out. He sent her over to
Barryroe to work the bins. It gave her something to do, got
her out of the nest for a few hours. The odd time she might
get something useful to bring home, like little bits of
cardboard that made for good insulation in the winter. All the
heat went out the gap at the front as in the morning the heat
of the sun warmed his feathers at the back. Froya was restless
lately, complaining about this and that, and Caw was in no
humour.

Also, rumour had it Jack Browne was leaving Wood Point
for good. He'd had enough. It didn't take much to put him
off, so he was on his way and good riddance to him. The
sheep were gone now from Lyall's field and the grass was
meadow. It was grand for picking slugs who stuck wet to the
hay stems, and if you wanted to have a rest you could lose
yourself within its confines and an old bird could grab time
to think about things.

Froya wanted to move back to the eaves of the old house
but he was against it, even if it was nearer to Barryroe and
her relations. He didn't want to relive the past. The place was
haunted as far as he was concerned. A few days earlier he
had gone up to see if it was in any way habitable but the
place was worse than ever. The driveway was overgrown and
the sycamore was full of squatting magpies they were
ignorant and they should go back to where they came from.
Sneering, watching him intently as he browsed.

There were loose slates lying on the old flower beds
surrounding the house and rats running across the roof with
impunity. As he flew on, the old tennis court had been
swallowed by marauding gorse. The old place was finished,
he concluded, and Froya just didn't quite get the majesty of
Abbeymahon. Caw flew to St. Peter's Point, landing on the

narrow grass verge, the shelduck busy along the sands. Small pools of water invited him to wade but the water looked too cold. He would leave the pleasure to the Redshank and the Greenshank. He wanted to tell the shelduck to feck off back to Germany, but he thought the better of it.

Times had changed and he had moved on. No longer was he regarded as lower order. After all he lived in the penthouse of the old abbey. What a nice address: Abbeymahon Mews. And the most important thing was that he had Froya, and he knew the other crows were jealous. He had moved on to live by dark country lanes, each morning watching the estuary come alive, and to gaze at the small prize cattle. They congregated amongst their own where they were safe. Caw felt exclusive, no longer having to fight or scrap for space, and now with Jack Browne going he was left as king of the castle. The daily flight low over the sand allowed him to see his own shadow. At times he was soaring like an eagle. What was it Jack Browne wrote and spoke aloud? It was a favourite thing for him to do and the only time Caw thought his writing was any good.

I might wait for you by the river and I will search the distance for you. There are hills and miles of earth to block my view, times then I think of you, when I am alone in my room. These images pass and the mundane emerges. My life continues. Then at night the moon lights up the water, and cargo ships sail by my window. I can feel them—ropes and ladders; small crew tied to quarters. The river continues. It disregards everything. It is only living to react.

I can stand all night at the window, imagining you, what you are wearing, what you look like today. Are you speaking? Are you quiet? Maybe you are sleeping softly. I can dismiss you too, like when the clouds open and I see the heavenly fires burn my imagination, presenting ordinariness, normal excursions. Then I understand that we are mortal, you and me. It is grand because I can go on about my business. I can admire women see the good in the world around me.

When I was ill they put me to sleep for a long time, different plumbers fixing pipes inside of me. When I woke I felt different, like not only was I repaired, but I was added on to. Yet they must have dressed my spirit and then cynically undressed it and left it bare, because I am no longer able to deal with the likes of you. Wrap you up and throw you to the dogs, because it is only when I see you, when our eyes finally meet it happens. Only then my heart rumbles to the taste of you. I am in love with you to the core of my soul, and don't get me wrong, because I have racked my brains for an explanation and for the life of me and, for the love of God, I can't find one, not a hint. Those soft eyes that burn a fire through my skin belong in here, in normality, like you are a goddess only visiting, staying long enough to mind us mere mortals and you have made humanity all your own.

I love thee by your eyes and they are one in sunlight or moonlight. I love thee by your beauty and I am sworn by the intensity of your stare. It is with you I shall lie. Come walk with me by the sea, and I will kiss you and you can tell me stories of old. I will warm to you on cold days. I will rise from the dead to view your pale skin, the mask of the mighty warrior, soul keeper, my lover, my river, you who lifts me from dead water to breathe once more.

Caw remembered them, meeting among the graves below him. How young and pretty Kate looked, and how much older and tired he was. Yet she was taken with him, and when they embraced he got the sense that she loved him. Why did he choose to go? He was a loser, always crying in his sleep, arriving home from the Fisherman's pissed and making midnight snacks to cheer himself up. What did she see in him? He was giving her at least twelve years if not more. Like, it wasn't like he was rich or famous or anything like that. He wasn't even any good at this writing business, for if he was he would have found a publisher and be making lots of dosh. Poor bastard, probably moving on because his funds are running low.

Maybe if he was loaded he might have brought her with him. You know, like eloped. Caw often thought of eloping with Mrs. Caw way back, but on reflection it would have been a pretty silly thing to do. To elope you have to really believe in love and all that goes with it. You have to have a pure heart and retain enough innocence to respect the world and what it offers. Jack Browne doesn't know what innocence is. If he eloped his lover would return home after a week. Glad to see the back of him, Caw concluded, wondering whether Froya would be home soon. She normally got back from Barryroe mid-afternoon.

He decided to follow the tide and he flew over the trees flapping his wings with a new sense of freedom. He almost touched the top of a pine tree. Below the small birds played silently in the meadow. The prized cattle lazed beneath the cover of the branches; they looked bored. Caw flew low almost touching the algae. He spread his wings gliding till he came to rest on the wet sand. Looking across, the estuary was emptying again, bringing with it all that was good and all that was foul. When it turns, the tide will bring us the same selection of fish and the flotsam and jetsam of the wild Atlantic. The giant roaring waves carried dark spirits wrapped within the spinning cotton wool, crash landing on the storm beach in Kilbrittain before it rounded on Wood Point, drowning all that is dry.

Later he and Froya will watch it fill as it reaches the incline at Abbeymahon. Dark mullet will scour the bottom, the curlews and shelduck will argue with the terns and the ringed plover. Above them the fox will roam the fields smelling the air, and the rat will bury his head in the dark ditches in search of scraps. The hierarchy of animals as the saintly sheep will return, and the pompous cattle will look up to the dark horses that stick their heads over bright hedges to gaze at country lanes.

This is my country, Caw thought now safely back in his turret. All of this my kingdom and I watch over it from here, for I am King Caw, king of the crows, the maker of all good things crow. They will flock to this place for centuries to read about me. Young crows will scream, 'Show me! Is that where King Caw lived? Was that his castle, his home? Did he rule the whole country from there?'

Caw cawed. Walkers stepping by on the path glanced at the turret to see what all the fuss was about. They saw Caw the raven stand on the grass ledge outside the turret, surveying his country for as far as they eye could see. King Caw, ruler of all crows.

Wood Point, A few years ago
34.

He left the key in Detta's for Mary Kearney to collect, but Mary rang and asked her to check the place over and make sure the windows were closed and that he had turned off all the electrics and the hot water emersion. Mary said she was busy but Kate knew her from old. She was always the same even at school. Not bothered; too much trouble.

Mary was cosy in life now; her husband was an accountant and they had a nice place in Passage West. When she entered the house she felt uneasy. He had paid a cleaner to leave it in good shape, and the floors smelled of disinfectant. She could see scrub marks on the walls where the woman had rubbed vigorously, her efforts yet to fully dry out. In the kitchen the tap dripped—plop, plop, but it wasn't that he had left it on; it was just faulty. All the fittings were cheap.

She tried to fix it using her strength till her wrist ached but the drip remained. Not as regular, but still there. Plop. He had closed the doors to the living room, so she decided to check out upstairs first. The emersion heater was off, and the bathroom scrubbed cleaner than her own. In the tiny bedroom he had earmarked for his daughter, the small window looked over the water that he sadly admitted that Jane had never seen. On the wall still dangled the wind chime with her butterflies. He had brought it upstairs to her room then left it behind.

His bedroom smelled of him. She had never been in it, but she remembered taking a peep one evening whilst she ran to the loo and he watched over the girls for a minute. She could see the mattress was old and worn; the base of it was torn with black foam peeping out. The small on-suite was gleaming. She imagined him shaving at the small mirror, the clouded water splashing on his skin, the razor gliding down his cheeks over the uneven bones of his jaw. His eyes looked deep beyond him to the dark wardrobe and the dead insects stuck on the windows.

Kate could hear the birds battle on the roof and the patter and flapping of their excited wings. How they must have entertained him on the still mornings when normal people engage in conversation or when lovers make love or tired partners chat about the weather. Husbands bring hard-working wives their tea, and children roll into the bed beside their mams and dads, little bodies, fragile, seeking the secure frames of their parents. Stories are told and songs are made up and sung. The world is busy with nonsense.

The front bedroom was cluttered with Mary's things—unneeded sheets and pillow case with curtain rings from the curtain rail that fell down each time the curtains were pulled. They lay harmlessly across the bed so he finally gave up on it.

She looked out at the green, which took up the centre of Seaview. It was a darkish morning. Even though it hadn't rained the whole place had a damp feel, like someone had let loose a hose over the plants and bushes. A neighbour banged a car door shut once and then again, but she couldn't see who it was as the view was very sharp. No engine sound, but another bang of the door and then nothing. She checked the utility room and the backyard. The gravel filled the space, but down by the walls moss had grown.

She suddenly remembered sitting there with him on the wonky seat drinking beer, the children playing and Sarah throwing the ornamental plane over the garden wall. Every time he got up she nearly went flying and vice versa. He spilled his beer twice, drowning the knee of his pants. They laughed. She liked his laugh. It was gentle and solid, but she wished he laughed more. Maybe some people are like that; they don't laugh very much. The living room was too small. He always said that but then he would comfort himself, saying it led to less hassle, the smaller the better, less cleaning and fuss.

Then she eyed the small table by the window where he sat day after day tap tapping. There was a small sheet of paper wedged between the leg of the table and the lamp stand, and on the wall his wooden cross hung from a nail that was far too big. He forgot his Jesus. She would give it to Mary to send on to him, but maybe he just left it there. It might not have meant so much, but he did say it went everywhere with him. She should text him but he was gone. Maybe he never wanted to hear from her again, not even by text.

Kate pulled the table back, and, straining, picked up the piece of paper. It contained scribbled notes, stuff he was working on for his book. She read them carefully and then re-read, as his writing was appalling. Stuff about crows on the gravel and a fox, then on its own the name "Caw" and then scribbled "the window" and "sideways," "autism" spelt incorrectly and then spelled right. He took the "i" from the "m." There were lots of little scribbles she couldn't read.

Near the top two names: "George Whelton" and "Diamond Jim." Four or five times he wrote the word "window," and she imagined him there tapping and typing as she passed by, he raising his head to wave at her, smiling as she pushed Sarah in her buggy. She should text him about the cross, but he was gone now. Young Hurley from the village took all his stuff in his sausage van, and they headed out the road. That was it; he was gone. She stood looking out the bay window. Outside the place was quiet, the occasional car noisily passing an old man walking his dog idled by.

She thought he saw her but soon realised he wasn't looking at her at all but at something on the roof—the birds or maybe the fire was going in the house next door. The window. He used say to her, "If only, Kate, you could sit at my window, see what it is I see, you would see the world as I see it. Do you know, my doctor says I suffer from a cognitive illness? He says that is why I write, to try and make sense of it all."

She thought of the day he was standing in his dressing gown hiding his scar. She wanted to tell him that she didn't mind scars, it is what makes people real. He never spoke of it much. She just noticed it sometimes, when he wore his shirt with one button too many opened.

She was about to go; the place was grand. He left it better than he found it. What should she do with the piece of paper? Maybe it was important. Hardly, or he wouldn't have left it on the floor. Probably slipped out of a file or something. She would put it with the cross and give it to Mary; she had his forwarding address.

Carefully Kate stretched, lifting the cross before removing it, the figure on the hardwood forever suffering under his crown of thorns. She used it as a paper weight. Time to go.

One last look out. No point in lingering. This part of her life was over. Things come and go. He was gone now from Wood Point, moved on. As he said himself, it was for the best. She would most likely never lay eyes on him again or be in this house looking out the window, as he did day after day, tapping away.

Kate heard his voice softly speaking to her: "Da da do do da da da da, doo doo da do..." The music he played. It was always the same tune every time she came to visit. "Da da da dah doo do do dad do da dooo..." Yes, he made a point of playing that music... Kate looked out the window one last time...

*

When she heard the loud banging and the fist on the glass panel of the front door, she left the bed sideways, resting her elbows on the sill to see who it was so early. She knew it was Thomas, his cap recognisable anywhere. He was oblivious to her and he continued with his banging. Kate threw on her dressing gown, the old faded one that Myrna had given her for Christmas going back years.

His face was flushed when she opened the door. "We staked him down off Burren. You would better hurry, Kate, the tide is coming fast."

Thomas choked for breath, his right hand shaking as he stood back to light a fag to settle his nerves.

*

Kate felt the tears swell as the light changed outside the window. The sun breaking through made little browns mix with dark blues, yet when the thick cloud reappeared the canvas was all grey. The water flowed fast, river rapids, the sea creating new funnels. New canyons were born. Taking a steak knife she undressed at the end of Burren pier, the water washing to the half-moon of sand where he was crucified. There was no time. The water, ice cold, accepted her as she swam towards him with the skill and shine of a fish.

*

I heard the music also and I knew it was time to return to Mammy Rosie. It carried with the wind skimming the water to reach my ears, and as I turned I saw the cattle still on the hill. They looked only perplexed. Time for them stood still. They had no sense of it, each day the same chewing the cud. The water splashed into my face, and I went under again into the vast darkness to find her.

I could see his face was covered and I thought of Mammy Rosie below, and I thought of him all those years ago standing in three feet of the Atlantic Ocean. So I returned to the darkness and as I came to the windscreen I noticed that Mammy Rosie was still struggling for breath, her enormous cheeks rodent-like, about to burst. As I swam to the open window there she was, her arms outstretched, beseeching me. One final attempt to save her. I crawled across the passenger seat, pulling her arms with all my might, her face full with blood. But then I saw her for real. I stared at her she was exactly like the picture that Michael Harrington kept on the sideboard, all fair haired and slim her eyes a light blue, and softly she wanted to take me into her bosom.

The car was by now full of water, and bubbles of air left her mouth and some of them hit off the side of my face. She hugged me so close, and I marvelled at the softness of her skin even if by now she was pale. She brought me back to when I was seven years old, and I felt no urge to let go as she held me so safe. Soon the water came into my mouth and Margaret's sweet voice reached a crescendo, and the view of me and Mammy Rosie was from the outside, drifting away slowly till it became lost in the darkness, fixed on us, sleeping my head resting on her chest.

Jack Browne read aloud:

I desire you, for you are of me! Feel the waves, angry ice when the sea washes your skin. Odd shapes caress the slime green of the jetty. I see the small stream, drains on tiny stones, filters through sea nettles, ripe berries to chew beyond the old sea walls ditches for you to hide. And me—I still desire old gentle by the turf fire.

By the fire the small caravan leaks on the headlands, green attire over ice cliffs, spillage, oil belly rusted, water yellow. You find the causeway to grief; you leave jumping rock pools beneath.

Where is it you go? By the sea road round the tracks, divided by dried dung, tiny blades of grass to guide you past the cliffs fall serenely to the sea over unkempt fields, scrub with ponies grazing. You are sad for the lazy beast who scratches her fat pregnant belly off rusted barbed wire.

Further a sleek-looking pony with a blue sheen and a strong tail comes close to investigate you. At thirteen years old you are unafraid, allowing the pony wet the palm of your hand with his tongue. You wonder at his sideway eyes. How does he make contact? Move a step away heavily only to return. This time you feel his nose wet.

On the winding road to the bridge you see a pheasant run, colours sparkly pink and brown like a giant hen on the loose.

He disappears and you peer through hedges till you reach the bottom of the hill. Climb. You will search the ocean at Dunworly, the freshness of the breeze. It is scooped by wooden spoons made in America.

The afternoon sun has broken the mesh of cloud to stroke the marbles in your eyes. People below run the rocks. Thin women giggle, trying to find a soft spot.

Like me you are consumed with sand grains of it. Like a million warriors fighting the tide, dragging, sinking, allowing small pools, encouraging genocide.

I advise you to leave. It is getting late. We best return to the headland, the caravan where we are safe, but you choose to go on without me.

I have tears running down my cheeks as you fade over the hill towards Butlerstown. I wave and shout at you, but you keep on going, never looking back.

*

Kate cut the rope at both ends and at the sides, lifting him up, their shoulders barely visible as the tide lashed against them. She let the knife fall to the sand before embracing him as a lost lover. He embraced her, his hands falling on her bare shoulders, the sea splashing their faces and the surf washing over their heads till she looks back down the estuary. She too heard the music and Margaret's gentle tones. She then saw the boy standing in three feet of the Atlantic Ocean, and she knew it was Jack.

*

Kate turned to go. She had seen enough. The window was now wetting with soft spits of rain. It was like a child had gathered rain drops to throw idly at the glass. She went to pick up the cross and the piece of paper but changed her mind as the window went dark with the caption "Snowfall in Wood Point for the first time in thirty years."

It fell first in tiny wet drops as it drifted over the salt marshes of Kilbrittain, announced by the sky larks appearing above the dunes to investigate. The wiser snipe sought shelter as the easterly wind carried its cargo over the sea. The kittiwakes are chasing the sprat as the first falls fresh cover the trees on the headland. Soon within the wood its beech trees are covered. Hiding their shame, it falls in sheets, condemning the seeds of orange Montbretia to remain in the earth.

Soon the whole village is white from the heights of Ramsey Hill down to the tiny cottages and solid houses that give a life to the main street. On it moves through Siberia and past the Marian year statue. The humble virgin looks lost in the pitiful cold till Kate sees herself drive down the slippery hill that leads from the Anchorage.

Jack Browne blocks her way. He sits in the middle of the road, the collar of his winter coat pulled tight around his neck. She stops, stepping out to the frosted road. She threads warily to him removing her gloves. Kate hears the music "Da da doo dad da daa...do dah do dah da..." She touches his skin with her ice finger. She sees it pink. As he rises to his feet placing her left hand on his right cheek, he stares into her eyes. Her hand feels the hard skin on his head, his receding hairline.

Soon he has transformed to different ages, standing in the cold Atlantic Ocean, the face a little boy lost. Kate hugs him close. The tiredness outs from him. She is making love with him in the ruins at Abbeymahon and then under the single tree in the field where the whole world can see you. She is curing him through the ages. She feels his strong fingernails embedded in the soft skin of her shoulder blades. Her mouth is open and she screams at him. Their eyes are unbroken. The boy stands in the ocean and Kate wants to be there. She wants to remove his scar with touch. She wants to stay at the

window and see the world the way he sees it, but the image is
dark, only his words remain, till one last time she sees a
flicker of light.

*

Where will she go now that there is nobody to love her in
the way she deserves to be loved? Once more she thought, if
it only happened at a different time, if only she had met him
seven years earlier. She closed the front door and walked to
her car. A neighbour was retrieving something from their car.
They banged the car door and then, unsatisfied, opened it
again before banging it closed with even more force.

*

Ted O' Reilly played with Sarah. He teased her with the
small tennis ball, hiding it behind him. Then when she
rounded to the rear, he would switch it back to the front. Kate
gave Fiona a biscuit. She sat on a blanket by the garden table.
She had been giddy but the biscuit calmed her. Kate lit a
cigarette. She was meaning to give them up, but like all great
things it would do another day. She poured herself the drain
of white wine from the bottle that Myrna donated the
previous Sunday.

She noticed that Ted had drunk all his beer as well; he
finally relented and allowed Sarah the tennis ball, which she
threw into the air, landing hard on the lawn, only to disappear
among the bedding plants. Ted got up to give his daughter a
hand to find it. Kate, checking on Fiona, took a drag on her
cigarette, remembering the final scene at Jack's window.
From the flicker of light she saw herself staring skyward and
wishing like a small child. The world took its time, removing
itself slowly, the music coming to a close and Margaret's

voice trailing off in final acceptance. After a close-up of her eyes, still and unemotional, the world drifts away to a rostrum camera. Removing from her it falls to earth as the sun sets over Timoleague, and the world is closing down for another day.

Author's note: Kate Donovan still lives in Wood Point with her husband, Ted O' Reilly, and her daughters, Sarah and Fiona. Jack Browne lives by a river. He has never returned to Wood Point.

The End

Also by this Author: Viaréggio

Available on Kindle

Reviews of 'Viaréggio.'

'The unexamined life is not worth living—this is ambitious novel that understandably took three years to write¬ and consequently, there is an overwhelming sense that a life in its totality has been compressed between its 300 plus pages together with a complex, dark thriller of innovative intrigue with a rewarding twist at the end.'

Angela M Cornyn - The Sunday Independent

'Dark journey of the soul- badgered by questions of life and mortality, in this dark shadowy and highly ambitious novel.'

Shelley Marsden - The Irish World Newspaper

Made in the USA
Charleston, SC
14 January 2012